The Marrowbone Marble Company

A Novel

Glenn Taylor

W F HOWES LTD

This large print edition published 2011 by
W F Howes Ltd
Unit 4, Rearsby Business Park, Gaddesby Lane,
Rearsby, Leicester LE7 4YH

1 3 5 7 9 10 8 6 4 2

This novel is a work of fiction. However, its places, for the most part, are real. Marrowbone Cut is not. It is a fictional hollow, and should not be confused with either Marrowbone Creek, West Virginia, or Marrowbone, Kentucky. Likewise, some of the events and individuals depicted herein were in fact real, as can be further studied in any of the excellent historical sources listed in the acknowledgments. However, the author has taken great liberties in the writing of this novel. Thus, all characters, their actions, and their speech are the product of the author's imagination and in no way represent any person, living or dead.

A CIP catalogue record for this book is available
from the British Library

ISBN 978 1 40747 054 2

Typeset by Palimpsest Book Production Limited,
Falkirk, Stirlingshire
Printed and bound in Great Britain
by MPG Books Ltd, Bodmin, Cornwall.

Black ground was fenced for men to till.
The dead of Gauley own this hill.

—LOUISE MCNEILL

PROLOGUE

JANUARY 1969

The ground was the color of rust. Holes the size of half-dollars were everywhere, some encircled by tiny mounds of dirt. This was hard earth, nearly frozen. Dried-up leaves and spruce needles turned brown. A hush had befallen the land, as still as the inside of a coffin. Such quiet recalled a time before timber had framed houses and a church, before plumbing hooked in hot and cold, before electricity snaked conduit. The trees slept. The creek was iced over.

At the back of the hollow, there was piled ash and shingle. Sheet metal lengths. Two-by-fours at peculiar angles, their surfaces bubbled and cracked and black. There was a furnace stack, fifty feet high and made from fieldstone. It towered above all that fire had taken, but its mortar was crumbling. A strong wind would soon enough knock it down and stir the ash and frayed black picture-frame wire and lampshade bones below.

Snow came. It landed silent on a thick sheath of glass, the size and shape of a backyard pond. This glass had run molten, but now it was cooled, its edges rounded, frozen in rolls. A woman walked a circle around it. She held in her hands a Bolex 16mm movie camera. She filmed the glass. Thought for a moment she had seen a fish eye looking up at her from beneath.

This tract of land had known many names. Bonecutter Ridge, Marrowbone Cut, the Land of Canaan.

A German hog butcher named Knochenbauer had settled it in 1798. He'd entered into common-law marriage with an Indian woman and they'd raised children and grandchildren and made their surname Bonecutter. The Bonecutters lived on these five hundred West Virginia acres for 150 years. They were hard, proud people who prospered some times and went hungry others. They witnessed love and murder, fire and flood, until only two remained. It was left to them to hold on to the land. They did so with the sure grip that hill people possess.

Loyal Ledford came to this place in 1948, and for a time people again walked the ground. They followed paths beaten by the feet of those who'd walked the same routes before them. House to church to meeting hall to woods' edge, and back to house. The people here made something real and good. They built with their hands. They put down roots. Ledford put his in deep. But his blood carried memories and his temper ran hot. In his dreams, hollows were flooded and people hid in holes they'd dug in the ground.

Ledford was apart from this world, and yet the people followed him. 'Tell you what,' he once said to them. 'We can stir the creek and wake up the trees. We can be a people freed.'

PART I

A LINE IN THE DIRT

OCTOBER 1941

Six brick chimney stacks stood at a hundred feet each. This was the Mann Glass Company, a ten-acre factory tract straddling the C&O Line at Huntington's western edge. Machine-made wide- and narrow-mouth bottles had been blown inside since 1915, and later, prescription and proprietary bottles. Eli Mann had opened the doors of a handblown specialty shop here in 1908. Now, at ninety, he owned a factory with one thousand employees and two 300-ton furnaces.

Inside, Loyal Ledford worked the swing shift, four to midnight. He'd done so since graduating high school in June, and before him, his father had done the same.

Ledford was a long, sturdy young man with big hands. At thirteen, he was a Mann Glass batch boy. At eighteen, he bid on and got his job as furnace tender. It suited him. He was careful to respect the fire, as heat will sometimes break even a young man down. Inside a glass factory, a furnace roared at 3,000 degrees.

Ledford squinted hard. Checked the gauge and

eyeballed the furnace fire one last time through the barrier window. As was his custom at the end of a shift, Ledford stared at the fire until his peripherals went white. Then he closed his eyes and watched the little swirls dance across the black stage of his eyelids. He pushed his scoop shovel into the corner with his boot tip and walked blind down the dark east aisle. The wall bulbs had surged again. Popped open like fireworks, muted by the rest of the racket inside. Ledford clocked off at a minute past midnight.

Saturday turned into Sunday, and Ledford sat alone in the dark in front of his work locker. The sweat sheen on his body dried up. His wet-collared shirt turned cold and stuck to him. He coughed. Pulled off his split-leather work gloves. They rode high, all the way to the elbows.

Inside the factory cafeteria, Ledford looked for Rachel. She was the plant nurse on the four-to-midnight shift, and they'd been eating together for two months. Rachel's mother was Mary Ball, formerly Mary Mann, Eli Mann's daughter. Rachel's father was Lucius Ball, plant manager.

She was three years Ledford's senior. She'd grown up easy in a big house on Wiltshire Hill. He'd grown up hard in a little one next to the scrapyard on Thirteenth Street West.

She was easy to spot. Her posture was spike straight and her hair was coal black. Ledford followed her from the milk bin to the table, put his tray down across from hers. 'What say, Jean Parker?' he said.

'What say, Pittsburgh,' Rachel answered. They'd had a date to *see The Pittsburgh Kid* a week prior. After, she told him he looked like Billy Conn, the Pittsburgh Kid himself. He told her she looked like Jean Parker, only younger. They'd kissed.

'Tired?' he asked.

'A little.' She wore a purple flower on the breast of her nurse's uniform. Her silver watch was loose on her wrist, thin as twine.

'Hungry, I take it.' Ledford cut his steak, as she did hers. They always ate the same meal. Steak, eggs, chocolate cake. It was the second thing he'd noticed about her.

'Did you read about the Navy destroyer? The torpedo attack?' Rachel chewed while she talked, blocked his view with her napkin.

'Off of Iceland? Didn't sink it though, did they?'

'No.'

She liked to talk about the war raging in Europe and in China. He didn't. Always, with wars, Ledford had liked to read, not talk. And so he did, in the paper, each day as he ate breakfast before class. But mostly, his reading came by way of books. History books, like the big old red one that had been his father's. *The Growth of the American Republic* it was called, and Ledford had read it thrice before enrolling at Marshall College as a history major.

The sound of stacked glass shifting echoed loud

from the kitchen. Mack Wells walked past. He was the swing-shift janitor and the only black man at the plant. He nodded to them and they nodded back. Rachel had bandaged his hand the night before. He'd been scorched by a valve exhaust.

'Mack Wells' wife is pregnant,' Rachel said.

'How do you know?'

'He told me while I wrapped his hand. She's due at springtime.'

'Is that right?' He shook hot sauce onto his eggs.

'Yes.' She'd stopped chewing and clasped her hands together on the table. 'I think springtime is the finest of the seasons for a baby, don't you?'

'I don't know.' He didn't look up at her. His pinbone sirloin was cut to gristle.

'What season were you born? I know you've told me, but I've forgotten.'

'July the eighth,' he said. He looked over at Mack Wells, who sat alone, his back to them. A line of sweat traced the spine of his coveralls.

'A summer baby,' Rachel said. 'Your mother must have hated carrying that weight in the heat.'

Rachel wanted to get married and she wanted to have a baby. Sometimes, she talked in ways that betrayed those facts. But when it went quiet, as now, she quit her talking and let it lie. They didn't yet speak on serious things. She hadn't told him of her mother's cancer, and she knew not to ask much on his family, his boyhood. He'd asked her on their first date if she knew what had happened to his mother and father, his older brother. Yes, she'd answered. 'Well,' Ledford had told her, 'good. We don't have to talk about it then.'

By all accounts, Bill Ledford had been a good husband and father, a baseball star and a glass-blower from Mingo County who gave what he could to his wife and children and gave the rest to the bartender and the bootlegger.

In August of 1935, Bill Ledford killed his wife and oldest son when he fell asleep drunk at the wheel of his Model A Pickup. Young Loyal had liked a hard wind, and so he rode in the bed. His brother preferred the warm space between his parents in the closed cab. One boy was thrown free and one wasn't. Loyal was thirteen when it happened. Eli Mann, his father's old boss, promptly bought the Ledford home from the bank. He told them keep their mouths shut about it, and he told the same to people poking around about the boy who lived there alone. Eli Mann gave Ledford a job, something to get up for every morning.

Ledford picked up the bone he'd been staring at and gnawed it. Rachel had walked away. She bussed her tray and approached Mack Wells, who stood and said, 'Miz Ball.'

'No need to get up, I just wanted to check on that hand.'

'It's just fine. That salve done the trick.'

She told him to change the dressing when he got home, and then she came back over to Ledford.

13

'You eat like a caveman,' she said.

'You chew with your mouth open.'

She smiled and her eyelids got heavy. Ledford wiped his mouth and loosed a cigarette from its pack. The matchbook was damp with sweat, and it took four swipes to flame.

'I can make us a pot of coffee,' Rachel said. She had a new apartment on Eleventh Avenue. Lucius Ball had wanted her to stay under his roof, but after nursing school and a couple of Mann paychecks, she'd packed her things.

'Watered down or thick?' he asked.

She watched him through the smoke. Everything about Ledford seemed older than he was. 'I bought a percolator just yesterday, and I'll make it any way you like.'

He winked.

Outside, the rain was picking up. It beat a chorus on the roof above them, and the people eating raised their voices to hear one another, and the dishwashers slept standing up.

Ledford stood in the entryway of the small apartment. He hung his wet coat and watched as she walked away barefoot on the hardwood. The place smelled of women's powders and hand cream. Such a scent reminded him of his mother's room and the small cracked mirror she sat in front of all those years before. Putting her face on, she called it. As a boy, he'd sneak up behind her when she sat in front of her mirror. But she always heard

14

him and scooped him into her lap and tickled him. She claimed that the ticklish among us were guilty of crimes. Over his laughter, she'd ask, 'You been stealin sugar, sweetie?' and then she'd hug him to her neck, and all was still and safe.

Rachel brought him a hand towel to pat dry. It was fancy, monogram-stitched, and Ledford hated to use it. She turned from him again and walked past the sofa to the kitchen. 'Should I take off my shoes?' he hollered.

'If you want to,' she said.

He did not. He walked to the fireplace mantel and studied the photographs there. They were lined up for the length of it. They told a story. Babies dressed in christening gowns and men with sly grins and bunny-eared fingers behind the heads of their gentle wives.

'Do you like music?' Rachel asked him. She'd started the percolator and was crouching at the cabinet beside him.

'I reckon.'

Her Philco had a phonograph right on top. She pulled a record from the cabinet and set the needle down. 'Do you like Claude Thornhill?'

'Never heard of the man,' he said. Piano keys tinkled soft over the quiet hum of clarinets. Ledford's neck and ears were getting hot.

When the horns came in, he nearly jumped out of his socks. She laughed at him, brought her hand to her mouth to stifle it. He rested his elbow on the mantle, knocking over two framed photographs.

When he went to fix them, Rachel grabbed his hands in hers. 'Do you want to dance with me?' she asked.

'Yes.'

When she laid her head against his chest, it seemed to Rachel that she'd danced with Ledford a hundred times before.

Ledford was trying not to upchuck his steak and eggs and chocolate cake. He'd not held a woman the likes of this one before.

'Do you know what this song is called?'

He opened his mouth to answer, but only swallowed instead.

'It's called "Snowfall,"' Rachel told him. They swayed. He looked at her hand in his, then down the length of her.

Barefoot in her nurse's uniform, she was the most beautiful thing he'd ever beheld.

NOVEMBER 1941

T he class was called 'History of the Revolutionary War,' and its professor was dull as drizzle on a windowpane. Inside the lecture hall, Ledford sat back row left. Try as he might, he could not stay awake. Swing shift will do that to a man.

Those who surrounded him were not of his kind. They were the variety of young people who, when they got smart-lipped in high school, Ledford had punched in the mouth. Young men wore neckties and argyle sweaters. Young women wore their boyfriends' jackets and spoke in tongues of Alpha and Omicron and Pi. When these students left the lecture hall, it was in groups of eight or more, hip to hip and laughing astride the downed top of a deluxe V-8 convertible. They drank beer.

Ledford walked alone from campus to Mann Glass, and if he drank, it was going to be whiskey.

But he'd long since decided not to go bad to the bottle, and truth be told, he liked his routine. Ledford had learned early to exist without friends, and his work and school schedules, though they'd run an average man down, gave him much-needed purpose. Besides, he liked glass. Especially in its molten form. To watch the stuff glow and channel outward from a 300-ton pot was a sight. He'd once watched his father, a real free-blower, puff up and shape that very material, and he remembered what he'd been told. 'Glass ain't nothing but the earth under your brogans, boy.' As his father had said this, he gripped his blowpipe in one hand and his punty rod in the other. He set them aside and scored a hot green ashtray with his dogleg jackknife. 'That there is sand, limestone, and ash,' he'd said.

Back in front of the furnace, Ledford watched the gauge needle blur and wobble. He smacked himself to stay alert. Late nights with Rachel were catching up to him.

There was a sting at the base of his neck. He turned to find Lucius Ball before him in black safety goggles. 'You want little babies to starve?' Lucius asked. Spittle flew. Landed on Ledford's cheek where the heat evaporated it.

'How's that?'

'Baby food jars. Isn't that what we make here son?' Sweat ran from the crease of Lucius's double chin, and his hair tonic smelled sour.

'I reckon it's one of the things we make, Mr Ball.'

'You can bet your last bits on that. And if that fire isn't tended right, then we don't stay on top of that quota board, do we son?' Lucius Ball liked to ask questions and not wait for answers. 'This plant out produces Los Angeles and Oakland, did you know that? Did you know we out produce Waco, Texas? I bet you didn't. I bet you take your eyes off the fire just as regular as you please.'

It wasn't about the fire. It was about Rachel. The man neither cared for nor understood his daughter's suitor, and he made no effort to hide it. Lucius Ball was an angry, greedy man. His father-in-law, the head honcho, was dying, and now it seemed that his wife Mary was dying too, unless they'd cut out all the cancer this time.

Lucius didn't like to look the young man in the eyes. Something was there that made him uneasy. He stuck his hands in his pockets and looked at the floor.

Ledford turned and tended the furnace.

When he turned back around, Lucius Ball had walked to the flow line, where Mack Wells had apparently missed a spot sweeping. Mack got an earful on dust and its potential to wreck all that is good and mechanized inside a factory's beating heart. Lucius walked away, shaking his head.

Ledford hollered for Mack Wells to come over. When he got there, Ledford said, 'I bet I can guess what he told you.'

'Man says the same things every week,' Mack said.

'Gave me a new one today. I reckon he used the same on you.'

Wells pulled out his handkerchief and blew. 'Dust take the durable out of duraglass?'

19

'No, but I like that one,' Ledford said. Behind him, a batch boy pushed a hand truck loaded with broken glass. Its peak rose from the stacked gallon buckets, cranberry-colored. Ledford said, 'Son of a bitch told me if I take my eyes off the furnace, the little babies'll starve.'

Mack Wells smiled and nodded. 'Suppose he thinks there wasn't no food fit for babies before the jar.' He wiped the back of his neck with the handkerchief. Ledford did the same with his glove, sulfur streaks left behind. Down the line, an operator screamed at a machine boy.

Ledford wanted to tell Mack congratulations on his wife's pregnancy, but didn't. They stood awkwardly for a moment, then nodded and went back to work.

Operators sulphured the blanks. Corrugators steamed the paper. Shippers stacked the boxes. Everywhere were hisses and clangs, roars and thuds. And Ledford wiped at his sweat and thought of his history professor and the way he stood silent in front of them all, waiting for an answer to questions like, 'What percentage of colonists backed the Crown?' And Ledford thought of Rachel, and how no one but him knew that she'd kiss a man on the mouth after only four dates, that she'd invite a man over after five.

He eyeballed the temperature gauge. He eyeballed the clock on the wall. He knew he was meant for something other than this.

DECEMBER 1941

Rachel watched him pace back and forth in front of the fireplace. Once in a while, he'd stop and stoke the embers, but mostly he checked his wristwatch.

She couldn't remember the last time she'd had a fire going in the middle of the day.

On the Philco, a man told any ladies listening that Lava soap would get their extra-dirty hands shades whiter in only twenty seconds.

Outside, a car engine roared, then cut out. Ledford could tell it was Lucius Ball's Lincoln Zephyr, but he walked to the window anyway. 'Your daddy,' he said.

'Well, what's he doing here?'

'I don't know.' He walked to the kitchen and opened the refrigerator. He closed it without having gotten anything, came back to the living room, and said, 'But he'd better not talk over this broadcast. So help me, if he interrupts the president—'

The doorknob turned and in came Lucius. He took off his fedora and brushed at the snow before he acknowledged either of them. Then the same with his overcoat. When he'd hung everything up and slapped his driving gloves against the end table to announce his presence, he shot his cuffs and said, 'Let's see what old Roosevelt's got to say on this one.'

Ledford walked back to the kitchen and stared inside the refrigerator some more.

'Shouldn't you be in bed Ledford?' Lucius Ball hollered. 'Aren't you on the clock in three hours?'

When the broadcast started, Rachel turned the volume knob as high as she ever had. She sat back down on the sofa with her knees pulled to her chest. Ledford poked at the fire, and Lucius stood with his arms crossed. His nose ran, and he sniffed hard every ten seconds.

The president's words were carefully chosen, and his voice carried vengeance and sorrow. The three in the small room were as still as the congressmen who watched their man before them. There was a cough through the radio's grate. There was a pop from the wet hickory in the fire.

Then Roosevelt said, 'Always will our whole nation remember the character of the onslaught against us.' Something had moved inside Ledford's gut, and now it surged upward as the congressmen beat their hands together like they never had as one. 'No matter how long it may take to overcome this premeditated invasion,' Roosevelt went on, 'the American people in their righteous might will win through to absolute victory.' The roar from the Philco caused Rachel's eyes to tear, and her heart seemed, for a moment, to stop.

She knew before looking at him that Ledford was gone from her.

He hung the poker on the cast iron holder and slowly turned. His teeth were grit behind his lips and his nostrils flared wide. He looked to Lucius, who was dumbstruck, unable for once to speak his mind. 'Mr Ball,' Ledford said, 'I quit.'

He put on his coat and told Rachel he'd ring her later. With his hand on the knob to leave, he stopped. She was crying on the sofa. Her father did not console her. He'd walked to the window and was watching the snow fall. It had picked up since earlier.

Ledford stood in the doorway and thought of their dance. Their song. He spoke her name and she looked up at him. He winked and was gone.

AUGUST 1942

He had joined the Marine Corps.

On December 10th, Ledford had walked into the recruiting station with a birth certificate altered by a Mann Glass secretary for a fee of five dollars. In the station's filthy bathroom he'd pissed in a test tube. Passed his physical. He was sent to Parris Island, South Carolina, where he found the weather utterly suitable to his demeanor. He watched the ocean any chance he got. He followed every syllable his drill instructor spat at him, as if the man was God himself. Ledford thrived on discipline. He got a reputation as a hard charger who didn't shoot the breeze.

When the men were issued their 782 gear, Ledford felt that old, joyous feeling from childhood Christmases. he loved his M1, and in no time he could fieldstrip and reassemble it like most never would. He grew to love the strain of calisthenics, whether at 0500 or midnight under floodlights. Drills became second nature. Hand-to-hand combat with short blades, plunging fixed bayonets into dummies – these acts were honed to reflex.

Ledford earned the designation of Sharpshooter on the rifle range. Even at five hundred yards, his targets came back Swiss cheese.

He smoked and played hearts with the other men, finding a peace in card playing he'd never lose. He traded insults, dimes, and nickels most often with a hard Mac from Chicago named Erminio Bacigalupo. Erm, they called him. Nobody could tell whether Ledford and Erm liked or hated each other. In truth, neither could the young men themselves.

Ledford wrote to Rachel twice a week.

Nights, he slept like the dead.

Once, drunk on his ass against the barracks wall, Ledford's drill instructor, an old Devil Dog from Alabama, had let his guard down. He'd seen action in the Great War. 'Enemy'll break, but only if you cut him,' he said. Ledford and Erm were the only men in listening distance. 'My CO taught me that. What you do is git inside their tent while they sleepin, cut one's throat and leave the other one to find him at sunup.' His words ran together. His eyes might have welled up. 'Must've done four or five Kraut boys thataway at Belleau Wood.' He fell asleep, then woke up. He looked at Ledford and Erm like he'd never seen them before. 'Take a picture, why don't you, you sons of a fucking whore,' he said. 'It'll last longer.'

In May, Ledford had boarded a troop train to San Francisco and seen the sights and then walked up the zigzag incline of the ten-thousand-ton transport ship. Aboard the Navy's vessel, sleep came interrupted, just as it would in New Zealand and in Fiji. A knot formed in the intestines. On August 7th, that knot came up the windpipe and nearly choked Ledford as he jumped over the side of the landing craft into the surf. He waded to the mud-colored sand of what they were calling Beach Red. He crossed it at a jog with the rest of his battalion. They could scarcely believe the quiet. It unsettled Ledford, and as he came to the jungle's edge, the knot broke loose, and he threw up the smallest bit of bile before swallowing it down again.

Back on the beach, palm trees grew as high as Mann Glass chimney stacks. They curled like fingers, waving the men inland with the wind.

This was Guadalcanal. The enemy was not to be found. Only silence. And in that silence, Ledford finally felt the weight of the last six months. He knew now what that time meant, what it had amounted to. Ledford was not Ledford any longer. He was just another Mac with an M1, First Marine Division, First Raider Battalion, B Company.

Nothing would ever be the same again.

Men sat shirtless, their backs against the vertical wood slats of the pagoda. Henderson Field was a flat, hot wasteland of a place. A wide cut airstrip in the middle of a jungled Pacific island. Nervous Marines walked around the pagoda, looking sideways at those without a helmet or a shirt, those able to enjoy their smokes and never look at the sky above them or the choked forest on all sides.

Like every other Marine, Ledford had become convinced that the Navy had left them on the island to die, that food and ammunition would never again be ample. By day, he repaired bomb craters left in the airstrip's grass and dirt runways. He leaned on his shovel and smoked and shot the breeze. He looked at that camelback ridge of mountains in the distance. From far off, it reminded him of home. But at night, in the jungle camp, the mosquitoes reminded him of where he truly was, and so did the Japanese fliers in the blackness overhead, dropping 250-pound bombs within spitting distance.

It was a Tuesday. Lunchtime with rations running short. Ledford slept alone on the dirt with his helmet over his face. He was dog tired and bug-bitten, from inside his ears to between his toes. He sat up, took out his Ka-Bar, and cleaned his fingernails. A skinny boy with a pitiful beard walked over from the shade of the pagoda's overhang. 'Ledford? You tryin to fry yourself?' His name was McDonough and he was from Chalmette, Louisiana.

Ledford didn't answer or look up from his fingernails.

'You want to get somethin to eat?' McDonough blinked his eyes at two-second intervals. He was seventeen years old.

'I'll eat with you, McDonough,' Ledford said, 'if you promise not to talk with your mouth full.'

But McDonough was one of the nervous ones, and when they sat down inside, he talked with his mouth full of canned fish and rice for ten minutes straight. 'Ain't had that sinus infection a day since maneuvers in Fiji,' he said, after chronicling his lifelong battle with a clogged nose and headaches. 'It's like I been waiting my whole life to come breathe this air in the Pacific.'

Ledford didn't even nod to show he was listening. At that moment, it seemed he'd do most anything to have steak and cake instead of fish and rice.

'My mother said I got the bad sinuses from her, and she got them from her daddy, and so on and so forth, back to my great grandfather, who stuck an old rotary drill up his nosehole one day and had at it until he killed hisself trying to unclog all of it.'

Ledford laughed a little with his mouth full of rice, but then he stopped, thinking such laughter might disrespect the dead.

'It's all right,' McDonough told him, smiling. 'It's a story meant to be funny. But it is true.' He held up his hand to signify Scout's honor or stack of Bibles both.

Ledford liked McDonough.

Back at camp that night, he looked over at the boy before lights-out. McDonough was flat on his bedding, looking up at the tent's sagging roof. The rain that pelted there came harder and harder until the sound of it drowned all others. A roaring quiet. A rain not seen or heard by any American boy before, even one like McDonough, a boy from the land of the hurricane. He just lay there, his finger stuck up his nose so far it almost disappeared.

Ledford thought of Mann Glass and Rachel. Of steak and eggs and the sound of West Virginia rain on the cafeteria tin roof. His chest ached. His gut burned. A drip from the tent's center point landed on his Adam's apple. He stared up at its source, a tiny slit at the pinnacle. The rain roared louder, its amplitude unsettling. Ledford opened his mouth and called out, 'Gully warsher boys,' but no one could hear him. He turned his head and watched McDonough dig for gold a while longer, then fell off to sleep.

In his dreams, there came a memory. He was a boy, and he fished on a lake with his daddy. The two of them sat in a row boat, oars asleep in their locks, their handles angled at the sky. Father and son bent over their casting rods and spoke not a word. There was only stillness and silhouette, quiet as a field stump.

Twice Ledford was awakened by the sound of Japanese Zeros zipping overhead. The rain let up. The bombs came down. He jolted when they hit, and in between, he wondered about the dream. He could not remember any lake near Huntington, nor could he remember ever fishing with his daddy. And the quiet. Why had it been so quiet?

In the morning, the men waded through calf-high

water outside the tents. It had gathered in the middle of camp, channeling the makeshift road they'd fashioned. Oil barrels floated by on their sides. A dead spider the size of a hamburger spun slowly, emitting little rings of ripples as it went. McDonough ran from it, got himself to higher ground at the muddy base of a giant palm tree. He had a deathly fear of spiders. The men laughed and pointed at McDonough, who, like many of them, had gotten the dysentery bad. The sprint from the spider had stirred things inside him, and he dropped his trousers right there at the base of the tree and let rip.

It was a sight. Ledford laughed heartily and shared a smoke with Erm from Chicago, who told him, 'You think that's funny, just wait till the malaria eats him up.'

SEPTEMBER 1942

The rations had grown a pelt of mold. Nightfall had come to resemble a wake, the men's mood shifting with sundown to gloom and the inevitability of death. Fever shivers gripped more than half, and on that Monday, orders came down that they all swallow Atabrine at chow time. Some said it would turn men yellow.

Saturday found them on the ridge Ledford had admired from a distance. Camel Ridge, some were calling it. They had no way of knowing that its name would soon change, and that the new name would be one they could never forget.

Bloody Ridge was high and steep.

They'd scampered through the jungle and then the ravines, on up through the head-high kunai grass that clung to the slopes, thick and tooth-edged. It sliced men's fingers and stung like fire. But they'd been told that the ridge would provide ease, a place away from the airstrip bombings.

Ledford's platoon dug in at the crest of a knoll. He and McDonough and a fellow named Skutt from Kentucky shoveled a three-man foxhole quick and quiet. Skutt got low, on his knees, and cut a shelf inside. He took a photograph of his daughter from his coverall breast pocket, set it gingerly on the ledge. He smoothed the dirt away from it with his bloody fingers. The girl was no more than two, fat like a little one should be. There was water damage at the corner, so that her stiff white walkers bubbled up at the ankle. Skutt licked his thumb and smoothed it.

'That your little one?' Ledford asked.

'That's my Gayle.'

'She a springtime baby?' Saying those words nearly caused Ledford to smile.

'Summer.' Skutt coughed. Once he started, he couldn't stop, and it became irritating in a hurry. The foxhole's quarters were tight. McDonough seemed to wince at every sound.

Night came, and with it the air-raid alarm. Bettys and Zeros filled the sky above the ridge, and they littered the hillside with daisy cutters. At first, it didn't seem real. The airstrip bombings had been one thing, but in this new spot, the feeling of exposure was almost too much. The earth quivered. The nostrils burned.

Ledford pressed his back against the foxhole's bottom and dropped his helmet over his face. Beside him, McDonough did the same. They waited.

But such waiting can seem endless inside all that noise, and some men can't keep still. After a time, Skutt leaped from them and ran, screaming, maybe firing his weapon, maybe not. He was cut to pieces.

When the raid was over, they surveyed the dead and wounded. All but two were beyond repair. Skutt was splintered lengthwise, groin to neck. Ledford's insides lurched. He turned back to the foxhole. He saw the picture of the baby girl on the dirt shelf. Somehow, she hadn't blown over.

The Marines were pulling back to the southern crest now, digging in there for more. Holding position.

Ledford looked at the picture again and left it where it sat. He followed.

Japanese flares with strange tints lit the sky overhead. Underneath, the enemy scampered ridgelines, closing quick on freshly dug Marine foxholes, where grenades were handed out, one to a man. Bayonets were at the ready. Brownings ripped through belts of ammo, humming hot and illuminating machine-gunner faces locked in panic or madness or calm. Mortars made confused landings, and everywhere, men screamed and cursed, and many of them, for the first time, truly wanted nothing more than to kill those they faced down.

Ledford wanted it. He bit through the tip of his tongue. He hollered and swallowed his own blood and stood and lobbed his grenade at the onslaught. Then he sat back down inside the hole. McDonough panted hard and followed suit.

After a while, Ledford climbed out again and got low. He set the butt of his rifle to his shoulder and looped the sling around opposite arm. Bellied down and zeroed in, he watched under the glow of a flare as a thin Japanese soldier ran across the ridgeline ahead. Ledford led him a little, shut an eye, and squeezed. The man buckled sharp, like a rat trap closing, and a black silhouette of blood pumped upward. Immediately, a hot sensation flooded Ledford from head to belly. A wave of sickness. A swarm of stinging blood in the vessels. He rolled back into his hole. His head lolled loose on his shoulders and he lurched twice. Killing a man had not been what he'd anticipated. 'God oh God,' he said. 'God oh God.'

Sunday-morning daybreak brought the battle to its end. The Marines had held. Their horseshoe line bent but never broke.

Ledford walked the ridge with McDonough at his side. Neither spoke. They looked at the bodies covering the ground like a crust. Hundreds of them. Nearly all had bloated in the sun. Their eyes were open, glazed, burning yellow-white in their staredown with the sky. Some of their faces had gone red. Others were purple or a strange green-black. The smell was too much for McDonough. He cried to himself and covered his face with a handkerchief and muttered about his sinuses, blaming everything on his bad pipes. Ledford tried not to breathe. He felt for the boy from Louisiana. This was too much for him to bear. He'd known it since McDonough had pissed himself in the foxhole. The smell had gotten bad, and

McDonough had apologized. Ledford had told him, 'You've got nothing to be sorry for.' He'd vowed in his mind to watch over the boy.

Two weeks later, Ledford watched McDonough climb the sandbar west of the Matanikau River. The boy turned back to stare at the water's surface, suddenly wave-white, alive with the plunk and stir of hand grenades, mortars kicking mud. He looked Ledford in the eyes, confused, and then his face exploded. His body sat itself down on the embankment, almost like he still had control of it and had decided to rest his legs. McDonough rolled the length of the embankment into the water and bobbed there, knocking against a tree root that had caught the collar of his coverall.

After that, when Ledford went flat on his bedding at night, he saw it: McDonough's confused face and the way it was instantly changed into something no longer a face, into something Ledford's brain could barely comprehend. His memory held no pictures such as this one. The only thing that came close was a sight he'd beheld as a boy. He'd come upon his father on the front porch, the dog whimpering and held off the ground by the scruff of its neck. His father swung a switch at the dog's backside, just as if it was a boy who'd done wrong. At the corner of the porch, where the chipped floorboards came together, sat a heap of ruined leather. His father's white buckskin mitt lay there, mauled almost unrecognizable.

He'd kept it oiled regular since his time in the Blue Ridge League in 1915. Now the dog had gotten a hold of it and it was ragged-edged and wet and ripped from the inside out. Same as McDonough's face.

Ledford played a little game with his brain for six straight nights in late September of 1942. The game played out on the back of his eyelids, where the furnace fires had set his mind on visions. Now he'd lay down, shut his eyes, and here would come McDonough's ragged-edged no-face and his daddy's exploded buckskin mitt and the squeal of the dog and the crack of the switch on short-haired hide. All of it would amplify against those eyelids until it became so loud that Ledford could not be still. He'd open his eyes and the sounds would quiet. But no man can hold open his eyes forever, and when they closed again, Ledford's heart beat against his breastplate double-time, and he sat up bone straight for fear his own mind and body were killing him. On it would go like this until he got up from his bunk and swallowed sufficiently from his own pint or somebody else's. Whiskey was the only thing to save him.

Erm Bacigalupo had won enough poker hands to own what little liquor the men had left. Some of it was Navy-smuggled, some of it was swiped from bombed-out Japanese camps. Either way, Ledford owed Erm for liquor. It was all written down on paper scraps Erm kept in his cigarette tin.

On the seventh night, the whiskey finally killed

the pictures and howls in Ledford's head. Rendered them temporarily gone.

He woke up the next day a new man. His voice had changed, gotten deeper. There was a whistle in his left ear. But from that morning on, Ledford was no longer visited by McDonough's exploding face.

In the days to come, he saw other men suffer similar fates to McDonough's. The enemy took to staking American heads on sharpened bamboo poles. It wasn't long before a Marine returned the favor.

After a time, Ledford found a quiet space inside the whiskey bottle. It was the same place his daddy had once found.

Ledford listened to the woods. He watched the treetops sway. He slept easy and ate well.

Rachel's letters saved him. He could get a hard-on just picturing the pen in her hand, moving across the paper he now held. *I love you*, she wrote, and he wrote it back.

OCTOBER 1942

He awoke in his foxhole at 0300 hours. It was black and quiet. The dreams had visited him again, but already they were gone. At the mouth of his hole, Erm crouched, smoking a cigarette. 'Let's go,' he said.

Ledford stood. He slugged hard from Erm's flask.

In front of him, Erm covered ground in silence. They put five miles behind them at a quick clip. Stopped, breathed, slugged the flask. Tucked themselves into the ridge folds west of the Bonegi and crept, then belly-crawled toward a small camp of sleeping Japanese. The rain beat in torrents. Its sound allowed them to move unheard. Its curtain allowed them to advance unseen. Single-file, they belly-crawled, stopping now and then to survey. Each gripped his .45. The mud sucked at their bellies and hips and knees.

Behind the enemy's line, Erm looked for sleeping pairs.

He found two such men tucked inside a makeshift tent of bamboo shoots and canvas. He peeked inside the open flap, then signaled for Ledford to stand watch. Erm slipped inside. Ledford kept his head on a swivel, once or twice glancing at the sleeping men inside. Each had dropped off while eating a tin of rice, now emptied and atop their chests. Ledford watched the slow rise and fall. He listened to the snore, recognized the exhaustion. The rain kept up. There was no sign of movement on the perimeter. Erm reached from the tent and tapped his shoulder. *Your knife*, he mouthed. Ledford holstered his .45 and fished the dogleg jackknife from his breast pocket. It had been his father's before him. Pearl-handled and well made. *Thackery 1 of 10* etched by hand on the flat. He'd spent hours honing the bevel on a pocketstone.

Ledford watched Erm crawl between the two men. One of them wore a thin mustache, the other was clean-shaven. They were rail thin. Young as McDonough. Ledford looked at the lids of their closed eyes, barely discernible in the low glow of their lantern, its oil nearly spent. He watched the eyeballs rolling wildly underneath. It was deep sleep. Dream sleep. He wondered for a moment what haunted these men, and then he watched Erm looking from one to the other and back. He chose the one on the left, put his hand over his mouth and drove the jackknife into his jugular vein, pulling it across the throat with all the muscle his forearm could muster. Blood came fast and heavy, surging in time with the young man's heart. Erm waited out the few soft gurgles, his eye on

39

the other soldier, who continued to snore. He wiped the blade across the dead man's still chest, one side and then the next, so that it made a red X next to the empty rice ration. He folded the blade shut and handed it to Ledford.

They left the tent and maneuvered back to blackness. On their way, Ledford considered the young soldier they'd left alive. He envisioned him stretching awake come morning, wiping the sleep from his eyes and turning to face his comrade. What horror the young man would experience – what confused detriment to arise to such a sight. This type of warfare could not be measured. It was more than payback for McDonough, more than putting a chopped head on a stick. More than taking a father forever from a baby girl whose picture he carried. This was what their drill instructor back in boot had told them would win wars. The man had sat in earshot until daybreak just to hear the screams of German boys echoing across the French forest. The awful screams. 'Nothing like it for defeatin the enemy,' he'd told them. That was so long ago now. Now here he was.

Before him, Erm walked in silence and thought of his cigarettes, dry inside a tin in his foxhole.

Ledford trailed behind. The jackknife jostled in his breast pocket as he walked. He thought of his father scoring glass.

He wondered how he'd come to follow such a man as Erm.

Rain beat his shoulders numb. Its sound was everything.

On a Saturday, in front of the pagoda at Henderson Field, Erm Bacigalupo said something he shouldn't have. What followed would confuse every eyewitness, for it showed them that in wartime, friends and enemies are difficult to discern.

Erm enjoyed messing with those he deemed 'country.' It was a hundred-degree afternoon, the last day of October, and Erm had picked a heavyset seventeen-year-old from Mississippi who'd just sailed over from Samoa with the Eighth Regiment. Three men sat on the skinny bench against the front wall, watching Erm size up the new boy. He up-and-downed his utility uniform, fresh-issued. 'Look at the sharp dresser,' Erm said, fingering the coat's buttons. Like everybody else, he knew the boy only wore the coat to hide his baby fat, and Erm wanted him to take it off so he could make his life more miserable than it already was. 'Look at the buttons on this thing. Anybody told you about the copper pawn, Country?'

'Huh-uh.' The pits of the coat were sweated straight through in circles the size of a phonograph record.

Ledford was under the pagoda's corner, his reading spot. He closed his Bible and slid out. The Bible's bookmark was a letter he'd gotten

41

from Rachel that morning. Eli Mann, her grandfather, was dead at ninety-one.

Ledford propped his elbow on the dirt and
watched the men on the porch.

Erm kept at it. 'Copper pawn'll give you ninety-
five cents a button. You know how to get there?'

'Huh-uh.' He tried to remember what he'd been
told about this kind of northern talk from this
kind of northern man.

'It's at the top of Mount Austen, but they're only
open from midnight to two a.m.'

Somebody laughed and somebody else told Erm
to shut up. Ledford stood up and started to walk
inside.

The boy from Mississippi said, 'Mount Austin,
Texas?' and everybody laughed at him. Ledford
looked at the boy's face, the way it wore a
confused, familiar look. He stopped and stood
behind Erm.

'This one isn't even worth it,' Erm said. 'This
one's dumber than Sinus.' Sinus was what some
of the men had called McDonough, as he never
shut up about his sinus problems. 'You watch out,
Country,' Erm said, tearing the copper buttons
off the boy's coat one by one. 'Sinus ended up on
a Jap spit with an apple stuck where his mouth
used to be.' All but one of the men quit laughing.
Erm stuck the buttons in his pocket and turned
to the two still seated. 'Old Sinus doesn't have to
worry about his clogged head anymore, does he?'
he asked them. 'Japs opened it up wide.'

Ledford grabbed Erm by the back of his neck, just as his father had done the dog that day on the porch so long ago. With a fistful of shirt-collar, he lifted the other man an inch or more from the ground and slammed him, face first, into the dirt. Then he took a knee next to the Chicagoan with a smart mouth and rolled him over, blood already thick with dust, front teeth already broken. Ledford raised his fist as high as he could and brought it down square on Erm's face. He got in two more before they pulled him off, the other man half-asleep and gagging on sharp little pieces of tooth, bitter little rivers of blood.

NOVEMBER 1942

I f there were any boys among them, Bloody Ridge and Matanikau had made them men. Bayonet-range fighting will do that, quick. Ledford didn't worry on the enemy any longer. If he kept an eye open, it was for Erm. The sureness of death's liberation had sunk in. Someone was coming for him, and it didn't matter much whether that someone was his comrade or his enemy.

When a man accepts that he will no doubt die, he is free to live.

The pagoda's shade was cooler. The rice rations tasted better. The whiskey was like drinking the sun.

Ledford grew accustomed to seeing things he'd not imagined stateside. One Marine safety-pinned six enemy ears to his belt. Heads stuck on a pole were not uncommon. Erm had joked of the sight, and now Ledford knew why. It was just another thing to look at while you smoked.

Still, Erm never spoke to or looked at Ledford after having his top teeth knocked out. He didn't speak much to anyone. He'd developed a noticeable lisp since the fight. The man's tongue knew not where to go.

Once, he'd gotten excited about a rumor that was spreading. 'The division is about to be relieved,' he'd said, lisping all the way. 'We'll be parading in Washington by Christmas.' The next day, his eyes were back to staring blank at nothing, all pupil. Black as jungle mud.

Some said Erm was shooting morphine he'd won in a stud game.

Ledford felt guilty for what he'd done to the hard Mac from Chicago. In some ways, he hated the man, the secret they shared of a maneuver in darkness. In others, he admired him. It crossed Ledford's mind to apologize, but he couldn't. He couldn't speak on much of consequence to anyone in those days of preparation. They were to push the Japanese out of the airstrip's artillery range.

Ledford found himself uncharacteristically hungover on the morning he marched toward Kokumbona on the heels of an Air Fleet strike. Positions were to have been secured and the movement through the jungle was to have been a safe one, but something was not right. Ledford felt it in his headache and in his bones. He looked at the Marines around him. They felt it too.

It was quiet. Ten yards to his right was Erm Bacigalupo. He looked as though he might vomit. His cheekbones stuck out. His lips were in a pinch.

Then came the hard clap of a single Japanese rifle, and Ledford's every muscle seized. He dropped and

45

rolled toward a thicket of green, but the noise had got to him this time. A burst of machine-gun fire originated somewhere too close, and then the thump of a mortar shell blew out his eardrums. All was still. Then ringing. His vision went seesaw. He stood, and just before another mortar landed before him, he made eye contact with Erm, who was running in his direction. Then another thump, and then silence. Ledford was aware of hurtling through the air. Something had gone through him, and he lay on his back, touching at a torn spot on his chest. Air emanated to and from this spot. It had gone clear through, and he breathed from it. He was deaf, but he could hear it plain as day, in and out, *pfffffffffff-hoooooo*. The left shin was also torn, smoking gray wisps and spilling black blood on the ground cover.

The thought came. *This is it.*

But then a corpsman was there, and he stuck in a shot of morphine. And then there was a stretcher and some movement, and then nothing.

The night ahead was something Ledford would never forget. He lay in a wounded dugout, eight feet deep, at Henderson Field. The heat inside the earth there was too much to take, and the men were packed shoulder to shoulder. They screamed. The smell induced gagging. Ledford tried to keep deaf, but his eardrums were healing. He tried to shut his eyes, but the swirls on the black stage of his eyelids erupted like they never had. His stomach jumped and his throat crawled

46

up his tongue. He breathed through his mouth, labored, like a dog.

Once, before passing out, he turned and saw Erm, three men away from him, his forehead wrapped in bloody gauze. He stared at Ledford, and a corpsman came by and stuck Erm with morphine, and he smiled, toothless.

The next morning they were flown out to a Navy hospital. Espiritu Santo it was called. It was there that Erm said to Ledford, 'I told you we'd be home by Christmas for the parade.'

The USS *Solace* carried the men to New Zealand. On board, an infantryman younger than Ledford cried with joy in his bunk. Everyone ignored him. They all spoke upwards, to the ceiling. Loud. Some perched on an elbow to see their surroundings. It didn't seem real that they could be out of the jungle.

'Think they'll have any KJ billboards up back home?' somebody said.

'What's a KJ billboard?' It was the teary kid.

'Ain't you had your eyes open doggie?' Ledford said. He was drunk and delirious. 'Kill Japs, kill Japs, kill more Japs. There's one plastered across every piece of plywood in the Solomons.'

The kid shivered. Jungle disease was in his blood. 'I'm done with killin,' he said. 'Japs or no Japs.' He looked down at his shaking fingertips. 'I just want my fingernails and hair to start growing again,' he said. As dysentery came, such growing went. The jungle blood could rot you inside out.

'Yeah,' Ledford said. 'You're done with it all right doggie. You go on and turn soft. Let those nails and hair grow real long.'

A couple Marines laughed. Another one said, 'Damned pansy Army dogs.'

Erm Bacigalupo said, 'Put some panties on while you're at it and bend over.' Everyone laughed hearty. There was no longer any room for soft. A code needed to be kept. Among men who'd done what they'd all done together, none could ever speak of going soft again. To do so would invite their nightmares to the waking world.

That night, Ledford made his way on crutches to Erm's bunk. He apologized for knocking his teeth out. 'I'm truly sorry for it,' he said. He held out his hand and they shook. Ledford pledged that once stateside, he would buy his friend some new teeth.

AUGUST 1945

It was Monday, the sixth. The grandstand at Washington Park Race Track was filled. Elbow to elbow they sat and waited, Southside Chicagoans and out-of-towners together. They'd come for the match race between Busher and Durazna, for which the purse was twenty-five grand.

Under the grandstand overhang, Ledford and Erm swilled from their respective flasks. They studied their short forms in silence. A fat lady in a flowered hat sat down in front of them and Erm made a farting sound. She turned, frowned, and fanned herself with a program. 'Excuse you,' Erm said to her. He flashed his smile and winked at her. His teeth were white as ivory, set solid and paid in full. When the woman left to find a more suitable seat, Erm hollered, 'Keep fannin honey, you don't know from hot.' He stood for no reason and wobbled a little on his feet. He sat back down. 'Did you see that broad? She was wide as she was tall.'

They were drunk. Had been so for three straight days, nine hours of sleep in total.

49

'What's the skinny on Durazna's trainer?' Ledford said.

Erm didn't answer. He was eyeballing the suits down front. 'Look at these cocksuckers,' he said. 'I paid good money for these seats. I gotta look at these silver-haired bastards all day?'

Ledford licked his pencil and drew a circle around the words *Oklahoma bred*.

'What's the point in standin? There's twelve minutes to post, for cryin out loud.' Erm's ears were turning red. He got like this, and there was no point in trying to stop it. 'Look,' he said. 'See how they all hold their binoculars with their pinkies out? How much you think they paid for those binoculars?' He stood up again. 'Hey, Carnegie. Hey.' The men down front knew not to turn around. They recognized that kind of voice.

'Carnegie came from dirt,' Ledford said. He didn't look up from his *Racing Form*.

'What?' Erm thought about sitting back down, but didn't. He ground peanut husks with the soles of his Florsheims.

'Carnegie came from poor folks. He was a philanthropist.'

'Philanthra-who-in-the-what-now?' Erm cleared his throat and spat on the ground. 'Pipe down, college boy.' He kicked popcorn at the empty seat-back in front of them and sat down. 'Choke those fuckin suits with their binocular straps,' he mumbled.

Ledford said he wanted to go to the paddock and see the horses running in the fourth.

Erm looked at his wristwatch. 'You go on,' he said. He'd set up a three-thirty meeting with his uncle and needed to be in his seat.

Down by the paddock, the horseplayers tried to blow their cigarette smoke above the heads of the tourists' kids. It was hot and drizzly. Undershirt weather. A track made soft by summer rain. Ledford was in the bag and it wasn't yet three o'clock. He drew another circle around the number nine in his short form, put it up over his head like a rain canopy, and walked inside, away from the paddock. He chewed cut-plug tobacco. 'Homesick Dynamite Boy,' he said as he walked. It was the name of the number nine horse, and at 7 to 1 it was an overlay if he'd ever seen one. He looked at his short form again. His left shoulder knocked against the side of a pillar, so he sidestepped, and his right shoulder knocked against a man in a black shirt and matching derby hat. There were no *Excuse me*'s. This was expected. Ledford felt the man's eyeballs on him as he walked away.

He had a fifty, three twenties, and a ten left in his billfold.

Since the war, Ledford had been lucky at the races. He'd once paid a semester's tuition with a single day's payout. Erm had helped him along with tips from men with no names. Ledford didn't ask questions. He stayed drunk much of the time. He'd finished college and proposed to Rachel and taken a desk job at Mann Glass. His life was a game of forgetting.

51

Housewives from Homewood were logjamming the betting lines. Ledford chewed the plug hard between his eyeteeth and studied his form while he parted all of them, instinct taking him where he needed to go. He stepped up to the counter and said, 'Five dollars to win on the nine.' There was no response.

Ledford looked up. A kid in a green golf hat looked back at him. His voice cracked when he spoke. 'This is the popcorn cart,' the kid said.

Ledford tried to recollect the previous half hour of his life. He remembered sitting inside a stall on a toilet that had seen too much action, drinking the last of the bourbon in his pint flask. But, like all memories, this one was a sucker's bet, because once he was in the bag, time and place were wiped and gone. He ended up wagering on three-year-old geldings at popcorn stands.

'Did you want some popcorn?' the kid asked. A red-rimmed whitehead pimple on his nose threatened to blow wide open of its own accord.

Ledford thumbed at the bills in his hand. The dirt under his nails reminded him of Henderson Field, digging. 'I'm a college graduate,' he told the kid, who was getting nervous because the man in front of him was relatively big and radiating alcohol and possessed eyes that had seen some things. 'Getting married on Saturday,' Ledford told him. 'Beautiful girl.'

He looked at the people going by. So happy. So unaddicted to booze and playing horses. So empty of parasitic memories. A short woman with legs like a shot-putter's rolled by a handtruck carrying a beer keg. It was held tight with twine. 'Hell of an invention, the handtruck,' Ledford said to no one in particular. 'Dolly, some call it. Roll three buckets a cullet around with one, no problem.' He watched the stocky woman go, her beer destined for some bubblegum-ass in the VIP Room.

As he walked away from the popcorn stand and the acned teenager who could no longer hold eye contact with him, Ledford's insides ached. He spat heavy.

He walked to the betting line and made it to the window with one minute to post. 'Five dollars to win on the nine,' he said.

He held the ticket between his thumb and forefinger. Kissed it. 'Come on, Homesick Dynamite,' he said, wedging himself through the crowd, jackpot sardines with dollar signs in their eyes. Ledford stood tall at the rail and waited.

Homesick Dynamite Boy came out of the clouds on the three-quarter turn only to falter at the wire. He placed by a head length.

Ledford littered his ticket for the stoopers to pick up.

Back at the seats, he was introduced to Erm's uncle Fiore, a short man with bags under his eyes and a tailored black suit. He had a large associate called Loaf.

'Erm tells me you busted his teeth out,' Uncle Fiore said.

'Yessir,' Ledford said.

'And you're from Virginia?'

'West Virginia.'

'You like to play the horses?'

'Yessir.'

'All right, son.' For the entirety of this exchange, Uncle Fiore had been grasping Ledford's hand, looking him hard in the eyes. He finally let go and said, 'I'm a patriot, by the way. I got the Governor's Notice for helping secure the port docks.'

Ledford nodded.

'How's the shin? Erminio tells me you took some shrapnel bad.'

'It's healed up fine. Little limp left.'

'Good. Good. My nephew's brain I'm not so sure about, but that didn't have nothing to do with the shrapnel.' Erm tapped the scar on his forehead where it spread beneath his hairline. They all laughed, except Loaf the associate. He had his hands crossed in front of him and kept shifting his stance. His feet were too small for his frame. 'Anyway, son, you stick with Erminio around the track. He knows a little something about ponies.' Uncle Fiore winked, and his eyebags seemed to disappear for a moment. He embraced his nephew, whispered something to him, and was gone.

Erm convinced Ledford to put everything he had on Busher in the mile race. Both men emptied their wallets, and both men cashed in four-figure tickets. They walked out of the racetrack feeling

54

as good as two medical discharges living on military pensions could feel.

They hit a nightclub, then Erm's mother's place for a meal. In the driveway was an Olds Touring and a red Packard sedan with suicide doors. After she had kissed him six times, called him 'country handsome,' and complimented his appetite, Ledford asked Erm's mother how much she wanted for the Packard. Without missing a beat, she answered, 'Five hundred cash for a marrying man.' It was a done deal. Instead of taking the train back to Huntington to be married, Ledford would ride in style.

Before he left the next morning, he phoned Rachel. She sounded tired. 'Well, we're in the money,' he told her. Said he'd be home earlier than planned, and that he had a surprise.

'Me too,' Rachel said. 'I'm pregnant.'

Ledford didn't know whether to howl or have a heart attack. But he smiled, and told her he was doing so. Then he told her he loved her. He meant it.

'A springtime baby,' she said.

'Nice time of year.'

He fired up the Packard and waved goodbye to Mrs Bacigalupo. In the passenger seat, Erm nodded off within three city blocks. He was coming to West Virginia to be Ledford's best man.

Crossing the flat expanse of Indiana, there was peace inside the car. Neither of them knew that across the world, the city of Hiroshima had already been erased by the atom bomb. Gone, all of it. One hundred thousand men, women, and children had been evaporated.

The war was nearly over.

The reception's buffet table was as long as a limousine. Folks who'd grown accustomed to rationing during the war lined up to get their fingers greasy. Here was a spread not grown in any victory garden. There was an apple and salami porcupine, chicken livers and bacon, cocktail sausages, dried beef logs, bacon-stuffed olives swimming in dressing, salami sandwiches, shrimp with horseradish, pineapple rounds with bleu cheese pecan centers, roast salmon on the bone, and anchovies with garlic butter. Ledford bit into the last of these and winced. This was partly on account of his toothache, but it was more than that. The little anchovies called to mind those long-forgotten fish-and-rice rations, stolen from the dead hands of the enemy. Ledford swallowed and smiled to a skinny old woman he knew to be Rachel's kin. He turned from the buffet table and bumped into Lucius Ball, his new father-in-law.

'How do you find the spread?' Lucius asked. His neck fat quivered as he hollered over the trumpet's blare.

'Plentiful,' Ledford said.

The man had spared little expense to host his only child's wedding in his own backyard, and he wanted it acknowledged.

Lucius tried to be friendly. He was nervous about the money Eli Mann had left to Mary in his will. Money she'd be doling out in short order. 'How's the leg?' he asked. The band finished a fast Harry James number. They'd only played three songs, but already they pulled their silk handkerchiefs as if choreographed, mopping sweat before the bride and groom's dance.

'It's just fine.' Ledford answered. 'Excuse me.' He'd spotted Erm talking up a curvy brunette he knew to be fifteen, if that.

Ledford walked away. He didn't care if it was rude. His father-in-law was fishing for gratitude, and he wasn't going to get it. Not so long as he was the way he was. Lucius Ball had never been able to keep his pecker in his pants, not even with a dying wife. Such things had kept right up. Everybody knew of his transgressions, and Lucius didn't give a damn. And now, the house on the hill was done up in grand fashion for the reception. If the church was dark and humble, this was white-linen and bulb-light flashy. Ledford had seen too much of nothing to be impressed by so much everything. He looked up at the tent's ceiling as he walked. There was a rust-colored water stain at the center post. A blemish amidst all that white. It called to mind the hole in his tent at Guadalcanal. That drip against his Adam's apple. McDonough.

He came up quiet behind Erm and kneed him in the leg. 'I see you met Rachel's cousin Bertie,' Ledford said. 'Bertie's a freshman in high school.'

Erm didn't care how old she was. He started to say so when the bandleader came over the PA. 'About one minute now, if we could gather up the bride and groom.'

Erm's dress blues had been in a box for three years. It showed. Ledford wore a store-bought black tuxedo, and that morning, when he'd asked his best man why he didn't do the same, Erm pointed to his brass belt buckle and grabbed his crotch. 'Eagles and anchors,' he'd said. 'She spreads eagle, I drop anchor.'

Ledford stepped from the crowded tent and looked up at the bedroom window. A light was on.

He nodded hellos and fake-smiled his way through the strangers on the porch, climbed the stairs inside and knocked before opening the door.

Rachel sat on the bed beside her mother, whose complexion was not unlike the white of her old hobnail bedspread. There was a coughed-blood stain on the hem of her bedsheet. Underneath, her shoulder and hip bones stuck out like stones.

Both women smiled at him.

In the glow of the table lamp, Rachel looked so tan and young next to her mother. Rachel pulled pins from the bun in her hair. Her veil sat next to a red glass bottle of codeine.

'Crowded down there?' Mary Ball's voice wasn't much more than a whisper, but Ledford listened to her every syllable. He'd come to love and respect his new mother-in-law. Once, when he'd come up short on tuition money, she'd stuck a hundred-dollar bill in his shirt pocket and told him, 'Any man who takes a degree in history needs a little help.' Then she'd laughed.

There was none of that now. Laughing always brought up the blood.

'Yes ma'am. It's packed to the tent poles,' he answered. He sat down next to Rachel and took her hand. 'They're calling us for our first dance.'

'Open the window wider,' Mary Ball told them, lifting a bony finger. 'I want to hear your song.' Ledford did as she said. She called him back over to the bedside. Looked him in the eye and squeezed his hand. 'You do right by Rachel,' she said.

'I will.'

'You don't ever forget what you've promised in marriage.'

'I won't.'

It worried the old woman that Ledford had no people there, no kin to speak of at all.

At the bottom of the stairs, Rachel wiped her tears before they went back out. She blew her nose and breathed in deep and kissed her man. 'I almost told her I was pregnant,' she said.

He nodded. 'I think she might know it anyhow.'

'I was thinking the same thing.' She laughed a little. Dusk had gone to dark outside the French doors behind her. Her gown looked almost silver against it. 'Still as hot out there?'

He nodded again. Stared at her.

59

'What?' she said. 'Are you drunk?'

'No.' Seeing her in the dress made him nearly as clumsy as the first time he'd gone to her apartment and knocked over picture frames. 'Can you dance in those?' He pointed to her high-heeled shoes.

'If I can't, I'll take em off.'

Though it wasn't as good as Claude Thornhill's orchestra, the band did a nice rendition of 'Snowfall,' and Rachel laid her head against Ledford's chest, and she knew they'd do what they'd pledged to do earlier that day. Richer or poorer. Sickness and health. This was forever. And Ledford looked down at the length of her and smiled at how the wedding gown could just as soon be the nurse's uniform he'd beheld four years before. For the length of that song, neither of them could see the people stuffing their faces at the buffet table, nor could they see Erm swallowing a highball glass of scotch in one swig, eyes shut, saying to woman after woman what he always said – 'How do you do?' Even the white linens and lights and cover of tent that had seemed in excess for a people at war, even these, for the length of that song became nothing more than snow falling all around as they closed their eyes and swayed. It was ninety-two degrees inside the tent, but the newlywed couple had ceased to sweat.

Above them, Rachel's mother nearly got up and came to the window. She knew better. Instead, she swigged her codeine and moved her fingers to the music and pictured them in her mind, just as they were outside. Her only daughter. The man she'd chosen. So much pain in him, but equal parts strength and virtue. She thought of her own husband, whose small storage of such righteous qualities had long since disappeared. He'd not been faithful to her, and that was unforgivable. She thought of her last will and testament, the changes she'd made unbeknownst to anyone, and she smiled.

Mary Ball would hang on for another day, long enough to see them off on the honeymoon. Long enough to read in the Sunday paper of a second bomb dropped, this one more powerful than the first. The smile she'd had from the music through her window was no longer. Her mouth wrenched downward at the corners. She mourned for man and wished only that she'd died the night prior. Her focus blurred, eyes shutting down like the rest of her. The last thing she ever saw were the words *Nagasaki wiped clean from the earth.*

MAY 1946

Little Mary Estelle Ledford squirmed in the crook of her father's arm. She had gas, and she couldn't yet pass it with efficiency. Ledford laughed at her grunts, the faces she made. Her eyebrow hairs were fine but dark and nearly connected to the hairline at her temples. He kissed her face all over. He sang to her a song that his mother had sung to him. *Was an old mouse that lived on the hill, mm-hmmm. He was rough and tough like Buffalo Bill, mm-hmmm.*

Rachel walked in from the kitchen. She eyeballed the beer bottle on the end table. Wondered how many he'd had. The throw rug under his feet stretched and tore with each step of the made-up dance he did with his infant girl. Their home was new, but their furnishings weren't.

Lucius Ball had gotten to keep his home after Mary died, but that was all he'd gotten.

As it turned out, the Federal Housing Authority liked to help out war vets. They'd only had to spend four pregnant months in Ledford's beat-up old house next to the scrapyard. In that time, Ledford had fixed things like cracked door thresholds and rotten windowpanes, but in the end he was glad to move into a new place. There were memories left behind in his boyhood home, but he hadn't yet sold it. He'd kept it as a place to go to on his own once in a while. These visits were less and less, as Ledford was skilled in the art of pushing on from the past.

His mother-in-law had been right about a man with a history degree. He hadn't done much with it. But, his mother-in-law had also left her family stake in Mann Glass to Rachel, and that meant a good deal. For one, Ledford had gone back to work. Not as a furnace tender, but as hot end manager. Desk job. He didn't care for the work, of course, but he could close his door even on the likes of Lucius Ball, who was now a broken man with the same pension to look forward to as everybody else. Rachel had sold the factory to a Toledo glass man who'd been a friend of her grandfather's. She and Ledford had put the Mann money in the bank for something they didn't yet understand. Rachel spoke to her father some, but only on the phone. He hadn't yet met his granddaughter, and she was three weeks old.

Mary grunted again. 'She's hungry,' Rachel said. 'Hand her over.'

Ledford did so, kissing the little one once more as he passed her to Rachel. Then he walked into the kitchen and opened another beer. *Church of the Air* was coming through the radio, but Edward R. Murrow would be on at one-forty-five.

Through the Philco, the preacher asked, 'How

63

long has it been since you labored in the field of God? How long since you bathed in his majestic waters?'

'Too long,' Ledford answered. He cleared his throat and spat in the kitchen sink.

The preacher's words stirred in Ledford a memory he'd not had in years.

There was a field, and he'd run through its weeds as a boy. Shoulder-high, the weeds seemed to know he was coming, bending before him and waking like water behind. There was a barn and an old preacher woman with a clay pipe in her teeth.

There was the lake from his dream, and his daddy, fishing from the rowboat.

Ledford went to the basement and looked at the half-full bookcase he'd built. It wasn't plumb to the ground. He stared at two books, side by side. *The Growth of the American Republic* and the *Holy Bible*. Both had belonged to his father. He picked up the old King James and looked for penciled underlinings. The marks of Bill Ledford's study. The marks of a man who could never outrun the engine in his head, but who would damn sure try. Ledford located one such passage. He took a belt off his beer and read the words, *I neither learned wisdom, nor have the knowledge of the holy. Who hath ascended up into heaven, or descended? Who hath gathered the wind in his fists?* Ledford liked that last line. He said it aloud. 'Gathered the wind in his fists.'

The phone rang. He slid the Bible back to its designation and picked up the receiver. It was Erm.

He had a tip on a horse in the eighth at Pimlico. 'This is the overlay of overlays, Leadfoot,' he kept saying. 'Don't back off the gas now.'

He told Erm to put him down for another five hundred and hung up. Stood in the center of the basement and looked around. His shinbone was acting up. Like someone had taken a hot poker to it. But Ledford would not sit down and prop it up. He'd ignore it.

Everything salvageable from his old house had ended up in the basement. There was a full tail fan of turkey feathers, gathered at the base in a knot of quills. It had come from his father's father. It sat on top of the bookcase, next to handblown blue bottles and three big glass scraps shaped liked diamonds. Against the wall there was an old brown trunk with quilts inside, one of them covered in swastikas. It was made by his great-grandmother, who, according to his father, had been half Indian. You'd always had to hide such a quilt, even before the second war, on account of Hitler. But Ledford's daddy told him that the quilt's true meaning was luck. Or love. One or the other, he'd never been sure.

The burn in his shinbone flared. He sat down on top of the trunk and picked at a shoot of splintering wood. Checked his watch again. Murrow would be coming on. He'd not listen today. He didn't want the news.

Above him, the floorboards gave as Rachel carried little Mary to her crib. He listened as

65

Rachel stepped light from the nursery and across the living room. He cupped his ear and picked up the sound of her knitting needles sliding and clacking. Ledford stood, opened the trunk, and felt beneath the swastika quilt. He pulled out a pint of Ten High. It was three-quarters full.

He tilted back, drained the bottle to a quarter, and put it back, next to the flat little box that housed his Purple Heart. He never opened that box. It may as well have housed a Cracker Jack prize. Next to the box he kept a burlap sack full of marbles his daddy had made for him. The shooter was black like tar, as if rolled and frozen in ice. 'One of these days,' his daddy had said, 'little boys and girls will line up and lay down every tooth-fairy penny they ever made for a marble like that there.'

Ledford stuck a piece of Beeman's in his mouth and stood in front of his crooked bookcase, smiling and looking for something to read. The pain in his leg subsided. He closed his eyes and fell asleep standing.

When he opened them again, the bookcase shelves were made of mud. Empty. Their surfaces cracked with tiny crooked lines like wrinkles in a roadmap. Ledford traced the cracks with his fingertip. He brought the finger to his mouth and tasted it. Dirt. Copper penny. Blood. There was a tickle on the palm of his hand, and there, worms wriggled forth from a hole the size of a button. Ledford pinched their ends and tugged, and the worms tore at the middle and whipped themselves side to side, split but still alive. He set them on the muddy shelves and watched them struggle to slide away. On the bottom shelf sat a single photograph, flipped, showing only its cotton white back. Ledford reached for it and turned it around. There was the fat Kentucky toddler in her white walker shoes. A hole had been burnt where her face should have been. Ledford smoothed the black ash with his thumb and the photograph roared at him. He fell on his tailbone and covered his ears, and the worms in his palms slid inside and burrowed deep, all the way up to his sinuses, and Ledford shook his head like a dog in water to loose them.

He awoke in this state on the hard basement floor in front of the bookcase. His fingertips were plugged up his nose-holes, and he lay flat on his backside like someone had knocked him out cold.

He crawled to the trunk for his Ten High. Tomorrow was a workday. He'd need to brave sleep again. He'd need to get through.

Upstairs, Rachel had frozen mid-stitch. The tips of her needles quivered as the baby grunted and banged against the crib rails in the nursery. 'Please,' Rachel whispered. 'Please stay down.'

Ledford's screams had come again, but she'd not go check on him this time. His nightmares were his alone. What he'd seen and done were not for her to question.

It was the baby she'd see through. It was Mary she'd listen for inside all the other noise.

JUNE 1946

When Mack Wells had returned to his janitorial duties at the Mann Glass Company, it was with little fanfare. Unlike the other GIs, his return was not featured in the company newsletter. Though he'd taken Honnigen with the 394th, he was not allowed to sail stateside with them after V-E Day. He'd been sent back with his service unit to an ill-lit port yard at four in the morning. No parades, no flashbulbs.

It was a Tuesday of his first week back on the job that Mack Wells made eye contact with Ledford. They remembered one another from their time before the war, and they recognized in one another's eyes the remnants of a shared shitstorm. They convened in Ledford's new office to talk over lunch. Each preferred the egg salad of the other's wife. They didn't speak much on the war. But as for life after its end, Mack Wells was not being offered what Ledford was, not by a longshot. Mann Glass liked its janitors black, the Federal Housing Authority liked their vets white, and neither party made an effort to hide such things.

Ledford didn't take to such small thinking. As

a younger man, like everybody, he'd played the game of white over black, but college had changed all that. History's study will somtimes enlighten the present. Theologians will sometimes speak openly in classrooms. At Marshall, Ledford had met such a man in Don Staples, professor of philosophy.

In Ledford's office, the rotary fan hummed metallic. He shut it off. Noises had begun to get under his skin.

Across the desk, Mack Wells had just asked about a new job.

'You want off the swing shift?' Ledford ran his fingers along the desk's beveled edge.

'That would help,' said Mack Wells.

'You want mold shop or hot end?'

'I think I'd make a okay flint.' Mack cleared his throat. He looked at the picture of baby Mary, stuck with a silver tack to a press board panel. Nothing else was hung on the wall.

'Mold maker it is.' Ledford took out a Mail-o-Gram pad and made a note to personnel. 'I'll speak to somebody in the 75 about you.'

Mack shook his head no. The Local 75 would sooner deunionize than offer membership to a black man. 'We could hold off on that,' Mack said. He wondered about Ledford's ways. Couldn't figure if the white man before him was on the level. 'But my wife will be lookin for work. My boy starts first grade this year and she was wonderin if selecting had a spot.'

69

The selecting department was all women. All women. All white. Ledford said he'd check into it.

They stood and shook hands, and each wanted to ask the other about what they'd seen over there. Neither could do so. Mack Wells nodded and put on his flat cap. He closed the heavy door behind him.

Ledford put his feet on the desk and lit a cigarette. He looked at the memo to personnel. Thought of all the men he knew at the plant who would spit at Mack Wells' feet if he wasn't pushing a broom. A knot took shape in his belly. He looked at the blank brown walls around him and rubbed his hands against his slacks. It was not yet ten a.m. Time to walk the floor, he decided. Time to watch the lava pour.

It was loud down there, but steady. Inside the sounds of a factory floor, there was the quiet that comes from constancy. The batch attendant unloaded the mixes. He wore the same split-leather gloves Ledford had worn years before.

Ledford nodded to the man, who he'd heard was a mute, but the gesture wasn't noticed.

When he turned to walk away, he knocked against the young man approaching. It was Charlie Ball, Lucius's nephew, who had been hired out of college as a supervisor. Charlie's father was county commissioner. His grandfather had been governor. 'Morning,' he said. His grin was of the shit-eating variety. His tie knot was fat and perfect.

Ledford had hated Charlie Ball from the moment he'd met him. 'Morning.'

'Loud, isn't it?' Charlie's eyes were set too close, and they looked right through you when he talked, on out to some empty designation beyond.

'It is.' Ledford glanced at his breast pocket to be sure he'd remembered his cigarettes. He had. He looked back at Charlie Ball, not much more than a boy, pudgy cheeks. Freckles. He had a face that stirred in Ledford the urge to whup him.

'You see the new blonde in corrugated yet?' Charlie's grin spread. He shuffled in his loafers. It was the third time he'd asked that particular question in an hour. He mistakenly thought such conversation ingratiated him with other men.

'I haven't,' Ledford said.

'Titties the size of footballs.' Charlie cupped his hands in front of his chest to elaborate.

'Uh-huh,' Ledford said. He stared sufficient to make Charlie squirm, and then he moved on.

Ledford walked past the flow line and through the side doors. It was warm out. Humid and cloudy. He sidestepped a stack of shipping palettes and lit a cigarette. Freight cars sat quiet on the line, waiting to be loaded. Ledford walked along the rail as if on a tightrope, his arms outstretched, his lips gripping his smoke. He fell off and kicked at shale rock between the ties. Picked one up and spat on it, rubbed it with his thumb. It reminded him of the pocketstone he used to carry for sharpening the dogleg jacknife. The knife he'd long since put away in the big trunk.

In the sunlight, the rock seemed to house glass, a shine inside the dust.

He threw it high at the batch tanks, above them the steaming chimney stacks. Through the steam, he could make out the green hills. They gathered up and cinched the valley shut. They were perfect.

It was quiet for a time. Then a shift whistle sounded to the east and Ledford's neck hairs stood on end. Every part of him seized up tight like a watch spring. The whistle, like the fan, had become an irritant of his soul.

When he got back to his office, Ledford tore off the Mail-o-Gram, walked to his secretary's desk, and said, 'Ernestine, I've got a note for personnel.' He watched her read it and nod her head. She wore a flower in her hair and a five-year service pin on her blouse collar. 'I'm feeling poorly,' Ledford told her. 'Taking the rest of the day off.'

She watched him walk away, pulling on his crooked tie knot and unbuttoning his shirt collar.

He gassed up the Packard and stopped at the ABC, where he bought two fifths of Ten High, a couple RC Colas, and a tin of cut plug for the trip.

At the house, he kissed Rachel and Mary hello. He phoned Erm, shoved a change of clothes into his gray leather grip, and kissed Rachel and Mary goodbye.

Rachel did not look him in the face. If this was

the last time she was to see him, she'd just as soon remember another Ledford.

Backing out of the driveway, he saw her silhouette through the window blinds. She still had that spike straight posture, whether she toted the baby or not. Most times she toted. He wanted to go back in and hold them both. Tell them he loved them. But he didn't. His foot found the clutch and his eye found the road.

On Route 52, Ledford rolled the window down and stuck his head out as he drove. He let the wind in under his eyelids.

His wristwatch read noon. He could be in Chicago by midnight.

The paperweight was ten inches of steel, the sawed-off end of an over-under shotgun barrel. Ledford stared at its two openings. From where he sat, slumped and fighting sleep, the glow of the desk lamp illuminated the gun barrels' insides, so that he watched a spider there, walking its tightrope. It was magnificent. The kind of thing he'd taken to noticing more of late. 'Hello,' he whispered to the spider. He wanted to lean forward and stick his finger in the barrel, but he was too drunk to move.

The air inside Erm's bookie office was stale. Wallpaper glue gone bad, whiskey molding in the floorboards. When the doorknob turned, Ledford's breathing seized. His back was to the door.

'Wake up Erminio,' someone said.

73

Erm jerked to attention in the slatback chair across the desk from Ledford. Erm swiveled and whirled and nearly fell to the floor. The creak of the chair seized Ledford by the nerve endings. He thought about grabbing the paperweight. It made a fine weapon. Instead, he stood and turned to face whoever had entered.

It was Loaf, the giant associate from the race-track. Uncle Fiore's bodyguard. His nose was red and swollen, and the buttons on his vest were mismatched. 'You going to sleep while your uncle gets an ulcer?' he said.

'I'm up, I'm up,' Erm answered. He fumbled with the papers on his desk as if to look useful.

Loaf sized up Ledford. 'Who the fuck are you?' he asked. His breath was rotten from four feet off.

'Ledford. We met at Hawthorne last summer.'

Loaf knew who he was. The question was a customary greeting. 'Yeah. Ledford.' He took out his handkerchief and wiped at snot and sweat alike. Loaf had little regard for his face.

On a leather love seat against the far wall, a naked woman shifted under the afghan that half-covered her. The curve in her spine was some-thing to behold. There was a birthmark on her hip. She sighed.

Ledford sat back down and looked at the gun barrel and wished he hadn't felt the impulse to use it for clubbing the head of an unknown man. The spider was gone. The glow from the lamp's green hood lit Erm a seasick hue. He coughed

74

hard and spat in the trashcan at his feet. 'I'm on it,' he said to Loaf. The door closed.

'Half-wit son of a bitch,' Erm muttered. 'You want breakfast?'

They walked to the diner on Ashland in silence. Both ordered coffee and corned beef hash and eggs. Erm kept coughing and spitting, this time on the dirty linoleum. He smeared it with his wingtip.

Ledford looked out the window. Chicago had not given him what he was looking for. The booze worked as it always had, but he wouldn't lie down with another woman. This didn't sit right with Erm. And that morning, at two a.m., a phone call had come that threw a switch in every happy man at the card table and the bar. The phone call made mugshots out of smiles. Erm's cousin had been hit by a car and killed.

The cousin, Uncle Fiore's favorite son, was a book-smart street enforcer with a straight job for appearances. A plumber who left behind a wife and three girls.

The waitress refilled their coffees. 'Listen to this,' Erm said. He had the newspaper quartered in his left hand, coffee cup in his right. The diner was getting crowded. Erm took quick looks at the front door over Ledford's shoulder. He tongued his bridge of porcelain teeth between swallows. He read aloud. 'Louis Bacigalupo, thirty-four years old, a union plumber, was injured fatally Tuesday morning just two days after his wife and three daughters had honored him with a Father's Day luncheon in his home.' Erm took a drink. 'What the hell does *injured fatally* mean? Who ever heard of *injured fatally*?' The waitress put their plates in front of them and Ledford said thank you. Erm kept on reading. 'The auto driver was charged with reckless driving and released under fifty dollars bond.'

Ledford knew what came next. It had been in the whispers that started after the two-a.m. phone call. It had been in the face of an associate who'd taken Erm aside at the basement card game. They'd left soon after for Erm's crowded bookie office, with Ledford down two hundred, his ace hand still on the way.

The naked woman had appeared from the hallway, lay down without a word, and slept.

There were meetings in the office corner to which Ledford was not invited, but he knew the good word. Murder was on the tongues of these men.

The 'auto driver' was out on bond. He'd be dead inside a day.

The corned beef hash steamed. 'I'm going to hit the road after breakfast,' Ledford said. He picked up his knife and fork.

Erm set the paper down. 'You just got here Leadfoot.' He broke bacon into little pieces and stabbed them with a fork.

'Yeah.'

Erm looked out the window at a couple walking by. They held hands and smiled. 'You feelin uneasy?

76

This kind of shit make you squirm these days?' He watched the couple turn the corner.

'You're the squirmy Ermie,' Ledford said. 'I'm just Loyal.' They both laughed a little, Erm's cut short. Ledford went on. 'Look, I been thinking too much lately. And now the baby and Rachel.' He felt like talking to Erm instead of just pushing bullshit back and forth, the only thing they'd ever done. He felt like telling Erm that he wanted to read books again like he had after the war, that a theology professor was on his mind, a man who'd told him of William Wilberforce and Mohandas Gandhi, that his mind was on God and birth and death, on Mack Wells and those who shared his skin color. He wanted to tell Erm that they'd been sold bad goods. That they didn't have to claw and tear and hate and kill and always, everywhere, win. But Erm wasn't the kind of friend you said such things to. Ledford had never wanted that kind.

He split an egg yolk with his fork. 'It doesn't have to be this way Erm,' he managed.

Erm looked at him, frowned. Then he said, 'Fuck you Ledford,' and got up and licked his thumb. He pulled two doller bills from a thick fold and dropped them on the chipped red laminate.

A leather strap of beat-up Christmas bells hung on the doorknob. It sounded as he walked away.

Ledford stood in the dark and looked at them. Mother and baby. He'd come in so quiet that Rachel hadn't stirred. She slept with her arm

77

across her forehead, her chest rising slow and even. Mary lay beside her, on her back, both arms up over her head as if stretching. She was a tiny thing. Ledford smiled. He'd hold them more, he thought. Tell them that he loved them. He'd make a change.

The hot dogs at Wiggins were fifteen cents apiece. Ledford sat at the countertop on a swivel stool, wiping chili from the corners of his mouth. The Very Reverend C. Rice Thompson sat to his right. He marveled at how young Ledford had eaten four hot dogs in the time it took him to put down two. 'You've got no problems with your appetite,' he said.

'Never have.' Ledford watched the proprietor move from the cash register to the counter-back. He pulled two cigars from an opened display box of White Owls. They were for the fat man in overalls paying his check. The elastic bands cut an X across the fat man's back. Ledford watched him breathe heavy at the register. 'Most times my stomach can hold its own,' he told the Reverend, 'it's my ears and brain that have been getting to me.' He finished off his second Coke and put the bottle on the counter. Looked at the White Owl box again. Next to it was a stack of Doublemint chewing gum, and next to that, a hanging display of powdered aspirin. Ledford could always use the aspirin.

'I hope that talking will help with that,' Reverend Thompson said. 'Rachel had the right idea sending you my way.' He took off his glasses and wiped at their lenses with his napkin. 'But I believe

I know someone you might speak a little freer with than myself.' He put the glasses back on and turned to Ledford, who stifled a burp. 'He's just over at the college here. You may have met him in your time there. Don Staples?'

Ledford shook his head in recognition. 'I had him one semester. Best teacher in the place.'

'Then you know he's a genuine theologian. Used to be with the Episcopal Church but he broke away and went to work for the CCC in the thirties. He's dedicated his study to the work of William Wilberforce.'

Ledford nodded. 'He spoke a good bit on Wilberforce in class.'

'Did you know he published a book on him?'

'No.' Ledford wondered why Staples had not laid claim to such a thing.

Reverend Thompson leaned in and spoke soft. 'The man is more committed to securing rights for Negroes than anyone you're likely to meet. Wears his beard lately in the style of John Brown. A true eccentric.'

'You think I ought to bother him?'

'Oh sure. He'd enjoy your company, just as I have. But he'd speak your language a little more fluent than I can, I'd imagine.' The Reverend, though older than Ledford, had not seen what the younger man had. He'd not lost so much for so long. He cleared his throat and signaled for the bill.

'How's that?' Ledford looked at the circle-shaped smears on the Reverend's lenses.

'Well, he spent time overseas in the First War, and he knows a great deal about a great many things.' He left it at that. It seemed enough.

After they shook hands, Reverend Thompson walked back to his church, and Ledford walked the length of Fourth Avenue to campus. He appreciated Rachel making the appointment with her Episcopalian man. The Reverend was a good sort, the kind who did not judge on attendance at God's Sunday meeting.

At Sixteenth Street, Ledford nearly knocked over a small boy selling newspapers. He wore no shirt, just a full satchel, bandolier-style. He squinted at the sun. Ledford bought a paper and walked on. A woman crossed in front of him, holding something wrapped in butcher paper. She smiled at him, and when he looked back to see her from behind, she looked back too.

It took three people to correctly navigate his path to Professor Staples' office. Its location was the basement of Old Main, just beyond the furnace room. An orange light emitted from the half-open door. Ledford knocked.

'Come on in.'

He pushed on the heavy steel door and stepped inside. 'Professor Staples?'

'Just call me Don, son.' The man looked at Ledford over spectacles worn low on his nosebridge. His beard was full and long. Blocked in black and gray like the coat of some animal. In his hand was a book. Everywhere were books. Stacked

in rows on his desk, the floor, in front of the full
bookshelves. 'What can I do for you?' he said.

'Reverend Thompson from Trinity Episcopal said
I might speak with you.' Ledford had trouble reading
the man's eyes, which were locked on him but else-
where simultaneously. The left one was lazy, off kilter.

'The Very Right Reverend,' Staples said. 'The
crème de le crème, the cream of the cash crop.' He
kept up his staring, sniffed hard. 'Oh, Thompson
is a good man of God. I'm only pullin your leg.'
He smiled. 'I had you in class once before?'

'Yessir.'

'Where you from?'

'Here.'

'What's your name?'

'Ledford.'

Staples thought for a moment. 'You have people
in Mingo?'

'Yessir. My grandfather was from Naugatuck.'

'You have people in Wayne County?'

'I believe I might.'

'Ledford,' the older man said, considering the
surname. He sniffed again, then set his book down
and wiped at his nose with his thumb. 'I knew a
Franklin Ledford up at Red Jacket.'

'My great uncle, I believe. Dead.'

'Oh yes, dead. Matter of fact, all the Ledfords
in those parts are long dead, aren't they?'

'That or moved away.' He was still holding the
door's edge in his hand. 'You're from Mingo?'

Staples shook his head no. 'Spent some time

81

there as a young man. But I'm a McDowell Country boy. Keystone.' He smiled again. 'Come on in and sit down. Just move those books off to the floor there.'

Ledford did so and sat. The seat of his chair was half-rotten. Under his backside, it felt as if it might go any time. 'I hope I'm not bothering you,' he said.

'Depends on what you're here for.' Staples leaned back and crossed his long legs. He took off his glasses and folded them shut. Held them two-handed across his belly.

'Well,' Ledford said. 'That's . . .' He couldn't spit it out. 'I . . .'

Staples did not move an inch. He sat and stared and breathed slow but noticeable through the nose he kept snorting. It whistled. The lamplight flickered under the orange scarf he'd laid across it.

'I have questions about God. And man.' Ledford cracked his knuckles against his thighs.

'Mm-hmm. Mm-hmm,' Staples said. 'And the Very Reverend, he didn't give you answers on those?'

'Well, he thought maybe I'd understand them a little better if they came from you.'

'Is that right? Well . . .' He came forward suddenly, slapped both his shoes on the floor. From his desk drawer he pulled a pipe and tobacco pouch. 'What's the weather doin?'

'Sunny. Hot.'

'You want to go for a walk?'

'Sure. Yessir.'

It was Sadie Hawkins Day, and coed girls chased boys across the green like they'd heard a starter gun salute. Staples ignored them and walked at a quick clip and talked with his teeth clamped around his pipe, which looked to be on its last leg. 'Are you married?'

'Yessir.'

'How long?'

'A year next month.'

'Child?'

'Yessir.'

'Boy or girl?'

'Girl.'

'Have you kept your pecker in your pants otherwise?' He did not break stride. They cut across the grass, dry and patchy.

'Yessir.'

'Good.' Staples stopped dead and pointed to a big maple tree ten yards off. 'This is the tree,' he said. The skin on his hand said he'd seen a good bit of sun. Long fingers. He was roughly Ledford's size, and he'd not stooped with age.

Ledford followed him to the tree. Staples sat down Indian-style next to a surfaced root. Ledford looked around. A Sadie Hawkins girl squealed and hurdled a green bench. In the distance, the GI dormitory trailers sat quiet and squat, brown rectangles in the sun. Ledford took a seat on a wide root.

Staples knocked his pipe on the tree trunk. 'You were overseas, I'd imagine?'

'Yessir.'

'Pacific or Atlantic?'

'Pacific. Guadalcanal.'

'Navy?'

'Marine Corps.'

Staples looked down at the black ash and made a strange shape out of his mouth. He'd not figured the young man for a Marine. He cleared his throat with a booming cough. 'You weren't drafted?'

'I enlisted.'

'Your mother and daddy were okay with that?'

'They died in '35.'

Staples had stuck his thumb in the mouth of his pipe. He shook his head. 'I am sorry son,' he said. 'You want to talk about booze now or save that for another day?' He pocketed the pipe in his jacket. Before Ledford could answer, Staples said, 'You read much Ledford?'

'I do some.'

'What are you reading now?'

'The Bible some. And a book called *The Growth of the American Republic.*'

Staples nodded and stood up. He'd gotten a case of the fidgets. 'Let's walk a while,' he said, 'and then you'll accompany me to my office, where I'll load you up with some new reading material.' He brushed off the seat of his brown slacks. 'How's that sound to you, Ledford?'

Ledford stood and brushed himself off in the same manner. He nodded as the older man had. 'Sounds good,' he said.

SEPTEMBER 1947

The child walked unsteady from one end of the little porch to the other. Her gait possessed a wild, untested confidence. Rachel stood guard, her foot on the first of three porch stairs. Boards were warped and nailheads surfaced. Rachel worried on splinters – Mary's feet were soft, though she'd been walking for over a month. She lifted her knees to right angles and pounded against the half-rotten boards. Ledford pushed open the screen door with the box he carried. He let Mary pass before him, winked at her, and stepped down from the porch. The Packard's trunk was up, Bill Ledford's blowpipe and punty rod jutting out the back. The suicide doors were swung wide open. A single spot remained among all the boxes crammed inside, and Ledford slid the last one there. He'd marked it *Attic Junk*, and its contents, mostly old books, had nearly caused him to sit down in the dark reaches of his boyhood home and reminisce one last time. But Mack Wells and his family were on their way over. The home had to be emptied.

Ledford slammed the Packard's heavy doors

tight against its contents. Inside those boxes were the remnants of a childhood in two parts – the first recalled in photographs, the second in pay stubs and grade cards that no one ever saw.

There was a sound from the porch.

'Oh dear,' Rachel said.

Ledford turned to see her bent and picking up Mary, who was on all fours, crying.

He pulled out his handkerchief on the way.

Little droplets of blood emerged round from the checkerboard scrape on her knee. 'Watch,' Ledford told her. He pressed the white hanky against the skin and pulled it back, showed it to her. 'What's that?' he asked.

Mary quit crying and stared at the crimson mark on the white square.

'That's a big girl,' Rachel said. She tickled Mary where she held her by the armpits, and the laughing came, harder than the crying. Ledford dabbed once more and the bleeding quit. He bent and brushed his fingers against the porch boards where she'd fallen. A truck backfired, then rumbled past on the street. Its muffler dragged. Ledford watched it stop at Sixth Avenue, and then, still kneeling, he looked back to the porch boards. To the corner, where they met up in a chipped V. He pictured his father's white buckskin mitt there, just as it had been all those years before, torn to hell by the dog. Then came McDonough's face. Ledford shook his head and stood up. Mary walked a circle in the front-yard square of crabgrass. Rachel stood by the curb with her hands on her hips. She was turned so that he could see her belly in profile, stretched to full with another child. Best they could figure, she'd gotten pregnant around New Year's, and here they were, on the precipice of another one.

A car turned off the boulevard and rumbled toward them. 'That's Mack,' Ledford said. He stepped off the porch, picked Mary up, and stood next to Rachel. He waved as the car pulled up the curb, and then he rubbed at the small of Rachel's back. She'd strained it pushing the stroller over railroad tracks.

Mack Wells stepped from the old Plymouth and nearly slammed the door on his boy, who had hopped the front seat to follow his father. The boy ran around the back of the car and opened the passenger door for his mother. She stepped out and thanked him kindly. For a month, he'd opened all doors for his mother. 'That's what a gentleman does,' his grandfather had told him.

Mack put his hand to his flat cap and nodded. 'Ms. Ledford,' he said.

'Hello Mack.' Rachel stepped toward them. 'You must be Elizabeth.' She held out her free hand to Mack's wife in greeting.

'Yes. Everybody calls me Lizzie.' Lizzie wore a rust-colored blouse and matching hat, tilted on her head.

The women shook hands.

'This Harold?' Ledford asked.

'This is him,' Mack said. He rubbed the boy's head from behind.

'Good to meet you Harold,' Ledford said.

'Pleased to meet you.' Harold looked up at the white family before him. The baby drooled, and he watched it stretch well past her chin, then give and fall to the sidewalk. It made a quiet splat.

No one spoke for a moment. Then Mack inhaled deep through his nose. 'Mmm,' he said. 'Smell that.'

'Bread factory,' Ledford said. 'You'll smell it everyday.'

Lizzie Wells sniffed the air and smiled politely. She looked mostly at the ground.

Rachel took Mary from Ledford. 'Let me show you the space in back for a garden,' she said. Lizzie nodded and followed, leaving the men and the boy by the car.

'If it isn't the bread smell stirring your stomach, it's the scrap metal clanging in your ears,' Ledford said. He turned and walked to the house, motioned for them to follow. His limp had come back with all the box hauling. He ignored the burn radiating up his shinbone.

Mack looked back at Harold. He knew the look on the boy's face. It was fear. Mack felt it too. There wasn't a black family for a mile in the West End, and he could scarcely believe he'd agreed to rent the house. But when his home loan had fallen through, and his mother had sold her house to move in with his brother, Mack had acted fast. Ledford had told him over lunch one day, 'I got a place in the West End you could rent real cheap.' Mack had quit chewing, looked at him like he was crazy.

Ledford went on. There weren't many neighbors, he'd said. There was the scrapyard and the bakery. There was the filling station on the corner, whose owner, Mr Ballard, was not a hateful type. He had a Negro in his employ, Ledford had told Mack. It had all seemed natural, what with Ledford's need to hold on to his old house and Mack's troubles with the Federal Housing Authority. Inside a week, they'd drawn up a lease and shaken hands on it. There'd been some looks in their direction, but neither man paid much mind. They'd become friends, as much as a black man could be with a white one. Mack was the only welcome visitor inside Ledford's office, the only glass man interested in hearing what Professor Staples had been teaching his young pupil.

The screen door squealed as Ledford opened it and stepped in. 'Gas and water and electric are all on and in your name,' he said. The staircase before them sagged at the middle of each riser. It would be good to have a boy running up and down again. Ledford smiled, 'Wasn't always that way with the water and electric. We used to barrel-catch rain and heat it.'

'I know about that,' Mack said. He surveyed the living room. 'You ain't taking that big chair?'

'It's yours if you want it.' Ledford regarded the wide upholstery. It had been his father's drinking chair. On payday, he'd pass out cold and spill over it. The smell still turned Ledford's stomach.

Young Harold walked over past the chair. He

looked at the built-in bookcase, the few books left there. He whispered, sounding out the spines.

'Book on baseball there. Go on and grab it,' Ledford said.

Harold took down the skinny book and opened it. He sat down cross-legged on the floor and turned pages.

'He's reading like a older child already,' Mack said.

'You like baseball?' Ledford asked the boy.

Harold said, 'Yessir,' without looking up from the book.

'Good.' Ledford smiled. 'That's your book then. But if that baby in Mrs Ledford's belly comes out a boy, I may borrow it back from you down the line.'

'Yessir,' Harold said, and then he went back to sounding out the words. 'The Red . . . Head . . . ed . . . Out . . . field,' he whispered.

Ledford fished the front- and backdoor keys from his pants pocket. His finger through the keyring, he whirled them a few times, Old West style, catching them mid-rotation with the snap of his hand. He held them out for Mack Wells to take.

The women came in the back door, Mary in the lead. She dropped to all fours on the cracked ribbon tile and picked at a loose piece of grout. Before she could get it in her mouth, Rachel reached down and snatched it.

'Harold used to put everything in his mouth,' Lizzie said. 'I caught him eating mud more than once.'

In the backyard, Rachel had asked her about

having more children, and Lizzie had explained she was no longer able. *I'm sorry*, Rachel had said, and it seemed to Lizzie that unlike some white folks, she meant it.

'Mary hasn't yet sampled mud, but I figured early I sure can't set out mouse traps.' They laughed together. They watched Mary pull herself up by a loose drawer handle.

'Strong,' Lizzie said.

Rachel pointed out the range's unsteady leg. She showed Lizzie how to bang on the refrigerator's monitor top if it quit running. 'Loyal put some work in the kitchen over the years,' Rachel said. 'Nothing's new, but everything's fixed.' She ran her finger over a long, glued crack in the table's porcelain top. It pinched at her insides to think of him alone in that house back then, still a boy, doing a man's job and a woman's too. She rubbed at her round belly through the silk.

Lizzie was used to some age on her things. The hand-crank wringer-washer next to the sink was the same one she'd grown up with, same one she still used. It was possible that Mack had not been crazy when he'd agreed to rent this place.

When Lizzie knew it wasn't obvious, she stole hard looks at Rachel's face. It seemed the woman was kind and genuine. She suspected the only black folks Rachel knew growing up were those who cleaned her house, those who followed the orders of her parents, but it was possible that such ways had not rooted in her.

'Loyal raised himself alone from age thirteen in this house,' Rachel said. She'd knelt to Mary, who was at the windowsill, pulling at an edge of unstuck wallpaper. She blurted something over and over that vaguely resembled 'flower,' the paper's pattern. Rachel looked through the windowpane, her eyes glazing over. 'I know he hopes your family will find the house suitable.'

Lizzie did not answer. She listened to the baby girl talking in her own language. Down the hallway, Mack and Ledford laughed at a joke. From the scrapyard there came an extended squeal and crunch. Lizzie's knees nearly buckled and her forehead popped with sweat. She was thinking how dangerous all this was. Her new job had come by way of Mr Ledford. Her family's new home, the same. White folks. Those whom her father had raised her to be wary of. And here she was, talking kitchens and children, vegetable gardens and barren wombs, all as if the expectant woman across from her had been born into the same world as she.

Charlie Ball was eager to hand out the cigars he'd bought. He walked the factory floor, sidling up to every man in sight with his box of White Owls, lifting the lid like it was a treasure trunk. 'It's a boy,' he said. 'Little William Amos Ledford. Saturday morning. Mother and baby are just fine.' Most men took a cigar and stuck it in a coverall pocket, then went back to work. Fishing for conversation, Charlie said to more than one, 'I'm not real sure where that middle name comes from, but to each his own, I guess.'

The name came from the Bible, a book Ledford had read yet again.

Ledford arrived at half past noon. It was Tuesday, the last day of the month, and he needed to get a few things done now that Rachel and the baby were home from the hospital. Her aunt, a retired schoolteacher, was helping out.

Charlie caught him as he walked toward the office door. 'There he is,' Charlie said, loud. His hair carried too much Royal Crown at the front. It clumped in spots. 'Cigar for the proud papa?' He opened the box with flair.

'Thank you Charlie,' Ledford said. He pocketed the thing as the others had.

'How's Rachel faring?'

Charlie spoke about his cousin as if he knew her. Ledford didn't care for such talk. 'She doesn't complain. Though as ever,' he said. He moved past the younger man and stepped into his office. Charlie followed.

Ernestine poked her head in the door. She'd just come back from lunch and carried a doggie bag. 'Congratulations Mr Ledford,' she said.

'Thank you Ernestine.'

Her smile was genuine.

Charlie watched her hips, and when she was gone, he leaned across the desk and whispered, 'How old is that gal?'

93

'What can I do for you Charlie?' Ledford hung his jacket on the back of his desk chair. The air smelled damp and old.

Charlie straightened back up. 'My uncle would like to know when he might stop by and see his new grandson.' Lucius had officially retired. He spent his days drunk at Chief Logan's Tavern. Nights he was in bed by seven.

'Well, he hadn't hardly come by for the first one, has he?' Ledford was running short on sleep.

'You can understand the excitement over a boy child, Ledford.' There was nothing but the sound of his own swallowing. 'Can't you?'

'Sure Charlie. Tell him his daughter will phone him.'

Ernestine poked her head in again. 'Mr Ledford,' she said, 'there's a man here to see you. Says his name is Admiral Dingleberry.'

Ledford laughed. Ernestine didn't, and neither did Charlie. It occurred to Ledford that they weren't familiar with the term. 'Well by all means, send in the admiral,' he said.

Erm stepped through the open door. He spread his arms wide, brown-bagged bottle in the left one nearly knocking Charlie in the head. 'Private Leadfoot,' Erm said.

'Squirmy Ermie,' Ledford answered. He couldn't wipe the smile off his face, and he didn't know why. The two had not spoken in more than a year, not since their awkward parting at the Chicago diner. 'What the hell are you doin here?'

94

Ledford came around the desk and they shook hands, clapped shoulders as if to injure.

'Visiting my old friend is what I'm doing.' Erm hadn't acknowledged Charlie, who stood by the hat rack and swallowed and smiled wide. 'Who's the broad?' Erm asked, motioning with his head to Ernestine's desk in the hall. His breath smelled of gin and chewing gum and cigarettes. He wore a new scar across his right eyebrow.

'That's Ernestine,' Charlie said.

Erm looked at him as if he'd insulted his mother.

'How old would you guess she is?' Charlie's voice was pinched.

Erm squared up on him. He cocked his head and smiled. 'Eighty-seven,' he said. 'What's your guess?'

Charlie laughed, then looked down at the cigar box. He opened it, looked in Erm's general direction, and said, 'Cigar, Mr Dingleberry?' His voice cracked on the last syllable.

'No, it's *Admiral* Dingleberry, kid. And yes, I wouldn't care to partake of your smoking pleasures.' Erm kept his expression straight. Ledford did the same beside him, though the urge to laugh was strong. Erm still hadn't reached for a White Owl. He said, 'That your position in this dump? You the cigar girl?'

With that, Ledford laughed out loud. 'All right, Erm,' he said.

Charlie frowned and closed the box.

'Hold it now, Kemoslabe,' Erm said. 'Big Chief White Owl want smokem.'

Ledford interceded. 'Charlie here is handing out cigars on account of Rachel giving birth Saturday.'

Erm spun his head. 'No foolin. You son of a bitch.' They shook hands again. 'Boy or girl?'

'Boy. William, after my daddy.'

'How about that? Big Bill Ledford. I bet he's a biggin. Hung where it counts like his old man.'

Charlie laughed.

Erm glared at him. 'Let's have at it then. Open er up and fire the torch.'

The three of them stood and smoked and Erm uncorked his gin and passed the bottle. Ledford couldn't bear to tell him how much he'd cut back, so he sipped light instead. He explained how they were doing just fine, careful not to badmouth his job too much in front of Charlie. 'Renting out the old house,' Ledford said.

'Yeah, to a nigger,' Charlie said. He laughed and took another swig off the bottle.

Ledford stared Charlie down and breathed slow and even. He contemplated his response.

Erm said, 'Well Sally, you just jump in anytime.'

Now both men stared at him, and Charlie set the bottle on the desk and excused himself.

'Jesus H. Christ,' Erm said. 'Who the hell was that pansy?'

'That's Rachel's first cousin. Her daddy's nephew. Pain in my ass.'

They both reached for the bottle at the same time. Laughed and exchanged *after you sirs*.

Erm sat down and explained he was passing

96

through on business he had in Baltimore. He got quiet after that. Neither spoke of their last meeting. Of Ledford's serious talk, of Erm's *fuck you* admonition, of the inevitable end of the auto driver who'd run over the wrong man.

Ledford still owed Erm six hundred on a straight play from the previous November, when Army had blanked West Virginia. The spread was two touchdowns. The final score was 19–0. Erm even made him pay the vig.

Ledford had been laying off the gambling like it was the sauce.

After a long silence, Erm said, 'I got married.'

'I'll be damned. When?'

'Last Thursday.' He looked around at the empty walls, tapped his shoes on the floor.

'Well . . . congratulations Erm.' Ledford nodded his head to convince himself such a move was wise for his friend.

'Yeah,' Erm said. 'She's got a bun in the oven.'

Ledford raised his eyebrows. 'Congratulations again.'

'A toast to married life,' Erm said. They drank again, and Ledford was about to ask what her name was when Erm hopped out of his chair and said, 'I gotta hit the road, but I'll be coming back through real soon.'

Ledford stood. He smiled uneasy. There was something in Erm's demeanor, something that said he was running from trouble. Ledford would not protest the abrupt departure. It was the way

97

things were for Erminio Bacigalupo. Always, he was running. Don Staples had been talking to Ledford about such movement through life. Away from things. Toward them.

'Listen,' Erm said. He was making sure his shirt cuffs stuck out beyond his jacket. 'I got something I need you to hold on to for me.' He pulled a fat-stuffed leather envelope from his inside pocket. 'Just make sure it stays where nobody gets their hands on it.' He held it out, but Ledford didn't reach. 'It isn't a bag of dogshit Ledford. It's dough. And a book.'

Ledford laughed and took it. Rubbed his thumb across the gold snap button holding it shut. 'I got a safe spot in the basement at home.'

'Good. And for your trouble, we'll wipe your paysheet clean. Get you out of my left column, back on the right.' Erm winked. Then he leaned forward. 'But listen,' he said. 'If I don't make it back from Baltimore, you see that money gets to my old lady.'

An alarm sounded from the factory floor. Erm stuck his fingers in his ears. 'Some job you got here,' he hollered.

'It's just a backup on the flow line,' Ledford hollered back. He looked at the half-full gin bottle, wondered if his friend would be leaving it behind.

'Whatever you say.' Erm licked his pointer and pinky fingers, then smoothed his eyebrows. 'For Ernestine on the way out,' he said. He turned, was gone, then stuck his head back in the office. He yelled, 'I'll be back in a week or two.'

The alarm shut down, and from outside his door, Ledford could hear the low murmur of Erm's voice, then Ernestine's giggle. The leather envelope in his hand was squared off, worn at the corners by whatever it held. It was smooth cowhide, a deep brown. Ledford wondered why Erm might not make it out of Baltimore alive. He wondered how much money was in his hands. He put the envelope in the middle drawer of his desk. In the bottom right drawer he set the gin bottle on its side. Then he sat down and stared at the pile of paperwork before him. At home, Rachel would be nursing or napping. Mary would be playing with her great-aunt. Ledford looked at Mary's photograph on the wall. He'd need to get one up of William.

OCTOBER 1947

They were calling him Willy within a week. Sometimes Ledford called him Willy Amos. He slept just fine in the daylight hours, but at night he fussed and fought his swaddling. Rachel was too tired to rise every time, so Ledford took to walking the house with the boy. He sang to him and he danced with him. He stared at the boy's eyes and how they locked on to an unknown point and stayed there regardless of swaying, all iris and pupil, black as cast iron. He had a darker tint to him than Mary. He was bigger than she'd been.

Ledford one-armed little Willy in the basement early Sunday morning. It was not yet four a.m. He pulled the lightbulb chain hanging from the rafters, and the boy squeezed his eyes shut. 'It's all right,' Ledford told him. 'Just a lightbulb.'

Willy cried some, so Ledford lifted him high and sniffed directly at the seat of his diaper. It smelled only of powder. 'That's a boy,' he said. 'You just stay that way until your mother rises and shines.'

He strolled the length of the basement floor, pointing to and naming the tail fan of turkey feathers, the glass scrap shaped liked diamonds, the map of the world he'd hung. He put his fingertip to the map and said, 'This here green chunk is the United States of America, and right here, West Virginia, is where we live.' He slid the finger to the right. 'And if you take a boat or a airplane across all this blue water, and you cross this pink Spain and over all these different colors in Africa, you get to here,' he tapped his finger against it, 'to these little specks of nothing on the blue ocean, to where your daddy was for a time.' Willy's head wobbled from his propped vantage point on Ledford's shoulder. He liked the tapping sound of his father's fingers on the paper map.

Ledford laughed. 'All right, little one,' he said. They stared at one another for a moment, and Ledford kissed him on the forehead. Then he looked back to the map.

He took a deep breath and told his boy that he'd not ever have to go to the little specks on the ocean, nor any other place like them. He put his hand on the boy's chest, his fingers nearly wrapping around the girth of him, and he said, 'I will protect you from all of it, William Amos.'

When the boy fell asleep, Ledford set him on a cushioned desk chair from the old house. He began unpacking the last of the boxes. *Attic Junk* it read on the side. In the box, and old black album of photographs popped and cracked when he opened it. With each turned page, it shed little black corner frames. Ledford gathered them as they fell. The photographs themselves were lined and chipped with age. They were not in the order they'd been intended. Their look made them his daddy's people, the Ledfords of Mingo, mostly tall and thin. Unsmiling faces and cheekbones that cast shadows. There were dates in faded pencil on the backs of some. Names like Oliver and Homer and Eliza and Wilhelmina. In one photograph, Ledford's daddy swung on a rope hung from a tree limb. He looked to be about six, his T-shirt dirty, loose around the neck. His head a blur of black hair and bared teeth.

Ledford picked up the other album. There wasn't much inside. Four pages filled out of twenty. An old woman who looked to be part Indian sat in a rocking chair and smoked a clay pipe. There was no name or date on the back. A baby picture of a child with eyes big and dark like his own children. On the back, somebody had written *Bonecutter*.

He picked up another book, leatherbound. It was small but thick, the size of a good Bible. It was his daddy's batch book from the early days at Mann Glass. Pages were organized by color. *White Batch* and *Opal* and *Best Opal* and *Shade Batch White*. There were penciled-in measurements of hundreds of pounds of sand and soda. Lead and arsenic. Ounces counted for borax and manganese. Bones. Bill Ledford had figured out how to make a transparent green by adding copper scabs. *Every shade of green may be obtained*, he wrote.

102

In the back pages, the batch book became an account of disparate times in his life. Bill Ledford had written in it almost daily, it seemed, from the years 1916 to 1925. There were passages about his days playing ball in the Blue Ridge League for the Martinsburg Blue Sox.

Lefty Jamison threw at my head today on account of me running off at the mouth last night when the likker oiled me up. I believe I had poked at his stomack to show how fat it was, and I may have called him a bench blanket.

The baby shifted and grunted on the seat cushion. Ledford eyed him a minute and knew he wasn't long for sleep. He flipped fast through the journal's pages, looking for something. In all those years alone in his house, he'd never been able to look. He'd feared doing so would make everything worse than it already was. But Ledford was the father now, and fear had been replaced by the single-minded need to keep his wife and children above ground. He'd protect them all.

On the next-to-last page the handwriting was easier to read, as if written slow. It read,

January 12, 1924, I am twenty-six today. Last night I dreamed the same dream again. I can't pick my feet up so I look down and I've got no feet. They are inside the ground. I fall forword and my legs bend the wrong way. A

cracking sound and a feeling of my bones breaking. I'm unable to put here in words what it is, but it is bad. Then comes the roaring sound like a glass furnace and I'm holding my punty rod in one hand and my blowpipe in the other. I get to my knees and I'm all cut up as I've been laying on cullet. It is raining and I have to keep my eyes shut. That's what the voice is hollering at me, not to open my eyes up. But I do, to see who's hollering in that awful familur voice, and when I look, it is our littlest one. Loyal. Nearly two now. And he puts the fear of God in me because his mouth don't open when he talks and his hands are afire.

Willy screamed out sudden. Ledford dropped the book back in the box and stood. The hair on his arms and neck was pricked and he couldn't get enough saliva to swallow. He held little Willy and felt his own heart race against the child's side, pressed to him. He could not understand what he had just read. The mind was not made to know such words as those from his daddy's pencil. Ledford breathed deep and looked out the single-pane window. The ground there was warming, sunrise gathering in its well. He watched a dwarf spider navigate the glass and wondered why he opened the books. He'd been getting by all right as of late, drinking less on the advice of Don Staples. Dreams visited Ledford with less frequency, their horrors dulled. But what he'd read had stirred anew the unquiet. He looked at his boy, no longer screaming but not yet settled, his eyes like those in the photographs.

Seven-card stud was the only game allowed in the home of Don Staples. Straight poker and five-card draw had no place. If a man tried to force such a variation, Staples would walk away from the table and hit the light switch on his way to bed. The group had changed over the years but had never topped five men. Its exclusivity was born in the idea that those light on brains and nickels, while always welcome in Staples' office or home, were not permitted to pull a chair to his round-top mahogany card table. In the fall of 1947, the group was down to three: Don, his younger brother, Bob, and Ledford. An exception to custom was made on the final Friday of October, Halloween night, when Ledford phoned ahead that Erminio Bacigalupo was passing through on his way back from Baltimore, and that he was a fine poker man. Staples said bring him.

Before they left the house, Rachel spoke very little to Erm. She had always mistrusted him, though not as much since her wedding night, when he'd told her, 'Ledford is the brother I never had, and I'd take a bullet for him.' Still, when he was under her roof, she watched him, close.

In the basement, Ledford pulled Erm's leather envelope from under the swastika quilt in the trunk. Erm opened it and pulled a hundred-dollar bill from the stack. 'For your trouble,' he said. 'And if you want to double it, look at the over-under on Maryland tomorrow. Now let's go play some poker.'

Staples' house was small, dark inside. From the record player in the corner, Louis Armstrong's 'Big Butter and Egg Man' played. The acorn ceiling fixture gathered smoke from below.

Each of the card table's four legs carried an ashtray. The men sat slouched over their elbows. They eyeballed the cards face up on the table and lifted the corner of those faced down. Ledford folded after Fifth Street, Bob after Sixth. Erm dealt in a manner bespeaking experience. The cards flipped from his finger and thumb and turned a singular revolution before landing flat. He was showing a pair of Jacks. Staples, a pair of sevens.

'Check,' Staples said. He tossed in a nickel, and down came Seventh Street. They showed their five and Erm took the pot, again.

Bob shook his head. He was ten years younger than Don, yet everything about them seemed identical – voice, movements, eyes, laugh. Bob was a less-wrinkled, clean-shaven version of his brother. He scooted his chair back. 'I gotta hit the head,' he said.

'Magnifying glass is in the top bureau drawer,' Don said.

Erm laughed and raked in his dollar seventy-five.

Staples packed his pipe and lit it. 'Ledford tells me you've recently married.'

'That's right.' Erm's nod was loose on the hinges, and his eyes were shrinking fast. 'She's a looker, but she's goofy up top, you know?' He tapped his temple with a finger.

Staples laughed. 'I know,' he said. 'Ain't we all?'

The clock on the wall read ten past midnight. They'd been playing for three hours. Ledford looked from the clock to his quarter-full rocks glass. He'd gone as easy as he could, but it was harder with Erm around.

The cornet sang a sad tune from the corner.

Bob sat back down and sighed. 'I'm about busted,' he said. He'd checked his pocket watch every ten minutes for an hour. Bob was a trial lawyer with a wife and three kids and his eye on public office. And though he'd gotten on fine with Erm that evening, he'd just as soon not know him past midnight. Like his big brother, Bob was a man of God, though he'd not taken the philosopher's path to knowing him, and he'd not wrecked his marriage and children along the way. He loved Don dearly, but he'd not gone overseas like his older brother. He'd never understood the demons.

'Looks like you can ante and stick for a few rounds.' Erm pointed to the little pile of nickels in front of Bob.

Bob pulled out his pocket watch again. He breathed in deep through his nose. 'I reckon I could play one more.'

'Big Bob,' Erm said. 'Big Bob, Big Butter and Egg Man.'

'Like the song says.' Staples stole a look at Ledford. They'd spent a little time in the office talking on Erm.

It was quiet for a moment. The kind of quiet that comes when a record has stopped playing and one man is drunker than the rest.

Bob shuffled the deck slow. Erm declined to cut. He poured another whiskey and sat back in his chair. 'Ledford tells me you're a scholar and a man of the cloth.'

Staples smiled easy. 'I've lived in both worlds. Even tried to mix the two.'

'Flammable is it?' Erm studied Bob's dealing motion, a habit of the suspicious.

'It can combust, if that's what you mean,' Staples said.

'I don't know what I mean half the time.' Erm laughed. It was loud. 'But if somebody had told me I'd be at a Virginia poker table with a preacher, a lawyer, and an office jockey, I'd have told him to climb up his fuckin thumb.'

'You're in West Virginia Erm,' Ledford said. He peeked at his down cards.

'That's what I said.'

'You said *Virginia.*'

'Tomato, tomahto.'

The Staples brothers looked at each other the way they always had when a card game went south. It was quiet, each man surveying what he had.

'Potato, potahto,' Erm said. Then, 'Shit or get off the pot, Preach. We got to go church in the morning.'

'I fold,' Staples said. His chair whined when he leaned back in it.

Ledford raised a dime and wished he hadn't told Erm about Willy's baptism the next day. Truth be told, he'd wanted to ask Don or Mack to be the boy's godfather, but one was lapsed and the other was black. Then Erm showed up, and without thinking Ledford had asked him.

Erm saw the dime and raised another. Bob folded. He dealt the rest of the hand in silence. Erm took the pot and kept his mouth shut for once.

Bob stood and stretched. He said, 'Well gentlemen.'

Don stood and followed his brother to the kitchen. On the way, he asked about a case Bob was trying. 'Any more on the Bonecutter dispute?'

Erm slapped his hand on the table. 'Drink with me Leadfoot,' he said.

Ledford ignored him. He was tuned in to the Staples brothers. *Bonecutter*, they'd said. It was the name from the back of the photograph. He got up and walked to the kitchen.

Don washed and dried his glass, his back to Bob, who leaned against the range, arms crossed. He was talking about arson.

'What was that name you used just now?' Ledford asked.

'Bonecutter,' Boh said. He yawned. 'They're a wild bunch out in Wayne County. Trouble. Had a land dispute with Maynard Coal for years, and

I've done some work for them, pro bono. Now all hell's broke loose.'

Bonecutter. It seemed to Ledford a name he'd known all his life.

'Well who set the fire?' Don wiped his hands with a yellow dish rag. He still wore his wedding ring, though he'd not seen his wife in fifteen years.

'Looks like the bad Maynard boy did it. He's come up missin since.'

'That's mass murder he committed,' Don said. His eyes were wide. He held the dish rag at his side, fisted, like he was trying to squeeze something out of it.

'What do you mean?' Ledford asked.

Bob cleared his throat. 'Five people died in that fire,' he said. 'It was in the paper.'

Staples just shook his head.

'Who died?' Ledford asked.

'The elders,' Bob said. 'I knew them a little. Mother and Daddy B is all they'd be called. They lived in the old ways.' He shook his head just as Don had. 'And their oldest girl, Tennis they called her. She was going on sixty herself. Burned in the house with them, along with her two grown children, who I didn't really know. Men, both of em. In their thirties, I believe.'

In the other room, Erm stood up and walked to the record player. He put the needle down unsteady. 'Big Butter and Egg Man' started up again.

Ledford cringed at the volume. He spoke louder. 'Who's left then?'

110

'The twins,' Bob said. 'Dimple and Wimpy. A little younger than Tennis was, maybe fifties.' He took out his handkerchief and blew his nose. Put it back in his pocket. 'They are tough to figure. Hard men. Real hard. Part Indian is what they'll tell you, among other things. But they will look you in the eye, and they will die before they give that land over to Maynard Coal.'

Erm stepped into the open kitchen doorway. He leaned against the jamb and smiled. His glass was full again. 'What time saloons close in *West* Virginia?'

The other three didn't answer. Erm had walked in at the wrong time.

Staples hung the dish rag on a hook next to the sink. 'Like you said, Erminio, church is bright and early.'

Erm nodded in that loose motion again. 'Yes,' he said. 'Church is early. Big Bill's big day. Big-balled Big Bill's baptism.'

Ledford laughed despite himself.

Erm continued. 'Big Bill will no doubt be a big butter and egg man like his Uncle Erm.'

Staples looked at Ledford. He wished the young man hadn't enlisted his Chicago friend as godfather. He wished he'd taught him a little more on life. There hadn't been time yet.

Erm kept up. 'Or like Big Bob over here.' He motioned with his drink hand and spilled. He tapped his foot in time with the piano keys from the other room. 'You got the kind of money that folds, don't

111

you Bob?' Erm laughed, said he was only fooling. Then he looked directly at Don and said, 'Where you get this music anyway?'

'Louisiana,' Don said.

'Louisiana?' Erm said the word as if he'd never heard it before.

'Louisiana,' Don repeated. 'This is Louis Armstrong, the finest musician we have today.'

Erm turned to Ledford. 'Leww-weeeez-eee-anna,' he said. 'Ain't that where Sinus came from?'

'Can it Erm,' Ledford said.

'Ooooo, yes sir.' Erm had straightened at the command, pried his eyes alert. He smiled at the Staples brothers. Then he paused and said, 'Armstrong's dark meat, isn't he?'

Nobody answered him. Bob pulled out his pocket watch again. Both he and Don straightened from their lean-tos. They'd not been talked to in this way by a younger man before.

Erm wore a look of contentment. He said, 'Ledford rents his house to dark meat,' and looked from one to the next, fishing for a response.

Ledford started to speak, but Don cut him off. 'Erm – can I call you Erm?'

Erm's grin spread one-sided and he nodded yes.

'Your friend Ledford rents the home he grew up in to Mr Wells because the federal government doesn't see fit to help out a Negro GI the way they might have helped me out, or the way they've helped you out, Erm. You follow?'

Erm didn't move a muscle.

'Well, see if you can follow this,' Staples said. 'You noted earlier that I'm both a man of scholarship and a man of God. An astute observation on your part. And do you know what I've come to learn from both? What is more clear to me now than ever?' He did not wait for an answer. 'That the poor, most especially the Negro poor, have suffered long enough, and that we are at a crossroads, right now, at this moment. And if we do not right our wrongs against them, a mighty eruption will come.' He started to continue, but didn't. Instead, he stared down the young Chicagoan, whom he suspected of carrying a pistol in his sock. He asked him again, 'You follow?'

Erm stared back and let his grin spread both ways. 'I follow,' he said.

'Good,' Staples said.

His brother let out a held breath. Ledford did the same.

Staples pulled the dish towel from its hook and threw it across the kitchen. Erm caught it with his free hand. 'Now,' Staples said, 'Clean up the shit you spilled on my linoleum.'

On the drive home, Erm passed out in the Packard. Before going inside, Ledford took off his overcoat and spread it across his friend. He left him there.

On his knees in front of the box labeled *Attic Junk*, Ledford picked up his father's batch book again. He'd not done so since reading of the dream, but now he scanned the pages for one word, *Bonecutter*. He soon found it.

June 5th. Old man Bonecutter showed up at the door again today. I will not do what he asks. I wanted to tell him it is his fault nobody will come out to Wayne and re-settle. He run them all off just like he did my mother. I will not leave the city of Huntington to return to the old ways. Something is not right out there.

Ledford read it three more times. He tried to remember his father as a man who might write such things, but nothing came.

He shut the book and put it under the quilt in the old trunk. It was a perfect fit inside the square where his Ten High used to be. As he closed the trunk's lid, he wondered if Erm kept his Purple Heart under a stack somewhere. He wondered why the two of them didn't keep in touch with anybody else from B Company. Why they'd never go to the VFW, or see about a First Marines reunion.

He supposed it had something to do with memory.

Ledford went to bed. Morning would get here quick, and Willy was to be baptized in front of the eyes of the church. He would have two Godparents. His Great-aunt Edna, a retired schoolteacher, and his Uncle Erm, a drunken criminal.

NOVEMBER 1947

I t had taken two months for someone to burn a cross in the front yard of Mack Wells and his family. At five in the morning, he was pouring a bucket of water on the last cinders when Lizzie asked him, 'Why did they wait so long to do it?' She pulled the lapels of her robe tight across her chest. She wore Mack's work boots on her feet, unlaced. In the yard, he was barefoot. He hadn't answered her question. 'You'll catch your death out there Mack,' Lizzie told him. 'No shoes on your feet.'

'The ground is warm,' he said. He stared down at it, watched an ember die. Tucked into the cinched waistline of his bluejeans was an Army-issue .45.

It occurred to Lizzie that whoever had done it might still be watching them, under the cover of early-morning dark. But the street was quiet. Only the bakery was awake, its assembly line humming, its slicers cutting loaves.

Mack looked around too. He had a mind to draw his pistol and fire at the first sign of movement. There wasn't any. He looked back at his house.

In the upstairs window, Harold pressed his forehead on the pane. The hall bulb behind him flickered. He knew what had happened. He'd awakened just as his parents had, confused by the dancing light from outside. 'Stay inside,' was all Mack had said to the boy.

Lizzie shivered on the porch. Her breath turned to condensation on the air. 'Mack?' she said.

Again he did not answer her. He stared up at his son's silhouette until his vision blurred. 'We'd better telephone Ledford,' he said.

At midnight on the eve of Thanksgiving, Rachel sat down on the love seat for the first time that day. She'd been on her feet for sixteen hours. Willy was finally down and Mary could be counted on to sleep through the night. The stuffing was made and the half-runners strung. Rachel looked at her watch. She stretched for the radio dial. The tuner spun loose and she couldn't pick up a signal. There was a hole in the grille cloth where Mary had punched the leg of a baby doll through. Rachel stuck her finger inside and for a moment wondered if she might be electrocuted.

She looked at the telephone, thought about how it had rung so early the morning prior. How it had awakened the baby. How Ledford had grabbed it and put his feet on the floor hard and said, 'When?' What they'd all known might visit the Wells family had visited them in the form of a fiery cross. The West End was white, and Ledford had changed that.

Now the Wells family was joining them for Thanksgiving dinner, at Ledford's request. Don Staples too. Rachel rubbed her temples and counted silently to herself, wagering that the telephone would ring again in twenty seconds. She got to sixty. Then one hundred. Ledford had gone for chewing tobacco at eight. 'Right back,' he'd said, like always. And, like always, he'd stayed gone.

She reached down beside the love seat and grabbed her knitting bag. It had been her mother's before her. From it she pulled her latest work, a half-finished sweater that would fit Willy next winter season. It was blood red and hooded with brown toggle buttons. She picked up the straight needles that had been in the family for two generations. Her pointer fingers found the taper. These were not metal needles, like so many. Nor were they wood. They were walrus tusk, brought back from Alaska by her great-grandfather, a fisherman.

Rachel's hands bony and worn. Her nails were chipped and her fingertips dotted with tiny cuts. She pulled the yarn's tail and looped, and soon found herself in a void of mechanical movement, orchestrating in her mind the tiny, scraping sound of the bone needles. She hummed, in time with the scraping, 'Amazing Grace.' Always, it was 'Amazing Grace.'

Downtown, on Fourth Avenue, Ledford was stride for stride with Staples. Their fedoras were pulled low and their coat lapels high. It was dark, save the headlights of a passing car or the office

117

lights above the storefronts. The Keith-Albee and the Orpheum were both running late pictures. A woman in a purple pillbox hat locked the ticket booth and walked west. Ledford thought he recognized her. He'd taken Rachel to see *Crossfire* the week before. Afterwards, they'd run into Mack and Lizzie, as they filed down from the balcony with the rest of the black patrons.

They walked up Tenth Street, past the darkened doors of Chief Logan's Tavern. On the sidewalk, there was a splatter of vomit in the shape of a daisy. They stepped around it.

The two walked fast and spoke to one another about the books. Staples loaned him. The American Indian was up for discussion. Ledford had not known such thought and conversation possible until meeting Don, and ever since, it seemed to him that his mind was expanding faster than it had in all the years prior, combined. They'd had conversations, like this one, that lasted five or six hours. Don had waxed knowingly on the laws of the Confederacy of the Iroquois. He spoke of the Indian League of Nations and their General Council's democratic ideals. He liked to say that nothing was new, that we spent our days committing the mistakes of those who came before us because we forgot to remember them. He liked to say, 'America will grab hold of the scientist's lab coat, and they will hold on for dear life as he rockets us straight to Hades.'

On this cold night, he answered Ledford's

question on work. On deeds. Staples said, 'Look here. 'Thou art the doer, I am the instrument.' And this is real important for you, Ledford, because you're the type that needs to keep himself busy.' The tip of his nose was red from the chill, and there was pipe ash caught in his beard. 'Now, busy like a businessman isn't going to cut it. Nossir. You've got to be busy like a bee, in the service of something besides *I*. See what I mean?' He grabbed Ledford by the coat sleeve and kept walking. 'You will only beat back what's chasing you if you forget about yourself. You work for your family, for your God, for those around you that need it most. Never for yourself.' He put his hands back in his pockets. 'Should've worn my gloves,' he said.

Ledford flicked the cherry off his cigarette one-handed and stuck the butt in his pocket. 'But what if the work a man does isn't real?'

'How's that?'

'Office work,' Ledford said. 'I'm not workin for anybody but those whose pockets is already lined, as far as I can figure.'

'Then quit,' Staples answered. 'You don't strike me as the type to fall in with the scotch-and-bridge crowd, Ledford. Get out while you can.' They were coming up on Fifth Avenue, Rachel's Episcopal church. 'Let's double back on Sixth,' Staples said.

The younger man had questions. 'Were you ever—'

Staples had stopped walking.

Ledford turned back to him. Staples was

119

squint-eyed and studying the church. Ledford looked there and saw, huddled against the double doors, the outline of a man.

'That doesn't seem right,' Staples said. He ascended the staircase. Ledford followed. The man's hand protruded from his shirtsleeve at a peculiar angle, pale and knuckled against the concrete. His neck bent hard against the door, and his winter coat lay beside him in a heap. 'That's a dead man,' Staples said as they got within five feet.

Hair grew wild and white from his earhole. His skin looked blue in the moonlight. 'That's Lucius Ball,' Ledford said. He took a knee and pressed his hand to his father-in-law's neck. Cold. There was blood on his chin. More beside him on the ground, mixed with vomit. Ledford stood and hung his head.

'Drank himself to death,' Staples said.

Ledford nodded.

'I am sorry, Ledford.'

'What was he doing here?' Ledford looked back down Tenth Avenue. The vomit outside Chief Logan's. He'd stepped around it. He'd had a bad feeling. Now here was Lucius Ball, at the doors of God's house.

'Refuge,' Staples said.

'What?'

'Refuge. Sanctuary. The church doors should have been unlocked.' Staples stepped forward and tried them. They did not give. Lucius's head slid a little from the movement. Both men watched him as if he might move again. 'You ought to get home,' Staples said. 'Let's get to the police and then get you home to Rachel.' He put his hand on Ledford's shoulder.

Neither of them were uncomfortable in the company of a dead man.

'All right,' Ledford said.

On the way down the stairs, he stopped. He turned and looked up at the steeple. It was tall and skinny, and it tapered toward the sky like a shiv, waiting on something to fall.

The Very Reverend Thompson joined them for Thanksgiving dinner. He felt a sense of shame for having locked the doors of his parish. It was a practice begun during the Depression, after someone had beaten in the communion cabinets and stolen all the silver.

For her part, Rachel had not shown emotion upon learning of her father's death. The night prior, when Ledford sat down beside her on the bed and gave her the news, she'd said nothing. Instead, she kicked off the bedsheets and walked to the bathroom. She stared at herself in the egg-shaped mirror, took out her bobby pins, and brushed her hair for a half an hour. When she'd finished, she hollered, 'Thanksgiving will still be Thanksgiving.'

They all joined hands in the kitchen. A prayer circle to offer thanks for their blessings and under-standing for their losses. Little Mary walked inside the circle, tapping knees as she went, saying, 'Duck duck duck goose.' Baby Willy slept on the porcelain tabletop, wrapped in a flannel blanket and wedged between the wall and a five pound can of Karo. All heads bowed. Reverend Thompson held the hand of young Harold Wells, who held the hand of his mother, who held the hand of her husband, who held the hand of Don Staples, and so forth. Harold kept one eye open and used it to see what white folks did when they prayed. The words sounded both different and the same as those spoken in his church. Staples had both his eyes open. He winked at the boy, who quickly shut his in response. Reverend Thompson said, 'Through Jesus Christ our Lord to whom, with thee and the Holy Ghost, be all glory and honor, world without end, Amen,' and they all repeated his final word, raising their chins off their chests.

The turkey was called a fine bird by all who partook of it. Lizzie Wells spoke quiet thank-yous to compliments on her cranberry dressing. She checked the time and worried on being late to her father's table.

Staples asked Harold about the first grade, about his take on the game of baseball. 'I like it,' was all the boy would say.

'How about ole Chuck Yeager,' Reverend Thompson said at one point. There was gravy on his cheek and his eyeglasses needed cleaning. 'They thought he'd blown himself up when the barrier broke.'

Truman became the topic of the hour, and all speculated on whether or not Senator Kilgore might well make a run at the White House in a year.

'My brother Bob could fill Kilgore's empty seat, I'd imagine,' Staples said. 'Specially since Bob's rear end is ample enough these days.' They all laughed, Mack the loudest. Harold smile with food in his mouth. He appreciated an adult's use of such terminology. Don continued, 'He'll probably smell this here turkey you've brined all the way across Eighth Street, Rachel. Be here by six to pick it to bone.'

Rachel smiled. She had her hands clasped under her chin. A calm had come on her since Lucius crossed over.

Ledford loved the way her crow's-feet came when she smiled. He put his hand on hers. He knew she was glad her father was gone. It meant one less worry on her mind. She'd loved her daddy, but he'd loved only things.

It was tradition in Rachel's family to dry out a Thanksgiving wishbone for a full year before pulling on it. After sweet potato pie, Rachel took the old wishbone from the kitchen window and replaced it with the new, grease-shined and chunked with meat. Harold and Mary would face off this year, the younger one with help from her mother.

Harold bent his knees and smiled at the toddler. Rachel gripped the bone with her. 'You two close your eyes,' she said. Mary giggled. She scrunched her nose at the boy whose knuckles brushed her own. Eyes shut, they pulled, and everyone clapped when the little bone snapped.

It had split dead center at the apex. None in attendance had ever seen such a break. Rachel asked Harold for his half and held them aloft, side by side. All leaned in and eyeballed. 'I'll be durned,' Ledford said. The halves were precisely equal in length.

Young Harold, who had squeezed his eyes as tight as he could, asked, 'What does it mean?'

No one answered him. Willy began to cry from the nursery, and little Mary, having lost interest, ran and tripped over the loose kitchen threshold. She landed on her chin and began to wail. Ledford went to her, Rachel to Willy.

Harold looked to his parents for answers. His mother licked her thumb and wiped at the crumbs on his cheek. 'It means both your wishes come true,' she said.

Harold looked around her to Reverend Thompson, who sipped from a coffee cup with his pinky extended. 'Is that right?' Harold asked him. 'Yes.'

Staples watched the boy. It was clear he had put some thought into his wish. 'What did you wish for?' he asked.

'Can't tell or it won't come true,' Mack said.

'That theory's been disproved,' Staples answered.

The boy didn't speak for a moment, and then he said, 'I wished I could play for the Dodgers, like

Jackie Robinson.' But this was a lie. Harold had wished nothing of the sort. As he'd pulled on that dry little bone, he'd asked God to help his daddy find the man who'd burnt a cross on their front lawn, and that when that man was found, to forgive his daddy for shooting him between the eyes.

It was the day after Lucius Ball's funeral that Ledford accompanied Bob Staples to the Bonecutter place in Wayne County. Bob drove a Ford Sportsman with an airtight convertible top. The car wore wood door panels like a boat. Inside, the two men shared Thermos coffee and Bob talked about his plans to run for office. 'Next year's elections won't be like any we've seen before,' he said. 'And I'm talkin about everywhere.' Bob's foot was heavy on the pedal, and he didn't watch the road when he spoke. 'My brother has told me about your stand on the rights of Negroes, and I'll tell you what, Ledford, high time is here.' The tires kicked rock hard around the wheel wells and Bob swerved off the shoulder.

'Your brother is a wise man,' Ledford said. 'He's helped me a good bit.'

They'd turned off 152 and were doglegging a steep county road. Knob Drop, Bob had called it. *Do Not Pass*, the sign said. Everything out here was steep, and every place name was followed by the word *Branch* or *Fork*. They passed a house where a man sold tobacco from the open trunk of a dead automobile.

Bob slowed to twenty miles per hour. He pointed ahead. 'Dead man's curve,' he said.

Ledford watched out his window as they rounded it. A drop-off of a hundred feet or more, no guardrail.

Some trees had emptied their color. Others were dotted here and there, red and yellow. Mostly, the hills of Wayne County were the color of mud, and it rolled down their inclines uncontained by streambeds. The mines had opened up new punctures, and folks had grown accustomed to what spilled forth.

'I aim to throw my hat in the ring,' Bob said. He'd slowed where muddy water crossed the road. The edges were crumbling away, the mark of habitual floodwater.

'Which ring?'

'Maybe Senate. Maybe governor.' The tires spun free for a moment, then found their footing. 'She's going to need a wash after this one,' Bob said. 'Should've brought the wagon.'

Ledford was thinking on senators and governors. It seemed to him they were usually white-haired and slicker than Bob. He looked down at the open file in his lap. Bob had told him to study up the case on the way. There was a letter from Maynard Coal & Coke dated February 1943 that read, in part, *It is our belief that your property includes coal reserves that would be conductive to the new surface mining methods of extraction* and *we encourage you to join your neighbors in the economic benefits that this offer represents.* There was a map of record from the county tax office. Tracts of land were sliced and numbered, lined and shaded. The Bonecutter tract was shaded the darkest gray, and it was the biggest plot by a longshot. *500 acre* somebody had penciled under it. The letters dated 1944 and onward employed increasingly threatening language. A handwritten one said, *You'll sell or you'll burn to the ground.* Another letter claimed the Maynards actually owned the Bonecutter tract, and that they had the deed to prove it.

Bob turned left on an ungraded road of dirt. Brown water rippled in potholes the size of tractor tires. Bob jerked the wheel right and left one-handed. He spilled coffee on his white shirt, cursed, and finished it off. Up and down they went, orchestrated by the thump and growl of axles and acceleration. 'The Maynard boy that came up missing since the arson was bad from the get-go,' Bob said.

'Is that right?'

'The youngest boy, Sam. Was a Golden Glove welterweight at one point. But he drank. His daddy Paul is Wayne County sheriff. Good man.'

'Do the Maynards own their own outfit?' Ledford shut the file and gripped the dash.

'They do. One of the few operators who grew from nothing. There isn't a New Englander on the payroll, even at the tippy top.'

After a quarter mile, it seemed to Ledford that they'd been swallowed by the branches growing over the road. Up ahead, he saw an old barrier gate of the swinging variety. Wood with iron hinges and hardware. For a moment, Ledford felt that he'd been to this gate before.

'These are good people, the Bonecutters, but they'll put you on edge some at first.' Bob laughed a little. 'Not even at first, really. More like all the time. But they're all right. And they just want to keep what belongs to them.'

Ledford hadn't mentioned his suspicion that he was somehow kin to the Bonecutters.

A man appeared from the brush behind the gate. He wore muddied brogans and blue jeans and a winter coat with the sheep's-wool collar up. On his head was a flattened engineer's cap whose grime had erased its stripes. The man undid a heavy chain and swung the gate open.

'I think that's Wimpy, but I can't be sure,' Bob said. He gave enough gas to push them through, then held up.

The man relatched the gate and walked slow to the driver's door. He stooped a little to peer inside. There was a rifle over his shoulder.

Bob said, 'Mornin.'

Ledford nodded hello.

It was hard to know if the man nodded back or not. There was some movement, but it was subtle. The bones in the man's face were right-angle sharp and ready to bust through skin, and his eyes spoke to the mastery of fear, the willingness to end a problem before it started.

'This is Loyal Ledford, a friend of mine,' Bob said.

Ledford nodded again. He watched the man's face as the name registered. It was hard to read.

'You want to hop in and ride the rest of the way?' Bob's smile was timid, and he blinked double-time.

'Nossir.' Wimpy stood up straight and walked ahead through the ditched wet leaves lining the road.

They drove past him down the steep incline. Rounding a bend, Ledford beheld Bonecutter Ridge and his insides shuddered. The sight of it brought Guadalcanal straight back to him, the camelback cutting the sky at Bloody Ridge. Ledford's breathing seized and he smelled scorched gunpowder and the effluvium of blown-open men. He tried to take deep breaths, settle himself.

If Bob noticed, he didn't say so.

They came to the bottom of a long, wide hollow. It ran low through the mountains like a trench.

The home sat at the head of the hollow. It was a single pen house of flat-planked logs, all different shades of gray. A bear hide, head attached, was nailed to the side. There was a sturdy-built outhouse ten paces out. Behind the house was a half-rotted crib barn, and next to that was a small, square dwelling. Bob cut the ignition and pointed to a scorched patch a ways off. 'That was the newer home,' he said. 'The one that burnt down.' Then he pointed to the little square building. 'That was the butcher's shop, I guess you'd call it. Where the hogs were quartered and all.' He pointed to the single pen house. 'And this house here is original to the Bonecutter family. Built in 1798.'

Everywhere, chickens pecked the dirt. Big ones and bantams, none the same shade. There was a small burial plot, fenced. Its headstones were crooked. Behind it, a gray goat clacked horns with a black one.

They got out of the car. Ledford noted only a single window on the place, high up, square, and empty. One of the two doors opened and a man stepped onto the jutting rock foundation. He was identical to the one who'd greeted them, who now approached from behind. Same right-angled face bones, same eyes. Same engineer's cap.

'That's Dimple,' Bob said.

When they got closer, Ledford took note of Dimple's scars. Plentiful. Deep. Skin where stubble should have grown. There was one on his cheek in the shape of a star that was no doubt the source of his nickname.

Short introductions were made before they went inside and sat on four chairs in front of the big black cookstove. Wimpy sat closest and fed the embers. He blew through pursed lips until it caught, then pulled logs from their floor stack between the stove's cast-iron legs. He leaned so close he singed his eyebrows. You could smell it on the air.

'There's beans still hot if you're hungry,' Dimple said. He chewed on a long kindling splinter.

Both visitors said thank you, no. The water pot boiled up.

Wimpy poured coffees all around. Ledford scorched his tongue on the first swig.

They spoke about the Maynards, and Bob produced the file folder from his briefcase. He pointed to parts of the text and handed the folder to Dimple, who read intently.

'They never did have nothin to go on,' Dimple said after a while. 'And I don't give a flat damn what anybody says otherwise.' He closed the folder and handed it back.

'I believe you're right,' Bob said. 'I believe Paul Maynard would agree with you. Seems to me he's lookin to leave well enough alone.' It was quiet. 'That only leaves the matter of the arson, and this Sam Maynard that's gone missing.'

'Well,' Dimple said. 'Paul Maynard knows better than to step foot out here, sheriff or not.'

'And no one's appeared to file a missing report on Sam.'

'I don't know about any of that.' Dimple worked his jaw in time with his heartbeat.

'Has any Maynard made further attempt to claim any part of your acreage since Sam's disappearance?'

'No.'

'Well, I wonder if the whole thing might just fizzle. If you two are content – what I mean is if they're content to . . .' Bob thought twice on speaking his train of thought aloud. He'd gathered

131

enough about hill justice to know when to keep his mouth shut.

Wimpy looked at his brother, then poked at the cookstove with a skinny log. Sparks kicked around inside like lightning bugs dying.

Ledford watched the hot square and let his eyes blur before Wimpy closed it back up. He thought about his furnace-tending days, how it was to be in charge of all that heat.

Wimpy brushed his callused hands against each other. He leaned his elbows on his knees and cocked his head to Ledford. 'We're kin to Ledfords,' he said.

It caught all of them off guard, as Wimpy had not said a word up to then.

'Yessir,' Ledford answered. 'I was reading through some of my daddy's things, and I came across your family name.' His voice was weak. He cleared his throat.

Wimpy said, 'Was your daddy Bill?'

'Yessir.'

The brothers looked at one another. Each was relaxed almost to sleep, one pitched forward, the other tilted back. Dimple had his hands clasped behind his head.

He said, 'Bill's mother, your grandmother . . .' He stopped and thought. 'Did you know your grandmother?'

'No, I didn't.'

'How old are you?'

'Twenty-six.'

132

Wimpy laughed and Dimple scoffed. He said, 'Boy, you still growin, ain't you?'

'Still growin hair on his pecker,' Wimpy said.

The brothers laughed hard then, and Bob and Ledford joined them. When it quieted, Dimple spoke. 'If I know right, your daddy's mother was Rose Coldsnow Bonecutter, my daddy's cousin.'

'That's right,' Wimpy said. He nodded and looked at his shoes, which he tapped softly on the floorboards. The light from the single window wasn't much. From inside, you'd hardly know if it was night or day. Firelight danced on the black bottoms of nail-hung cast-iron frying pans.

'Rose taught me in the second grade,' Dimple said.

Wimpy had a peculiar look in his eyes. 'I can see her now,' he said. 'I was back in the woods a playin and I looked down and it was her funeral, and it cast a pall on ever thing. When you see something like that, it casts a pall, don't it?'

'She died of the cancer,' Dimple said. 'Her husband was Alfred Ledford.'

'Your granddaddy,' Wimpy said.

'Al, they called him.' Dimple watched Ledford close. 'You never knowed him.'

Wimpy said, 'Al was from Mingo County, and he was visiting one day with Bill Butcher out here at Fort Gay.'

'Fine man, Bill Butcher, friend of my daddy's,' Dimple said.

'And Al had your daddy with him, must have been

four or five years old.' Wimpy held his hand out over the floor to signify height. 'And Al started to lay a hard whupin' on that boy and Bill Butcher stepped in front of him. They got into it and Al Ledford shot him.' He shook his head and pocked the fire. 'Them Mingo Ledfords were rough people.'

'Kilt him,' Dimple said.

Wimpy cupped his ear. 'He what?'

'Kilt him.'

'Yeah, kilt him.'

Dimple's eyes chased an ember that jumped through a crack in the cookstove. 'Al Ledford went to the penitentiary over that.'

'Died there a year later,' Wimpy said. 'After that, your daddy lived out here for a time.'

Ledford's daddy had never spoken a word on such things.

Bob coughed and fidgeted.

'We been wonderin when you might come out here to us,' Dimple said. He unclasped his hands and set the front legs of his chair to the floor.

Ledford didn't know what to make of the last words spoken. He didn't know what to make of anything. These men, it seemed, were his people.

Wimpy was nodding his head in agreement with his brother. 'I knowed you would come,' he said.

Ledford wanted to ask if there had ever been a lake on their property. If they remembered him and his daddy fishing from a rowboat, like in his dream.

The words got stuck in his throat.

After a long quiet, Dimple asked Ledford if he knew that the Bonecutters were part Indian. Before he could answer, Dimple said, 'Shawnee. Trace our blood straight back to Tecumseh. You know who Tecumseh is?' When Ledford said he did, Dimple stuck the kindling back in his teeth and chewed. Then he said, 'Maynards think Indians wasn't nothin but animals. Most folks wouldn't argue em, I reckon.' He stared at the fire. Finished off his coffee and spat to the floor the remnants of his kindling splinter.

Outside, the Bonecutter brothers pointed to the land around them, the rising inclines on either side. The hollow, snaking north, fairly wide and cut by a stream, its endpoint the big camelback ridge. Each twin used one hand as a brow visor, the other a sweeping survey tool. For every divot and clearing, they had a name. 'This here,' Dimple said, swinging his hand at the earth below their feet, 'all this here we call Marrowbone Cut.' Their grandmother had once told them why. She said that the soil was rich like marrow, and that the Lord had dug deep here, just for them to settle on.

Their mother said different. Everybody thought she was crazy. 'This here Cut in the hills,' she used to tell them, 'it ain't from no God, and it ain't for you. It's for polecats and slugs, and it'll swallow ever one of us that stays.'

Ledford pushed his boot soles against the ground. The words repeated in his head – Marrowbone Cut.

He took a long look at the ridge. What had happened to him upon first seeing it was over. Hills looked the same the world over. Ridges rose and fell, east and west. People gave them names. One was not the other.

He studied the ridge, its empty trees packed tight and reaching skyward. He almost asked Bob if they could stay and climb to its pinnacle. It called to him. But they both had wives and children in town. And it would be unwise to climb the ridge. The Maynards were on the other side, mourning the one who'd come up missing.

A dream visited Ledford that night, and in it, the Bonecutter brothers walked the chalk lines of a baseball infield, and an airplane flew overhead. When it passed, the brothers turned for the visitors' dugout and sat down on the bench. They said something he couldn't make out. He read their lips. 'You couldn't even afford an ankle,' they said, and pointed to the outfield. Ledford turned and looked to where they pointed. A man with a camera took pictures of another man, who had been crucified. He was skin and bones and wore an unkempt beard. His wrists and ankles were bound with twine to the skinny crucifix. It was made from braided vine, and it leaned against an outfield fence fashioned from chickenwire. All at once, the fence buckled under, and the man on the crucifix went down with it. Ledford looked away. A terrible feeling came over him. The dugout went dark inside.

There were sinister movements from its floor. Ledford knew he was dreaming then, but he could not pull himself awake. He could not sit up in bed. His father's voice spoke clearly: 'Raise your hand to your chest, boy. Put your hand on your heart.' Ledford could not open his eyes. He could not raise his hands from the bed. It occurred to him that he was paralyzed, that even his breathing had stopped. There was panic in his blood vessels, silent and without motion. There was the sensation of being eight feet underground, shoulder to shoulder with things he could not turn to see. He could hear them sighing. Then, another voice came. It told him *Make marbles*, and then his hand came to his chest and he breathed in deep and sat up straight and waited for his heart to blow open from the pressure.

The voice that had spoken the two words was one he'd not heard in five years, but it was unmistakable. It was the voice of McDonough. It was Sinus from Chalmette.

Ledford went to the nursery and watched his children. They slept in white-railed cribs against opposite walls, Mary on her stomach and Willy on his back. Arms sprawled wide and mouths open. He placed his hand on their chest and back to feel them breathe.

It seemed to Ledford then that something had changed. That he could no longer go on as he had been to now. He would live for his children. He would make something real for them.

In the basement, he opened the big trunk's lid. He knew that under the swastika quilt, there was nothing but the past, an empty impression of a bottle of Ten High. He closed the trunk and turned to the little desk he'd built against the wall. He sat down at the desk, pulled from its drawer a pencil and a blank-paged, leather-bound journal. He'd bought it a week prior, upon noticing its likeness to his father's.

Ledford stared at the empty page before him. His fingers trembled a little. They steadied when he pressed lead to paper. He wrote one word. *Marbles.*

FEBRUARY 1948

They sat together on the west steps of Old Main, the cold concrete numbing their tailbones. The campus sidewalks were salted. 'See her?' Don Staples said, pointing with his emptied pipe. Across the green, a woman walked fast and determined. 'She's the new director of physical education for women. Can't recall her name.'

Ledford squinted for a better look. 'Pretty,' he said.

Staples nodded. 'I believe I'd let her direct my physical education any old day of the week.'

'I believe you would.'

'She could measure my growth.' They laughed. Staples said, 'I'm not as old as you think I am.'

Marshall's campus was shaping up. Folks talked about it going from college to university status.

Staples pointed his pipe at another walking the cross-cut path. 'See him? That little son of a bitch is the one that stirred the pot on me fall semester. Said I offended his morals.'

'How?'

'I can't remember.' Both men looked at their shoes. Staples continued, 'He didn't like something I said about marching tanks through downtown to commemorate Armistice Day.'

'What did you say?' The young man in question was coming their way.

'I can't remember.' Staples watched the young man approach, his spotted bow tie sharpening with each step, his scarf tucked just so into his lapel. 'I may have said something that to his ears was unpatriotic. He may have thought me a Communist.' He straightened his back and stuck his pipe in his pocket. 'Hello there young fella,' he said.

The young man stopped at the foot of the stairs. He'd wanted to move past them without altercation. 'Hello Professor Staples.'

'I can't recall your name.'

'A. P. Cavendish.' With a leather-gloved hand, he pulled out his pocketwatch and checked it.

'Cavendish,' Staples repeated. 'How could I forget a name like that? Your old French ancestor discovered hydrogen, didn't he?'

'I'm not aware of any such thing,' Cavendish said. Another boy hollered from across the green and Cavendish smiled momentarily, waved, then went straight-faced again. His complexion was splotched.

'Well, sure you're aware,' Staples said. 'You're full of more hydrogen than most, aren't you Cavendish?'

'Professor Staples, I've got to—'

140

'You blow hot air from both holes, don't you son?'

Cavendish had crested a step to keep moving, but stopped dead at this comment.

'Let me introduce you to my *comrade* here, Loyal Ledford,' Staples said.

The two shook hands and nodded.

'Cavendish is both managing editor of the *Parthenon* and president of the Inter-Fraternity Council.'

'Is that right?' Ledford said.

Cavendish nodded affirmative.

Staples said, 'Wrote an article, if memory serves, advising President Truman not to intergrate the military.'

'It would be disastrous, in terms of security,' Cavendish said.

'Is that right?' Ledford said. A bell sounded inside the building behind them.

'Ledford here is a glass man,' Staples continued. 'A fire-eater. Raised by Indians. You know all about fire-eating, I'd imagine?'

Cavendish did not respond.

'What with your hydrogen ancestry, and hot air rising and all. You ever put flame to your flatulence, Cavendish?'

There was an awkward silence, as Cavendish looked from one man to the other, both seated yet towering, both boring holes with their hooded eyes. The wind picked up. 'I've got to get to class,' Cavendish said.

'By all means.' Staples pointed his open arms

141

up the stairwell, designating a clear path. 'Walk the path of enlightenment young man.'

They watched the doors close behind him, then looked at one another and shared a laugh.

Neither spoke for some time.

'Dreams after you lately?' Staples stared out beyond the college gate at Sixteenth Street. A car sounded its horn.

'Some.' Ledford lit another cigarette.

'Any more with McDonough?'

'No.'

'Your daddy?'

'No.' Ledford squirmed at the thought of how much he'd shared with the man. It both frightened and freed him. He watched the traffic turn on Third Avenue, gray exhaust dancing on the frozen air. He said, 'But the other night, I woke up and Rachel wasn't in bed with me. I walked to the nursery and the cribs were there, but the rails were all broken and splintered and they were empty inside. I went back to bed, laid down, shut my eyes, opened em again, and there was Rachel. And I went back to the nursery, and sure enough there was Willy and Mary, cribs just fine.' He cleared his throat.

'Well, you weren't awake the first time. You were dreamin.'

'Sure didn't seem like it.'

Staples nodded. He knew the feeling. 'Your job?'

'I'm liable to kick a hole in the office wall. It's all scheduling and getting on the phone with men who think the dollar is salvation. And now, the old man up in Toledo has died, so his sons are taking ownership, and word is they play golf with Charlie Ball.' Along the bricks, a lone squirrel scurried. It cut across the grass and climbed the trunk of an oak tree, spiraling its length as it went. Ledford wondered why it wasn't in its nest. He went on, 'I'd rather be back at the furnace.'

'Maybe you ought to be back in school. Get your doctorate. Teach.'

Ledford laughed and thumbed up the stairs behind them. 'I'll join ole Cavendish in the fraternity house. Get on as delivery boy for the paper.' He wiped his nose with a coatsleeve. 'No. I'm done with school, just like I'm done with the Marine Corps.'

Staples thought hard about what to advise. The younger man at times seemed a contemporary of himself. 'Whatever you do, don't ever fancy the idea of politics like my brother.' The race for governor was on, and Bob Staples was a longshot.

'Is it not going well?'

'He thinks of me as his advisor on matters of faith, and right now I'd advise him to remain who he is. He's tampin out his fire, got his compass set to some direction I can't figure.' The wind picked up. Staples pulled his lapels. 'It isn't righteous or noble, that's for certain.' He tapped his shoe soles against the stone and shook his head.

'I was afraid something like that might happen,' Ledford said.

'Yes, yes. My brother.' Staples changed gears. 'Well, I have thought a little on it, and maybe you *ought* to do this marble company idea.'

'That's what I'm thinkin.'

Staples patted Ledford on the back. 'I wish I could tell you how to go about all of it,' he said to him. By *it* he meant life. 'I know it's got something to do with holding on to the ones you've got, and if you can, on top of that, make a little music and have a little fellowship. Build something.' He thought for a moment on the word *build*. 'But not like they do nowadays,' he said. 'I mean *build*, like they did before all this.' He took his arm away and waved it toward Sixteenth Street, Third Avenue, the mill, the boxcar foundry. 'You got to do what you know is right,' Staples said. They looked at each other then. 'And I mean right by your family, not by you alone. And your family, in the end, is everybody.' He often spoke this way. He called it soapboxing. 'Or, you can do right only by yourself, like most do these days. And Mack Wells' child will grow up to hate your child and both of them together will grow up to hate the little Russian children, and a few silverspooners like Cavendish there, and a whole lot of regular boys will run off shortly to Korea, and you know what happens then.'

Ledford nodded. He knew.

MAY 1948

The returns were in. The *Daily Mail*'s Evening Edition ran photographs of the primary winners, stone-faced and staring at something beyond the camera lens. 'Why don't any of these men smile?' Rachel asked. She bit into an apple. Baby Willy was at her breast, half asleep. He was big at eight months, and most young mothers would have long since weaned their babes from the breast, if they'd ever breast-fed at all. But not Rachel. To her, such separation seemed wrong. 'Bob Staples would have smiled,' she said. Her feet were crossed on the opposite kitchen chair. Mary sat beneath her mother's legs, a kitchen tent of sorts, under which she whispered secrets to her one-legged Raggedy Annie.

'Bob Staples didn't even come close,' Ledford said. He was leaning against the counter's edge, swirling the beer in his can. His tie was undone. Just home from work. 'He played the big boy's game and lost.'

Mary laughed at something she'd whispered to Raggedy Annie. A strand of her hair tickled the back of Rachel's knee. 'Well, no one was going to

145

beat Okey Patteson,' Rachel said, 'and Bob's a good man, Loyal.'

'If you say so.'

'He is and you know it.'

'I *did* know it. Not no more.'

'Not *any*more,' Rachel said. She'd eaten her apple to the core, spitting out the seeds as she went. She pushed the little seeds around on the tabletop.

'Uh-huh,' Ledford said. He finished his beer and threw it in the trash. 'Anymore, no more, same thing. That man talked a big game, but when it came down to it, he balked.' Ledford got to his knees on the linoleum. 'Hello,' he whispered to Mary, then the same to Raggedy Annie. They ignored him. He winked anyway, kissed his daughter's cheek, and stood back up. As he did, his vision went black and he nearly fell over.

'What do you mean he balked?' Rachel said.

Ledford steadied himself against the counter. His vision came back, starry, then whole. 'What I mean is, he said he was dedicated to the Negro's cause, to equal pay, to housing reform. Did he forget? He hasn't even spat a word about the half-assed decision the Supreme Court just handed down.'

'Well, he tried his best Loyal.'

'He did nothing of the sort. What he tried was to get votes. And a man doesn't get votes unless he sells out his principles.' He opened the fridge and cracked another beer.

Baby Willy rolled, open-mouthed and asleep, away from his mother's breast. She looked down at him, the curl of his little lip. The way it still searched, sucking though nothing was there. Rachel looked up at Ledford. She hoped that, like her, he'd be staring at the boy, but he wasn't. He had his back to them. Hands at the sinktop, braced and straight like tentpoles. He spat in the disposer.

'Not a good day at work?' she asked.

'Is there such a thing?' He didn't turn when he spoke.

The Diamond T dump truck was rust-colored and well used. The stencil on the doors read *Mann Glass Co. 10 Ton Limit.* Mack Wells drove it as he had on past deliveries, one-handed and carefree, as if the dented bed behind him didn't carry 16,000 pounds of broken glass. As if Route 2's center line were a barrier wall, protecting oncoming vehicles from his tendency to weave.

He looked at the river outside his window. It followed the road like a serpent. Or rather, the road followed it. Here and there a coal barge churned along, slow and dirty. Each one pushed a mighty load, flat and stacked side by side, front to back. Black mounds rose in skinny ridges from each pallet as if mountains had grown from the water and learned to swim. Tug horns sounded and stacks pumped gray tails that disappeared on the river air. The water these behemoths cut was dark muddy brown. A V-shaped ripple, churning, on its surface a reflective film.

Ledford had the passenger window down. He

held his open hand against the wind, then closed it in a fist.

Mack Wells took note. He said, 'You'll never catch it.'

'How's that?'

'The wind. Ain't no man can gather it in his fists.' Mack turned back to the road ahead. 'Proverbs.'

Ledford nodded. He made his hand flat and extended his fingers. The wind's resistance subsided and his fingertips cut the air quiet. He considered Mack's knowledge of the Bible, his ability to quote and name verse. 'I've always liked that passage,' Ledford said. 'Can't say I've understood it, but it sounds about right.'

Mack nodded. The speedometer read sixty. 'Means we're fools,' he said.

Ledford rolled the window up so he could strike a match. He lit two cigarettes and handed one to Mack. On the bench seat between them sat a pair of lunch pails and coffee Thermoses. Ledford's had a rotted seal, and at each pothole, coffee trickled from the lid. He watched it trace the upholstery stitching on the seat, searching out the holes there, soaking into the popped stuffing.

Mack had made plenty of these Saturday delivery runs. The pay was decent, and he usually rode alone. It gave him time to think, something that proved alternately fruitful and damning. On Tuesday, Ledford had told Mack he'd like to ride along on this particular run. Mack had told him it would be good to have the company, though he wasn't sure he meant it. 'Why you want to go anyhow?' he'd asked. Ledford had answered that he was interested in the destination, the factory at Marble City. Mack had told him, 'Well, you know we just dump the cullet and go on our way?' Ledford had talked of staying a little longer, having a look at the place. When Mack had asked him why he was so interested in a marble factory, Ledford told him, 'Because a voice in a dream told me to make marbles.'

They traveled Route 2 in relative silence. After a time, Ledford asked Mack about his Army unit. Conversation came easier. Mack told of a college boy he'd learned under, how in a year's time, he'd become proficient in fixing damn near any mechanical thing that broke. 'They could've given me a degree in engineering for all the shit I done fixed,' he said.

Ledford laughed. 'Sounds like they ought to have.'

Beyond place names, neither man broached the subject of combat.

They were in the town of Friendly by noon, the sandwiches and coffee long gone. Marble City had opened its factory doors in Friendly two years prior, and it now produced so many marbles, both industrial and gaming, that folks had taken to calling the whole town by the name of the company. The factory had brought jobs just as miners had started to lose them. Men who had spent twenty years underground now found themselves sitting on buckets, sorting green glass from blue.

A dwarf in maroon slacks swung open the factory's service gate. Mack eased the big truck through.

The sign on the fence pictured a smiling red marble, backgrounded by the silhouettes of skinny buildings and chimney stacks. This was Marble City.

Mack nodded to the little man, a gesture that was not reciprocated. Instead, the man frowned and eyeballed Mack all the way through the gate. Even ten yards in, when Mack checked his side-view mirror, he had his stink-eye locked in.

'Guess they ain't too friendly here in Friendly,' Mack said.

'Guess not.' Ledford watched as another man emerged from the factory doors. He stood in front of the truck and walked backwards, guiding them with hand signals as if on an airstrip. Ledford thought of Henderson Field, how he'd watched men do the same there, easing patched-up Hellcats off the broken apron.

They hit their mark and got out of the truck and stretched.

When Mack turned the crank, the winch made a popping sound and the cable groaned as if protesting the weight of its haul. Glass shifted and tinkled on top of the stack. Like a swarm of silver minnows, Ledford thought. When the truck bed went forty-five degrees, there was a rush of sound and dust and the glass began its quick descent to the waiting ground below.

Twenty sorters emerged and surrounded the shining mountain. They gripped five-gallon buckets in each hand, stacked three deep. They sat on metal stools and milk crates and began what seemed to Ledford an impossible job.

The dwarf walked a circle around the sorters, his arms crossing his chest, his brow still furrowed. Ledford cut off his path and asked where he might find Mr King, the man in charge. 'Check furnace three,' the man told him.

Inside, there was a familiar smell. Sulphur-like and old. But there were other smells Ledford couldn't categorize. Sounds too. Men rolled handtrucks stacked with full buckets to three awaiting furnaces. At the back, they poured in the glass. At the front, a machine worked, cam-operated and precise. Ledford could see the thin neon trickle there as it drained into a metal box and came out perfectly round, a glowing molten ball riding a chute to the rollers below. On the floor was a wooden cooling barrel, half full.

A wide-backed man wearing suspenders stooped beside an industrial fan. He closed an eye and aimed it at the opening in furnace three. Ledford approached him. 'Mr King?' he shouted over the fan's roar.

The older man turned and sized up Ledford over the brim of his steel-framed glasses. They sat on the bulb of his sweating nose. 'What can I do for you?' he asked.

Ledford introduced himself and they shook hands. Mr King was glad to give him a tutorial. They walked the length of furnace three, back to front. King pointed at the metal box from which the molten balls emerged and said, 'That's the head. A shear cuts it to size inside and it comes down the chute there to these rollers.' The finger he pointed with was stained a permanent gray. Blistered at the tip. 'See how those rollers are in motion? That insures they're perfectly round.'

'How many do you make in a day?' Ledford was mesmerized by the man's operation.

'Oh, that depends. Last year we made four hundred thousand.'

Ledford tried to picture four hundred thousand marbles. He wondered how many it would take to fill the dumptruck.

'It'll be a million when we get these new furnaces built, get these new machines put together.' Mr King whistled loud at a teenaged boy who was tipping a batch of yellow cullet into a hole. The boy looked at his boss. 'Don't pour quite so fast,' King told him. 'Slow er down some.' He winked and smiled, and the boy heeded the advice. 'That hole he's pouring into is the crucible,' Mr King told Ledford. 'It's where you add your striking colors.' He began to walk away. 'C'mon,' he said. 'Let me show you some finished product.'

On the way to his office, they passed an unlit furnace, its machinery gathering dust. Ledford asked, 'What about this one?'

Mr King regarded it with nostalgia. 'Built that in 1931,' he said. 'See how the shear's chain operated?' He ran a finger along the rusted links. 'Had to service it more than I would've liked. New ones save us a lot of money.'

The walls of his office were covered in framed

photographs of employees and family alike. Men and women with their arms around each other, their hands gripping blowpipes and punty rods. Children knelt at circles drawn in the dirt. They had marbles at the ready, their thumbs the triggers. Ledford walked in a square around the small room, eye-balling their faces, the wrinkles of their joy. At his waist, in custom-built display cases lining the walls, were handmade, oversized marbles of all colors and designs. There were clear crystal paperweights with tiny flowers inside. There were handblown ashtrays like the ones his father had once made.

'Kids love to play Ringer,' Mr King said. He'd taken a seat at his desk and was watching Ledford closely. 'And now that folks have a little money to spend, they want games, collectibles, you name it. Back when I started in marbles, there wasn't demand at all. Folks were lucky to put food on the table.'

Ledford turned and faced him. 'If you don't mind me askin, what do you plan to do with the old machine out there?'

'The chain-driven? Why do you ask?' He took off his spectacles and pinched the bridge of his nose.

Ledford sat down in the only other chair. 'Well,' he said, 'I reckon if it's for sale, I'd like to buy it.'

Mr King laughed a little. Then he said, 'You know, I like the cullet we buy from Mann Glass. The coefficiency mixes real well with what we buy from up the road here. But I hear that pair of Toledo brothers that's bought you out is cuttin the fat, maybe movin to a cheaper batch. There truth to that?'

'I believe there is,' Ledford answered.

'Even heard they're lookin to cash in quick, turn right around and sell the whole caboodle to Illinois Glass. I don't suppose you know if there's any truth to that?'

'Wouldn't surprise me. I've heard rumbles.' Ledford watched the older man nod and work his lips together in thought. He wondered what mechanisms turned inside King's big head. He wondered how Mack was faring outside.

'Well,' Mr King said. 'Let's talk.' He opened a desk drawer and took out pen and paper.

The ride home was relatively quiet. Ledford told Mack that Mr King was a smart and honest man. That he was privy to the inner workings of Mann Glass management, and that things might change for the worse at the factory. When Mack didn't say anything in response, Ledford said, 'I'm lookin to get out while the gettin's good.' Still nothing from Mack in return.

The sun was setting over the treetops ahead. Its glow cut through their skinny tips and danced atop the river's churn. Ledford had his elbow out the open window. It was cold from the wind. He looked at the wide river rolling past, marveled at how different it looked from that morning. Purer. Wiser somehow. After a while, Ledford said, 'I'm lookin to start up my own thing. An outfit that doesn't run on the idea of money alone.' He waited a moment, then said, 'Be honored to have a man with engineering skills along.'

'Well,' Mack said, 'I'll keep it in mind.'

JULY 1948

Erm Bacigalupo had bought his family a Hallicrafters television set with swinging mahogany doors and a picture tube he dusted with his handkerchief. On the last, hot Chicago night of the Ledford family's visit, he dusted it five times inside an hour. Everyone watched the screen. Even Rachel had her eyes on the television.

The favor of godparenting had been returned, as that morning, Ledford had stood at the altar inside St Mary of Perpetual Help, renouncing Satan and all his works and pomps. He was now a caretaker of the soul of baby Fiore, Erm's son.

Erm's new place was a two-story red-brick rowhouse in Chicago's Bridgeport neighborhood. There was crystal on every flat surface in the place. Brandy decanters in every room, half full and circled by balloon glasses. Ledford noted the fine glasswork, but he didn't pick them up. The contents of such craftsmanship were hell on a man sticking only to beer.

Erm's wife Agnes had been a nightclub singer – a canary, Erm called her. She didn't say much, and she slept when she pleased. As she had for much of the Ledfords' visit, she lay alone in her upstairs bedroom. The rest of them crowded around the television down below. Little Fiore cried in his Moses basket astride the bar. Erm didn't notice. The wall-mounted phone in the kitchen rang, and he went to it.

Rachel picked up the baby, her own boy crawling free on the floor. She swayed and bounced on the balls of her feet and sang, 'Mama's little baby loves shortenin shortenin.' She longed for the drive home the next morning.

Willy reached up and grabbed at the fireplace set. Soon he was standing, steadying himself with two fistfuls of cast iron. Poker in the right, broom in the left. 'Loyal,' Rachel said.

Ledford had Mary on his shoulders and was doing a little dance to keep her happy. He eyed Willy, bent his knees, and snatched him up around the waist. Ledford made the sound of a plane throttling, one-handing each of his children, whose laughter came up from the belly and shook their little bodies. Ledford kept his eyes fixed on the television as he spun. It amazed him that such a thing was possible. A moving picture, as it occurred, so that a body in Chicago might see what those inside the picture tube were seeing, at the same instant, in real flesh and blood in Philadelphia. He watched the delegates fanning themselves, the gray screen blurring their features so that each fat man in attendance looked identical to the next. Folks sat

156

talking and laughing, wearing horn-rimmed glasses and mopping sweat. This was the Democratic National Convention, and a speaker was approaching the podium.

Rachel had gotten baby Fiore to sleep, and she placed him back in the Moses basket on the bartop. He'd felt good in her arms, and she wondered when she'd have another one that size. She eavesdropped on Erm in the kitchen. He was talking loud with a cigarette in his lips, something about a wheel.

Ledford set Willy on the floor and pulled a satchel of marbles from his back pocket, one of the dozens of bags he'd bought in recent months. He emptied them on the rug by the boy's fat feet.

'You watch him close,' Rachel said. 'He's liable to choke.'

'Hasn't put one in his mouth yet, has he?' Ledford swung Mary down and faced her to her brother. Both children began grabbing at the little glass globes, Mary with precsion, Willy with bad aim. Ledford glanced at them every so often, but he was enraptured with the man on the television. Hands clutching the podium, this mayor from Minnesota commanded attention. He said he was speaking on behalf of a minority report on civil rights. There was a howl from the audience. Some of it good, some of it bad. Ledford leaned in and spun the volume knob. The man's voice raised and he said 'vicious discrimination' and he spoke of Jefferson and the freedom of all colors of men and

157

the Democratic Party's dedication to such. He said that there would be no watering down when it came to civil rights. He began to shout and shoot his fist toward the ceiling. 'The new Emancipation Proclamation,' he boomed.

Ledford forgot where and when he was as he stared at this little man on the box before him.

'To those who say we are rushing this program, I say we are one hundred and seventy-two years late,' the man said. Ledford felt a rising surge behind his ribs, and it was as if he was back at Rachel's apartment in 1941, in front of the Philco.

There came a chuckle from behind. Ledford turned to find Erm, stabbing a cigarette into an ashtray he held level. 'What the hell is that supposed to mean?' he asked.

Ledford tried to tune him out and put his eyes back on the man with the strange pronunciation who had stirred his very soul. The speech was wrapping up. Erm shouldered past him and rolled down the volume. 'Got to be a ball game on,' he said.

On the floor, Willy kicked his sister hard in the thigh and she cried. Ledford picked her up and rubbed her back. He took her to Rachel. Willy stared at the marbles before him as if they might move unassisted, then kicked at them wildly with his feet.

'C'mon to the basement with me Ledford,' Erm said.

In the basement, they smoked and Erm poured a whiskey and a beer. He pulled a brochure from his desk and handed it to Ledford. *Charles Town*

Race Track it read. 'I like this little West Virginia track,' Erm said. 'I'm going to get in on the ground floor, stable a couple horses there, maybe own my own track someday.' He regarded Ledford through the smoke. 'There's money to be made for you and that business you're starting up.'

Ledford wished he hadn't told him about the marble company.

'Listen, I saw your face upstairs,' Erm said. 'Your college-boy face.' He bugged his eyes and hung open his jaw. 'Them politicians get your motor runnin, like your buddy the professor.' Erm shook his head. 'You got slow down on that dinge horse-shit, Ledford.'

'Dinge?'

'Niggers,' Erm said. The lamp on his desk flickered and hummed. It was dark down there, the paneling a deep amber, the ceiling low. 'Don't get me wrong, I work with em. Just got off the phone with one who runs a wheel in Bronzeville. Dresses first class, got a billfold full a spinach.' He stopped to light another cigarette, the flame dancing purple under his hollowed eyes. 'But he lives in the black belt, he runs his numbers in the black belt, and he keeps to the dinge canaries chirping in the Black Belt clubs. You know why?' It was quiet. They breathed hot mildew, stagnant basement air. Erm switched on the table fan. 'Because the second he steps out of Bronzeville lookin for a house to buy, he's a dead man. The first customer he calls on outside of Bronzeville, he's a dead man.

159

The first white broad walking down Halstead he does a double take on, maybe stares a little too long? He's a dead man.'

Ledford listened to the hum of the fan. He watched its silver propeller turn inside the cage.

Erm leaned into his highback leather chair. He put his feet on the desk. 'Your man on television can say what he wants.' He spread his arms wide and faced his open palms in. 'But white is over here, and black is over here.' He looked from one hand to the other, spoke slow and deliberate. 'And that is how it will always be.'

Ledford leaned into his own chair. He fingered the brass nail heads that gathered leather taut across the armrest. Across from him, Erm set his cigarette in an ashtray and took out his front teeth. They weren't as white as before. Looked more wood than porcelain. Erm dropped them into a glass of clear liquid on his desk. Ledford watched them clink and settle. He glanced down at his knuckles, the white scar from the punch that had taken Erm's teeth. Ledford rubbed at the coffee-colored leather and contemplated his friend. He'd been right to hit him all those years ago, and he was of a mind to do it again. Instead, he said, 'You're wrong, Erm.'

'About what?'

'About black and white and how they will always be.'

Erm smiled. The empty space in front gave him a look of stupidity. Toothless for all his riches, he was a sight. 'Whatever you say Ledford.'

160

Each man was troubled then, and each wore a grin that both showed and concealed such trouble. If they'd been in a Guadalcanal foxhole, they might have drawn short blades or choked one another. But they were here, wives and children walking and talking and breathing upstairs, babies newly cleansed by God, absolved of what would surely come. So Erm and Ledford sat and stared.

Erm was the first to look away. He shuffled a stack of papers, whirled the teeth circular in their bleach. 'Listen,' he said. 'We think different, me and you. We even drink different these days, now that you gone square on me. But that don't matter. We're friends, Ledford.' The fan shut off and the desk lamp cut out. Blackness enveloped the basement. 'Goddamnit,' Erm said.

Upstairs, the fireplace set overturned and cast iron clanged loud. Willy cried out, but it carried the sound of fear, not injury. Mary joined in. Then baby Fiore. Ledford listened to the calm stride of Rachel above him. She walked blind to each of the children, her hands true and strong despite the darkness.

Erm tripped over a case of wine and cursed. He was looking for a candle.

Ledford stayed put, still rubbing at the armrest nail heads. He could hear everything in the dark. Down the alley, someone kicked over a trash can. Two floors up, Agnes called weakly for help. A mouse ran across the ceiling joist above his head, its tiny feet clicking splinters.

Erm struck a match and held it to the candle's wick. He lit up yellow, all shirt front and forehead. 'What the hell are you just sitting there for, Ledford?' he said.

Ledford laughed. 'You're yellow,' he said. 'Too much chow-line atabrine.'

Erm tripped over the same case of wine. He cursed again, raised his foot, and brought it down hard. Thin pinewood split wide open, loud as a firecracker, and bottles popped and shattered. Their contents pooled and ran a wide trickle across the concrete, searching for the grate. Ledford closed his eyes to be rid of the candle's glow. He listened to the wine moving slow across the floor. A perfect sound, like a low creek before sunrise, only slower. Wine slow, he thought, and then he thought of Jesus and Cana, how the Methodists of his father's church had only drunk grape juice, had known Jesus' wine was unfermented. He thought of Reverend Thompson and the Episcopal Church of his wife. The free-flowing, fermented wine they sipped. He thought of the man on the cross in his dream, the blood of the Christ in his Bible, the blood on the pages of his history books, the blood of the African slaves as it spilled from the ships that brought them here and into the cracks of auction blocks and platform parades and the dirt of the cotton field and the drain on the street. He thought of the blood of the sleeping Japanese boy with the thin mustache, how it surged and fell in sheets and

162

spoke to him in the language of animals. He wondered how a man could ever get past such a sight and sound as that.

Erm switched on a right-angle flashlight and shined it in Ledford's face. Then he trained it on the wine trail, which had routed itself between the legs of Ledford's chair and was fast approaching the floor drain. Ledford turned and watched it follow the cracked contours of the foundation. Blood red but thin like water.

'Twenty dollars a bottle,' Erm said.

Rachel hollered for a little help. Ledford stood up and walked to the staircase. He stopped on the way and put his hand on Erm's shoulder. 'You're right Erm. We're friends, always will be,' he said. 'But I can't use your money for what I've got to do.' He handed back the racetrack brochure. In the exchange, the flashlight's beam wobbled between them. 'We'll be hitting the road tonight,' Ledford said. He ascended the stairs and gathered his wife and children.

It was the bottom of the seventh inning in the league championship game against International Nickel. Mann Glass was up 6 to 5. Ledford sat on the dugout bench and cleaned out his cleats with a Popsicle stick. Next to him was Charlie Ball, who whimpered like a child over the hamstring he'd pulled running down a fly to right. He'd made the catch and gotten them to the stretch. But now the top of the lineup was due at the plate. Ledford was batting lead off and Charlie followed. It was clear he wasn't going to make the batter's box, and they were already down to nine men after two machine boys had to leave in the sixth to report for Saturday C shift.

Ledford saw his chance to gain ground in a battle he'd lost at season's beginning. Back then, the other men had voted down his proposal to integrate the team, ignoring his insistence that Mack Wells was a fine shortstop. Now, watching Charlie Ball's ugly grimace, Ledford put in a plug of tobacco and said, 'Charlie, your uniform'd fit Mack Wells just fine.' He nodded his head in the direction of Mack, Lizzie, and Harold, who sat on the far end of the left-field guest bleachers, ten feet between them and the other spectators. Mack had brought his brother and mother to watch the game. Harold was reading a book.

'Didn't anybody ever tell you not to crack jokes that isn't funny?' Charlie said. He stopped bellyaching long enough to look at Ledford and spread his one-sided smile.

Ledford spat heavy on the toe of Charlie's left cleat. 'I look like I'm joking?' he asked.

Charlie rubbed at his hamstring with both hands. 'You're crazy if you think I'm lettin a dirty nigger wear my uniform.'

Ledford scrunched his lips and sucked in his cheeks. He worked up another load of tobacco juice and spat again, this time on the left pantleg.

'Hey!' Charlie Ball turned red.

164

'What you going to do Charlie?' Ledford asked him. He stuck his finger in the man's soft stomach and said, 'You're too fat to get around on the fast ball anyhow, bench blanket.'

Charlie Ball showed his teeth then. He furrowed his brow and cocked back his fist like the might throw it at Ledford, who just smiled in response and said, 'Let it fly rich boy.'

An older man from corrugated came over and sat down between them. He said all this could be figured without the tough talk.

'I got it figured,' Ledford said. 'There's a Mann Glass employee settin right over there on the bleacher, and his average was .350 in the colored leagues.' Ledford pointed to the Wells family, and the rest of the team looked. 'If he tightens the belt by four holes, he can wear this invalid's uniform and keep the game movin.'

Nobody said a word.

Then, the mute batch attendant stood up. He stared for a moment at a bat someone had stuck through a hole in the chain-link. He grabbed it by the barrel, walked to the end of the dugout, and tapped it hard against a metal fencepost. From the bleacher seats, another man jogged over, and the mute batch attendant started telling him something in sign language. The other man, who had no shirt on and wore a wide surgeon's scar from his sternum to his bellybutton, said, 'Jerry says the colored boy can wear his getup, and he'll put on the rich boy's.'

Ledford smiled. He nodded *thank you kindly* to both the scarred man and the mute.

'Forget it,' Charlie said.

'Forget what?' Ledford stood, his temper rising. 'Forget that another man just offered to fix your problem? You tellin me you won't let a Negro *or* a mute wear your fat suit?'

Charlie stood to face him, but sat back down when his hamstring gave. He looked at the spit-soaked dugout floor and shook his head. 'I won't let that nigger put on a Mann uniform. Don't care whose it is.'

Ledford knocked the older man from corrugated aside and went for Charlie Ball. The older man managed to grab him by the right shoulder, but with his left hand Ledford seized Charlie's throat and hooked in hard. He could feel the Adam's apple spasm against his palm. He could tell his fingernails were breaking skin. Charlie looked like his eyeballs might explode, and Ledford stared at them, teeth grit, willing them to do so. There was the sound of metal cleats gripping ground, and men circling and jostling for position and pulling and saying, 'Whoa whoa whoa now.'

They pried Ledford off and Charlie sucked at the air like an upright vacuum. It sounded as if his throat had collapsed, the opening there crushed to the circumference of a termite hole.

The man with the chest scar laughed heartily. Harold Wells stood beside him now, fingers interlaced on the chain-link, the look on his face showing nothing.

Ledford was shuffled to dugout's edge. He caught sight of Harold and then the rest of the faces in the bleachers. He'd choked a man in front of them all, and he could not take it back.

The home-plate umpire was hollering about a disqualification for delay.

Ledford walked across the field to the nickel plant's team captain. He and the rest of the team hadn't left their dugout since the stretch. The man wore no expression, as if none of it had happened in the other dugout before his very eyes. Ledford said, 'We might need a few extra minutes for a wardrobe change.'

The man's eyelids were like those of a bloodhound. He let his jaw drop open before he spoke. 'We won't play against no team what fields a colored.'

Ledfored sized him up. Bony. Slow. Backed by ten men with cocked ankles and fisted hands. Ledford smiled at them. Then at the man before him. 'Will you play against a team that fields eight?' he asked.

'No sir.'

'Well,' Ledford said, 'I reckon we've got ourselves a forfeit situation.' He walked to the pitcher's mound and stood on it. Looked up at the sky above for a plane. None flew. Both teams stared at Ledford and a few spectators got up to leave. He watched Lizzie Wells pull her boy away from the fence by his shoulders. Mack had already headed for the car. Ledford saw the back of Don Staples as he walked past the concession booth to the parking lot.

The umpire hollered, 'Game's called on account of forfeet.'

Ledford decided to stand on the mound until nobody was left.

When they were gone, he looked down at his jersey, the black-felt letters stitched tight to the chest. Four of them, forming one word. *MANN*. Ledford began unbuttoning. He pulled off the jersey. The clouds had thinned and the sun felt good on his shoulders.

Next to his backpocket tobacco was his jackknife. He pulled it out and sat down on the mound and began to rip at the stitching of the last *N*. When he'd loosed nearly all of it, he gripped the big felt letter in his teeth and yanked his head back. It tore loose clean, as if it had never been there. Ledford spat out the *N*, stood up, and put his jersey back on. He was careful to line it up right, hole to button. He smoothed it with his hands and looked down. *MAN* it read across his chest.

'Big things, bad and good, happen in threes,' Ledford's mother once told him. She'd been more talkative than usual, and was made somewhat numb by the three things that had befallen her in the winter of 1933. She'd lost her job at the grade school, Bill's hours at Mann Glass were cut in half, and she'd found a lump in her breast.

Now, three things were upon Ledford, almost all at once. Inside a week, he'd put in his notice at Mann Glass, filed business papers with the state tax department, and decided to move his family to Marrowbone Cut. The first two came relatively easy. It was the third, explaining such a change to Rachel, that worried him.

They lay in bed next to each other, quiet but breathing heavy from what they'd just finished. Even after three years of marriage and two children, they met in a controlled fury almost nightly. The only prompt necessary was the brush of one's skin against the other's under the sheets.

Ledford sat up and lit a cigarette. 'I think we ought to move to the hills,' he said.

Rachel lifted her hand to his back. She rubbed at the scar there, to the left of his spine, where the shrapnel had come clean through. It was shaped like the letter Z, sloppy-edged, as if drawn by a pink crayon. 'The hills?'

'I've had enough of town.'

She was quiet for a time. 'Do you wonder about too many changes at once?' She reached around him for a drag off his cigarette.

'Yes, I've wondered that,' he said. 'I've wondered mainly for your sake, and the children's. How would you all take to it. But to my mind, it couldn't come fast enough. These are things we should have done from the get-go.'

She wasn't sure she followed him, but she thought for a moment about living in the country.

About walking out her back door and seeing no neighbors, and about taking strolls through the woods until a path was beaten. This made her happy. 'I'm game,' she said.

Ledford turned to Rachel. She was smiling. He'd expected her to cry. Her eyes were mostly pupil in the low lamplight. 'We'll have to sell the house,' he said. He watched for her expression to change. It didn't.

'I've always felt it was poorly constructed anyway,' she said. 'Like Lincoln Logs stacked too fast.'

Ledford laughed. She was looking at him the way she had just minutes before, as he'd moved on top of her. It was a stare that possessed neither fear nor angle, only the want to be as one. 'I love you,' he told her.

They talked for two hours. Rachel wanted to sell her parents' house too. It had been empty of people since her father died, its insides gathering dust. Now it had a purpose. She told Ledford they could use Mann money from the bank to help. There was a lot of it. She said she'd knit colorful little bags to hold the marbles he'd make. Said she was fast, and that her bags would be royal blue and red and sunflower yellow.

She went quiet when he told her that by settling in the hills, he meant the Bonecutter property. That he aimed to set up both shop and home there. She put her head on the pillow and looked at the ceiling when he told her he'd been out to visit the Bonecutters again and gotten their okay on things.

Men like those frightened Rachel, and she wondered, briefly, if this was all a mistake. She considered that she was running from something. Ledford was easy to figure – he'd been running from his past since the day she met him. But for Rachel, it may have been the future. She didn't want to join the Junior League or the PTA. She didn't want girlfriends, never had. She didn't even particularly want to go back to nursing, as it had brought little in the way of fulfillment. What she wanted was to raise her children up right, those she had and those to come. To bandage them when they were hurt, to teach them their lessons. To hold them pressed against her face for as long as they would let her.

It was decided. 'I'll call the realtor tomorrow,' Ledford said.

SEPTEMBER 1948

Selecting was bad work. It was liable to strain the eyes, watching all those little glass jars come by on the belt. And it was loud. Always loud. Lizzie Wells, like all the other women on the lehr, sometimes found her eyes jumping left to right long after work was done.

She checked her wristwatch. Almost six a.m. She reached down and discarded a faulty medicine dropper. Across the room, Faye had a sneezing fit. She was the oily-haired one everybody said was crazy. When her sneezing subsided, Faye stood still for a moment, shoulders sagged. Lizzie noticed the tag at her collar was up, a little white square at the base of her neck. Then Faye shot out her arm and picked up a misshapen baby food jar. She reared back and threw it across the room. A couple women ducked the shattering ricochet. 'Nobody can't do this type a thing for fifty cents a hour,' Faye hollered. 'No man would stand for it!'

Somebody told her to shut her mouth. Otherwise, none spoke a word. There was just the metal hum of conveyance.

Lizzie took quick glances and otherwise kept her

eyes on the belt. A nice woman who was older than the rest patted Faye's back and pushed her along, back to her selecting spot.

The shattered baby food jar lay in a scatter at the far end of the room. Lizzie took note of its jagged condition, pictured Mack in his old duties, sweeping it into a dustpan. At least he'd had security then, she'd thought. Word was, the new owners were looking to lay off anyone they saw fit. A greed had come over the upper offices of Mann Glass, just as it had come over the rest of the white world. It was a greed Lizzie's father had foretold. Always, he had told her, after a time of hardship or war, the white man will seize the opportunity to re-establish his place on the throne.

As was usual, Lizzie walked home alone, right along the railroad tracks. She cut across at the overpass and walked through the empty lot behind the hardware store. She didn't pass a single house on this route, and that was how she liked it.

At home, she kissed Harold good morning. 'Sleepyville,' she said, using her fingernail to scrape at the morning in the boy's eyes.

She kissed Mack at their crossing spot in the bathroom. 'Got home fast,' he said. He stood on one foot and pulled a sock on the other.

Lizzie reached up and took a seashell from the tank lid on the wall. 'Fast as I could,' she said. She took the pins from her hair and set them in the seashell. 'You know that one girl who's plumb crazy? Well, she *went* plumb crazy today. Threw a jar against the wall, smashed it. Yellin about how men wouldn't do this work.' Lizzie sat down on the tub's edge. 'That's life on the lehr,' she said.

Mack didn't respond. He finished dressing in the bedroom, then went downstairs to heat enough oatmeal for himself and the boy. Always, it seemed, they ran out of time. Harold had to be across town at 7:30. First bell at Frederick Douglass was 7:45.

When they pulled into the driveway of Lizzie's parents' home, Mack's wristwatch read 7:32. Her father, Mr J. Carl Mitchum, sat in a highback wooden chair on the porch. He checked his own watch and stood. He was a big man, and he didn't like to be kept waiting, especially by his son-in-law. What he did like was to walk his grandson Harold to school in the mornings at a slow clip, and with conversations on God and demons. Douglass was only two blocks away.

'Morning sir,' Mack said. His father-in-law did not answer. Harold ran up and gave him a hug around the waist.

'You eat a good breakfast?' J. Carl's voice was low and commanding, like a sousaphone chirping. He had his hands on the boy's shoulders.

'Yessir. Two bowls a oatmeal.'

J. Carl rubbed his thumbs against the boy's collarbones. 'Good,' he said. 'But you still a scarecrow short on stuffing.'

Mack handed over Harold's lunch pail. 'I've got to get to work,' he said.

J. Carl took the lunch pail and set it on the wide

handrail. He pulled a small tuning fork from his pocket and handed it to Harold, who walked away, flicking it. J. Carl watched the boy. He didn't look at Mack when he spoke. 'You know he can just stay here with us on weeknights. Make things a whole lot easier on you.'

Mack didn't answer.

He backed out of the driveway and watched the old man resume his seated post in the highback chair. He put the boy on his knee. Inside the screen door, Mack saw a shadow pass, then another. The whole family was most likely there. They all lived within a block of each other. Lizzie's older brother taught math at Douglass, and her sister taught music. Both had gotten master's degrees at Bluefield State.

J. Carl was the music director at the Sixteenth Street Baptist Church. He didn't like his daughter living among poor West End white folks, and he did't like her working at Mann Glass.

At the factory, Mack waved at Ledford, who was backing out the main doors, both hands on a cardboard box. It was his last day, and after three years in an office he'd never brought enough to fill a single box.

It occurred to Mack that the day was not shaping up. Lizzie's talk of the crazy woman on the line had spooked him. Harold hadn't spoken to him on the way across town. Ledford had left for good.

He put on his gloves and took his place on the main line. His hands moved from memory, sulphuring the blanks as the molten glass was drawn up.

175

Up above, less than five minutes after Ledford cleaned out his desk, Charlie Ball moved into his office. The Toledo brothers were running things now, and they liked Charlie. What they didn't like were expenses allotted for company picnics or holiday parties or baseball teams. They didn't like employee fellowship or company newsletters, or unions, or Negroes.

Charlie stood in the doorway with his hands on his hips and winked at Ernestine, who ignored him. 'King of the hot end, Ernestine,' he said. 'King of the hot end.'

Ernestine rolled her eyes.

Charlie walked the platform. He oversaw the lines now, and he intended to keep the men under watchful eye.

At noon, Mack Wells took his lunch break. He sat down alone in the cafeteria corner and had just forked in a mouthful of dumpling when Charlie Ball pulled up a chair across from him. Mack nodded and chewed.

'Word is, your wife is part of an uprising on the selecting line,' Charlie said. He pushed the salt shaker back and forth between his hands. 'Women who were happy to have work when the war started all of a sudden think they're making slave wages. Now doesn't that seem strange to you?' He smiled and waited on an answer.

Mack finished chewing and swallowed. 'Well, I don't know about any uprising Mr Ball, and Lizzie—'

'Here's what's going to happen boy.' Charlie leaned in close. The salt shaker was squeezed in his fist. 'Your wife is going to lose her job on the lehr for Communist insubordination. That, or you lose yours for insubordination as we sit here right now.' He waited for a reaction and got none. 'Either way, I don't need two coloreds inside this plant. That's the bottom line. No Ledford here to say otherwise.' Charlie eased back and thumbed a clump of hair off his forehead.

Mack just looked at the younger man who'd called him boy. He wasn't sure he'd heard right, was contemplating lost dollars in his head. He felt the urge to reach across and use a handful of Charlie's hair to slam his face to the table. Instead, he sat still and said nothing.

'I didn't hear you,' Charlie said. He cupped his hand to his ear. A couple of men returning their trays had taken notice of the conversation. Charlie cocked his cupped ear at Mack. 'What do you say? Your job or your wife's?'

Mack swallowed, stood, and took his tray to the return belt. He brushed against the gawking men as he went, and they moved along.

Charlie frowned and laughed a little. He watched Mack Wells walk away. 'Back to work,' he said to no one in particular.

Mack kept walking. The words repeated in his ears. *Back to work*. He had other ideas.

When he'd typed it, slow and painful on the green

177

Remington typewriter he'd picked up at a rummage sale, the words had seemed inspired to Ledford. Now, in the lantern light on the back stoop of Dimple and Wimpy Bonecutter's place, he wasn't so sure. He'd spilled coffee on the paper. The typeface was light.

Both brothers stood and read at the same time, Dimple with the lantern held above them. They squinted hard and moved their lips in whispered study. The top of the page read merely *The Plan*. Underneath, there were passages like *Ledford monies will be sufficient to run electric, H_2O, and gas, and decisions will be made co-operatively to consider vegetable gardens and farming endeavors*. Another part read *Home and dwellings shall be built with standard plans from US Department of Agriculture (24' x 10' A-Frame Cabin, for instance)*.

Wimpy looked from the paper. It took him a minute to locate Ledford, who'd sat down on the chop block. 'Where you goin to git these federal plans?' he asked.

'Already got em,' Ledford said. 'Library.'

They went back to reading. When they'd finished, they walked off to a lone fencepost and Wimpy leaned on it and they talked in hushed tones. It had gotten so dark that Ledford would not have known they were there save for the whispers.

After a time, Dimple picked up the lantern and they walked over to Ledford. He stood from the chopblock and brushed sawdust from the seat of his pants. 'That's just a draft,' he said.

Dimple spoke. 'We'd like to welcome you and yours to this land.'

Ledford looked at the brothers, then down at the ground. A sense of relief had come over him. He nodded. 'Thank you,' he said.

'We don't see no problem with the house plans and what have you. And the hookup to power and gas and water – you know Mother and Dad B had it up at the main house.' Dimple pointed in the direction of the charred flat square. 'Lines is already run. But do I figure right that you plan on building a glass factory on this ground?'

'Well, I envision a relatively small dwelling,' Ledford said. 'Maybe a fifty-by-fifty-foot deal? High ceiling. I'd put a big furnace in, just to make the batches worth our while.'

'Mm-hmm.' Dimple rubbed at his stubble. He and his brother had never set foot in a factory. They didn't like the sound of the word.

From the woods came the sound of a deer traversing dry ground cover, snapping twings. In response, Dimple's ears moved like a cat's. 'And you say this marble idea come to you in a dream?' he asked.

'Yessir.'

'A voice?'

'That's right.'

Dimple started to inquire further, but Wimpy cut him off. 'What did the voice say?'

'Make marbles,' Ledford answered.

Now they both rubbed their stubble. Then, simultaneously, they stopped. Dimple put his hands in his pockets. Wimpy rocked on his heels, swinging the lantern in his grip.

The dream was enough for them. 'Okay,' Dimple said.

'There's one more thing,' Ledford said.

'What's that?'

'I work with another man at the glass plant who may be losing his job. His wife too. I don't know for certain, but they might be interested in movin out here with us. Working. Raising their boy.'

'That'd be just fine,' Dimple said.

'Well, I ought to mention.' Ledford cleared his throat. 'They're Negroes.'

'How's that?' Wimpy stopped rocking on his heels. The lantern kept swinging.

'They're Negroes.'

'Colored?' Wimpy asked.

'Yessir.'

The brothers nodded that they understood. Dimple said, 'You do know this here's *Wayne* County?'

Ledford nodded that he did.

'What's this fella's name?' Dimple asked.

'Mack Wells.'

'Has he ever worked for Maynard Coal?'

'Nossir.'

'Then I don't give a damn what color he is. He and his are welcome here.'

Ledford shook hands with both of them. They didn't invite him in. He got the impression they went to bed not long after sundown.

NOVEMBER 1948

No one thought Truman had a chance. The *Chicago Daily Tribune* had even printed the headline DEWEY DEFEATS TRUMAN, but that was a bald-faced lie. Truman had triumphed. 'I'll be durned,' Ledford said. He stared at the newspaper and wondered if Truman would live up to the promise of Mr Hubert Humphrey's speech.

He lit a cigarette and read onward. The article predicted price controls and an increase in minimum wage. Next to it, Truman himself spread his arms wide and smiled, his hat in one hand, his patented wave in the other. Nowhere were the words *civil rights*. Ledford's breath condensated on the cold morning air. He sat cross-legged on a tarp just outsided the front flaps of his tent, reading the newspaper that Jerry the mute had brought from town. For almost a month, Ledford had been sleeping four nights a week inside the square of canvas. Days he spent building his family's new home, all the way at the back of Marrowbone Cut. In their backyard was a hillside covered in oak trees and ash and poplars. In their side yard, a mountain stream. Ledford was happy.

He stood up and stretched. Jerry the mute and his cousin Herchel the scarred had already gotten a fire going. A straight-seam coffeepot sat on one of the rocks circling the pit. It jiggled as its contents boiled. Herchel used a sweat rag to pick it up and pour. At his ankles was a Plott hound pup. It had been born two months prior to a bitch belonging to his uncle, an East Tennessee man who knew hunting dogs. Herchel was calling the pup Jack Dempsey.

Ledford held out his cup and Herchel poured. They stood and sipped and sighed. Ledford bent and petted Jack Dempsey's little head. The pup took his wrist between its two little paws, cocked its head, and bit his finger. Ledford pulled loose, stood, and laughed. Shook the sting from his hand. He stepped around his tent and beheld the nearly finished home they'd erected. It was a fine house. A two-story A-frame with a covered front porch and spruce siding. A tin roof and ten windows. Fifty yards east sat an identical one, only it was one-story. It too was nearly finished, and it was to be the Wells family home. Both sat at the back of the hollow, nearly out of sight from Dimple and Wimpy's dwelling.

Ledford watched Herchel pour another round of steaming coffee into Jerry's cup. He could hardly believe his good fortune at having hired on these men. After the baseball forfeit, he'd approached Jerry at work, asked him if he'd be interested in a new job. A construction job. Dollar an hour. Jerry wasn't deaf, he'd simply never spoken. He'd listened and nodded yes. He'd written on a scrap of paper that his cousin Herchel, *the one with the scar on his belly*, was out of work, and that he owned a Ford tractor with a backhoe attachment. The three of them had worked hard together after that, along with Mack and Dimple and Wimpy. And now, Jerry and Herchel would stay on permanently as employees of the unnamed future marble company. They would help build its factory, and at the same time, they'd build a house for themselves.

Jack Dempsey had the cuff of Jerry's blue jeans in his bite. The little dog got back on his hunches and whipped his head side to side. Jerry paid him no mind. He held the tin cup in his teeth and signed something to Hercheal, who nodded lazy.

There was a shotgun blast from the woods. Jack Dempsey let go of the blue jeans and took off like a shot, tail-tucked and dropping turds all the way. He whimpered while he ran, high-pitched and patterned like a wolf whistle, and hid in the recesses beneath the new Ledford porch.

Herchel laughed so hard that coffee came out his nose. 'Did you see that damn dog dropping his mess?' he said. 'If he gets lost, he can follow his own crumbs back.'

Ledford thought this was the funniest thing he'd seen and heard in years. And the little dog possessed true speed. 'I tell you what,' he said, 'he ran so fast he burnt the wind.'

There was another shotgun blast. Dimple and Wimpy had gone out early to hunt rabbit.

Lizzie's father stood on the front porch with his big arms crossed. He did not uncross them to recognize her departure, nor did he come down from the porch as her mother and sister and brother strolled along the driveway, waving goodbye. Mack and Lizzie waved back from inside the car. It was loaded with the last of their things.

The Plymouth's front windshield was streaked in mud. Lizzie watched her girlhood house get smaller as they backed away. Tears had welled in her eyes, and everything looked rounded. Her father's squared stance even softened at the edges. She wiped her eyes and looked for Harold.

Behind big J. Carl, where his mother and father could not see him, Harold cried harder than he had in some time. He pressed his face against his grandfather's double-holed leather belt and stuck his fingers in his ears. That way he wouldn't hear his parents drive away.

It had been decided that Harold would live with his grandparents during the weekdays. There was school to be considered. His aunt and uncle were down the street, and they were in the classroom too. Their children, Harold's cousins, were eager playmates. On the weekends he'd stay out at Marrowbone Cut.

J. Carl kept his arms crossed and let the boy cry. He did not watch the Plymouth as it drove out

184

of eyeshot, trailing a Packard driven by a white man he couldn't figure. J. Carl shook his head. He turned, knelt, and pulled Harold tight against his shoulder. His big hand pressed the boy's head there and cupped it, so small and perfect. 'It's all right son,' J. Carl said. 'Sometimes mothers and daddies got to do foolish things before they find a righteous path.' In his mind, he prayed that his youngest daughter would someday cease forever testing his patience. Unlike his other two, Lizzie had always chosen what he forbade.

Inside the Plymouth, Lizzie let herself go. She bent her head to her knees and shook. Mack rubbed her back between shifting gears and kept his eye on the Packard. It started to rain. 'It's not that bad now,' Mack said. 'We'll be seeing him. Every few days we'll see him.'

She sat upright. 'Every few days? He's our son, Mack.' She wasn't taking the time to breathe right. She put her hands out, pointing ahead. 'Why are we following *them*,' she said, 'when *they* are back there?' She swung her arms back toward Sixteenth Street.

He didn't have an answer.

'Loyal Ledford is not some different breed of white folk,' Lizzie said. 'He's been trained like the rest of em, eyes shut and ears plugged. Have you thought about that?' She smacked her hands against her lap.

Mack had thought about it. It seemed all he thought about was the uncertain future, and when he did so, he'd get to thinking on the past. Always, it was the past. Alone on the road, he'd thought long and hard on Lizzie, how she'd not been the same since Harold was born and the doctor told her she would not bear another child. Her state since had been one that seemed, to Mack, only half awake. Her mood could turn on a dime. He also thought about how he'd run away from his wife and baby boy and the world they had to face. He had run to the Army and served his country, fixing roads and bridges and trucks and tanks. And after a while, when black men could fight along-side white, Mack had hugged his rifle tight and rocked on train and truck wheels across France and into Germany. When they arrived, he saw the look in those white boys' eyes on the banks of the Rhine. It was a look of utter confusion, and later, for many, it was a look of camaraderie. Mack had crossed the Rhine with his new comrades in the Ninety-ninth. He'd charged German nests while emptying his M1. Some in the Ninety-ninth were even white boys from Alabama and Mississippi and Georgia. He'd celebrated alongside all of them when they reached Leipzig. But as quick as it had appeared, the look in those white soldiers' eyes was gone when they stood at the door of the Leipzig rec hall and said, 'No niggers allowed.' And then, Mack was shipped back to his engineers unit, and everything was the same as it had been before. So it was that he'd decided then, as he had again and again in his life, to hate all white folks.

He'd returned to face their world with his wife and son.

And then, at Mann Glass, he'd looked in Ledford's eyes.

The windows were fogging inside the car. Mack took out his handkerchief and wiped in a circle before him. 'Yes,' he said. 'I've thought about it.'

Lizzie had forgotten what they were talking about. She dabbed her eyes with the cuff of her blouse and looked at him. 'Thought about what?'

He stared out the windshield. The wiper blade was torn. It dragged a mud-colored smudge back and forth across the glass. 'About all of this we're doin.' He thought before continuing. 'I don't have no answers, Lizzie.' He squinted. 'I just want out of the West End.'

Ledford had sold the house to Mr Ballard from the filling station down the street. He was a good man, and he needed a second home. He had four boys, the youngest fourteen and the oldest twenty-two, all of them Golden Gloves contenders.

Mack thought about the house, the spot in the yard where the cross had burned. He thought about the job at Mann Glass. He told Lizzie, 'I just want out of the factory and onto the land, and I ain't lookin to spend my own nickels to do it.' They turned and went under the viaduct. 'Ledford is putting up the nickels,' Mack said, 'and he and Rachel got a mite more than two to rub together.'

APRIL 1949

Ledford had quit reading the newspaper. It gave him a stomach-ache, reading words like *38th Parallel*. When a paper rode in with a lumber delivery, Ledford would toss it on the pile. He had a furnace stack to build.

He was hand-laying the stack in fieldstones he collected walking the property with a wheelbarrow. Around his growing chimney were wall studs and roof trusses, the bones of an unnamed marble company.

It was a Friday evening. April Fool's Day. Ledford stood in front of the empty-walled factory and sipped his coffee. He walked inside, lifted the corner of a tarp on the floor, and threw the evening edition underneath, next to all the other papers he'd been saving.

His wheelbarrow was in the back, where he'd left it, half full of stones. Next to the furnace, under another tarp, sat the old marble machine he'd bought from Mr King. Mack's brother Herb was reshaping the rollers on a lathe, and Mack was working on the cams and shears himself.

Ledford finished his coffee and set the cup on

the furnace bricks. He put his hand to them. Cold. He imagined them hot, a fire inside. He imagined that liquid glass running, orange as the sun.

For two weeks, the electric, water, and gas men had been on the property hooking the whole place in. Their handiwork was everywhere. Copper tubes and conduit stuck up from the ground like organ pipes. There was a hole in the ground where the natural gas line would come in to fuel the furnace. Ledford bent to the hole. He stared into it. He cocked his head and listened to its hollow call.

Across the Cut, Don Staples stood under a tree, planing wood he'd laid across two sawhorses. He'd retired from Marshall and moved out to Marrowbone in August. He was building a chapel at the clearing by the creek.

Rachel walked over to Staples with a canteen of cold water. 'It's quittin time,' she said.

He smiled. 'Particularly for old-timers.'

Rachel assured him that he was a spring chicken. He sat on a sawhorse and split open his pouch of pipe tobacco. The smell caused Rachel to lurch. Smells were getting to her of late.

She'd gone to the doctor on Monday. She was pregnant again.

Mack and Lizzie came over and sat on the Ledford porch at sundown. The air was strange with the feeling of April Fool's. Ledford wore a look of contentment on his face. He watched the children where they congregated at the roots of a tree. He opened his mouth and said, 'Rachel's pregnant.'

No one said a word at first.

'You pullin my leg, Ledford?' Mack said.

Ledford assured him it wasn't a joke. He shook his head and smiled. 'Hell, all I got to do is shake it at her.'

Both men laughed out loud.

Lizzie smiled, but it wasn't genuine. Though they'd become friends, she couldn't look at Rachel then. For the life of her, she couldn't understand why some were so blessed with children while others were not.

Rachel smacked Ledford on the arm. She smiled, but hers was as false as Lizzie's. A palpable guilt weighted on her for the way Ledford had told them, and she wished Lizzie would look at her. Rachel understood why she couldn't. She poured herself more tea and the ice in her glass cracked and settled. The sound made her stomach lurch again. Her mouth began to water. This pregnancy was different from how the others had been.

In the front yard, Harold chased Mary in a figure eight between two maple trees. When he caught her, he tickled her armpits, and she laughed so hard she peed herself a little. Willy rumbled over from where he'd been kicking a ball against the house. At a year and a half, his gait was not unlike a drunk man's, knock-kneed and zigzag. He came to his sister's rescue. Harold allowed the little ones to pin him to the ground, no longer warm from the day's sun. 'Help,' Harold hollered, and the adults on the porch watched with one eye while they talked.

Downstream, Staples and Herchel were thirty feet up, on all fours on the roof of the chapel. They'd worked past quitting time once again, and the chapel was nearly finished, towering on its stilts. Dimple and Wimpy had suggested they build it up high off the ground. They'd seen what floodwater could do to the Cut, and the chapel's location put it square in the path. Every other dwelling was built back from the creek, but Staples had envisioned his place of worship, and none could argue it. Already, a spring rain had come, and already, the stilts wore the mark of high water.

The two men drove nails into the rafters through sheets of tin and wood. Staples was tired. He bent four spring-heads before driving one home. On the next hammer swing, he came down hard on his thumb. He gasped, dropped the hammer, and brought his thumb to his mouth. 'Son of a bitch,' he said.

Herchel smiled. 'Goin' to turn purple,' he said. 'Then black.' He drove in the last nail of his line. 'Means your pecker's still a growin.'

'How's that?' Staples frowned and blew on his thumb.

'When you hit your finger like you done, means your pecker's still a growin.'

Staples laughed. Made sense to him.

The Bonecutter brothers rode by atop their new horses, tipping their hats as they went. They'd fixed up the crib barn and cut hay and gathered sawdust into head-high piles. The horses were a gift from the Ledfords.

The brothers said 'Evening' to all, and when they passed the Ledford place, Dimple clucked his tongue and dug his bootheels in his horse's side. Wimpy did the same, and they tore off up the hillside through the woods, the horses following a path they'd begun to cut on the brothers' nightly rides.

The Bonecutters had once kept horses, long ago. Both brothers knew that a horse's eyesight was unpredictable at night, and they wanted theirs to know the land by touch, even in blackness. It was something their grandmother had taught them to do, and it was something needed now more than ever. Behind the smiles of the new residents of Marrowbone Cut, black and white alike, was a palpable fear. An edginess evident in the eyes. More than once, some unknown hill neighbor had snuck onto the property and shot their guns to the sky. The still, pre-dawn air had carried throated calls of *Niggers go home* and *No niggers in Wayne*. The same had been painted in white on the trunks of big old oak trees. These were cowardly acts. None in thirty miles would do such things in the open. All knew the reputation of Dimple and Wimpy Bonecutter. Still, the brothers wondered if any of this was the work of the Maynards. Or maybe some ridgerunner family squatting on the edge of their acreage. The twins had always been happy to let such squatters be, but the recent displays of anger, however gutless, had put them of a mind to protect. To guard those who'd come to their land. It was a role they relished. It made them feel young again. High up on a horse, the brothers felt as strong as they had in the old days.

Dimple's horse was a big buckskin gelding named Silver, like the Lone Ranger's. Wimpy's was a brown-and-white paint horse named Boo, shorter-legged than Silver and wider around the middle. She was a moody mare, and Wimpy's balance wasn't what it had been as a younger man.

As they disappeared into the woods, the sun dropped behind the hills and the children were called in to their homes.

After Mary and Willy were asleep, Ledford set the phonograph needle to a record he'd borrowed from Mack. It was Mahalia Jackson. Her voice filled the ten-by-twelve space they'd designated as dining room. Boxes were stacked on the big cherry table from Rachel's girlhood home. They were full of cullet samples, broken glass from three different factories. Rachel stood over a box of red glass, her fingertips at their edges, her mind on her own mother. Ledford took her hand and led her to an open spot of floor by the stairs.

They danced. Mahalia sang, *Going home one day and tell my story, I've been coming over hills and mountains.*

It didn't feel right to Rachel.

Ledford could feel it in her arms around his neck, the way they hung there, limp as wash on a line. 'What's wrong?' he asked.

'Nothing.'

'I heard this playing at Mack's. How about that voice?' He kissed her forehead. 'Wait here,' he said.

She had an unexplainable urge to cry, but didn't. She stood alone by the stairs. She looked at the front door of their new home. It had been hung crooked and stuck every time you tried to shut it. From the dining room, the needle scraped and the music went dead. Then silence, and then the tinkling of piano keys and the soft whir of a clarinet. He'd put on Claude Thornhill's 'Snowfall.'

They swayed together, Ledford pushing his hips against hers, but Rachel never came around. When he asked again what was wrong, she said only that she felt poorly.

'I'm just going to go lie down,' she told him.

After midnight, Rachel awoke to a pain in her stomach. She walked to the bathroom and turned on the light. She pulled up on her nightgown and down on her underwear. Spots of blood, some tiny, some the size of a dime, marked the white cotton.

She sat down on the toilet and cried. She had known it all along in her bones, but still she cried.

For a moment, she wished to God she wasn't here, in a bathroom that smelled of sawdust in a house with a shallow foundation, on land she'd never known. She wished to be back in her mother's house on Wiltshire Hill. She wished her mother alive so she'd have someone to talk to.

There was a thump at the bathroom window

and a quick, shrill sound. Rachel closed her knees together and gathered the nightgown to her chest. Again, the thump at the window, but this time she was looking. It was a redbird, smashing itself against the glass and chirping an awful call. Again the bird pounded itself to the pane, and again. Then all was quiet.

'Rachel?' Ledford called out. He'd jumped out of bed and pulled his .45 from atop the highboy.

'It's okay,' she said. 'Just a bird flying into the window.' She wondered why it was flying around in the middle of the night.

Ledford lay down again. 'You all right?' he asked. Since the first neighbor fired a gun and hollered hatred from the woods, such wakings had become customary.

'I'm fine.' She'd wait till morning to tell him about the blood. She'd have to put a pad in overnight, go to see the doctor in town on Monday.

Rachel couldn't sleep after that. She looked at Ledford, his chest rising and falling, his hand there on top of it, wedding band scratched and dull.

At the back door, she put on his rubber boots and barn coat and went outside. In her hand she carried a flashlight. She walked to the end of the house, just below the bathroom window. She switched on the flashlight. The redbird was not there. She bent for a closer look, thinking he'd crashed to the ground, but there was nothing. Not even a feather.

Then came a flapping up above. Still bent at the knee, Rachel shined the flashlight at the window. The bird had come back. It was perched on the roof's edge, just above the sill. It looked down at Rachel, cocking its head this way, then that. In the flashlight's beam, its eye was black and wet like glass. Rachel was still.

She stared at the eye of the redbird and it stared right back at her.

Then, it quit its perch and dive-bombed.

The occurrence was too fast for Rachel to move, and it was upon her. She managed to shut her eyes and raise an arm, but the bird's beak found the split between her ring and middle fingers, and it pierced the skin of her temple.

And then it was gone.

Ledford stumbled from the back door barefoot with his .45 in hand. He trailed a red flutter into the treetops, gun raised and oscillating right to left. He stuck it in his waistband and ran to Rachel. 'Are you all right?' he asked. He knelt to her.

She'd rocked onto her backside and was touching gingerly at her wound. She laughed, loud and nervous. 'It was a redbird,' she said. 'It dive-bombed me.'

Ledford picked up the flashlight and turned her head in his hand. He lit up the small pockmark at her temple. Bluish, leaking a drop of blood. He turned the flashlight on the trees where the red blur had sought refuge. 'What in Sam Hill?' he managed.

It was then that he remembered a dream he'd had, though he wasn't sure when. In it, a cardinal had perched on a fencepost covered in locusts. They awoke and swarmed the cardinal, who did not move. The locusts twitched and shivered and ate and left behind a pile of bones the size of toothpicks.

Back in the kitchen, Ledford stuck a dish towel in the opened top of a peroxide bottle and tended Rachel's wound. 'It's not anything to worry over,' she kept saying. He resoaked the towel and dabbed nonetheless.

When they'd sat down at the table, he asked, 'What were you doin out there?'

Rachel looked at the mantel clock on the back of the range. It was almost two a.m. She looked down at her hands. Dirt had caked under the nails on the left but not the right. 'I've lost it,' she said.

'What?'

'I've lost the baby.'

Ledford stepped around the kitchen table to her. He pulled her to him tight. His hand moved up and down her back by memory.

She did not speak further, nor did she cry. After a minute or two like this, she said, 'I'd like a drink of liquor.'

His hand stopped. He could hear the tick of the clock behind him. 'All right,' he said. There was a full pint of Ten High in the attic. Ledford had bought it but never cracked the seal. He walked to the stairs.

When he came back with the bottle, he didn't look at her. He set it on the table and turned, pulled at the cabinet doorknob. It was stuck and only gave when he put muscle to it. He'd hung the magnet latches too close to the hardware. He wasn't yet accustomed to his new hand drill.

Rachel wished she hadn't said it. None had spoken a word on his not drinking liquor, and now she'd conjured up what she'd been glad to be rid of. Her hands clasped before the bottle.

When he turned, he held only one coffee mug. It rang sharp against the enamel table top when he set it before her. Their eyes met, and he winked at her. Smiled. He patted the gun in his draw-strung trousers and said, 'I'd better go put this thing up. Liable to shoot my pecker off.'

She listened to his bare feet pad the hardwood as he walked away. She broke the seal on the bottle and poured.

Upstairs, Ledford checked on Mary and Willy. He put his ear to their noses and listened to the air going in and out. He cupped his hand to their foreheads to check for fever. The bedroom window was cracked a half inch – he could feel the crisp draw. A screech owl called from someplace way off. The children did not stir. And then, through the cracked window, Ledford heard the un-mistakable blow and snort of a horse. It did not originate from far, and if he had to guess, it came from the muzzle of Boo the mare.

★　　★　　★

198

Above the chapel door hung a sign. It was a four-foot length of broken siding, painted white and strung on roofing nails. Staples had found the wood in the scrap pile reserved for campfires, and the heavy-gauge wire had been left at the foot of an electrician's ladder. He'd finger-painted on the white sign the words that came to him one day while perched atop the chapel roof, beholding his surroundings, and he'd spoken them on the air.

Land of Canaan Congregational the sign read.

Staples stood outside the chapel, nodding at Mack and Lizzie and Harold, the last ones to crest the stairs and enter. He scanned the perimeter, as if hoping to spot more potential new fillers, as if there were folks roaming the wooded Wayne hills on this Palm Sunday morning. He spotted Dimple and Wimpy coming across the holler on their horses. Staples stuck his finger and thumb in his mouth and whistled. They trotted over.

'Why don't you come on and join us boys?' he asked them.

Dimple coughed and brought up a heavy load, spat it on the ground. 'Nossir,' he said. He let his horse bend to pick at a patch of grass still living amidst all the mud trample.

'Well, if you change your minds, I'm here. Every day.' Staples' living quarters were in back of the chapel.

'Every day?' Dimple asked.

'Every day.'

'What religion do you preach?' Wimpy asked.

Staples pointed to his sign. 'I use the terms loosely,' he said. 'This land of yours is as fine as any I've come across. And I've given our chapel this name of Canaan because, like all of God's earth, it belongs to each of us who are the offspring of Abraham.' He smiled at the blank stares before him. 'And by the offspring of Abraham, of course, I mean everyone.'

'Everyone?' said Wimpy.

'Everyone.' Staples thought for a moment he might have convinced them to come inside. Dimple had cocked his head to have a look. Staples continued. 'And the word *congregational* I use just as loose, for it refers to our independence from all other denominations.' He'd decided to simply go on reciting what he'd practiced for that morning's sermon. If the two men before him decided to come inside, they could stand to sit through it again. 'And just as important,' he went on, '*congregational* refers historically to our commitment to the abolition of slavery's ugly remnants upon this great country.'

They looked at him like he'd spoken in French.

Inside, the church pews shone with lacquer. They were solid white oak, six feet long and twenty inches deep. Plain. Stained to a golden brown. With six against the west wall and six against the east, the little church could seat seventy. On this day, nine were present.

Herchel could hear Jack Dempsey barking from clear across the Cut. He'd left the dog in the house, had assumed canines weren't welcome at worship.

200

He looked up at his handiwork. They'd decided on a scissor truss for the ceiling, and Herchel had stained the beams to match the pews. He smiled and noted how the peaks were perfect, the butt cuts too. The air inside was like a lumber mill. Dusty and new. He looked at the heads of the Wells family in front of him, so still and accustomed to worship.

Herchel hadn't been in a church for ten years.

Beside him sat Jerry, who was clinching his cheeks to stifle a fart. He sweated though it was temperate. Pressed his boot sole to the floor and bounced his leg up and down.

Jerry had never stepped foot in a house of the Lord.

It was quiet as the agnostics and atheists and Baptists and Episcopalians shifted on the hardwood. Willy broke free from his mother's lap and bounded up the steps to the pulpit, a simple lectern made from pew scrap, no insignia. Sawdust danced under his clumsy saddle shoes. Ledford stood to give chase, but Staples said, 'Let the boy be.' He was coming down the aisle with a cardboard box in his hands. He pulled from it and handed, to each in attendance, a King James Bible and a hymnal. *Hymns of the Spirit* it read, gold embossed.

Staples bent to Willy, who jumped up and down on the plank steps, the smack echoing from the trusses above. He stopped when he saw the sugar cube being handed his way. The boy snatched it and stuck it in his mouth. Staples told him, 'There's more where that came from if you sit on your mama's lap and be still.'

At the pulpit, Staples stood tall. He wore a white dress shirt and black tie, and he'd made an effort to comb his hair and tame his beard. They looked up at him, and he smiled, nodded. Said, 'Welcome.'

He began his sermon with the same explanation he'd delivered out front to the Bonecutter brothers, who were not in attendance. Then he put on his spectacles. He took a wad of paper from his shirt pocket and flattened it on the lectern's face. Braced his palms there and cleared his throat. 'When we think of eternity,' he read, 'and of the future consequences of all human conduct, what is there in this life that should make any man contradict the dictates of his conscience, the principles of justice, the laws of religion, and of God?' He looked out at them over his spectacles.

Ledford recalled the words as those of William Wilberforce.

Outside, the wind picked up. It rattled the panes of the single-hung windows, each cracked open to let the place breathe.

The preacher closed his eyes and inhaled deep. Then he looked at the faces before him and began. 'My name is Don Staples,' he said. 'I was born in McDowell County in 1893. I came up mean and nasty. Broke the Hindenburg Line in the First World War.' He let that sink in for a moment. 'Then I came home and was married and became a father.

I failed in both endeavors. I ran wild for a time before I was called by God to the Virginia Theological Seminary, where I first read of William Wilberforce, the man whose words I spoke to you just now.' His bad eye rolled slow. 'At the seminary I meet the great-great-great-grandson of the abolitionist Absalom Jones. I followed Will Jones to Mingo County in 1927, and together we built a church where black and white miners worshipped side by side for a time. That time ended in fire and hatred, and the hard years came, and I left that parish in 1933, worked all over as a preacher with the CCC for four years, and then I came to Huntington, helped on flood relief. Took a job teaching at Marshall.' He paused. Took another deep breath. A nuthatch bird lighted on the window pane and called. 'In all my travels on this earth,' Staples went on, 'from France to Germany and from the ocean shore to the coal mine, I have seen the ugly capabilities of man.' He took off his spectacles. 'I have seen ignorance and fear where the principles of justice should be. I have seen oppression in the name of religion, and of God. I have seen a den of robbers.' He stood stock still. 'But here, today, I see no such things.' He looked at Ledford and then Rachel. Mack and Lizzie. Herchel and Jerry. Mary and Willy. He looked long and hard at Harold. 'I see no ignorance in your faces, no fear in your posture.' He smiled. 'I see liberation.'

Staples spoke then of Jesus entering Jerusalem on a donkey, and of the people laying down palm tree branches. Jesus tossed over the tables of the money changers, Staples told them. 'Drove em on out,' he hollered, pointing to the doors.

Willy got loose and ran up and held out his hand for another sugar cube. Staples obliged with two. The boy returned to his mother's lap and Staples went on. 'Righteousness is not always mighty, and power is not always rich.' He folded his papers and stuck them back in his shirt-pocket. 'Who wants to sing a song?' he asked.

They turned to 'Bring, O Morn, Your Music' and sang of the ocean's laughing rapture and the people's thousand tongues calling for light.

Staples promised them that he'd never afflict their ears with boredom. He said clapping was welcome, as was hollering and the stomping of feet. If any played an instrument, bring it, he said.

Rachel raised her hand.

'Speak freely here,' Staples told her.

'We have a piano being delivered.'

'Amen,' Staples said.

Rachel was at peace with what had happened to her. She had two healthy children. She'd have another one day.

Staples asked if any would like to step to the lectern. Said that all were welcome to speak their minds, no matter the subject.

There was only quiet. The nuthatch bird had gone from the window and the wind had ceased to blow. Mack Wells checked his wristwatch. Jerry prayed for the service to convene. He couldn't hold his monumental fart much longer.

A marble fell from Mary's dress pocket and rolled to the center of the aisle. Harold sprung from his seat and retrieved it. He held it to his eye. 'Blue cornhusk,' he said.

Ledford nodded. He'd given the boy a book on marbles. Ledford hoped to be manufacturing such a variety within the year.

Harold handed the marble to Mary and walked back toward his seat. He stopped short, thought for a moment, then climbed the stairs to the lectern. Staples stood aside.

Lizzie leaned forward in the pew, thought for a moment about stopping the boy. Instead, she reclined and reached for her husband's hand.

None could see the boy wholly where he stood behind the wooden stand. Only pantlegs, shoes, and shoulders. The top of his head. 'Next week's my birthday,' Harold said. His voice had come out softer than he'd thought. He could feel a tremble in his hands. Still, he spoke. 'I want a ball glove.' The adults smiled. 'I want more Negroes to be allowed to play ball with white men, like Jackie Robinson.'

He turned and looked at Staples, who nodded and told him he was a natural.

'Boys at school say mother and dad is crazy for moving out here. They say white folks isn't no good.'

Mack watched his boy close. He was fascinated by his only son.

Lizzie started to correct his grammar. *Aren't any good*, she thought to herself. Then she sighed and sat back in the pew.

Harold said, 'I only know Baptist. And I don't know any white Baptist.' He coughed and inadvertently knocked his head on the lectern. He rubbed it away. 'Stretch, this boy at school, says white folks . . .' He met the eyes of Loyal Ledford, who wore a look much like his own father's. 'I don't think that Stretch knows what he's talking about,' Harold said. 'I think God made all people good and then some of em get taught bad.' He lit off fast down the stairs and into his seat. Mack put his arm around him.

'Amen,' Staples said again.

OCTOBER 1951

Mack walked the length of the Cut with a notepad and pencil in hand. Back at the chapel, he'd noticed Jerry following him but paid him no mind. He'd come to expect such things at Marrowbone. Jerry followed Mack, and the chickens followed Jerry.

In front of the vegetable garden, the two men made eye contact and nodded. Mack began writing down greenhouse dimensions, and presently Jerry approached him, making signs with his hands. 'Sorry, I don't understand,' Mack said.

Jerry motioned for the pencil and notepad. On it, he wrote, *What are you scouting?* and handed it back.

'Oh, I'm trying to figure a system for the whole place. We need a water station in case of fire. Could double for irrigation.'

Jerry nodded. He was impressed. He took the notepad again and wrote *How do you know all this?*

'Army,' Mack said. 'Engineer unit.' Across the creek, there was a trampling of leaves from the woods. Mack trained his eyes in its direction. The sound had come from out beyond the empty A-frame that would house his brother and mother.

Mrs Wells had been a cook all her life, and when her sons told her the pay rate at Ledford's new outfit, she quit her job at Smalley's Cafeteria and said, 'Sign me up.' Mack's brother Herb could swing a hammer, and he was the type to wander where whimsy led.

The leaf trampling grew louder, and Dimple and Wimpy came out of the woods, riding double astride Silver. Dimple was at the reins and Wimpy behind him, a rope in his grip that trailed back and lashed to Boo's bridle. The mare was acting as pack-horse. Her load was no ordinary supply. Tethered to her saddle, jutting up like a stalagmite, was the severed head of a ten-point buck. Its blood ran down Boo's barrel and flank, zebra stripes on a paint horse. Big ancient saddlebags rocked with her gait, and they too dripped blood. The handle of a meat cleaver stuck out from a pocket. On the opposite side, a canvas bag hung like a close-quartered hammock, shoulder to flank.

They'd hung, bled, and dressed the mighty deer in the woods, and now they were bringing it home.

Jack Dempsey the Plott hound followed along. The horses had gotten used to him as a pup, and he slept most nights in the barn. He stood almost thirty inches and weighed sixty-three pounds. A fine dog. He'd once gone after a black bear and faced it down. Herchel had come running when he heard the awful snarls. The young bear nearly sliced Jack Dempsey dead before Herchel shot his 20-gauge in the air.

Even Dimple couldn't help but pet the dog, and Dimple hadn't touched a canine since one bit him in the face as a boy, granting him a nickname for perpetuity.

The brothers eased their mounts over the footbridge slow and steady. The creek beneath was low. The footbridges, built just after the '49 flood, had yet to be tested.

The twins rode to Mack and Jerry, nodded. Mack and Jerry nodded back.

'We'll roast at Ledford's pit tonight, that's all right by him.' Dimple wore no gloves on his hands. They held the reins bloody red, fingernails outlined in dried black scab. Across his forehead was a crimson smear where he'd wiped at sweat while cleaning the deer. 'It's a biggin,' he said.

Wimpy nodded.

'That sounds good,' Mack said. 'There's plenty a firewood stacked.'

'Your mother have any venison recipes?' Wimpy asked.

Mack shook his head no.

'Well,' Dimple said, 'they'll be some good stew bones from it anyhow.'

They rode off to the head of the hollow, where the old butcher's shop awaited.

That night there was a bonfire and a feast, and afterwards, Herb Wells produced his guitar. It was a big old Stella twelve-string, the only worthwhile possession their daddy had left behind when he disappeared in '31. Herb hummed low and used a steel thumb pick to walk the sound out. Rachel had set up folding chairs in a circle around the pit. They sat close and tapped their feet on the dirt, and watched the blue-tips dance. Their backs made a wall to keep the children from the fire while they duck-duck-goosed in a round, oblivious to the night's cold air.

The goats were free again. They'd bent the wire on the pen fence and hurdled. Now they circled the gathering, clacking heads and testing their horns on Jack Dempsey the dog, who ignored them, then bit their hides without breaking skin.

Herchel laughed.

Mrs Wells didn't care for the goats. She excused herself to the Ledfords' bathroom.

Herchel was a little bit drunk. He sang a made-up line along with Herb's guitar. *Jack Dempsey blues, goat horn blues.*

Ledford said, 'Herb, if you stand and play that guitar in a wide stance, those goats'll come over and scratch your balls for you.'

Herb laughed while he played. He wound down his picking and they congratulated him and Staples said, 'It's no wonder I've not seen you at worship, Herbert. Man plays like that has already inked in blood.'

Ledford watched the easy laughter on the faces of those around him.

Herchel pulled a flask and tilted it to his lips. He passed it to Jerry and Herb, who did the same. The firelight played across their foreheads, and it shone in the lines of the face of Mrs Wells. It reached clear to the wrinkles of the Bonecutter brothers, who stood apart from the circle and listened.

Staples sang a song for the children, who patted their laps in time with Herb's picking. *Was a tiny old man that lived at the dump, uh-huh. He was short and squat like a sycamore stump, uh-huh.* Harold Wells laughed genuine. His mimickers, Mary and Willy, followed suit. Staples sang on, *Had a mile-high trash heap bed for his head, if you like city livin just go on ahead, uh-huh, uh-huuh, uh-huuh.*

Ledford recognized the tune his mother used to sing him.

Jack Dempsey moseyed over from the porch and sat at Herchel's feet. Herchel rubbed hard at the dog's ears. 'Watch his eyes,' he said. They shut slow with each touch, reopened, and shut again. 'He cain't stay wake when you rub him like that.' Herchel then demonstrated what happened when he scratched the dog's snout. Jack Dempsey's top lip curled, showing his teeth. Then he sneezed three times fast and explosive. Herchel did it again with the same results. It sounded like a light-bulb busting. Everyone laughed.

'Ledford, you remember that time he was a pup and heard that shotgun blast?' The liquor was warming all of Herchel's extremities now. 'Jerry, you remember?'

Both men acknowledged that they did.

'He tucked and run like the sky was a fallin.' Herchel slapped his knee. 'I never seen nothin, man or beast, what proved the turn of phrase like Jack Dempsey done. I seen those little brown droppings with my own two eyes. That dog had the shit scared out of him.'

Everybody laughed harder then, but Herchel cut his short. 'Beg pardon ladies,' he said.

'I heard worse,' Mrs Wells answered.

Wimpy walked over to them. It grew quiet. Some were not yet accustomed to the brothers, as their presence was primarily from a distance. 'Enjoy the venison?' Wimpy inquired.

All nodded. 'Truly delicious,' Rachel said.

Wimpy kicked at a pebble with his boot tip. 'I come up with a name for your company,' he said. His gaze was to the ground, eye sockets deep, shrouded from the firelight.

'Let's hear it,' Ledford said.

'Well, I reckon you could name it for the place where you built it. Could call it the Marrowbone Marble Company.'

The moment the words were spoken, Ledford found them both peculiar and perfectly suited. Destined, he decided, and he wondered how he hadn't thought of it himself. 'That's just about perfect,' he told Wimpy. 'Thank you. Very much.'

Wimpy nodded, turned, and walked away.

'I'll make a fine sign,' Staples called after him. He finger-painted on the air.

Wimpy waved without turning.

It was nearly ten when Rachel called bedtime for the little ones. They begged for one more ghost story.

212

Herchel leaned into Herb Wells. 'They want the shit scared out of em,' he whispered. Herb agreed.

The fire threw less light. Dimple and Wimpy left their positions and went off to bed.

Staples gave the children one more. 'This tale's called "Hickory Nuts,"' he said. 'Heard it from my mother.' He leaned forward in his chair and drew a house in the dirt with his finger. The children sat close. Staples spoke, 'An old man down in Switchback wanted to sell his big brick haunted house, but nobody would bite. So, he offered a reward to anybody who could stay in it all night and prove it wasn't inhabited by ghosts. My granddaddy volunteered.'

'Really?' Harold asked. He sat on his knees with his hands in his pockets. Beside him, Mary and Willy did the same.

'Really. So, my granddaddy sat in the haunted bedroom that night and stared at the big fireplace with a candle on the mantel. He lit a match and stuck it to the candle.' From behind his back, Staples produced two kitchen matches and struck them on his front teeth. They blazed up big and he bugged his eyes above the glow. None cried or ran away. 'Tough crowd,' Staples said. 'How old are you Willy? Seventeen?'

'Free and a half,' Willy said. He held up his thumb and two fingers.

Ledford and Rachel stood by and chuckled. He pulled her to him, her back against his chest, his chin on her head.

Staples licked his thumb and finger and squeezed the matches dead with a hiss.

At this, Willy beamed.

'There we go,' Staples said. He winked at the boy. 'With the candle, my granddaddy lit a fire in the fireplace from wood that was already stacked and dried. It lit up the hearth, which was built from rough stone. It also lit up the floor, and there he found a burlap bag of hickory nuts and a hammer. So, he cracked some nuts. Soon enough, a human finger stuck out from the stone hearth.'

'Not really,' Harold said.

'Really,' Staples answered. 'A whole human hand. And it caused the candle and the fire to flicker and dim. And my granddaddy knew if he asked the hand a question in the name of the Creator, it would be obliged to answer. So, he asked, "What in the name of God do you want from me?" And the hand showed its palm, and a tiny mouth opened in the center of the palm and said, "Raise this rock."'

'It said what?' Mary was shivering by then. She pulled her knees to her chest.

'It said, "Raise this rock."'

Willy asked, 'When you goin make that fire on your toof agin?'

That tickled Mrs Wells, who set off a rumble of laughter from Herb and Herchel.

Staples smiled, then righted his ship. Put back on his grave face. 'And so my granddaddy took that hammer and worked all night busting up that stone hearth, and beneath it, inside a hole, he found another burlap bag, but this one wasn't full of hickory nuts. It was full of a treasure of old coins, enough to keep him rich the rest of his days.' Staples leaned forward, and, one by one, pulled a quarter from behind the ear of each child. 'And from that treasure he gave me these, and now I'm giving them to *you*. Save em now. Use em for good.'

Even Harold, nearly ten, was impressed.

Leftover venison was divvied, foil-wrapped, and handed around. Goodnight embraces abounded. Little Willy took a leak on the smoldering fire and his parents shook their heads. Pants at his ankles, he turned and said, 'Daddy teached me.'

'I bet you he did,' said Mrs Wells. She turned to Rachel. 'You best keep an eye on that one,' she told her.

Just before midnight, Ledford and Rachel found themselves locked together at the middle again, bucking under the quilt and trying to keep quiet for the children down the hall. They rolled from one another and lay panting, sweat on the tips of their noses already going cold. 'I love you,' Ledford said, and they rolled back together and kissed.

He'd found something at Marrowbone he'd not known before. It was in the fire, the music, the stories. The children. His wife beside him. He didn't even miss the liquor.

In the crook of his shoulder, Rachel felt nearly the same. Her discomfort with the place had passed.

She'd come to know it well. But something was missing. Her family was not yet full. She'd been checking the calendar, studying the pattern of her cycle. She breathed in the fire smell of her man beside her and rubbed her finger over his belly scar. She closed her eyes and prayed that what they'd just done would bring her another baby.

In his dreams that night, Ledford encountered a stone fireplace hearth like the one from Staples' ghost story. There were no hickory nuts or human hands. A pull string hung from inside the chimney shaft. He knelt, leaned in, and pulled it. There was no click, no light. He pulled again. A sound came, like ice cracking. He pulled again. There was a shift of some sort above, and small pieces of rock and ash fell onto Ledford's hand. He gave a final tug and something gave, and there arose from way up the chimney a hollow, empty sound. An old light socket fell and knocked against his hand. It left a red impression, circle-shaped, and it settled in the fireplace ashes. Then, a voice came from up the chimney, nearly lost inside the hollow howl. 'Orb,' it whispered.

Ledford scooted the light socket away and lay down on the ash. He stared up the shaft into darkness, a coal-black pinpoint. 'What?' he asked.

'Orb,' said the voice. 'You shall call him Orb.'

JUNE 1953

T he test batches came out of the furnace ugly-colored and easily cracked. Among them, here and there, was passable marble, enough to fill fifty hand-knitted bags, twenty-five count in each. They were banded swirl marbles of green and blue, amber and red. Shooters – taws, some called them – were bigger than the rest. Ledford made these by hand, one at a time.

Lizzie Wells sat in a frayed wicker chair on the Ledford porch, her sundress a catch-all for yarn. Her wooden needles clicked as she knitted and purled, knitted and purled. She kept it loose in back and finished up the twelfth row, wrists rolling loose and regular, talking while she worked. 'You sure you feelin up to this?' she asked.

Beside her was Rachel. She cast off and regarded the candy-striped marble bag she'd made. 'This one ought to be for Christmastime,' she said.

Lizzie was about to cast off herself. 'I just wonder if it's a good idea for you to go.' The two women had spent hours of their weeks and days knitting together. They'd spoken of babies and war and canning and getting out sweat stains and husbands and mothers and daughters and sons. Sometimes they didn't speak at all. They hummed. Sometimes, like now, they conversed without really conversing.

'I wish we had peppermint swirl marbles to fill this one,' Rachel said. She stuck the tusk needles in her hair bun.

Lizzie snipped yellow yarn with rusty shears. 'I'd go with you if I thought they took kindly to Negroes.'

Ledford came out the front door buttoning his shirt collar. He smelled of aftershave, and there was a daub of soap foam in his earhole. 'You ready?' he asked.

'Here.' Rachel handed him the latest marble bag. He took it inside and threw it on the pile with the rest, a mountain of drawstring satchels waiting on their filling. They spilled forth from apple baskets lining the dining room wall. The big table was a mess of papers and bills and a calender with a pencil slash through every day up to this one, June 19th.

On the porch, Rachel readied herself to rise. She put one hand on her swollen belly and the other on the armrest.

'Honey that chair won't hold,' Lizzie said.

'You sayin I'm fat?'

'I'm sayin that chair is old and you about to pop.'

Ledford came back out and the two of them helped Rachel stand. 'I'm not an invalid,' she said.

'Not yet anyway.' He kissed her forehead and rubbed at her belly.

The Packard was acting up. They bumped across

the lot to the gate, clutch slipping. Between them, a giftbasket bounced on cracked leather. Rachel had woven the basket and filled it with ten full marble bags, her best ones. Blue and green for boys. Pink and red for girls. It had been her idea to make such a peace offering to the Maynards.

It took ten minutes to wind around the ridge on Knob Road. Ledford worried all the way that Rachel would get carsick. In her state, it seemed likely. She was due in August.

The sign at the turnoff was in need of repair. *Maynard Coal and Coke* it read, and under that, *Beech Fork Gap, W A*. Some bug or fungus had made a hole where the V had been.

At the bottom of the steep paved lane, a man in coveralls leaned into the open hood of an old Chevy Standard, his socket wrench fixed on a stubborn spark plug. A brown dog stepped from the corrugated shed at the sound of the approaching car. The man straightened and looked. His skin had seen its share of sun, and he looked past middle-aged.

'Which one is that?' Rachel said.

Ledford put it in park and regarded the man through the windshield. 'I believe that's Paul, the sheriff.'

'And you're sure he's a good man?'

'That's what I gather.' Ledford stepped from the car, called 'Afternoon,' and went around to help Rachel. He knew her thinking in all this. Even a Maynard wouldn't shoot a pregnant woman.

The dog cut short its approach and growled, its hackles raised in a line.

Ledford took Rachel's arm and eased her out. She shut the door behind her and Paul Maynard saw that she was pregnant. He whistled and the dog turned to him. He pointed to the shed and said, 'Go on.' The dog obeyed.

Rachel carried the giftbasket and they strolled over to him. Her shoes sunk in the mud. Floods had visited again the week prior. Beech Fork Gap, unlike Marrowbone, was always hit hard by floodwater.

Paul Maynard stuck the socket wrench in a hip pocket and clasped his hands together.

When they were a couple yards off, Ledford said, 'I'm Loyal Ledford, this is my wife, Rachel.' He extended for a handshake.

None came. 'I know who you are,' the man said.

'Are you Paul by chance?' Ledford had heard Paul was the wisest of the family, the slowest to percolate. The least ruffled by the color of some of his new neighbors. As sheriff of Wayne County, he was one of the few men in local politics who'd never been called crooked.

'I did know your daddy once,' he said. He unclasped his hands and went cross-chested. Took short looks at Rachel's stomach. 'Good ballplayer.'

'He was,' Ledford said.

Rachel glanced at Paul Maynard's knuckles. They were covered in nicks, and the nicks were greased, filled in black like cracks in the street.

'For you,' Rachel said. She gripped the basket with both hands, extended it almost to touching him. 'Well, your little ones really.' She smiled.

He didn't. 'What is it?' he said.

Her arms shook with the weight of the outstretched load. 'It's marbles,' she answered.

'Marbles.' He considered the word. 'Playin marbles?'

They nodded.

He uncrossed and took the basket from her. Had another sideways look at her condition. 'Thank you kindly,' he said. A frown settled in at his brow. He wanted to say more, but couldn't.

From far off there was a hollow screeching sound. Ledford looked over Paul Maynard's shoulder at the hillside in the distance. There was a square-cut black hole in its face, and emanating from within was a growing rumble and whine. A mantrip emerged and rolled forth, rounding a tight curve. With a thud, it hit track's end at the top of a skinny tipple. The men aboard jostled and grabbed at their headlamps.

'Fridays are halfdays now,' Paul Maynard told them. He hadn't turned around at the noise.

Rachel watched the men step from their low-lying vehicle. That far off, they looked to be boys, their silhouettes long and awkward, their limbs wispy. It seemed to her they'd been dipped in some giant inkwell, not a splotch of light to be found.

Ledford knew the Maynards had dug about as

much from their seam as they could. For a little out fit like theirs, he imagined the coal boom was long since over. He cleared his throat. 'We won't keep you,' he said. 'Just wanted to say hello, let you know about our little factory that'll be up and running tomorrow.' He pulled an envelope from his back pocket and stuck it in the basket. 'That's an invitation to the party we're having. State's birthday and all.'

Paul Maynard nodded.

A week before, Ledford had driven rutted roads for a five-mile radius, putting such invites in the mailboxes of country people who'd loathed his presence since the day the Wells family moved in. He regarded the man before him, thought maybe he wasn't such a person as that. 'Was I right in thinking you were Paul?' Ledford asked him.

He nodded again.

'Well, Sheriff, I hope your little ones like those marbles. Made em ourselves, and if any Maynard wants to come on over and see what we've done with the place, or even come to worship at our chapel, that'd be most welcome.'

'Most welcome by who?' Paul Maynard's voice was tired, his eyes the same.

'By all of us,' Ledford said. Beside him, Rachel smiled and unstuck her shoes from the mud.

'What about them Bonecutter brothers?'

Ledford said, 'I told them we were coming here today, and that I aimed to invite you. They won't give you any trouble.' As he spoke these words, he realized that they were only half true. He *had* spoken to Dimple and Wimpy about his plans, but they'd made him no promises.

Paul Maynard turned and looked up the hill. The men filed down the mountain in two small packs, their knees bent and their frames clumsy against the uneven slope. 'Well,' he said. He thought it best if the couple leave before his nephew and the other miners walked over. 'I thank you for comin.'

This time he shook Ledford's hand.

When they'd gone, Paul's nephew walked over. 'Who was that?' he asked.

'That was Loyal and Rachel Ledford.' He set the gift basket on the roof of the Chevy. 'Good people.'

Shorty Maynard glared at his uncle. He could hardly believe his ears. 'They're nigger lovers is what they are,' he said.

Shorty was as mean as his dead cousin Sam, and drank nearly as much. He stood six and a half feet tall. Hands the size of a ball glove.

Paul ignored his nephew. He watched the Packard turn onto the main road.

On the way home, Ledford smoked a cigarette and blew it out the window, close to laughing at how easy it had all been. For so long, they'd been scared to make contact with the Maynards, and now, there'd been a handshake. 'You could see it in his eyes,' Ledford said. He watched the road, steered with both hands. Raindrops shook loose from the canopy above and landed fat on the windshield. 'He wasn't half bad after all.'

Rachel didn't respond.

He looked over at her. That was all it took to know.

He jammed the brakes and pulled to the shoulder. 'Rachel,' he said. His vocal cords had tightened. He couldn't swallow.

A single blue vessel wound a crooked path across her forehead. Everywhere her skin had gone bloodless. Sheet-white and open-mouthed, she wobbled in her seat. Her hands gripped her stomach. The sound of her breath was throaty, like an old woman.

Ledford put his hands on her cheeks and turned her face to his. She winced, and a high-pitched cry came up. The bags under her eyes darkened before him and she said, 'No.'

Ledford put his hand next hers on the belly. He smelled the blood then. Pulled back the hem of her skirt. A flat roll of red coursed forward on the seat, widening as it went.

Ledford's breath caught. Inside his head were so many buried visions of blood running, yet none had struck him as this one had. He pulled off his shirt and undershirt, balled them. 'It's going to be all right,' he said, stuffing the whole thing between Rachel's legs.

He went hand over hand on the wheel and shifted reverse to forward. The tires spun once in the ditch and kicked free. He knew the Packard would not let him down. He knew he could get to the hospital in fifteen minutes flat if he kept the pedal mashed. He'd only have to slow at dead man's curve.

Orb Ledford was born by cesarean section at 12:02 a.m. on June 20th, the state's ninetieth birthday. He weighed five pounds even.

Rachel had nearly died in the ordeal. She'd been transfused twice, her skin the color of egg whites.

The doctor told Ledford that she'd bear no more children.

Ledford watched his wife sleep under the veil of morphine. He held her hand and did not cry. She was alive.

He walked down the hall and looked through chicken-wire glass at his new baby boy. 'Little Orb,' he whispered, and indeed the boy was miniature. But he looked fine inside his incubator, his arms moving, his feet kicking.

Mack and Lizzie came to the hospital. Lizzie flicked a pill bug off the purple rhododendrons she'd arranged inside a pitcher. She brushed at the sweat-crusted hair on Rachel's forehead.

A nurse looked on wide-eyed. She whispered to the others at the nurses' station about the strange white folks and their strange colored visitors.

Ledford took Mack aside in the hallway. 'I want the festivities to proceed,' he said. He looked at his watch. It was eight a.m. 'Maynards might even show up, and I want folks to see that marble machine at work.' He tried to count in his head how many he'd invited. They'd told Bob Staples about the grand opening, and who knew how many he'd told. They'd given ten invitations to J. Carl Mitchum to hand out as he pleased. But J. Carl was more than a little wary about sending black children to Wayne County for any reason.

Mack nodded. He put his hand on Ledford's shoulder. 'You just worry about your wife and son, I'll look after all that other,' he said.

Soon after, he and Lizzie headed back to Marrowbone.

By noon, the molten flow had started and Jerry poured green striking glass into the crucible. Herchel eyeballed the furnace belly. Ledford had taught him to gauge the temperature by sight. On this day, Herchel reckoned 2,000 degrees on the button.

Outside, a few neighbors had shown up after all, silent and overwhelmed by the sight of white and black living and working together. They were guarded in their holey shoes and faded Sunday-go-to-meetin clothes. Some were barefoot. One boy wore a circle of dirt around his face. He'd taken a washcloth to it at his mother's behest and only bothered with the middle. Now she guided him by the shoulders and whispered when it was okay to move. They had never been within ten feet of a black person, and their kin had been among those to fire rifles in the air and shout epithets they'd heard since birth.

But these two, along with some others, had ignored the warnings of their kin. They'd come to see the marble company for themselves.

They ate with relish and speed the white-iced cake Mrs Wells had made. They drank in gulps the punch she'd set out, a concoction she called Rum-Tum-Goody. 'There's plenty now,' Mrs Wells said. 'Don't be bashful.' She smiled from behind the picnic table, just as she'd done all those years behind the cafeteria counter. She couldn't begin to count the number of hateful white faces she'd looked at in that time. But these were country people. Their expressions were harder to read.

Mack used Lizzie's sewing shears to cut a red ribbon strung across the factory's main doors. Staples' sign hung true above, bolted to the corrugated steel. *Marrowbone Marble Company* it read. *Established 1951.*

Back at the front gate, the brothers nodded to Bob Staples as he pulled to a stop. The top on his Ford Sportsman was down, and in the passenger seat next to him was a man with a movie camera. The man raised it and pointed it at Dimple.

Dimple trained his shotgun on the black-and-silver contraption, lined his sight to the middle of its three lenses.

'Hold on, hold on,' Bob Staples said. He put his hand on the camera and pushed it back to the young man's lap where a small circle of piss had just leaked. 'He's just documenting this for me. Like he did my campaign.'

The young man's knees quivered, and he used his camera to cover his accident.

Dimple lowered his weapon. 'You keep it turned off till you get to the back of the Cut,' he said. 'You hear me?'

'I hear you,' Bob said.

'Talkin to the other one Bob.'

'Yessir,' said the cameraman.

Inside the factory, the small crowd gathered and watched the thick flow of glass as it was sheared, dropping in little globes of perfection on the rollers. Mack had retensioned the chain drive, and now he stood watching with the rest of them as marble after marble proceeded hot down the line, trailed by shadows of orange. It was a sight to see.

Little Willy had seen all the test runs. The furnace no longer impressed him. He regarded the boy with the circle of dirt on his face, stuck his tongue out at him.

Bob Staples came through the open doors and greeted his older brother. He introduced his cameraman, who said, 'Pleased to meet you. Is it all right to film in here?'

'I don't care if you do a dance and sing a song, son,' Staples told him. 'Just don't turn what you see here into something it isn't.'

Mary stared at the camera the young man held. She moved close to hear its sound over the hum of the fans. When the man went outside, she followed him.

'You want to look at my camera?' he asked. His sideburns grew down past his ears and his accent wasn't local.

Mary nodded yes. He knelt and held the camera before her. She read the letters on its side. Sounded them out. 'Pa-lard. Bow-lex,' she said.

The young man laughed. 'That's right,' he said. 'Close enough at least. How old are you?'

'Seven,' Mary said.

'Reading big words like it's nothing.' He watched as she studied the camera close. 'You'll speak French by the time you're ten,' he said.

Later, four came from the Maynard clan, only one male among them. At the gate, Dimple and Wimpy greeted the truck on horseback and eye-balled the boy. He sat with his sisters in the truck bed. He was too young to rough up or even have words. His pretty sisters cowered, and up front at the wheel, his mother sat, a bowl of ham salad next to her on the seat. She nodded to the twins respectfully.

No words were exchanged.

Dimple used his shotgun to wave safe passage and spat on the ground when they passed.

At two o'clock, Jerry and Herchel pulled a tarp off the marble circle they'd made for competitive games of Ringer. It was official size. Two-inch plywood, packed dirt on top. 'C'mon up and grab you a bag a marbles,' Herchel said to the children among them. 'Jerry here'll show you how to knuckle down, shoot a little.'

Lizzie handed out the little bags she'd come to know so well. The boy with the dirt-ringed face chose the candy-striped that Rachel had finished the day before. Lizzie pictured her friend on the porch, hands working the needles. They didn't seem the same hands she'd seen that morning, still and pale across a hospital bedsheet.

'What do you say?' one boy's mother instructed.

'Thank you,' the boy said, his eyes on his new bag.

'You're welcome,' Lizzie said.

Mack brought out something he'd built in secret. He set it down on the flat patch next to the Ringer circle. 'I call this the Marble Zigzag,' he said. A pair of two-by-twos ran vertical from a base, reaching four feet high. In between the verticals was a series of back-and-forth channels, scrap wood that Mack had bowl-gouged to carry marbles. He dropped one in the top and the children crowded to see it roll to and fro to the bottom.

They lined up to try.

The cameraman rolled film through all of it. He crouched and sidestepped, shooting faces wide and close. Mary followed him.

Back at the gate, a tan Cadillac Coupe de Ville came to a stop. The brothers were astride their mounts on opposite sides of the road.

Wimpy took in all that chrome, the way his reflection warped in the bumper. Boo's reflection made her a dinosaur. He squinted at the windshield, but the sun's glare obscured whoever sat inside.

A man stuck his head out. His hair was slick

and his skin was tan. 'Afternoon gentlemen,' he said. 'My name is Erm Bacigalupo. I'm an old friend of Ledford's.'

They stared at him. He had a boy in the passenger seat.

'Don't tell me he hasn't mentioned me,' Erm said.

Dimple regarded the car, the high starched collar of the man driving it. 'He spoke of you. Said you was in the war together.'

Erm held up his hands. 'Got my proof of invite in my jacket pocket here gentlemen,' he said. 'Don't get itchy with those long guns, paper's all I'm pullin.' He reached in and produced the invitation he'd received in the mail two weeks prior.

'No need for that,' Dimple said. 'But Ledford ain't here.'

The boy fidgeted in his seat. 'I gotta pee-pee,' he said. He grabbed at the crotch of his trousers and rocked back and forth. He was five years old and looked like a miniature Erm.

'Hold it in,' Erm said.

The boy slunk in his seat and kicked the dashboard hard, left a mark. Erm turned to him and smacked him across the face. 'Hold it in,' he said again. Then he turned back to Dimple. 'Where is he?'

'Hospital. Rachel had a baby. Came a month early and they had to cut him out. Nearly killed her.' Dimple watched the man's reaction close. It seemed to be one of concern.

'If I get back on 52 to Huntington, can I find the hospital?'

Dimple nodded yes. He tilted his head and looked at the boy, who cried quietly, his hand on his red cheek.

Wimpy had maneuvered Boo to the passenger window so he could get a look at the boy, too.

As the Cadillac reversed to turn around, the twin brothers' eyes met over its roof. For days, they'd discussed who might show up, who might be trouble. Neither had predicted the Italian from Chicago.

They watched his whitewall tires kicking mud as he drove away. When the car was just a spot in the distance, it slowed and swerved to avoid a man walking. His tall frame sidestepped and came on. His edges were blurry. 'Throw me the field glasses,' Dimple said.

Wimpy rooted in his saddlebag and tossed them over.

The eyecups were rough-edged and the lenses were scratched. Dimple did his best to re-locate the man through the worn prisms. When he had him dead center, he said, 'Well ain't that a kettle a shit?'

'What?'

'It's Paul Maynard. Train your rifle.'

Wimpy pulled his Winchester from the saddle scabbard. It made a dry sucking sound, barrel scraping leather. He tucked the butt plate to his shoulder, put his thumb on the hammer spur, and cocked it. He centered the ivory bead on Paul Maynard's chest. He watched the man's outline get bigger and clearer until he filled the rear sight's V. That's when Paul Maynard raised his empty hands over his head.

When he got in shouting distance he said. 'I'm unarmed. I'd just like a word.' He kept coming.

'Anybody with you?' Dimple asked.

'I'm alone.'

Wimpy kept him in his sights until he got within five feet. 'That's close enough,' he said. Maynard stopped walking, hands held high. 'Cover him,' Wimpy told his brother. Dimple raised the shotgun while Wimpy put his up and dismounted. He patted Maynard down, then stepped back and stood next to Boo.

'You ain't the law on my land,' Dimple said. 'And even if you was, I wouldn't give a flat damn.' He spat on the dirt. 'What do you want?'

'Just a word.'

'Put your hands down,' Dimple said.

Maynard did so and was then overtaken by a deep coughing fit. At its end, he managed 'Excuse me.' He spat into the stickweeds lining the road. His eyes watered. 'I come to say that if you two are able, I'd like to put trouble behind us. I know that's a good bit to ask of you, considerin all that's happened, but—' He coughed again, then righted himself.

The three men found themselves in a predicament. Each knew but could not say out loud all

233

that Paul referred to, but it was there. Paul's son Sam had burned the Bonecutter place to the ground with five inside. Dimple and Wimpy had come home from town to find their family gone, and they'd not called on the law, the law being Paul. Instead, they tracked Sam Maynard, and then they took care of him.

Maynard cleared his throat and spat again. Nerves had always produced in him an allergy and an abundance of phlegm. 'You know as well as I that Sam was bad to the core. He was only ever good at one thing and that was fightin. The liquor took him from bad to worse.' He decided then that it was time to look the brothers in the eye. 'I ain't making excuses,' he said. 'I just . . . well. I just met Loyal Ledford and his wife yesterday, and a few from our place already come over here this morning, and I wondered if we might not use this thing you got here as a means to . . .' He couldn't finish the thought.

'Peace?' Wimpy said.

Maynard swallowed, and then he nodded. 'I reckon,' he said.

Dimple tucked his shotgun in the crook of his elbow and dismounted. He stepped forward and held his hand out for Maynard to take it. He did. They shook. Then Wimpy stepped up and did the same.

For a moment, the three men stood facing each other, not a word between them. Paul Maynard nearly asked about the living situation at Marrowbone. Nearly told them of the other

234

Maynards, who, as his nephew had put it that morning, would never offer peace as long as niggers were in the mix. But he didn't speak to this. Instead, he nodded, said 'Afternoon,' turned, and walked away.

They watched him go.

When he was out of sight, there came the faint call of a child's laugh from opposite direction, at the back of the Cut.

'They're rollin marbles,' Wimpy said. 'Havin a big ole time.'

Dimple tied Silver to the gatepost. He put in a wad of tobacco.

'You want to go have a look-see?' Wimpy asked.

'Better keep our post here. You go on if you want.'

Wimpy looked across the Cut as far as his eyes would let him. He could smell the furnace smoke. Then, he could smell the chimney of his family's home, no longer there.

He sniffed the air some more. His mother's biscuits. He cocked his ear. The laughter of his sister and his nephews, the high whistle of his father, the song of his grandmother on the wind.

None of that was real. But there were other sounds. New ones. And there were homes dotting the land again. And the people who dwelled in them were righteous and hardworking, and they were bringing others into the fold.

Maybe, Wimpy thought, it would work this time around.

His grandmother had once told him that a man

would come to Marrowbone. His name would be Ledford, she'd said. He'd always assumed it would be Bill, not his son. He looked over at the burying ground beyond the house.

'I'd just as soon stand guard here with you,' Wimpy said. He watched a red-tailed hawk circling above. Its wingspan was wide and frozen in a balanced glide. Dimple looked up, and he, too, followed the hawk's route, the two brothers craning and twisting their necks to see, waiting for the bird to spot a field mouse, and tuck its wings, and dive.

PART II

A HOUSE ON THE SAND

JUNE 1963

The slug bellied over wet dirt, a stripe trail left behind. Its feelers had the look of tiny wet matchsticks. Four skinny tentacles reaching out to morning air, reading the sunlight above, sniffing the ground below. The feelers bent left and right. They retracted and extended. The slug came to the edge of a drop-off. It hesitated, then carried forth, vertical now, called below by smell. Other snails had set their compasses the same, and three were in stride with this one, intent on drowning. Nineteen of their brethren already lay dead at the bottom. They floated and sank, U-shaped, still and brown and bloated.

Mrs Wells bent to the trap and dug her fingers under its rim. She pulled it from the dirt, leaving a circle impression behind, three inches deep. Ledford had handblown these for her, extra-depth ashtrays, six of them. Sunken along the vegetable garden's perimeter, they were slug death chambers. Every morning, she emptied them into a slop bucket.

'Twenty-three,' she said aloud, counting the number of dead in her Thursday morning

239

roundup. She knocked the glass trap against the side of her gallon bucket. An inch of beer swirled at the bottom, and the little wet bodies dropped like turds. 'Plunk plunk plunk,' Mrs Wells liked to call out as they landed.

At the garden's far end, Mary stepped lightly along a row of cabbage seedlings no bigger than clover. From her cupped palm she dropped black pepper dust onto the soil. It would keep the cats from pissing in the rows. They'd initially welcomed the unkempt felines, who proved their worthiness with gifts of dead mice. They'd sit at the front door with a limp tail between two teeth, hanging like a drowned nightcrawler. But lately they'd taken the vegetable garden as their personal toilet, and this would not do.

Mary sneezed from the pepper's rising dust cloud.

'Bless you,' Mrs Wells called to her. She nearly had to shout across the garden, which had grown this season to the size of a baseball field.

Mary was barefoot. She wore a sundress stained by blackberry juice and a gardening belt made from a potato sack. Rachel had made it for her. 'How many dead?' she hollered to Mrs Wells.

'Twenty-three. Two more than yesterday.'

Mary tossed the last of her pepper.

At seventeen, she'd already graduated high school and was enrolled at Marshall for fall. She would study political science, just as Harold had done before her.

She wriggled her toes in the dirt and watched him. He was thirty yards off, tending to the chickens in his undershirt. He opened a door on the back of the coop and checked the nesting boxes. A broody hen squealed at him.

Harold liked the chickens. Especially when they were quiet. He'd rub his knuckles against the backs of their necks and watch the sheen move across the brown feathers, like gasoline on a puddle.

When the time came, he could snap one of those necks as easy as he could pet it.

Inside the run, he threw grain with the same motion Mary had spread pepper. Chickens pecked at it all around him. He latched the door and looked to the garden. Shaded his brow with a hand. His eyes met Mary's. He walked over, a gait like his father's, only Harold was taller.

'Sun's hot already,' he said.

'Tomatoes need it.' Mary flicked at pepper flakes caught in the lines of her hand.

'You decided on that dormitory?' He took note of her calf muscles. Hard, already tan from working outside.

'I'm going to stay out here.' Mary had trouble looking him full in the face. He'd grown a mustache. He'd grown handsome. She glanced at the old burn scar on his left biceps. It was oval and smooth, pinched at the edges.

'I figured,' Harold said. 'Same as I did. You won't make many friends that way.'

Mary shrugged. She wasn't interested in friends.

241

When she looked at people, she imagined them through the lens of her movie camera.

Harold had lived at Marrowbone during his years at Marshall, but he'd joined the Civic Interest Progressives. In the CIP, Harold became known by everyone. 'Your daddy tell you we're picketing Smalley's again tomorrow?' he asked her.

She nodded.

Mrs Wells walked over.

'Morning Grandma,' Harold said. He kissed the top of her head.

'I hear you say you're picketing at Smalley's again?' She set her bucket down and wiped her hands on her apron.

'Yes ma'am.'

Mrs Wells shook her head. 'I worked for those people for eighteen years,' she said, then she picked up her bucket and walked away.

They watched her go. 'She's slowing down some,' Harold said.

'Still murders slugs by the dozen though.' Mary smiled and watched the old woman amble. She considered what Mrs Wells had said. She pictured her working all those years at Smalley's Cafeteria, serving all those white faces, never once a black patron. Now her grandson and his fellow students had staged a sit-in at Smalley's. And when they were banned outright, they'd started marching the sidewalk with signs.

'Well, I'll see you Mary,' Harold said. He reached out and brushed her arm as he left.

In August, he'd be leaving for law school up at Morgantown. She wondered what she'd do then. Who she'd watch.

Above her, in the high branches of a staghorn sumac tree, the birds jostled. Six hollowed-out gourds hung there, half-dollar holes their entry-ways. They were birdhouses, strategically placed by the garden to ensure the bugs didn't take over.

Mary watched Harold walk away and listened to the birds chatter.

Up the Cut, a crowd of children had gathered. They stood around the dirt-and-plywood platform in silence as the wooden cross-rack was lifted from the center. It left behind thirteen marbles, three inches between each, their lines cutting an X on the well-worn surface. This was the game of Ringer.

Two boys toed the pitch line and knuckled up. The fat one, Hambone Maynard, shot first. His taw quit rolling two inches short of the lag line. A couple of girls in the crowd whistled their approval. Then Orb Ledford unleashed his big sulphide shooter, a black-painted dog inside. His unorthodox release caused some to shake their heads, but those heads went still as the marble quit rolling half an inch short of the lag line.

Orb knocked seven out of the circle before Hambone Maynard cleared one. The game was over quick. It was for keepsies, but when Hambone held out his banded clearie taw, Orb nodded no and walked away. His daddy had told him never rock the boat when it came to Maynards.

It was time to let the dogs run.

Orb was one week short of ten years old. He was tall for his age. Skinny as a rail and topped by a thick shock of black hair. He didn't talk much, and he didn't give or take affection, not from anyone. He'd always been that way.

Orb was encouraged to always and everywhere be careful, for he had the kind of blood that ran and didn't clot.

He didn't speak his first word, *dog*, until he was four. By that point, they'd long since known that he was different. Special. Slow, some would say. But when it came to singing, or a marbles circle, Orb was anything but slow. To him, music was an involuntary fire. It pulled from him what waited deep inside his belly. Orb could sing like Little Jimmy Scott. It was easy as chewing gum.

And it was the same with marbles. He saw the lines and angles in the Ringer circle as if they were drawn there. He merely had to connect the dots. It had always been this way for Orb. He'd always been around church music, and he'd always been around marbles. He merely took them up.

The dogs were different. He felt something for the dogs.

He walked first to woods' edge behind Jerry and Herchel's place. There, he lay down four pieces of deer jerky, spaced ten paces apart and placed at the line where backyard became forest.

Then he headed across the Cut toward his own house. His shoe soles banged the bridge planks and he didn't use the hand ropes.

It was quiet at the back of the hollow. None were home. Not his mother, father, sister, or brother. When he walked up the hill to the pen, the dogs stood from where they slumbered and began to pant. Four of them inside. Plott hounds, all. Offspring of Jack Dempsey, all sixty pounds, give or take. Jim-Jim, Tug, Pug, and Doo-Dad. Orb had named them himself. The pen was ten-by-ten, chain-link. A rusty corrugated roof. Herchel and Jerry had built it for the boy's dogs when they were still pups.

Orb undid the latch and the dogs jumped all over him. As always, he went to the ground and let them lick his hands and face and sniff at his creases and the bottoms of his shoes. He lay prone and expressionless as they stepped on his skinny arms, their claws lining him in white. It comforted the boy to be held down, and he shut his eyes and nearly smiled. After a while, the dogs were sated. Orb stood and clicked his tongue twice. They sat down in a circle around him.

Then he made a strange sound that originated in his throat and came up slow, ending in 'Tooooooooo east woods!' The dogs shot from their seated positions as if catapulted. They chugged across the Cut like Thoroughbreds packed in a bunch.

At woods' edge they lowered their snouts and

traced a line. The treats were not in the same spot as the last time, but the dogs had come to expect this. They kept moving, and eventually, Doo-Dad, the only female among them, found the first of the four pieces. She called, and the others bounded over, each filing in to find his own jerky. They swallowed their jerky whole. Then Doo-Dad broke for home, and the others followed suit.

Orb stood at the open gate of the pen as they came back across the Cut. They strode like racing dogs, eyes on a jackrabbit. They jumped the creek with one glorious bound apiece, single-file and stretched. They didn't put on the brakes till they'd nearly hit the back of the pen. Orb closed the gate, latched it solid, and walked away.

The dogs panted and slurped at their water trough.

Lizzie's sister Effie crossed the footbridge and waved her hand over her head. 'Orb!' she hollered.

He glanced in her direction, then away, then walked with greater speed toward his house. He leapt the porch stairs in two strides and slammed the front door behind him.

Effie was used to it. She crossed her arms and stared at the Ledford home, so still at the back of the hollow, not a trace of the boy's movement inside. She wondered what he did in there alone.

The clouds covered up the sun. Effie's shoulders cooled. She uncrossed her arms and turned around, traversing the bridge she'd just come across. Her own home was quiet that morning as well, her daughters having stayed in Charleston for summer school.

In October 1953, Effie's husband Joe had died aboard a Skymaster troop carrier en route from Korea to Japan. There'd not been enough of his blood type to transfuse. Effie had kept right on raising their two daughters, just as she'd kept on teaching music at Douglass. But then came integration, and by 1957, her student numbers were halved. In 1961, they shut Douglass down and Effie was out of a job. She'd moved to Marrowbone Cut and assumed the post of choir director for the Land of Canaan Congregational.

Back on the porch of her A-frame, Effie sat down in a rocking chair. Next to it lay the pale canvas bag her sister had given her, full of red and blue and yellow yarn. Knitting needles stuck out like tiny goal posts. Effie sighed and left the bag where it lay. She was tired of making marble bags. She rocked, her eyes fixed on the wide billow of gray smoke from the factory. It never ceased, this smoke. It poured toward the heavens morning, noon, and night, the furnace below reflecting orange off everything inside. Effie had never cared for marbles.

It was one of the things that fascinated her about Orb. He played Ringer for hours each day. She looked from the factory to his house again, not much land separating the two. She imagined she heard him singing inside, but it was not so. Effie longed to refine the boy's vocal technique.

She'd never encountered such raw talent in a singer. Not in her pupils who'd been labeled 'prodigies.' Not even in her father's choir.

J. Carl had finally come around on Marrowbone. In a week, he'd be coming out for the celebration.

Willy Ledford stepped from the doors of the factory. Effie could tell it was him by his gait, the way he raised and lowered his cigarette hand. Not yet sixteen, and the boy had ceased to hide his foul habit. Willy was a boxer, and the only time he didn't smoke was the week before a fight.

He crossed the yard and stepped heavy up the stairs of his house. Slammed the door behind him, just as his younger brother had. They'd learned early on that it had been hung crooked, and that you had to swing hard to get it closed. Once, Ledford had hung a screen door for the temperate months, but as pups, Tug and Jim-Jim had busted right through the screen. Ledford staple-gunned it back to the frame, but the dogs came through again and again, and little Orb soon followed suit. Everyone had laughed about the dog door and Orb's fancy for it, but eventually Tug and Jim-Jim got so tall that they split the door's cross piece, splintering it beyond repair. There'd been no screen door since.

Ledford stepped from the factory smoking his own cigarette. He checked his wristwatch. Dimple and Wimpy would be along soon with two horse-drawn trailers. Twice a week, every available man formed a line out the factory doors. Hand over hand, they passed cinched burlap marble bags, twenty-five count each, and loaded up the box trailers until the tires nearly flattened. Then, Dimple and Wimpy would mount up and pull the heavy loads to the front gate where they met the distributor truck.

Ledford's one-furnace operation was no Marble City, but Marrowbone marbles were shipped to stores across West Virginia, Kentucky, and Ohio too.

He looked up at the house, the boys' bedroom window. A threadbare shade hung inside, thin as paper. Ledford watched the silhouette of his oldest boy, curling too much weight on a long bar. Willy's torso rocked as he heaved the thing to his chest. Behind him, Ledford could see the outline of Orb's head where he sat on the bed, watching his older brother build muscle.

The goats ran past. A blur of black and gray. They bleated, loud and trumpet-pitched.

Ledford stubbed his cigarette on the bottom of his boot and went back inside. In the corner was the tarp, a mountain of newspapers underneath. The tarp's peak was shoulder high. He lifted its edge and grabbed a paper from the stack. Glanced at its date. Two weeks old. An article caught his eye. 'Buddhist Crackdown by Viet Nam Charged,' it read. He eyed the first few lines. Buddhist monks were being forced to sign petitions against their cause of religious freedom. Ledford shook his head and began folding the paper, his hands quartering it tight and precise, by memory. On his way back to the furnace, he dipped the folded paper in a bucket of dirty water. It dripped a serpentine trail along the sawdust floor behind him.

One-handed, Mack Wells gripped a punty rod at the lip of the furnace window. On the end was a small bulb of molten glass. In his other hand, he held a red delicious apple from which he took man-sized bites.

'Liable to drop that rod,' Ledford said.

Mack chewed his apple. 'Not with these forearms,' he said. 'Been putting up the weights, sparrin some with Willy.'

'Mmm-hmm.' Ledford took the rod from Mack and choked up on it. He cupped the wet newspaper in his right hand and set the molten bulb into it, already rolling his left wrist. The paper sizzled and smoked and charred, and the bulb turned. 'Kennedy is fucking up in Vietnam,' he said.

Mack put his boot on the edge of a wheelbarrow full of broken blue glass. The sorters had done their job – he couldn't spot a single shard of green. 'Kennedy'll be just up the road in Charleston next week,' Mack said. 'Why don't you grace the centennial, tell him what a fuckup he is.'

'Humphrey had my vote,' Ledford said. He watched the rolling bulb slowly lose its glow.

'I know he did.' Mack took a last bite of his apple, spit two seeds on the floor, and threw the core across the room at the head of a new employee. He missed. The young man was from the neighborhood, one of Effie's former students at Douglass. Hayes was his last name. Folks called him Stretch. 'Anyway,' Mack said, 'I thought you were back to quittin the papers,' he said.

'Well.' Ledford had no answer for his friend. It seemed every time he tried to shut out the world, it gave him cause to open his eyes again.

The hot bulb rolled, and layer by layer the newspaper disappeared.

It was a small, four-square building with a stair-step roofline. Painted above the door were the words *Boxing Gym*. Herchel and Jerry had built the place, with Paul Maynard's help, back in '59. That was the year Paul had boarded up Maynard's Boxing Gym, where he'd once trained his son Sam to prominence. But Sam was long since dead, and the Maynards no longer had the money to run a gym. Their open shafts whistled empty on the hillside. All the coal had been dug. Everybody had left, save Paul. His nephew Shorty stayed closest to home, moving his family just up the road. Shorty was Paul's deputy, an arrangement rife with trouble.

Inside the gym, Willy sat down on a dugout bench against the wall. He was heaving, elbows on his knees. Under the bare lights, he dripped sweat and watched it pat against the floor in dark circles. Behind him, the barnwood paneling shone blood red. Jerry had washed down the walls a week prior, dry-locked them, and rolled two coats of the red stuff. *Orient Bay*, according to the can.

Mack Wells drank water from an Army-issue canteen and breathed hard through his nose. He tugged off his headgear and tossed it into a corner bin. 'You're faster with that straight right,' he told Willy.

'Thanks. You still whupped my ass.' Willy had been regional runner-up at 112 pounds the year before. He liked to train alone, and he liked to spar with Mack.

'Might have more wind if you quit smoking them squares,' Mack said.

'I know it.' Willy stood and stretched. His muscles tightened, outlined in shadow as if cut from stone. 'I'll be seein you,' he said. He walked out shirtless, a wet towel on his head.

Gym rules were posted by the door: *You spit on the floor, you go home* was one of them. Others were observed and learned over time: no posters, no murals, no music. No talking during the three-minute work sessions. Windex wall mirrors nightly – anyone who'd shadow-boxed before them. Get gloved up to hit the heavy bag or get out. Amateurs only, Junior Division only. No pros. No dues.

Paul Maynard walked in at five till five. He stuck his head inside the cramped back office. 'Coach,' he said, nodding.

'Coach,' Mack said, likewise. He had his feet on the desk and a notepad in his lap. On it, he'd sketched a criss-crossing marble highway design. He regarded it. Paul hung his hat on a hook. In the corner, an industrial fan with a skin of brown dust ran hard.

Two boys came in the door. There were never more than four on a Tuesday. Never more than eight, no matter what the night. They were all from the area. Country tough and white. Most in Wayne wouldn't allow their boys to box at Marrowbone. Some called it *Nigger Gym*. Most could scarcely believe that Paul Maynard was a part of it. They vowed not to reelect him sheriff.

At five-thirty Don Staples walked in and took his spot in the rotten leather barber's chair. Mack hit the bell with his ball-peen hammer. Work sessions commenced. There was the slap of the rope against poured concrete. The snapping, exhaled hiss of the shadow-boxer before the mirror. Heat gathered and sat quick. Wet. It was something, the way sweat could stink. Even a boy's.

Stretch Hayes walked in a little after six. He'd come in once before, thinking he could spar from the get-go. Thinking that because he was city tough, because he had the interrupted eyebrows of a street fighter, he'd somehow bypass the two-month rule. He found out different, quick. And here he was again, fresh off his first shift as furnace tender. He hovered in the gym.

Staples one-eyed him over the book in his hands. It took guts to be the sole black fighter in the gym. Only Harold had held that designation before.

Paul watched the footwork of a skinny boy from

Echo Creek, kicked at his sneakers to keep his square small. He didn't acknowledge Stretch's presence.

Staples liked Stretch. He showed enough respect, whatever Paul may have thought, and he didn't seem the type to cause trouble. It was known that his daddy had once killed a man, but to Staples, this was neither here nor there.

The bell sounded again. There was a little chatter. The boys passed a water jug and spit in a bucket. Mack called Stretch over. 'Furnace work suiting you?' he asked.

'Yes.' Stretch, like a young Ledford, had been drawn to the fire. He liked to stare at it and close his eyes to see what happened on the backs of his eyelids.

'You like it out here?' Mack asked.

'Yes. Can I spar?'

'No.' Mack knew of the boy's family. None before him had graduated high school. The men died young or lived behind bars. Stretch's daddy was up at Moundsville. His brother, Huttonsville. Mack couldn't yet decipher if their trouble ran through Stretch.

Paul put in a dip two-handed. One hand to squeeze-shape the stuff, the other to pull out his bottom lip. He disliked messiness.

Staples stepped down from the barber's chair and over to him. 'Don't do that shit in front of the kids,' he said.

'They've seen worse.' It was the same conversation they'd had last practice.

Staples waved him off and walked over to Mack and Stretch. 'You're looking to spar?' he asked the young man.

Stretch nodded. The guidance counselor at school had suggested it before he graduated. She'd said it was better than a fistfight.

Mack understood Staples' intention. 'Kids finish up about seven-thirty,' he told Stretch, pointing to the clock on the wall. It was the kind that came standard in schools, old and round and hanging on a nail above the light switch. Electrical conduit snaked the place, tacked down in loops and painted over red like the walls. 'What's wrong?' Mack said, eyeballing Stretch. 'You can't stay that long? You got someplace to be?'

Stretch kept his mouth shut and his chin high. A sparse goatee was coming in slow. He shook his head no, though he was supposed to catch a ride back to Huntington at seven. He had people to see.

'Good,' Mack said.

Paul had never let anybody spar until after two months' worth of three-days. The mirror was your sparring partner, the medicine ball your opponent. He stepped to the office and motioned for Staples to follow.

Before Paul could shut him down, Staples said, 'I'm just going to put on the mitts. Let him take a few swings.'

Paul sighed, then nodded his okay.

The gym bell sounded again and again. Stretch watched the clock. He didn't work out like the others. Instead he sat on the dugout bench and eyeballed the conduit on the wall. Corrugated casing over all that electric charge. Like a snake-skin, he thought. Like the rubbers he bought at the druggist's.

Stretch wanted to beat the shit out of somebody.

At seven-thirty Paul used his tongue to pry out the dip in his lip. It dropped in the yellow spit bucket. He walked over to Stretch. 'Better wrap your hands,' he said.

Mack came over to show him how. The other boys had left.

Harold came in the door and said hello.

Stretch didn't say it back. The two weren't on speaking terms. Stretch's older brother had never liked Harold, had once called him an Uncle Tom. But now that brother lived inside a prison cell, and it seemed to Stretch that maybe he'd been wrong about Harold. He'd been wrong about Marrowbone, too. And in those days, Stretch was going to take a job where he could get one.

Harold went to work on the double-end bag, then the speed. Like Willy, he did things alone inside the gym.

When he wasn't throwing punches, Harold watched Stretch Hayes. Wondered if he was as tough as he looked. The day before, inside the factory, he'd overheard Stretch and Willy talking about him over the roar of the fans. 'Harold thinks the CIP means somethin. It don't mean a damn thing to nobody I know from the neighborhood,'

Stretch had said. 'And why he got to talk like a white boy?' Later, as he fell asleep, Harold had whispered words aloud in bed. 'Don't mean a damn thing,' he said again and again, accenting different syllables, trying to wash out the white.

The floor ring had a soft enough cover. It was twenty by twenty, and the corner posts were padded sufficient. Tattered and tethered, the rope covers sagged, wrapped here and there by duct tape, like everything else in the place. Stretch stepped through and squared off in front of Staples, who smacked his punch mitts together flat-faced and hard. Their gunshot sound flinched Stretch's eyes.

Staples felt his age inside the ring. He didn't have the wind he once possessed.

For the first minute and a half, he let the young man throw his one-two, one-two, one-two-three's. Then he started counterpunching with the mitts. Soft at first, then zippy enough to raise red welts across the young man's brow. He wanted to see if the Sixteenth Street tough would lose his temper. He wanted to tell him what Paul Maynard told his fighters, sage advice for boxing or CIP sit-ins alike: 'Lose your temper, lose the fight.'

Stretch strained and winded himself and threw haymaker hooks that missed their mark. He went two three-minute rounds without losing his temper. Then he puked in the spit bucket Mack had put in his corner. After the first heave, Stretch dropped to his knees and let loose two more spigot-gushers – chicken salad and RC Cola. Nobody said a word.

Mack threw him a bloodstained towel. He'd wait until Stretch left to laugh at the boy. He'd wait to express his newfound respect.

Paul stood at the ropes and watched Stretched heave a last time. 'It ain't basketball,' he said.

When Stretch did walk out that night, gray-faced as he'd ever been, they all nodded to him in a manner that believed their optimism. In their book, he'd passed some sort of test.

Willy was outside smoking. He'd lifted the keys to the Packard. 'Need a ride home?' he asked Stretch.

Roba Quessenberry Stood at the front window of his restaurant, his fat arms crossed and his hands fisted. He worked his jaw and ground his teeth on a toothpick. Spat the toothpick upon his own floor, where it lay next to the others he'd chewed. 'Goddamned niggers,' he said. 'Goddamn pinko commies.'

Outside the window, twenty picketers walked a calm line. Their signs read *Boycott Smalley's* and *Serve All or Serve None.* Among those walking the line were Lizzie and Harold Wells, along with Ledford, Rachel, and Mary. They cut a small circle on the hot pavement, and they were joined by J. Carl Mitchum, his wife, and Effie. Ten members, white and black alike, of the Civic Interest Progressives also walked in stride, as did Bob Staples, their counsel in the injunction brought by Smalley's to block such picketing. Don Staples brought up the rear. He watched his brother, proud that he'd come back to law from politics.

All were relatively cheerful. The sun beat their shoulders and squinted their eyes. Passersby ignored them for the most part, and the newspaper had again failed to send a reporter. But inside, Quessenberry's face told them all they needed to know.

Orb sat cross-legged, his back against a concrete planter from which a sapling waved in the wind, half dead. He'd brought two cigar boxes with him, each filled with marbles fresh off the rollers. He turned one between two fingers. Sunlight exposed its inner workings, layers of red and orange and blue. It was an 'end-of-days' marble, named for the glass that made it – leftovers from the factory floor at day's end. These were his father's new favorite to concoct, and Orb could see why. He stared at the thousands of flecks inside the glass. He saw in its swirl a hurricane. A butterfly. The teeth of a rabid dog. It seemed to Orb that he could see everything inside that marble.

He got up to show it to his father. On his way, the sole of his sneaker snagged on a wad of gum and he fell to his knees. Blood split the skin's surface quick. Orb sat and stared at it, the welling pools, the running streams. Then he turned to look at what had tripped him. It was off-white, Wrigley's, maybe Beeman's, and in it was the pattern of his sneaker sole.

No one noticed Orb at first. They had their eyes on Don Staples, who, as he was known to do, had jumped up on his milk crate and started a 're-invigoration ceremony,' as he called it. The purpose was to remind picketers of their aim. He wore an old straw hat and had sweated through his shirt at the armpits. He said to them, 'And so you can steal glances at Huntington's version of Bull Connor over there,' he pointed to Quessenberry's fat red face behind the glass, 'but don't forget that confrontation must always remain non-violent. No matter how hot the sun, how long the hour, we must—' He'd spotted Orb, the bloody knee. He hopped down from his perch and pointed. 'This boy needs attention,' he said.

Harold got to him first. He loved little Orb, had since the day they brought him home from the hospital, so small and fragile. Harold kneeled, his hands catching the fast drips of blood. 'What happened?' he asked the boy, though he knew better than to expect an answer to a question.

Orb pointed behind him to the gum. 'Trilobite,' he said.

Harold looked at the gum. The lines left by the sneaker sole did resemble a fossil. Sometimes he thought he could understand the way Orb's brain worked.

Ledford bent next to Harold. 'Damn if it isn't comin faster this time than last,' he said. They all knew he was a bleeder. Had found out the hard way.

260

Harold stripped off his T-shirt and wrapped it tight around Orb's knee.

'I believe we might need some tape,' Ledford said.

The picketers had gathered in a horseshoe behind him. 'Maybe we should phone an ambulance Loyal,' Rachel said. 'Last time we couldn't get it stopped.' She winked to her boy, who stared past her at something no one else could see.

'I'll get tape,' Harold said. 'And I'll get on the phone.' He jumped to his feet and ran for the front doors of Smalley's Cafeteria.

Roba Quessenberry saw him coming, shirtless and streaked in sweat. He picked up his cattle prod on the way to the door.

Mary watched what was happening. 'Daddy,' she said.

Ledford gripped the shirt tight on the boy's bony knee. The thin cotton was turning white to red in a hurry. He looked over his shoulder at Mary, then at Harold, who'd made it to the cafeteria door. 'Hold this,' Ledford told Rachel, and she did so.

The pavement radiated heat through her shoes as she tended to her boy. She hummed and applied pressure. She hoped to God that behind her Ledford would heed Don Staples' words.

All the picketers stared at the entrance to Smalley's. There was a feeling that something was about to happen there. Don Staples began to holler stop when the door flung open, nearly hitting Harold in the face. Quessenberry exploded forth and maneuvered his cattle prod fast and practiced, its twin electrodes finding their target in the center of Harold's wide chest. There was a quiet, ugly sound, and Harold took two clumsy steps back and dropped to the pavement.

Mary rolled film, feet planted, breath caught in her throat.

Ledford was upon Quessenberry before the man could look up from his victim. He took the prod in both hands and shoved it lengthwise under Quessenberry's jawbone. Now they both clung to the weapon, and Ledford used their shared inertia to swing the man against the doorjamb of his own establishment. He stuck him there and pressed the prod hard against all that fat, the Adam's apple giving way beneath it.

It was like a dance for Ledford, one he'd choreographed through repetition twenty years prior in boot camp, one he'd mastered.

There were some steps a man never forgets.

He watched the eyes bug, listened to the esophagus panic and click. 'You son of a bitch,' Ledford said. 'I ain't a preacher. I don't have to turn the other cheek.'

Behind him, Don Staples was saying, 'Hey now, hey hey. Ease off there son.' He patted Ledford's shoulder gingerly.

Ledford stepped back and Quessenberry dropped to the concrete like the closing bellows of an accordion. He whistled and wheezed as the instrument might, split at the seams, lying in a heap.

His wife came out screaming. She looked down at her husband, then at Ledford and those behind him. 'You nigger lovers,' she shouted. 'Goddamn every one of you!' Her gray hair had come out of its bun in wild wisps, a spiderweb torn by the wind.

Below her, Quessenberry was beginning to move. He felt at his neck as if worried it had disappeared.

Ledford spat on the ground at their feet. He turned and saw the distraught faces of Don Staples and the CIP youngsters. Lizzie was nearly in tears, tending to Harold on the hot concrete. J. Carl Mitchum knelt beside her. His expression was unlike the rest. He nodded to Ledford. Had the cattle prod been in J. Carl's hands, he likely would have killed Roba Quessenberry.

'I'm fine,' Harold was saying, pushing away the worried hands of his mother and getting to his feet.

They checked the prod marks on his chest. Ledford ran to his own boy.

'It stopped,' Rachel said. 'Can you believe it? He clotted up this time.' She had gathered Orb in her arms. He stared at the end-of-days marble.

'I'm calling the police!' Mrs Quessenberry yelled, pulling her husband to his feet.

Bob Staples looked around. A couple had stopped to gawk on Fifth Avenue. A teenager had laid down his bicycle to watch. 'Go on and do it,' Bob said. 'Got witnesses aplenty that saw your husband assault an unarmed man.'

Quessenberry slipped from his wife's grip and

dropped to the concrete again, this time on a sore tailbone. He made a whimpering sound, and his wife squawked, pulled helplessly at the neck of his shirt, then slapped him across the head.

Ledford felt alive. His blood coursed like it had as a younger man. Then he looked to his wife and youngest child. He began to realize how close he'd come to killing another man. The life in his blood shut down. He nearly vomited. The whir of Mary's camera ran loud in his ears.

When her father turned to her, his face framed in a close-up through the viewfinder, Mary saw for the first time the desperation he possessed.

He said, 'Shut it off.'

She did so.

He stepped closer to her and whispered, 'I never want to see that film.'

He helped Orb to his feet. The boy pointed to the gum. 'Trilobite,' he said.

'That's right Orb,' Ledford told him. He hugged him close. The boy's arms dangled loose at his side, an end-of-days marble in each hand.

In the woods, Wimpy stood at the mouth of a small cave and pointed inside. The children clustered around him, squinting for a better look. 'See there,' Wimpy said. 'See them eyeballs?' The children wore searching looks. 'Don't nobody cough now. If you cough, it'll come after you.'

A small girl, six years old, grabbed the hand of an older boy standing next to her. It was Hambone

Maynard. He shot her a mean look and yanked loose. 'Don't you know he's pullin your leg?' Hambone had chocolate around his mouth and a slingshot in his back pocket. His daddy had told him he'd tan his hide if he went to the nigger commune again.

'*Am* I pullin your leg? You *sure* about that?' Wimpy grinned at the boy.

'Sure as shit stinks,' Hambone answered.

Wimpy's grin went straight. 'You watch your mouth in front of these girls,' he said.

Orb walked toward the mouth of the cave. The ground cover was wet under his sneakers, and sunlight was scarce through the canopy above.

'Orb, I'd stop right there if I was you.' Wimpy swatted a mosquito on his neck. He watched the boy stop, then start walking again. Orb was only five paces from the cave mouth when Wimpy decided to cough.

At this, there arose a furious growl and the sound of shale kicking as some beast erupted from its rocky perch inside.

The children, with the exception of Orb, screamed like banshees and turned tail. Hambone Maynard ran headlong into a hickory tree.

The thing emerged fully from the cave, roaring. It had an oval-shaped open mouth, canine teeth like bleached daggers, jutting wide. A pink tongue and flared nostrils, black fur that carried a sheen. It was hunched, with dead eyes and empty, swinging arms. Its long nails drug the ground, lifeless.

Wimpy watched the children scatter and scream. He laughed so hard he bent double. Hambone stood at the base of the hickory tree and shook his head. He took to running again, this time with a left-bound tilt, fingers grabbing air. His balance was askew. Top-heavy and leaning hard, he fell again, and this sent Wimpy's laughter to new heights.

Orb started at the thing before him. He smiled. 'Hey Uncle Dimp,' he said.

Dimple, on all fours, raised his head so that the bear's face looked skyward. He regarded Orb. It was odd to see a smile on his face. Rare. Even rarer to be greeted, called by name. 'Boy,' Dimple said, 'if that's what it takes to make you smile, I reckon I've got a full-time job on my hands.'

Orb stepped to him and ran his fingertips over the bear's eyeballs. They stared back at him, black in the middle, brown at the edges. Like the eyes of his dogs, he thought. He wondered if his daddy could make marbles look like these.

Dimple stood. 'Whew,' he said. 'Hotter'n blue blazes under that thing.' He pulled the pelt off, tucked the bear's head, and began rolling up the hide. 'Tell you what, though, it's cool in that cave.'

Orb watched him fold in the claws and tuck the flat arms carefully. He got the pelt to the size of a bedroll and shoved it under his arm. 'Let's go,' he said. 'Your mother'll be waitin on you.'

Wimpy had gone off down the hill after the children. 'It ain't real,' he hollered to them. 'Just a mind trick.'

266

Friday Summer mornings had become Wimpy's time to school whatever children were around. It had started with just him and Orb, woods-walking. Wimpy had shown the boy how to track. Orb liked to scan the ground for deer tracks especially. He'd plant two fingers beside the imprint and press. Wimpy always watched and said one of three things: big one, little one, or medium one. He'd pointed out which berries could be eaten, which could not. They'd pulled wild onions and dug ginseng. They'd picked purple horsemint and Wimpy had tied its leaves and flowers to the Ledford porch rafters, where Orb liked to sit and watch them curl and flutter in the wind, bunched husks wrapped with twine. When the time came, Wimpy would cut them down and grind them up with his old mortar and pestle. From this, he'd make tea.

Rachel stood behind the house, watching the children run from the woods. Their faces were stuck in expressions of horror. The Maynard boy cupped his head where it swelled.

Rachel took the last clothespin from its clench between her teeth. She hung the bedsheet's corner and watched the line sag. There was no sign of Orb from the woods.

Inside, she made him a bologna sandwich and thought about the Bonecutter brothers. Their insistence on frightening the children both tickled and irritated her.

She heard a twig snap. Through the dirty

kitchen window, she saw Orb's white knee bandage bobbing through the trees. He emerged and ran for the wash on the line. Rachel knocked hard on the window and he stopped. She shook her finger at him. He'd intended to use the bedsheet as canvas, his dirty fingers as paint.

While he ate his sandwich, Rachel went to the pantry and taped two Band-Aids to the inside cover of *Doctor Dan the Bandage Man,* the only book Orb would try to read, and only if two fresh Band-Aids awaited him each time. The book had come with two originally, and Orb believed it should be eternally replenished so that he might be kept in Band-Aids at all times, anticipating his next bleeder.

He'd never been able to see letters and words like everybody else. They did not go together and form sounds of any meaning. For Orb, reading was not to be.

Still, his mother tried.

'Eat your crust,' she said. 'It's got vitamins in it.'

He bit and tore and chewed. She pulled her chair next to his at the table and patted her lap. Orb climbed up. He'd not follow such a command from any other.

Her arms enclosed him as she held the book open before them, one-handed at the spine, like a hymnal. With her free hand, she pointed to the first word.

'Dan,' Orb said. Above the type, four boys had their six-shooters drawn. One was on his back.

Rachel pointed to the next word.

'Fell down,' Orb said.

'No Orb. Look at the word.' She tapped her finger under it – *is*. Orb sat and stared. Rachel told him to sound it out. This command had never made sense to him. 'Is,' Rachel said.

'Is a busy fellow.' Orb spat the words out from memory. 'He is always on the go but one day in a big backyard cowboy fight he fell and—'

'You're not sounding them out.'

'*You* read it.' He swung his feet forward and back, kicking Rachel in the shins.

She resituated to avoid the blows, sighed, and gave up. 'He fell and scratched his finger on his make-believe gun,' she read. She turned the page. 'And what do you think the big cowboy did?' She waited for Orb to answer.

He'd gone still. Always, when read to, his tendons and muscles would relax, and Orb was finally still. 'He cried,' Orb said.

'Right,' Rachel said. She went on reading. 'Boo hoo hoo—'

'Why does he cry?' Orb stared at Dan's sad face, his hand to his leaking eye, his mouth open in a wail.

'Because he hurt himself.' They'd had this exchange a hundred times.

'But why?'

'Because little boys and girls cry when they hurt themselves.'

Orb had never cried. Not since a newborn, on the night he came home from the hospital.

Rachel read onward, and Orb sat, his little fingers interlocked across his belly. His tailbone pressed into her thigh. His head was to her breastbone. When she took a breath, she smelled dried sweat in his hair.

Rachel never contemplated the words she read aloud. Not anymore. While reading to Orb, she was able to ponder the laundry and the weather and the payroll balance. She planned her days and organized her thoughts while some other part of her brain took care of sighting and spouting words. On the last page, she read, 'And he shook Dan's hand. 'I have a new name for you. We'll call you Doctor Dan, the Bandage Man.' And they do so to this day.' Rachel closed the book and set it on the table. She said, 'So we will too.' She picked up a piece of breadcrust and ate it. With her other hand, she stroked the patch of skin behind Orb's ear. 'Sweet boy?' she said. 'You going to finish your crust?'

There was no answer.

Rachel took Orb by the shoulders and turned him to face her. His body complied, but not his head. The eyes were wide and glazed over. Gaze fixed on the back of the stovetop – the mantel clock.

'Orb!' Rachel said. She snapped her fingers and pinched the end of his nose. She waved her hand in front of his face. 'Orb!' she shouted.

He came out of it.

This happened once in a while. They called them his 'episodes.'

'I don't feel good,' Orb said. 'I'm tired.'

'All right sweet boy,' she said. She pulled him to her and rocked. Rachel had always loved the moments just after an episode. They were the rare spaces in time where he would let her hold him.

She tucked him in bed and pulled down the window shade. He breathed through his mouth, dead asleep in seconds. The sun cut through the space between shade and still. It illuminated his chin, his little mouth. The too-big front teeth stuck out like Chiclets, crooked and white. Rachel watched him sleep for a moment before pulling the door shut.

Downstairs, she washed and dried Orb's plate and poured herself a whiskey. She drank it fast, rinsed the coffee mug, and stuck it back in the cabinet. The whiskey pint she tucked below the sink in a basket, under the Ajax can. There was a slow drip from the sink trap. Rachel leaned in for a closer look. Two Band-Aids wrapped around the pipe at the spot where the water drops sagged and fell. She smiled. Thought of Orb's brain, the way it worked to right wrongs. She left the Band-Aids where they were and stood back up.

Orb had been a puzzle from the get-go. Even for the doctors. He'd been small, of course. Fragile. Reverend Thompson had baptized him at the hospital, for fear that he'd die before he made it out the door. Rachel remembered the day they brought Orb home. How everyone, including her, wondered if he was meant to make it. Dimple and Wimpy had seen this kind of baby before. They sat Ledford and Rachel down, insisted that they contemplate a certain old way of doing things, a way that had kept many a sick baby alive. And Rachel had gone along with it. Orb swaddled against her, she'd followed the twins to the crib barn, and inside, Wimpy had led Boo the mare from her stall. While Dimple rubbed Boo's muzzle and hummed to her, Wimpy positioned Ledford and Rachel on either side of the horse. Orb cried, loud and raspy. 'Now,' Wimpy had told Rachel, 'I want you to pass him under Boo, clear across to Ledford. Ledford, you take him, then pass him back. I want you all to do this three times.' And they did as they were told. And Orb ceased to cry.

When he was two, he fell and split his forehead wide open on a coffee table corner. It was Christmas Eve. The blood refused to clot, and Orb was drained to a pallor the likes of a ghost. Ledford wrapped and rewrapped the boy's head, using first his own shirt and then Willy's. At the hospital, the doctor said the boy had hemophilia. Later, another doctor said that was hogwash, that the boy had von Willebrand disease. None could figure over the years why some of Orb's cuts and scrapes clotted and others didn't. The only thing they uniformly agreed upon was that internal bleeding was to be feared, and that the boy ought never be jostled hard, as one might be in a fall from a height or an automobile crash.

Rachel had looked at her husband when this

was spoken. His blank face told of the thoughts inside. Thoughts of his own family's end in an automobile.

By five years old, it was clear that brain doctors could not figure out the boy's episodes. They spoke of electrical currents, explosions in his mind that rendered him useless, but there was no evidence of seizure.

Orb was a mystery child. The only thing they knew was that he couldn't read worth a damn, and that he didn't belong in regular school. So, Rachel had kept him at home, where she and Ledford let him be who he was. Turned out he could shoot the daylights out of a marble and sing like an angel from heaven.

The light in the kitchen shifted. Rain clouds were moving in.

Rachel walked out back to unpin her wash. She'd just reached for the bedsheet corner when something caught her eye. Wimpy was thirty yards off, at woods' edge, and he was talking to someone who wasn't there. Rachel took a few steps in his direction.

At the foot of a sumac tree, Wimpy regarded the redbird, perched on a high branch, side-stepping and wagging its head. 'I don't know,' Wimpy said. 'You tell me.'

The bird whistled back, 'Whoit, whoit, whoit, whoit,' and Wimpy laughed out loud.

Rachel got within twenty yards when Wimpy and the redbird turned and looked at her. She stopped, thought about turning around. Instead, she raised a hello hand and quickened her pace. Wimpy smiled nervously and turned back to the bird. He said something she couldn't make out. When she got within a few feet, the redbird shot from its perch and disappeared into the woods. Rachel stopped. 'I'm sorry,' she said.

'It's all right.' Wimpy started to walk away.

'Wait.' She didn't know what to say after that. In her bones she knew this to be the same bird that had stared her down and dive-bombed her more than ten years before.

Wimpy turned and looked at her like he'd done something wrong.

'I think I know that bird,' Rachel said.

Wimpy cocked his head and regarded her. He stepped in close. 'I've knowed him for twenty years,' he said. 'Now what kind of cardinal lives for twenty years?'

'How do you know it's the same one?'

'Cause he's missin the middle toe on his right foot and his eyes is twice the size of most.' Wimpy used his tongue to excavate a clump of snuff from his jaw. He spat it on the ground. 'What do you mean you know him?'

'About ten years ago, that bird dive-bombed me in the backyard over here.' She pointed back at the house.

Wimpy laughed. 'He had the horn for you, I reckon,' he said. 'Was it in April?'

Rachel felt momentarily as if she were in a

dream, as if this conversation could not occur in waking life. 'It was April Fool's Day,' she said.

'Well, there you go. He was foolin with you.'

Rachel felt faint. 'I need to sit down,' she said. And she did, right there on the dirt and grass.

Wimpy sat across from her. 'Maybe it's that whiskey I smell on your breath.' He winked at her. Then he looked to the woods, where the bird had disappeared. 'Dimple thinks I'm touched in the head for how I feel about that bird, but he's been visitin me so long, talking to me like he does, that I just don't care what Dimple thinks.' He pulled at a hunk of crabgrass and tossed it over his shoulder. 'As I recall, that bird used to visit in April, then it was May the next year, then June. He comes every year, and he tells me things.'

'What does he tell you?'

Wimpy pulled the leaves off a crabgrass shoot and stuck it in his teeth. He sized Rachel up before he spoke. 'When he's happy, he weets and whoits and dances, like he done today. That tells me there'll be no flood, no deaths in the family and what have you.' He watched her react. There was nothing there but genuine interest. Belief even.

Rachel swallowed. Her throat was dry. Lips the same. 'And when he's not happy?'

'Well, then he chips.'

'Chips?'

'Chips.' Wimpy proceeded to imitate the bird's unhappy sound. 'And he don't dance, and he stares at you a good bit.'

'Has he ever flown at you?' Rachel asked.

'Can't say that he has.' Wimpy stood up. 'But I ain't a beautiful creature like yourself.' He reached down and helped Rachel to her feet. 'Redbirds is horny for women that smell good and keep a little money in the breadbox.' He laughed. Rachel joined him. 'I got to git,' Wimpy said. He tipped his hat and and walked away.

Staples stood before them, his Bibled hand raised above his head. The pews were nearly filled. In the back sat Paul Maynard and his family. Paul had combed his hair and trimmed his mustache for the service.

'How many here know the story of Shadrach, Meshach, and Abednego?' Staples asked. He waggled his Bible and watched the hands raise before him. There were only three. Ledford, Lizzie, and Paul Maynard.

Staples spread his Bible on the podium and combed his fingers through his beard. 'When Nebuchadnezzar had a giant golden statue erected in Babylon, he made it law that all should fall down and worship it upon hearing the sound of a musical instrument. Those who did not obey this law would be thrown in a furnace and burned alive.'

In the very first pew, Jerry sat at attention. His hymnal was in his lap, and upon it were paper scraps and a pencil. Jerry had long ago begun to take notes at the Land of Canaan Congregational.

He hung on every word that split Don Staples' lips, and he'd come to like church more than anything else in his life. With his pencil, he wrote, *Nebakudazzer?* and vowed silently to crack open his Bible that evening back at home. He checked his wristwatch. It was nearly eleven. Herchel was still in bed, no doubt snoring, too hungover to keep his word and come to church.

Staples said, 'But Shadrach, Meshach, and Abednego were wise, and they knew when man's law was foolish. They knew that when God's law conflicted with man's, only one could be obeyed. And so it was that they refused to fall down and worship the golden statue, and so it was that Nebuchadnezzar had them thrown into the furnace, which he'd stoked to seven times its normal temperature.'

Ledford looked out the window at the smoke rising from his own furnace. He wondered if Stretch Hayes was eyeballing the fire as he should. Wondered if the temperature was too high or low, if the batch on the rollers would be prone to cracks.

Staples leaned forward on his elbows, the podium seams creaking under his weight. He pulled his spectacles from his shirt pocket and put them on. 'The three were not burned,' he said. 'They walked from the furnace just as they went in.' He put his finger to its designation on the thin, greasy page and read, 'And the princes, governors, and captains, and the king's counselors, being gathered together, saw these men, upon whose bodies the fire had no power, nor was a hair of their head singed, neither their coats changed, nor the smell of fire had passed on them.' Staples looked out at his congregation over the bridge of his spectacles. His bad eye rolled wide, then he blinked and found his focus. 'And Nebuchadnezzar blessed their God who had delivered his servants, for these men had yielded their bodies and changed the king's law.' Then Staples, as he was prone to do, slammed shut his Bible on the podium and removed his spectacles. The thud emitted would awaken any drowsers among them, and he would search out their dozing eyes with his own. 'Why do I tell you of this story?' he asked. 'Why today?'

None knew the answer to this question better than Ledford, who had ceased to look at the column of smoke out the window. He knew that the lesson was meant for him especially, as Staples had taken him aside after the cattle prod incident at Smalley's. He'd questioned Ledford's discipline for non-violent protest. Staples had told him, 'We will never find the change we seek if we give in to our baser instincts.' He'd gone on to say that Ledford might need some soul-searching, that he might need to reconcile his past. His parents, his brother, the violence that took them away. The war, what it had done to him. Staples had tapped Ledford on the chest and said, 'Son, you'll never make it unless you turn all that war inside you into something else.'

Now he looked at Ledford where he sat. He smiled to the younger man before continuing. 'I tell you this story today because I was reminded of it by a magazine article. I'm a subscriber to the magazine, and in last week's issue, I read one of the most extraordinary pieces of writing I've ever come across. Its author was Dr Martin King, who Ledford and I had the privilege of meeting a few years back at the First Baptist Church in Charleston.'

Paul Maynard shifted in his seat and pulled at the crotch of his slacks. He sighed and worked his jaw. He'd sat his family closest to the door on purpose. They'd taken to attending services about a year prior. The rest of the Maynards had not followed suit. When Staples got to talking like he was now, about King and his cause, Paul always got up and walked out. On this morning, he did not.

'While imprisoned in Birmingham Alabama a few months back,' Staples, went on, 'Dr King penned a letter in the margins of newspapers and on smuggled-in scraps. That letter was addressed to the six Alabama clergymen who had denounced his tactics of direct, non-violent action.' Sweat gathered in Staples' graying eyebrows. He wiped them with his thumbs. 'In the letter, he points out that such non-violent stances against the unjust laws of man trace back to the story of Shadrach, Meshach, and Abednego, and that the acts of civil disobedience we see practiced by oppressed Negroes today serve to remind us all of what many have forgotten.' He looked Paul Maynard dead in the face, and then he looked over all of them, his brow furrowed, his jaw set. 'That the immoral ways of segregation and the oppression of the poor must be met head-on with the strength of God's moral law, and if done peaceably, with yielded bodies, the unjust kings on their bloodied thrones will no doubt change their ways.'

'Amen,' Lizzie said. Beside her, Harold and Mack nodded their heads.

Staples gathered up his Bible and his papers. Then he said, 'And now, I believe our young preacher has some words for you this morning on the same subject.' He smiled at Harold. 'He'll be leaving us for law school in Morgantown soon, and I for one will miss these too-rare sermons of his, one of which some of us witnessed at our very first service here, nearly fifteen years ago.' Staples smiled. 'You could hardly see his head over the pulpit back then, but he's a real pawpaw knocker these days.' He waved Harold up.

Paul Maynard slid from his pew and left just as Staples was about to take Harold's empty seat. Instead, Staples followed. As he went, Harold was saying, 'I believe Preacher Staples was right, and I believe that history will show us who has truly exhibited great power and righteousness in these times of trial.' Harold could feel the burns on his chest with each breath he drew. 'As Dr King wrote in his letter, "One day the South will recognize its real heroes. One day the South will know that when these disinherited children of God sat down at lunch counters, they were in reality standing up for what is best in the American dream.'"

Outside the doors, Staples called after Paul Maynard. 'Hold on now Paul,' he shouted. He descended the stairs and gave chase.

Down at the lot, Paul swung open the door of his truck but did not get in. Instead, he fetched his cigarette pack from the seat and lit one. When Staples was in talking distance, Paul blew smoke in his direction. It pounded from his nose and mouth as he said, 'I swear Don . . . by God, if I'd known you were back to this type a thing . . .'

Staples regarded the bigger man. 'It isn't a type of thing, Paul,' he said. 'It's everything. Weren't you listening?'

'You can git off your high horse with me, buddy. I live right here.' He pointed to the ground below his feet. 'Right on this here, and it's a place I was elected to protect.' Elections were coming up again, and Paul was worried. With the family mine shut down, he counted on the paychecks. 'Now what do you think people's going to do if they find out I'm attendin services where a colored boy takes the stage to spout off about King?' He pulled so hard on his cigarette you could hear the paper sizzle.

'I think it doesn't matter what people do. I think from the sounds of it, you ought to have listened to the sermon a little closer Paul.'

'Oh hell,' Paul said. He threw his cigarette on the ground and got in his truck. He'd wait there for the rest of his family. 'Look here,' he said, elbow on the open window well. 'I'm glad to support the gym, and I'm happy to train white fighters alongside colored ones, but I'm done with your church Don.'

'Paul . . .'

But Paul had already started cranking his window up. He'd seal himself off and fry inside the cab before he'd hear another word on it.

Staples turned and walked toward his church. His bones ached and a cough came over him.

The sign had gone crooked above the door. Staples looked at it for a moment, then decided to sit under a shade tree on the lawn. He pressed his back into its bark and scratched at an itch on his shoulder blade. He wished he had his pipe with him.

Above him, tied with twine and dangling from the skinny branches, were chunks of scrap glass from the factory. One hundred or more. They twisted in the wind and sparkled like costume jewelry. They were hung in the tree years before by Harold and Mary and Willy after Staples had told them that glass trees warded off evil spirits.

Now he slouched and watched the sun glint white on the weathered edges of blue, red, and clear glass.

From inside the church, he heard only silence. Harold had finished preaching. Then came the sound of the piano, Effie's fingers so knowingly finding their mark. It was 'Wade in the Water.'

Staples closed his eyes and listened, and when Orb began to sing in his high and haunting way that God was going to trouble the water, Don Staples nearly wept.

President Kennedy had come to Charleston like he promised. The state's one-hundredth birthday was not an occasion to be overlooked. Bob Staples had gone to witness the sight that morning, and at five p.m., when he pulled up to the gate at Marrowbone, he was still smiling.

'Evenin Bob,' Dimple said, nodding from on horseback.

'Evenin Dimple.' The top on Bob's Impale was down. He nodded to Wimpy, who was taking a leak beside his horse. For the first time, the brothers looked old to Bob. 'Rained much here today?' he asked.

'Off and on,' Dimple said.

'Cats and dogs in Charleston. Ole Kennedy just stood right there in it.'

'Did he now?'

'See this hand?' Bob said. He took his right hand from the steering wheel and raised it before him. 'This hand shook the hand of the president.'

Dimple nodded. He was not impressed.

'He came right down the Capitol steps and onto the sidewalk. Shook hands with anybody in reach, including yours truly.' Bob marveled at his own hand. 'Those Secret Service men must have a real time trying to do their job.'

Wimpy zipped up and walked over to the car. 'You say you touched the president?'

'That's right.'

Dimple spotted a tick burrowed in Silver's mane. He leaned back and fetched from the saddlebag his needlenose pliers. He secured the tick with the pliers, struck a kitchen match on his thumbnail, and burned it alive.

Bob watched, his brow furrowed.

'Did you speak to him?' Wimpy asked. He stared at Bob's hand as if the presidential seal might appear.

'I can't recall. It happened fast.'

'I reckon you ain't warshed your hand yet,' Wimpy said.

Bob said he hadn't.

Dimple dropped the burned tick into his open palm and blew it into the air. He stuck the pliers back in the bag and said, 'Did you pull his britches down and kiss his rump while you was at it?'

Bob drove on in and parked.

It was hot. A breeze came steady through the Cut, making it bearable for those raising the circus tent. Herchel swung the butt end of a maul into the last stake. He stood and beheld it. Double-peaked and striped red and white, it would seat two hundred. His new girlfriend had gotten the tent cheap. Bendy was her name. Russian. She'd once been a flying trapeze artist. After she broke her hip and found God, she moved out to Marrowbone and began teaching Herchel the fine arts of acrobatic love-making and marijuana cultivation.

Bob Staples nodded to Herchel and looked over the tent. He felt a little foolish leaving the state capital festivities for this particular centennial affair.

He walked to the Ringer circle, where Orb had just won his fourth straight game. He patted the boy on the head and asked him where his father was. Orb didn't answer.

Mary watched her little brother through the viewfinder of her movie camera. She wore a pair of her father's old slacks, cut off just above the knee. She found that men's trousers, when cinched at the waist with rope, made the best Bermudas. Two Band-Aids stretched across her ankle where she'd cut herself shaving. As always, Orb had been glad to supply the Band-Aids.

She quit rolling film and lowered the camera to her side. Harold walked over from the porch of his house and shook hands with Bob Staples. Mary waved to him, but he didn't see her. She turned the hand crank on her camera, winding the motor's spring. Fixing Harold through the lens, she rolled film again.

Ledford was up at the dog pen. He stuck his fingers through the chain-link and watched the tongues lap. 'Simmer,' he told them.

His neck hairs stood on end. He could feel someone watching him. When he turned to find out who, it was Orb. They boy stood twenty yards off, still and blank. Ledford thought for a moment he was having an episode, but when he whistled, Orb came over. 'I think they're hungry,' Ledford said. 'You feed em yet this evenin?'

Orb shook his head no and dropped two full bags of marbles at his sides. They'd been playing for keepsies again. He pulled the tarp off the food bin, swung open the lid, and started filling bowls.

'I don't believe we'll be able to let em run tonight Son,' Ledford told him. 'Too many folks that might be scared of dogs.'

'Okay.' Orb was inside the pen, setting the bowls before anxious snouts.

'Did you rake em for ticks this mornin?' Ledford asked.

'Yessir. There was two on Tug. I burnt em.' But he hadn't burnt them. Orb would not kill any bug, ever.

'Good boy.' Ledford put his hand to his brow and looked down the Cut. There was movement around the chapel and the circus tent. Jerry and Herchel were snapping kindling across their knees and tossing it in an old oil drum. Bob Staples was laughing at something Harold had told him. 'I'm going to head on down,' Ledford told Orb. 'Your mother's in the house.' The boy just stood there, as he often did. Ledford bent to him. 'Happy birthday Son,' he said. He pulled a newly handmade taw from his pocket, three-quarter-inch and shiny. It was a sulfide, clear, a clay man inside.

Orb took it and turned it over in his hand. He studied the marble. It was still warm.

Ledford hugged Orb hard. Then he took him by the shoulders and looked him in the face. 'I love you Son,' he said.

He headed toward the circus tent.

Bob hadn't seen Ledford in such a getup before. His white shirt was pressed and the polish on his loafers had yet to fully dry. 'Well, I'll be damned,' Bob said, shaking Ledford's hand, 'you own something other than overalls after all.' They laughed. Bob said, 'And I see your beard is aspiring to grow as wild as my brother's.'

Ledford pulled at the whiskers on his chin. 'It's coming in okay,' he said.

'I was just telling Harold about the Smalley's case. The judge threw out their injunction. Ordered them to file another one if they want to proceed. He recognized that we have the right to picket.' Bob was pleased with himself, and he didn't care to hide it. 'My phone's been ringing off the hook, I'll tell you what. There's a lot of civil rights attorneys with an eye on this one.'

Ledford nodded. 'Glad to hear it. How was the party in Charleston?'

'Well attended.'

'How many?'

'I heard five thousand. In the rain.' Bob held up his hand. 'Kennedy shook it,' he said.

'Is that right?'

'Firm grip.'

'I bet it was.' Ledford loosed a cigarette for himself and another for Bob. They cupped against the wind and lit up. 'Did he have much to say?'

'It was a short speech.'

'I bet it was.' Ledford watched Mary, who watched everyone else.

'He said the sun might not always shine in West Virginia, but that the people sure do. Said any other place, they would have all gone home to get dry.'

'Well,' Ledford said, 'I reckon there's enough out of work to fill the esplanade and Washington Street too. Maybe the coal dust has fortified their skin, made em waterproof.'

'What in the hell are you talking about Ledford?'

Ledford looked up at the sun. 'I believe we're out of the woods here. Isn't a cloud for miles.'

Bob looked up and squinted.

The dogs bayed in the distance. A fox had scampered by.

'Listen Ledford,' Bob said. 'Charlie Ball was up in Charleston today.'

Ledford flicked the cherry off his cigarette and stuck the butt in his pants pocket. 'What the hell for?'

'Well.' Bob cleared his throat. 'He's going Democrat.'

'What do you mean he's going Democrat? That boy is a spoon-fed Arch Moore brownnoser.' Ledford had heard about Charlie's rise up the ranks. He'd gone from hot end manager to city councilman to mayor.

'Not anymore. He's planning a run for the legislature, and he's switching teams to get elected.'

'Son of a bitch.' Ledford rubbed at the back of his neck.

There was a roar from the oil drum. Jerry had dropped in a fiery rag.

'You might be surprised Ledford. Ole Charlie may have grown up on us.' Bob was smiling his politician smile, an ugly remainder from his run in '48.

'Ole Charlie can grow up as much as he wants to,' Ledford said. 'But he's dumber than dirt Bob, and you know it.'

'Well,' Bob said. He took out his handkerchief and wiped his nose. 'I thought I ought to mention it.' He hesitated. 'And I'd better mention that he said he wants to make peace, and, seeing as he has family in the area, said he might show up here today.'

'What?' Ledford could hardly believe his ears. Bob was too predictable, always an eye out for a political up-and-comer, but never a discerning one.

'Well,' Bob said. He looked around nervously. 'Where is my brother anyway?'

'He's in bed. Feelin poorly.' Ledford looked over Bob's shoulder at two approaching figures. It took him a moment to make them out. 'I'll be durned,' he said.

Erm Bacigalupo stepped stride for stride next to his boy Fiore, who had grown tall for fifteen. The two of them had shown up once or twice a year ever since their first visit on the day Orb was born. Oftentimes it was unannounced, a side trip from Erm's dealings at the Charles Town Race Track.

At first, Ledford hadn't wanted him around, but after Erm's wife Agnes shot herself in '55, he'd mostly felt sorry for the man.

From twenty yards off, Erm called out, 'What time do Mr Barnum and Mr Bailey arrive?'

Ledford hollered back, 'Soon as Admiral Dingleberry gives the go-ahead call.'

They shook hands. There had been no hugging or backslapping in years. 'Fiore, you're a regular beanstalk,' Ledford said.

'It's Fury,' the boy answered.

'You look at a man when you speak to him,' Erm said. He put two fingers under the boy's chin and pushed up, hard.

Fury wore double-kneed blue jeans and a fine plaid shirt, buttoned to the top. His hair was parted and held in place with ample oil. It reflected the sun. 'Hello Mr Ledford.' The boy looked like he never smiled.

'What time do the titty dancers take the stage?' Erm asked. He smiled. His tooth bridge had darkened a shade. His nose wore burgundy vessels matching those in his eyes.

'Erm, you remember Bob Staples.' Ledford stepped aside and Bob leaned in for a shake.

'How are you Erm?' Bob said. That politician smile was on again.

'I'm up a grand thanks to your Shenandoah bangtails,' Erm said.

'Say again?'

'Erm plays the horses up at Charles Town.'

Ledford wished Bob would skedaddle. The mention of Charlie Ball had turned his stomach.

'Oh,' Bob said. 'You enjoy the races?'

'That your convertible in the lot Bob?' Erm thumbed toward the gate.

'It is. Bought it new last year.'

'How many miles you put on it?'

'Oh, I think about two thousand or thereabouts.'

Fury spit on his finger and bent to rub mud off his brogans.

Erm breathed in the smell of damp burning timber from the oil drum. 'Ledford,' he said, 'you got shit burgers on the menu tonight?'

Ledford watched Fury. The boy rubbed and rubbed at his shoe until no trace of dirt could be found.

'Well, I'd better go check on my brother,' Bob said. 'Nice to see you again Erm. Nice to meet you young man.' Bob ambled off in the direction of the chapel.

Erm called after him. 'We'll catch up later big Bob, big butter and egg man.' He laughed and produced his flask. Spun the top off with a flick of the thumb. 'Convertible Bobby,' he said to Ledford. Then to his boy, 'Stand up straight Fury.'

'I didn't think the state's centennial was your style,' Ledford said.

'C'mon now, Ledford. You know I love Virginia.' Erm winked. He liked to get under the skin of his old friend.

Ledford looked at Fury. There was something

291

unsettling about him. Ledford tried to make eye contact. 'Fury, Willy's up at the gym if you want to go see him.'

The boy walked off, slow and silent.

'Goddamned teenagers,' Erm said.

Herchel and Jerry slid on their work gloves and tipped the fiery barrel into a trench they'd dug that morning. They tossed foil-wrapped squashes and onions into the coals. Sparks danced invisible on the evening air. The sun was getting low on the ridge, and the lot was filling with cars.

By five-thirty, people were walking in from the woods.

At six, two Corvair vans pulled in, trailed by a station wagon. Each van wore a white stripe down the side, and inside the stripe had been painted the words *Radiant Light Gospel Choir*. J. Carl Mitchum was at the wheel of the first, his wife the second. Eighteen singers unloaded – men in dark suits and women in pink-and-purple dresses. Their hats reached high and their heels made tracks in the mud. Each member hung a dry-cleaned choir gown over their arm, still in the bag. They strode up the Cut in a pack. Their children jumped from the crowded station wagon and followed.

Effie was the first to spot them. She ran over and hugged her mother and father. All around, white folks stared. Many had come for the free barbeque and punch. Few of them had known what to expect from the strange folks at Marrowbone, and fewer still had ever seen so many black folks in one place.

One local man, a skinny, out-of-work miner, took a long look at the parade of gospel singers and promptly swallowed what punch was left in his Dixie cup. He told his wife and daughter to do the same, and then they all set them down on a picnic table and walked back into the woods.

Mack turned the hand crank slow and steady on the rotisserie he'd fashioned for the occassion. The pig's flesh was reddish brown and split at the armpits. The skewer ran through it, ass to mouth, and Mack had rigged up its legs with coat-hanger wire.

He checked his wristwatch. The pig had been over the coals for just shy of five hours. That morning, Dimple and Wimpy had told him six would suffice. They'd taken Mack and Ledford to W. D. Ray's place, where the pig was asleep under a bench on the porch. Bedded down on an old dirty quilt. They'd paid Mr Ray a hundred dollars for it and returned to the old butcher building, where Mack and Ledford had watched one brother hold the pig still on a block-top table while the other one stuck a ten-inch knife in its neck and rolled his wrist. The pig screamed for a full minute, a sound not unlike a child's, while a wide jettison of blood rushed forth from the hole. It spattered the boots and pantcuffs of the twins, who paid no mind. It gathered and ran in a line to the pitched floor's daisy drain.

Ledford had walked out. Mack had nearly lost his stomach.

At 6:30, inside the tent, Ledford took the stage. He tapped the microphone and said, 'Evenin.' People meandered in. Ledford estimated their number to be 150. The TV station had sent a reporter and a cameraman. They stood in the far right corner, whispering and fanning themselves with newspapers. In the far left was Mary, perched on a folding chair and rolling her own footage. 'I want to thank all of you for comin,' Ledford said. The microphone whistled. 'Tonight we celebrate the centennial birthday of this great state.' A few clapped and hollered. 'And we also celebrate the ten-year anniversary of the first official batch of the Marrowbone Marble Company.' There were a few more celebratory calls. 'But that is not all this day will mark. As some of you know, mine and Rachel's youngest boy Orb claims June twentieth as his birthday. And this one makes ten.'

Down front, Willy hoisted Orb on his shoulders and began to dance in a circle. He whooped as he went, and the crowd applauded the boy. Orb looked this way and that, then up at the tent's center post. He put his hands to his ears and a few people laughed.

'Orb's got his own way of things,' Ledford said. 'And that's something else I'd like to speak on, if you'll permit me, for just a moment before we get to all the eating and music.' His voice was loud through the PA. It seemed to echo. 'What I mean is, Orb has his own way of going about life. He doesn't see things the way most do.' Ledford cleared his throat and shuffled his feet. 'And I for one admire that breed of sight. Vision, you might say. I see it at work every day around me here at Marrowbone Cut, a new vision of how life can be.' His voice quivered. He looked at the floor. 'I am a glass man,' he said. It had grown quiet. The katydids called from the trees.

The choir members and their children had all grouped at the left of the stage. All except the littlest ones stood close and looked around, as if expecting an ambush.

Ledford coughed into his hand. 'There's some literature on the table up here by the stage. It tells about our profit-sharing system for employees, our food and clothing pantry in the chapel.' He'd wanted to say more on the vision he had for Marrowbone, but couldn't. He looked out at the people, their faces tinted orange, evening sun through tent walls. He went on, 'We can't hardly keep up with the demand for playing marbles, and Mack Wells' invention of the Ringer cross-rack has caught on. So, if anyone's out of a job, come on in and see me.'

He searched the crowd for J. Carl Mitchum, but instead found fat Charlie Ball, who stood next to Erm, of all people. The two of them whispered back and forth, laughed a little. It was unnerving. Ledford shook it off and continued. 'And we put out heads together with others as much as we can. The West Virginia Human Rights Commission, to name one. We're happy to have the vice president of that commission here this evening, Mr J. Carl Mitchum.' Ledford pointed to him and J. Carl waved a hand. 'We're honored to have you sir, and your gospel choir.' He surveyed the crowd again. Looked back at Charlie Ball, who was handing a business card to Erm. The spotlight Jerry had rigged up was getting hot. Sweat ran cool down Ledford's spine. 'The Radiant Light Choir is going to sing for us a little later,' he said, 'and we've got a boxing exhibition and a marble surprise for the children. So go on and fill up on the barbeque and all, and have a good time.'

Some applauded and some did not. Bob Staples looked at his pocket watch.

Rachel had made her famous coleslaw. She and Lizzie stuck slotted spoons into it, four bowls' worth. 'Enough to feed an army,' Rachel said.

Lizzie nodded. Around her, the choir members shuffled to find a place in the buffet line and white folks in hand-me-downs kept their eyes on their own. A quiet had befallen all.

Stretch Hayes had brought along his mother. He introduced her to Rachel as they came through the line. Mrs Hayes wore gauze over one ear, an elastic bandage circling her head. She spoke loudly. 'Does my son talk with respect out here?' she asked. Rachel said he did.

At seven-thirty, Jimmy Ballard arrived in a

black Cadillac. He was a pro fighter, a contender for the welterweight title. He was the youngest son of Mr Ballard, the filling station owner from Ledford's old neighborhood, and he'd spent his formative years in Ledford's boyhood home.

Jimmy Ballard was a celebrity.

A makeshift ring had been set up on the lawn by the big garden. Ballard stepped inside and raised his arms over his head. He unbuttoned his pressed shirt and winked at the women. Mack gloved him up. Ballard cracked his neck. He wore pinstripe suit pants, black wingtips, and no shirt, and he waved his gloved hands at the gathering crowd.

Willy climbed through the ropes across from him. His mouthpiece was already in and his headgear tied tight. He punched himself in the jaw a few times and danced on his toes.

Paul Maynard had declined the invitation to oversee the exhibition. There were a few others from the Maynard clan present, including Hambone and his older sister, Josephine. Josephine had her eye on Willy, whom she'd kissed the previous Saturday night.

Ledford stood between his son and Jimmy Ballard. 'This is all in good fun folks,' he said. 'Mr Ballard here has been nice enough to make a contribution to our food and clothing pantry fund.' There was clapping. Ballard waved again. 'And boys,' Ledford spun on the balls of his feet and surveyed them. They were black and white, young and lean. 'If any of you care to work hard and follow rules, our gym is open Monday through Thursday, five to eight.'

When Mack struck the bell with his hammer, Willy came out of his corner like a bull at the gate. Ballard slipped the left, but Willy caught him with a roundhouse right. It stunned the older fighter, and it stunned everyone watching.

Ballard kept him at bay after that, working his jab and trying not to let one go on the kid. His expression went from charitable to frustrated.

In the third and final round, Willy again sent one home, this time a left hook. Ballard's knees gave momentarily, and when he righted himself, he had to dance to avoid another one. When Mack sounded the final bell, Ballard hugged Willy and whispered to him, 'You're really good kid. I almost had to beat your ass.'

Everyone whooped and hollered and some of the anxiousness fell away. Wayne County white boys and Sixteenth Street black boys jumped the turnbuckles and shot their skinny arms forward and back, shadow-boxing around the ring and laughing.

Before he left, Jimmy Ballard gave his autograph to any who asked.

At eight-thirty, Mack led a procession to the twenty-foot surprise. A patchwork cover was draped over what looked to be a giant Christmas tree in the Wells front yard. Lizzie and Rachel had stitched together moth-bit bedsheets and holey paint tarps to cover what waited beneath. The sun was setting, and its last rays peeked over the ridge, illuminating the faces of the children. They craned their necks and looked up, wide-eyed. Mack gathered a length of rope attached to the top. 'All right, children,' he said. 'I want you to count down from five.'

They did so, gaining volume as they went. At the shout of 'ONE!' Mack pulled the rope and the musical marble tree appeared. None knew quite what it was, but the young ones oohed and aahed anyway. 'Orb,' Mack said. 'You're the birthday boy. You do the honors.'

Orb stepped front and center. He looked up at the fixed wooden planks of the giant marble tree. They spiraled the thick center pole, jutting like dorsal plates on a dinosaur, thick and smooth. Mack and Herb pulled up a twenty-foot A-frame ladder. It seemed to sway at the middle.

'Be careful,' Rachel said. Her hand was to her mouth. She couldn't help but picture Orb falling from that height, his insides bleeding out.

'I'll stay right behind him,' Mack said.

And he did. He followed the boy to the top, one hand on the ladder, the other waiting and open under Orb's backside just in case. On Mack's back was a heavy satchel. Inside the satchel were five giant marbles, hand-rolled by Ledford and weighing five pounds each. There were more down below.

At the top, the two of them leaned over and braced against the uppermost leaf plank. Together, they held the satchel aloft and let the giant marbles fall, one at a time. Mack's spacing was perfect, as was the angle of the planks. The marbles rolled

299

and plunked and played a tune as they went, spiraling downward and singing out *ploink ploink ploink* as they went, deeper and deeper in pitch, faster and faster, like some giant xylophone.

When all had dropped to the ground, there was a moment's silence, and then the children ran forth to touch the marbles, big as softballs and swirled blue and green.

Each of them took a turn, two at a time. They began to carry with them their own bags of Marrowbone marbles, dropping the small along with the big, bending their ears to the intricate differences in song, marveling that such an instrument was real.

When it had gotten too dark to safely scale the ladder, all were called back to the tent, and the Radiant Light Gospel Choir took the stage. At the end of the first riser, Orb stood among them, the only one without a robe. In the audience, black and white stood shoulder to shoulder and listened as Herb ran the bow across his new fiddle and turned the pegs. J. Carl stepped to the microphone and said, 'This state is the only one born of the Civil War, a war whose end saw the cessation of slavery.' His voice came from deep down, low and steady. 'Tonight marks a hundred years since those times, and it reminds us how far we have yet to go.' It was quiet. Then, J. Carl said, 'This one is for Medgar Evers.'

He stepped back, turned to his singers, and raised his arms. Effie came in on piano, then Herb on the strings. And the robed singers lifted their heads and sang. Their sound inside the tent was immense.

For the final verse, Orb sang solo, his eyes shut tight, his face to the tent's pinnacle. Effie had assured the other singers he'd be fine.

Orb sang of the time when people had been here for ten thousand years. He sang of us all, shining bright as the sun.

It was the most beautiful rendition of 'Amazing Grace' that any in attendance had ever heard. Women wept where they stood, and the TV cameraman forgot to roll film, his mouth agape, his breath caught. Mary filmed it all, imagined the silent footage of Orb's lyric.

By eleven, the crowd had thinned and the katydids could be heard again. Erm wandered drunk past a stack of folding chairs. He found Ledford coiling electrical cord in a loop. 'You were right Ledford,' Erm told him.

'How's that?' Ledford was bent over, yanking at a length of duct tape on the plywood runner. He stood and kept coiling.

'All those years ago, when I told you black and white could never come together, and you said they could? You were right. I can see it now.' He'd been at the flask all night, but after what he'd seen, he meant what he said.

Ledford put his hand on Erm's shoulder. 'Well, I'm glad to hear you say that. Thank you, Erm.' It occurred to Ledford that he could no longer read his old friend. He knew not when the man was telling the truth. Maybe Erm himself didn't know. Ledford asked him, 'What were you and Charlie Ball talking about earlier?'

Erm took another slug from his flask, twisted the cap, and returned it to his back pocket. 'I told him I almost didn't recognize him under all that fat. Told him when I build my first racetrack in West Virginia, he can resign as mayor and be the cigar girl.'

At woods' edge, Fury and Willy crouched in the brush. Fury produced a fat, lumpy cigarette. 'This is what I was telling you about,' he said. 'You never smoked a reefer before?'

Willy shook his head no.

Fury swung his silver Zippo across his thigh, popping its top against his blue jeans. He swung it back up, spinning roller to flint in the same spot.

'Where did you learn that?' Willy asked.

Fury didn't answer. He was putting flame to paper. He drew deep and held it in, then blew smoke in Willy's face and handed over the joint.

Willy drew just as hard, but he coughed everything up and clutched his throat. Fury laughed at him and they passed it back and forth in this way until nothing remained.

After a time, Willy lost his ability to speak, and he lay back against the ground and looked to the sky. The tree branches were moving above, and beyond them the stars seemed to pulsate. Fury was going on and on about his great-uncle Fiore, the power he wielded. 'He once tore a man's nose off his face with a pipe wrench,' Fury said.

After a while, Fury asked, 'Do you know what my dad does for a living?' He looked down at Willy, whose eyes were nearly shut.

Willy wanted to answer *bookie*, but he couldn't even manage the word. He wondered if this is what it was like for Orb. For Jerry.

'He kills people,' Fury said.

Willy began to see tiny men dressed in white, descending by parachute from the pulsating stars on high. They tilted to and fro as they fell slow to the earth, like seahorses dancing in a tank. Willy shut his eyes.

The television aerial was planted near the top of the ridge. From it, a heavy-gauge cable ran for a quarter mile to Don Staples' Philco set, the only television at Marrowbone. On Friday night at eleven, they all gathered around it for the local news. Staples' living quarters in back of the chapel were anything but ample. Elbow room was hard to come by.

The women sat on the twin bed pushed against a wall. Rachel knitted a toboggan for Orb's growing head. She'd finished a pair of them that morning, black winter hats for the Bonecutter brothers. Lizzie and Effie laughed the way sisters do when reminiscing. And Mary petted the black-and-white cat on her lap and wondered how long until he bit her. Beside her stood her father. Orb sat at her feet.

Harold was in the corner by the door, sifting through a crate of Staples' record albums.

Herchel was drunk, same as every Friday. He and Jerry played catch in the dark outside the chapel, Herchel humming 'Amazing Grace' like so many had been all day. He stuck his head in the open door and asked, for the fifth time, 'Is it on yet?'

Nobody answered.

Herchel hummed some more and tried to focus on the television. 'They say that thing adds ten pounds,' he said.

'Quiet,' Staples said. 'Here it comes.'

The anchorman's glasses obscured his eyes, and his tie knot looked to be choking him. He said that not all the centennial parties were to be found in the capital. 'Just outside of Huntington, in Wayne County, local entrepreneur Loyal Ledford and his Marrowbone Marble Company hosted an event complete with games for the children, a tour of the factory, and live music.'

On the screen, the anchorman disappeared and in his place was a silent vision of the circus tent, folks milling around inside.

'Those stripes just ain't the same in black and white,' Herchel mumbled.

The anchorman said, 'The residents at Marrowbone believe in co-operative living, regardless of color. Negroes and whites work and live together.' There was a quick shot of Orb dropping his marbles atop the massive tree.

'There you are Orb!' Rachel said. Everyone in

the room cheered. Then came a blurry flash of the choir swaying onstage, followed by Ledford alone at the microphone, looking down.

The anchorman said, 'While some applaud this style of communal living and working, others have voiced concern that the Canaan Congregational Church, located on Marrowbone grounds, may be comprised of agitators engaged in Communist practices.'

Staples laughed out loud.

A commercial came on for triple-waxed Cut-Rite waxed paper.

Ledford lit a cigarette and sidestepped Herchel to get outside. Herchel followed. He shook his head and said, 'Communist my hairy ass.'

Staples was glassy-eyed and nodding his head in agreement with someone who wasn't there. 'Folks saw it,' he said. 'They aren't stupid. Those in the know will come.'

AUGUST 1963

Willy couldn't get his pants off. He tried, with opposite foot, to loose the bunched blue jeans from his ankles, but it wasn't to be. The jeans would stay where they were. Under him, Josephine Maynard had her arms and legs splayed across uneven ground. She moved them to and fro as if to make a dirt angel and said to him, 'Go on and do it.'

And so he did. With considerable trouble.

There was trouble finding where to put it. Trouble with moving too fast once he did. It was as if his hips were piston-driven, unable to cease pumping until everything fell apart.

The two of them had met there at noon. It was a patch of hard hillside near the top of Bonecutter Ridge. On the east face of the ridge there was a jutted rock – Big Shoe, they called it. The size of a truck. It hung over them, dark.

Willy didn't know what to say when he rolled off Josephine. He just went for those blue jeans at his ankles, buttoned up quick as he'd come undone. He pulled out his cigarettes, the pack squished, doubled back. He had to tear one in half at the crack to smoke it. He tore off half another one and offered it to Josephine. She shook her head no, was pulling up her own trousers.

'Let me put a hickey on your neck,' she said. She was brushing the dirt off her back.

'No.' It hadn't been what he thought it would be.

'Do you want to put one on me?'

'No. Let's go up top of the Shoe.' He clambered up the incline and she followed.

You could see further away up there. You could see clear across the Cut. Willy figured whose house was whose. Out back of Herchel's, Willy saw someone watering the tomatoes. 'Flea-sized,' he said.

Josephine kicked at loose rock. 'Well,' she said. 'I'll see you.'

Willy reached for her hand, but he had trouble looking at her straight. He kissed her on the cheek. 'See you.'

Josephine headed down the other side of the ridge. She side-stepped the rocky length until the grade leveled, and then she moved faster, worried her daddy would smell cigarettes on her clothes.

Willy lit another half cigarette and started down his side of the mountain.

When he got to the bottom, he cut across his own yard under cover of trees. He stopped behind a big oak and watched his mother through the kitchen window. She was hanging green beans on fishing line, tacking them to a ceiling joist. They hung heavy, their lengths lined up and pointing every which way. They swayed when she bumped her head against them, like wind chimes.

Willy walked to Herchel's. In among the wildflowers, at yard's edge, he bent and smelled the thick buds he now knew to be marijuana. He broke one off and stuck it in his pocket.

Herchel was still watering. Willy came up behind him. 'Boo!' he yelled.

Herchel didn't twitch. 'Got to do better than that, punchy,' he said.

Willy wanted to tell Herchel what he'd done with Josephine. But he didn't. 'Tomatoes were picked three weeks ago at the big garden.' He pointed across the stream.

'Different variety,' Herchel said. He hadn't turned around yet. He had his thumb stuck in the hose hole to get a fan spray. When he'd given another once-over, he took the thumb out and had a drink. 'Aaah,' he said. Turned and looked at Willy. 'You want a drink?'

'Shit Herchel,' Willy said. He stared at Herchel's right eye, in which the white had been made red. 'What happened?'

'Bendy poked me with a two-prong turkey fork.' He cocked his head. 'You look like you're all hot and sweaty.' He stuck his thumb back in the hole and shot a jet stream at Willy's face. He laughed and hollered after the boy as he ran. 'Stay off that ridge young man, I know what you done up there.'

From the kitchen window, Bendy looked out at

her man. He was laughing hearty, bloody eyeball and all. She didn't feel bad for sticking him. They'd been in the kitchen when it happened. He was washing, she was drying. When she'd again suggested that Jerry might finally move out, he'd told her, 'Honey, you'll hit the curb long before Jerry.' That's when she grabbed for the turkey fork, so shiny where it lay drying on the dishrag. It shouldn't have surprised her that her arm moved so quick. She'd stabbed a man before.

Herchel walked across the yard to water his marijuana plants. He took note of the missing bud, shook his head. While he watered, he unzipped his fly and pissed on a ladybug traversing a lamb's ears leaf. He farted, said, 'Aaah' again, and spoke to the ladybug. 'Forgive me,' he said, and she flew away.

When he'd finished watering, he turned and saw Bendy in the kitchen window. He blew her a kiss.

SEPTEMBER 1963

Mack Wells had bought the old school bus for three hundred dollars. He'd found it sitting on four flat tires in the scrapyard next to Ledford's old house. Jimmy Ballard had told him about it – a 1942 Ford Short Bus. 'Same year my son was born,' he'd told the scrapyard's proprietor as they gazed upon it, still mostly black and yellow, its insides ripped out by hobos looking for a spot to bed down.

It had taken Mack all of August to rebuild the engine and fasten seats to the floor. Stretch Hayes was his apprentice, rolling under the bus on a creeper board and listening as Mack pointed to and named brake line, fuel line, axles, and suspension. He'd set up a metal shop in back of the factory, and he taught Stretch to weld and cut. They outfitted the bus with a new fuel tank and hoses. They painted it blue.

Harold had gone off to law school, and Mack found solace in the company of Stretch. Their work was fast, and it derived from necessity. After the local news covered the centennial celebration, folks had begun to show up. They were white, black, and in between, and they were looking for work and a place to live. Their children would need to get to school, and the road to Marrowbone was not on the district driver's route.

The new folks were country and city, young and old. They were willing to bend their backs and help raise a house. Seventeen of the new arrivals were children, and they ranged in age from two to thirteen. Eleven were white, four were black, and two were a little of both. Mack was to be their bus driver, and Ledford his co-pilot.

At 7:00 a.m., on September 3rd, the children lined up and filed on board. Willy waved to them as he ran off down the road. It was four miles to school. He was training again and aimed to beat the bus.

Rachel and Lizzie had repaired and refreshed many a child's wardrobe for the occasion. They looked on, blowing sassafras tea steam from the rims of their mugs. Their faces were worried and proud. For on this day, almost ten years after *Brown versus Board of Education*, they watched a bus set out to integrate a Wayne County school.

Mack pulled to the curb of Poke Branch School at 7:30. Word had gotten around, and there were two dozen on the lawn with signs they'd plagiarized from memories of Little Rock newspaper pictures. One read *Race Mixsing is Comunism*.

Ledford stood in the bus's aisle. 'All right,' he said. 'Let's do like we talked about. Keep your eyes forward and hum your favorite song as you go.'

Orb had sat in the back. He was the last to step off the bus. Ledford winked at him and rubbed his head. 'You'll like school,' he told him. 'They know more math than me and your mother put together.'

Only one woman in the crowd had the nerve to step in spitting distance. This was evidenced by the phlegm Mack wiped from his shoulder with his handkerchief. Afterwards, though it was his favorite red hanky, he threw it in the wastebasket outside the school's double doors. Behind him, the woman kept at her insults. Her voice was hoarse from screaming at her children and her dogs and her husband and the mail carrier. 'Antichrist!' she hollered. 'Sodomites!'

The children all crowded into the hallway outside the principal's office. They stood tight in a pack, their eyes fixed on a bulletin board. It was sparsely tacked with class schedules and teacher names, sign-up sheets for bake sales and food drives. Poke Branch School enrolled grades one through twelve inside nine rooms. The gymnasium's floor was rotting. In the wintertime, the furnace coughed black smoke through floor grates. When it rained for more than three hours, there were fifty tin pails at the ready to catch drips.

Inside the principal's office, Ledford and Mack were pleasantly surprised with the man's demeanor. 'Yes,' he said to them, 'I'll have Miz Buskirk sort out the new enrollee papers.' He'd suffered a burn on the right side of his face and he had to dab at his eye periodically on account

312

of a faulty duct. 'There's ample room here for all your children, and our teachers are up to the task.' He looked at both Ledford and Mack when he spoke. 'My brother is a pipe fitter for a chemical plant up in Baltimore,' he said. 'He went to the March on Washington last week, called me afterwards, said he'd cried tears of joy. Now, here's a man whose first wife grew up in the Klan.' He raised his eyebrows and ignored the duct welling up. It threatened to overflow as he looked from Ledford to Mack and back again. 'You show me a body who says things aren't changin, I'll show you a damned fool,' he said. 'Some of us aren't as backwards out here as they make us out to be.'

Miz Buskirk the secretary got the paperwork in order. The children were assigned to rooms by age.

Ledford watched his youngest boy walk down a narrow corridor with a blinking ceiling bulb. Orb walked stride for stride next to Chester, a black boy whose family had come to Marrowbone from Jenkinjones, McDowell County. Orb had liked Chester from the start because he could shoot marbles and he did backflips off most anything, including the porch rail and the dog-pen roof. Ledford liked Chester because he called folks by their professions, not their names. Chester never remembered names.

Ledford watched the two boys turn the corner. He wondered if Orb would speak a word all day.

DECEMBER 1964

Some men didn't breathe their pipe smoke in. Don Staples was not one of those men. It was cold, and the coughing had gotten worse. He spat phlegm, red-striped by blood, into his tiny pedestal sink. He moved the stuff around with his finger, measuring the red evidence. He wondered what inside him was rupturing.

Outside, it was a clear night. He turned away from the window and sat down on the bed. His one-room chapel abode was frigid. Staples put his back against a bed pillow. Behind it, cold came through the wall. The pillow's down feathers might as well have been ice cubes.

A book, pen, and paper lay on the bedspread beside him. He read his own writing: *Dearest Annie and James*, the letter began. *How can I say all that must be said here?* He picked it up and wadded a ball. Threw it across the room.

If Staples had a nickel for every time he started a letter to his estranged wife and son in California, he'd have been a rich man.

He pulled the television knob and waited for the picture to blossom. The local news anchor spoke through static about the Economic Opportunity Act. He said, 'Many believe that the War on Poverty will work best right here in West Virginia.' He wore his hair in a comb-over that wasn't fooling anybody.

Staples had high hopes for President Johnson's newly declared war. It seemed to him that even with Kennedy gone, a promise made to the poor might finally be carried out. Federally funded Community Action Agencies had sprung up in every county, Wayne included, and folks were showing up for meetings. Staples had been to a few himself. He'd sat and listened to out-of-work miners and stooped grannies and angry mothers as they stood up and told commission members about impassable roads and run-down school-rooms with no windowscreens. Folks were fed up, and somebody was finally listening to them. In Huntington, black people were mobilizing, and somebody would hear them too.

Outside, the dogs were running loose. Staples could hear their anxious snouts against the ground. Hogs on the trail of a truffle.

Orb had taken to turning them loose before he went to bed, which was ten or eleven o'clock in those days. The boy seemed to require less sleep all the time. He'd grown five inches inside a year. Thin as a broomstick, his head had grown most of all. There was no way around it, Orb had a big noggin. Prevailing thought among his family was that his brain was finally expanding. This was evidenced in his newfound ability to read. School had helped him along, and so had Chester. Orb had cracked the code, and in moments of solitude, Rachel would find him sitting in the corner of a room, whispering the words on the page before him. First it was *Doctor Dan*, and later, his big Mother Goose book. His favorite rhyme was 'Taffy Was a Welshman' because it contained the name of his home. Book propped in his lap, he'd whisper, 'Taffy was a Welshman, Taffy was a thief. Taffy came to my house and stole a piece of beef.' Inevitably, Orb would smile as he got to the end, relishing in the words he could now see before him. 'I went to Taffy's house, Taffy was in bed. I took the marrowbone and beat him on the head.'

There was a knock at Staples' back door. He got off the bed, coughed, spat one last time into the sink, and opened up. Orb stood there, shivering, his head uncovered, his hands stuffed in his armpits. Behind him, the dogs snorted and circled.

'You're liable to ice up and crack,' Staples told him. He waved the boy in. The dogs followed, and Staples slammed the door before they made it. 'You want coffee?'

'No sir,' Orb said. 'Can I watch television?'

'Well it's on isn't it?'

Orb sat down on the floor. He rubbed his hands against his corduroys for heat. The news anchor was talking about a fire in White Sulphur Springs that had caused one hundred thousand dollars in damage. Orb turned to Staples. 'You ever seen that much money?' he asked.

Staples shook his head no. He'd picked up a toothpick and was dislodging a stubborn piece of corn.

'In other news,' the anchorman said, 'State Senator Charlie Ball was hospitalized today with a liver ailment. He is expected to be released tomorrow with a clean bill of health.'

'We'll see how clean his bill is,' Staples said. He chewed up the toothpick and swallowed.

'Is that the man Daddy and Mr Wells used to work for?'

'You could say that. But a man won't really *work for* another man if he doesn't respect him.'

Orb tried to figure that one and couldn't. *Respect* was a word that had always confused him. *Respect the fire* his daddy had always told him, whether they were looking at the marble furnace or the barbeque pit. Orb wondered if the hundred-thousand-dollar fire had felt disrespected.

A commercial came on. Two children sat on the floor in front of a television, just as Orb did. He watched them watch a Gemini rocket launch. Inside the rocket, an astronaut drank Tang from a zero-gravity bag, and then the children stirred their own Tang into a glass and gulped away. 'Have a blast . . . and some Tang,' the announcer said.

'I wish we had Tang,' Orb said.

'It isn't natural.' Staples checked his wristwatch. 'Time for you to get home Orb,' he said.

On his way out the door, Orb turned and hugged the old man around the rib cage. Staples patted the back of his head. It still took some getting used to, Orb's newfound tendency to hug. If you watched him close, he was expressionless as he did it. The hugs were mere mimicry, a habit picked up from his mother, but he offered them nonetheless. All were grateful.

Before he took off, Orb used his hands to sign 'Goodbye.' Jerry had been teaching him sign language again, though Orb talked more than he ever had before.

Staples watched the boy run up the Cut, the dogs on either side of him. It was the kind of cloudless dark outside that moved the heavens closer, the kind of cold that brought no snow. He stepped out into the yard and walked a circle around the chapel.

The creek was frozen solid. The glass tree was quiet. Icicles the size of sewing needles hung from tree branches and glass scrap, like teeth on a jawbone.

Staples regarded the moon. It was full, its edges crisp against the blue-black night as if scissor-cut. Around it, the stars mapped their claim on the night sky like buckshot. He wished he knew their pattern, their meaning, but he didn't. He wished to be free of the thoughts such nights produced, but he wasn't. Staples was overwhelmed by the world and the mess people had made of it. There was much to be done. He hoped he had the energy.

He listened. There was only the still of winter. No frogs, no birds, no crickets, no wind. He breathed deep through his nose and a cough came upon him again. It hadn't quit when he stepped back inside and shut the door behind him.

State Senator Charlie Ball sat and swirled sugar in his coffee with a spoon. He admired the new ring on his pinky finger. It was thick and fat, gold with maroon inlay. BPOE it read below the Elk head. As an elected official, Charlie made a habit of visiting every community organization he could stand to, particularly when they handed over honorary hardware.

Jim's Spaghetti was crowded as usual. Lunch rush. And, as usual, Charlie was seated in the back corner booth. He tapped his feet and checked his watch. Thought about slipping his coffee under the tabletop and adding the contents of his flask. His cousin came through the door just in time to stop him.

'Good to see you, Noah,' Charlie said.

The thin man slid in across from him and struggled to remove his overcoat. 'Sorry I'm late Charlie,' he said.

'I'm accustomed to it.' Charlie had always felt sorry for his younger cousin, Noah Ball, though there was no real reason to anymore. Noah was rich, the busiest mortician in Wayne County. He was also influential in politics and had once been county commissioner. Now he headed up the War on Poverty Commission in Wayne.

But Noah was skinny and frail, and he'd never

dated a woman. Charlie watched him knock his funny bone on the table's edge. He grimaced. 'Well, Noah,' Charlie said, 'what was so awful important you couldn't tell me over the telephone?'

Noah looked around, nervous. 'How long they been letting coloreds in here?' he asked.

'This isn't Wayne,' Charlie said.

The waitress said how do you do and poured two more coffees. Charlie winked at her and watched her hips sway as she walked away.

'You see how she tied that apron string in the back?' Charlie said. 'Like buttermilk biscuits rising under there.'

Noah made a late attempt to crane his neck and gander. 'Yeah, like big ole biscuits.' He cleared his throat. 'Listen, there's some things going on you ought to know about.'

'I ought to know everything. That's my job.' Charlie slurped his coffee and eyeballed a black patron at the lunch counter. The young man was laughing with a mouthful of apple sauce. Charlie shook his head.

'It's that Marrowbone compound,' Noah said. 'That crazy Don Staples is getting more involved with the community action groups, and he's no dummy.'

'Spit it out,' Charlie said.

'He's been making known his suspicions that federal funds are not being allocated properly.' Noah had lowered his voice to a whisper.

'Jesus Christ, Noah, did you pick up that lingo

in a Lyndon Johnson handbook? Tell me what the hell is going on.'

The waitress came back to take their order, but Charlie held up a hand and she retreated.

Noah leaned across the table. He whispered. 'Well, I been puttin people on the payroll, supervisory positions, you know, making sure I go to community meetings and nod my head. And most of the welfare and AFDC types are happy to have anything come their way. Shorty Maynard keeps them in line.' He looked around again. 'But the local Communists, like Staples and Ledford and all the crazy coloreds they got around 'em, well, they know a lot about the federal bylaws, I guess. About the poor having a say and all. They're makin' noise, Charlie, stirring up meetings with talk of committees made of these local nuts.'

Charlie reached across the table and patted his cousin's bony hand.

'That's a fine ring,' Noah said.

'Thank you kindly. Now look here.' The waitress was coming back. Charlie stopped her short again, but this time he hollered, 'Two cheeseburgers, two coleslaws, two cherry pie. Okay, sugar?' He returned his gaze to Noah and said, 'I've heard rumblins of this stuff myself. Preciate you tellin me. I need to do something, it's simple as that. Just like here in town.' He glanced back at the black couple, lowered his voice. 'You'd think it was Columbus or Detroit the way these niggers are organizing, with the CIP and the Human

321

Rights Commission and old man Mitchum with his righteous speeches.' He smiled. 'Everybody wants a piece of this federal money, Noah, but we're the ones doling it out.' He winked. 'So you sit tight and go on fixin' up your dead people, and I'll do my job.' He patted Noah's hand again, then raised his own in a fist between them. 'This may be a District 5 meat hook, but it reaches all the way to Wayne,' he said.

On Christmas Eve, Ledford put the children's things under the tree and looked up at the star on top. He'd made it himself. Blue glass, hollow and handblown, an opening for the bulb inside. It was beautiful, the way it threw light across the ceiling.

There were still a few presents to bring down. He grabbed the newspaper from the coffee table and climbed the creaking stairs to the attic.

There were, among newspapers, certain bits that Ledford would not use to cool hot glass. He saved them instead, cut them out and pasted them into the old empty album he kept in the trunk. He still cracked open the trunk now and again, sat up in the attic with memories. Some were his own, and some were his daddy's.

He sat cross-legged on the bare wood floor and pasted in the latest article – *Marrowbone Marble Co. Feeds Hungry on Christmas Eve.* It was from that day's evening edition, and there was a photograph of Harold setting a plate of turkey and stuffing before a smiling old woman with a patch over her eye. Harold looked so serious in the picture, his face aged beyond his twenty-one years. Ledford was happy to have him home for Christmas. Such stays were rare in those days. If he wasn't up at Morgantown carrying eighteen hours a semester, he was on the road. He'd spent the previous summer registering black voters in Mississippi, and he'd been lucky to come back alive.

Ledford flipped the heavy pages in reverse, through two years' worth of articles. Like always, it occurred to him that the headlines recorded a pattern – for every step forward, there came another one back.

He sipped from his glass of milk. He longed to be tired, to find slumber's peace. But the dreams were visiting again, and it was best to wait for exhaustion's peak.

It was two in the morning.

More Than 100,000 Marchers Stage Giant Parade in Nation's Capital. He ran his fingers over the words, the miniature dots of all those faces across the field's expanse. Ledford wished he'd been there for it. He turned the page.

Four Children Die in Birmingham as Explosion Levels Negro Church. He remembered how Staples had called a special ceremony that night at the chapel, a Monday. How he'd cried openly in front of all of them.

PRESIDENT'S ASSASSIN STILL NOT APPRE-HENDED, an Extra edition. Ledford remembered that day too. He'd been in town, making a deposit at the bank. Everywhere, folks crowded around radios and televisions. They wept unguarded when the final word came, and Ledford walked past them to his car, his face unreadable to passersby, his mind wondering how many of them had shed such tears for the little girls in Birmingham.

He shut the album and stood up. Stuck it back in its place under the swastika quilt. Each time he did this, his eye moved to the empty, squared-off imprint where his pint bottles had rested. His taste buds stood at attention and his nose-holes filled with the scent of Ten High whiskey. He longed for its burn. But those days were long behind him, and so he swallowed the rest of his milk, pulled the lightbulb chain, and descended the attic stairs with a present under each arm.

Orb would be up by five. He'd asked Santa Claus for a new set of marbles, shooter included. He reckoned that marbles made by the fingers of elves were infused with magic, and there was no telling what kind of Ringer would come of that.

FEBRUARY 1965

Community meetings in Poke Branch had always been held at the school. After Charlie and Noah Ball had a talk with the superintendent, this arrangement ceased to be. 'If you ever want to get elected again,' Charlie Ball had said to the man, 'you'd better padlock the doors on those people.'

The superintendent told Poke Branch's principal that he'd be wise to comply. 'If you want to keep you job,' he'd said to him, 'you'd better do as you're damn well told.'

An alternate site had to be found, and Staples promptly suggested the new community center at Marrowbone. The place wasn't quite finished, but it would do. Sawdust collected in the corners where broom bristles couldn't reach. Basketball backboards piped down from the high-arched ceiling beams, rimless and blank. But the place sat two hundred easy, and on the night of the meeting, Dimple and Wimpy lost count of the rusted-out cars pulling through the gate.

More had been expected than actually showed,

and everybody knew why. There were those who still refused to set foot on land housing black folks.

At a little after six p.m., Ledford walked to the microphone stand. He asked everyone to quiet down and take a seat. He estimated more than a hundred in attendance. Most of the Marrowbone residents had stayed away, but Herchel and Jerry and Mack and Lizzie sat in the front row of folding chairs, alongside Staples and Rachel. Mary crouched at the end of the aisle, her camera running, as always.

'Thank you all for comin,' Ledford said. 'Since Mr Martingdale has to be in Charleston tonight, I'm going to let him come up and speak first.'

Martingdale was the field representative from the Office of Economic Opportunity in Washington. He walked to the microphone with a few people applauding. Ledford put his back against the wall and looked out on the crowd. The right half was peppered with important types. Noah Ball sat next to Shorty Maynard, who had finally stepped onto Bonecutter land. He and Paul had ceased to speak to one another, though they shared an office.

Lately, Shorty had been using his badge to strong-arm support for Noah. He'd pistol-whipped a pool hall owner up Hog Holler. The man had questioned coughing up twenty dollars a month to sell beer without hassle.

Martingdale was shaky at the microphone stand, and he hadn't taken off his overcoat. 'I've heard there's been some trouble between the people and the politicians down here,' he said, 'and our offices are currently investigating that claim.'

Most in attendance were silent. One man in the rear stood and pointed at Noah Ball and Shorty Maynard. 'Why don't you ask them two about it,' he hollered. There were cheers and applause.

Paul Maynard leaned against the back wall with his thumbs in his gun belt. He chewed a matchstick, expressionless.

Martingdale tried to regain control. 'Please,' he said into the microphone. 'Please try to keep things civilized.' He said a few more words about what a good sign it was to have such turnouts at a meeting. 'If everyone can work together,' he said, 'we'll all get somewhere.'

He was out the door by six-thirty.

After that, Ledford lost control of the crowd. They took turns standing up and shouting about the lack of bus service to their hollers, the unpassable roads and swinging footbridges with half-rotted boards. One man, a retired miner with advanced silicosis, stood and said, 'I want to know what is being done with all that money coming in from Washington.' He took a deep breath. 'I got a feeling that Deputy Maynard over there is padding his new boxspring with it.' There was approval, and some chuckling. The man went on, 'I reckon he figures to pad enough greenbacks he won't feel that pea poking him no more.'

At that, laughter erupted, and so did Shorty Maynard. He shot from his seat and went for the old-timer, leaping over the seated laps of those in his row. Somebody stuck a foot out and tripped him, and when he sprawled across the wide middle aisle, the laughter grew louder.

Shorty stood, his height extended, his face almost purple with anger and embarrassment. At a loss for words, he nearly drew his sidearm. Noah Ball sidestepped across the row and suggested they go outside to cool off.

Paul Maynard snuck out before they turned to the door. He rounded the corner of the community center and waited in the dark. When the door opened, he listened. A metal lighter opened and struck flame.

'These people have gone plumb crazy if they think they can get away with this here,' Shorty said. 'I'll ride ever one of em out on a rail.'

'I know it, I know it,' said Noah Ball.

Paul watched his own breath condensate on the air. He craned his neck forward to get a better listen.

'And I will end this place quicker than Loyal Ledford can say marble.' Shorty was fuming.

'Keep your voice down now.'

'Why? What the hell for? You think I give a good goddamn what these welfare cases and nigger lovers hear? You think I won't do what I say I will?' Shorty looked down at Noah Ball. He wanted his questions answered.

'Well, I just think we ought to remember that Loyal Ledford is a war hero. He's a decorated Marine who—'

'You think I'm scairt of Loyal Ledford cause he fired a rifle at some slope-eyed midgets? You got another thing comin, Noah.' Shorty only shut his mouth long enough to pull on his cigarette.

'Well,' Noah answered, 'those Bonecutter brothers are rough people too, now, and I think we also got to remember that your Uncle Paul is the law around here, and he—'

'I'll tell you what about my uncle,' Shorty said.

Around the wall's corner, not five feet away, Paul quit breathing. His ire was building quick. His heartbeat slowed and he thought of his son Sam, how he'd talked this way.

'That old man has lost it if he ever had it in the first damn place. His time is comin to an end.'

Paul wondered what his nephew meant by those last words. He could have been talking about the next election, in '68, making his own run at sheriff. He could have been talking about something more. Paul had always wondered if Shorty had the property deed Sam had talked about. Some old relic that claimed all of Bonecutter Ridge, including Marrowbone Cut, belonged to the Maynards.

Paul imagined what Shorty would do if he found out his daughter Josephine was dating Willy Ledford.

Up the Cut, the gym door opened and a swath of light and sound poured forth. Stretch Hayes was laughing and egging on Chester, whom he'd dared to backflip off the gym roof.

'It ain't even that high. See?' Stretch pointed to the stair step roofline.

Shorty glared in their direction. 'See that,' he said to Noah Ball. 'That Hayes boy is just what I mean. Comes from a family of criminals.' He shook his head. 'I'll git him and the rest of em fore too long.'

Orb followed Chester out the gym door. 'Don't do it, Chess,' he said. 'You'll break your neck.'

Chester looked up, calculated rotations in his head. 'I won't Orb, don't worry,' he said.

Paul thought not of his dead son then, nor of his no-good nephew. He was listening to the voices of the boys up the Cut. The boys from the gym he'd come to love. There was promise in their sound.

MARCH 1965

Herchel had once seen his uncle play a stand-up bass made from the gas tank of a milk truck. The instrument was part of a Tennessee jug band, and Herchel had never forgotten its sound or size. He'd vowed to one day make such an instrument, and when Mack was rebuilding the Short Bus, Herchel got his chance. The bus's immense gas tank was corroded in two spots. Dime-sized holes spread wide. But it was made from thick-sheeted steel, and it was made to carry a tune.

They'd been bolting and soldering for a month. On Sunday night, inside the Marrowbone Community Center, band practice was set to commence. Mack held the gas-tank bass off the floor by its long maple neck. Herchel rolled underneath on a creeper board and fastened there the rubber head of a toilet plunger. When he finished, he rolled back out and stood up. Mack was testing the plunger bottom, wiggling the big bass around by the neck. The suction had worked. Their contraption did not skid against the floorboards – its foundation was airtight.

'Works like a dream,' Mack said. 'Care to try it out?'

Herchel plucked at the strings they'd fashioned from clothesline soaked in melted candlewax. His new bass played loud and deep. He smiled at Mack and them at Jerry, who sat in a folding chair and picked at Herb Wells' old guitar. Over in the corner, Herb tuned a trade-in fiddle he'd gotten that morning in town. Like everyone in the corner, his eyes were on the new RCA Victor. Ledford had bought it the day before. No longer would residents have to cram into Don Staples' dorm room for news and entertainment. Now they could watch in color. The wide cherrywood cabinet had hinged-top doors, and underneath was a stereo phonograph and an AM/FM radio. The thing had set Ledford back six hundred dollars, but the marble business was good, and his people loved television.

Staples was the only one standing. He stared at the screen and shook his head. 'Why on earth did you buy this monstrosity?' he said.

'Price has come down on televisions.' Ledford scratched at his ever-growing beard. 'I figured we could afford it after the run on cross racks at Christmas.' Mack's invention of the Ringer cross rack had been a gold mine. Children no longer had to hand-space their marbles – the rack was precut with holes.

'Just keep up your inventory,' Staples aid. 'Next thing I know you'll steal the only cross I got.' A few years back, he'd nailed a cross-rack prototype to the top of a walking stick. If any children were interested, they could carry it down the aisle during church procession. Staples liked to joke that the drilled holes in the cross were perfect for a church such as theirs. 'When the persecutors get to chasin you,' he'd always say, 'there'll be less wind resistance.'

Across the gym floor, Chester let out a cheer. He'd done the impossible and scored on Orb. The two of them crouched on their knees over the Ringer circle and eyeballed angles.

Herb looked in their direction, then back to the television. He thumb-plucked his strings and set the fiddle on his lap. 'Bonecutters won't even look at a television,' he said.

Lizzie told him to hush. She and Effie and Rachel sat closest to the screen. They knitted marble bags while they watched. ABC's Sunday Night Movie was *Judgment at Nuremberg*, and on the screen Marlene Dietrich strolled along a thoroughfare in a fur coat. 'The German people love to sing, no matter what the situation,' Dietrich said.

Mack had finished up the last of his bass adjustments and strolled over. 'I never heard no Kraut carry a tune,' he said.

Lizzie told him to hush.

Marlene Dietrich's face filled the screen in a close-up shot. 'The words are very beautiful,' she said. 'Very sad. Much sadder than the English words.'

Mack scoffed. 'Sadder my black behind,' he said under his breath.

Dietrich's character went on, 'The German soldier knows he's going to lose his girl. And his life.'

'How old do you think she is?' Effie asked. She'd lost count of her stitches.

'She's sixty if she's a day,' Rachel said.

'No. Can't be.' Lizzie frowned and shook her head. 'Look at that skin on her face. Woman doesn't have but one wrinkle.'

Mack said, 'She sang on the USO Revue in the war. I met a private in France who said he stole her stockings right from the dressing room.' He got a far-off look, laughed a little. 'This boy used to sniff em.'

'That ain't true,' Herb said.

Mack went on. 'She wasn't no spring chicken back then, either. I say she's a old woman. I say that's a makeup job.'

Dietrich disappeared from the screen and in her place was a black circle, ABC written across its face. The network was interrupting for a special report.

Over by the water cooler, Herchel was walking his fingers across the strings and bobbing his head. Jerry strummed along with him, improvising what sounded like the old tune 'Oil It Up and Go.' They both stopped dead at the sound that escaped Effie's throat. There was something familiar about the sound, something terrible that Herchel couldn't place.

Effie stood up from her chair and put her hands to her open mouth. Lizzie followed suit. Their

334

unfinished marble bags fell to the floor in silence. On the screen, police in Selma Alabama trampled a column of people who'd crossed a bridge.

Ledford's heart rate quickened. He found it difficult to breathe. 'Oh no,' he said.

A policeman swung his club against a bloodied fallen woman. Effie turned away.

Tear gas clouded most everything. Limbs scrambled, searching for a foothold, for escape. There was none.

Unseen white folks cheered from the roadside.

Staples sat down in a folding chair, put his elbows on his knees, and prayed.

Effie headed for the door. She'd not watch another moment. She needed to call her father.

Mack held Lizzie's hand. On the screen, a policeman in a hard hat and gas mask unknowingly stepped in front of the camera. His head was on a swivel. He watched his fellow officer ride into the crowd on horseback. As he rode, he swung a bullwhip in a figure eight, like a medieval knight. Like a Horseman of the Apocalypse.

Mack worked his jaw. Lizzie let go his hand and followed her sister out the door. Mack watched her walk away, then turned back to the television. 'Ain't nothing new,' he said.

Rachel looked over her shoulder at him, then at Ledford. His teeth were grit behind his lips and his nostrils flared wide. She recognized this face. She'd seen it before, more than twenty years prior, and for a moment, she was back on the

335

sofa in her very first apartment, a fire going in the middle of the day, a voice on the radio calling for righteous might.

In the opposite corner, Orb and Chester had ceased to shoot marbles. They were still on their knees, each holding his taw and staring at the adults, whose actions they could not figure.

'Somethin bad happened,' Chester said.

'It's the Sunday movie.' Orb wanted to finish the game. 'It's about war.'

Chester stood up. He tried to make out the picture from across the room. He watched the old white preacher pray, and he watched the black engineer cross his arms on his chest. The scarred man and the mute put down their instruments and walked to the television. There was a ringing in Chester's ear. 'That ain't a movie,' he said.

The grounds of the City of St Jude were covered in the sunken shoeprints of five thousand souls. Two days of rain had turned the lawn to mush, and when the people filed in on Wednesday afternoon, the mush went to mud. They'd come for the final leg of the Selma-to-Montgomery March, and among them stood Don Staples, Harold Wells, and Mary Ledford. Don had rolled up his slacks to keep them dry. He and two other men held the rope of a field tent while Harold repaired a snapped pole. Mary stood by and reloaded her camera.

Harold had blown off an exam and left Morgantown Monday morning. He'd seen what the rest of them had on television, and then he was at Marrowbone, asking who wanted to go with him. There was no sense trying to talk him out of it. His eyes bespoke determination, dedication to the cause. Even Lizzie had held her tongue. Like all of them, she knew that such a trip south held in its path the very real possibility of death. They'd shot Jimmie Lee Jackson. They'd beaten Reverend Reeb until he no longer drew breath.

When Ledford had taken Mary aside and said to her, 'I won't let you go,' she'd responded, 'Daddy, it's not for you to decide.' When he'd expressed concern over Staples' health, the older man told him, 'You're going to take over the pulpit sooner or later, son. If it's sooner, so be it.'

Tuesday, when night had fallen on Tennessee, Harold had crouched in a ball on the car's floorboard. At a stoplight in Lenoir City, Mary put a blanket over his back. A man in the crosswalk eyeballed her, walked around the car, and checked the plates. He had a package of Pall Malls rolled in his T-shirt sleeve. She could read the writing through the worn cotton. He spat on the ground and kept walking. Mary's hands trembled.

They spent the night in Chattanooga, in the home of Herchel's uncle, and they made it to Alabama alive.

The City of St Jude was God's domain, a campsite for those who'd descended upon Montgomery to do his work. As dusk fell, Mary pointed her camera to the sky, where a helicopter droned and circled before doubling back. 'Why does it keep flying over?' she asked.

Harold wiped his hands on his blue jeans. The tent pole was repaired. 'Looking for snipers,' he said.

All around were Army troops and Alabama Guardsmen. Mary filmed their helmets and rifle tips, so cold and dull, dancing above the heads of nuns and schoolchildren and men and women from north and south and in between. White and black were together in her viewfinder. They were jammed on the lawn like sardines.

They passed sandwiches hand over hand. The setting sun glinted off the foil wrapping and Mary's lens filled with white light.

She filmed a U.S. Marshal standing out front of Women's Tent Number 4, his senses trained to know an assassin.

Dr King's convoy of black sedans had been hurried through a gate in back.

The sun set over the red brick St Jude's Spire.

Darkness set in. Folks in the crowd spoke on numbers. They'd heard they were ten thousand strong.

By nine o'clock it had gotten cold, and the mud in the field sent shivers through anklebones. Everyone waited before a big flatbed truck. Celebrities were to appear there. Their songs and jokes and words of wisdom had been promised. Behind Staples, a man asked, 'Did I hear right? Is Tony Bennett here?'

Harold had his eye out for Nina Simone. He hoped she'd sing 'Mississippi Goddam.'

The crowd pressed forward, and exhaustion got the better of some. Mary managed to squeeze out the side and find some peace at the children's playground. A rusty carousel squealed as it spun. Four little black girls with braids in their hair gripped the bars and propelled it with their feet. When it hit top speed, they jumped on and giggled at their dizziness. Mary smiled at them. She filmed them as they spun, around and around again. Beyond the playground, a dull orange light emitted from the windows of St Jude's Hospital. A small boy stood in one of them and waved to Mary. She raised a hand back.

In the pressing crowd, Harold lost track of Staples. He heard the old man's cough and tried to locate him, but the people were too many, too loud, too anxious for something to happen. There were shouts here and there for help, for a doctor. Harold worried that one of them might be intended for his friend. The mood was beginning to sour.

By the time Harold found Staples, the entertainment had begun. Anthony Perkins spoke into the microphone about the importance of the night. Feedback whistled, assaulting the eardrums. Harold locked elbows with Staples in order not to lose him again. 'You all right?' he asked.

'I'm just fine,' Staples answered.

Dick Gregory and Sammy Davis Jr rattled off jokes at the expense of Governor Wallace. Pete Seeger and the rest led the crowd in a rendition of 'We Shall Overcome.' Harold closed his eyes and sang. He wished he knew where Mary had gone.

Staples stifled his coughs as best he could. His feet were wet. For the first time in his life, he felt old and small.

They did not find Mary until two a.m. They slept sitting upright in the car. The windows fogged and the air inside went stale. Harold wished Mary would lay her head on his shoulder. He wished he could kiss her and press his skin against hers, but it was not to be.

Morning came quick, and as the march filed out of St Jude's, Mary, Harold, and Staples found themselves in the middle of a pack that stretched before and behind them for miles. The clouds broke up and the sun warmed their bones. Beside them, a young black man carried an enormous American flag atop the wind-bent arc of a tree limb. He led them all in a chorus of 'Onward, Christian Soldiers.' Helicopters flew over twice and the chopping of the blades nearly drowned out their voices. They sang louder. Among them were a myriad of nuns and men in clerical collars. Staples walked straight-backed. His shoes had dried. He nodded to a priest. 'Peace be with you,' he said.

Soldiers dotted the highway. They donned helmets and leaned against the hoods of their jeeps. Rifle straps lined their shoulders. They wore looks of disinterest, their faces revealing nothing, as if they watched a parade of thirty thousand every day.

Harold took note of the sneakers on a young black woman to his left. They were worn to nothing, the soles separated from the toe and flapping loose on the blacktop. He pointed to them. 'Looks like you could use a new pair,' he said.

'I'm an original,' the young woman answered. It was what they called the three hundred marchers who'd walked all fifty miles from Selma.

'No shit?' Harold said.

'Watch your language.' She unscrewed the cap of her Thermos. It was strung bandolier-style across her torso. Under it were three or four layers of clothing in various stages of disrepair. She squinted at Harold. 'Where you from?'

'West Virginia,' he answered.

She scrunched her nose and frowned. She looked at Mary, who carried her camera at her side. 'You from the press?'

'No, just filming.'

'You two together?'

'No,' Harold said.

'Good.' She took another swig from her canteen. 'That might fly in West Virginia, but down here they lynch you for that.'

Harold wondered why she didn't wear an orange vest like the other originals up front.

She shook her head at them and peeled off.

The young man with the flag turned and handed it to Harold, then started passing out oranges from his knapsack. Mary rolled tape of

Harold shouldering the flag. She nearly tripped on the heels of those in front of her.

Fields of dry stickweed lined one side of the highway, and spectators looked on through sunglasses. Some stood and some sat. One man slept with his arm over his head. Another crouched low and filmed the procession, at one point aiming his camera at Mary, who aimed hers back at him. They waved.

As they came into Montgomery, the fields turned to houses and filling stations. Black folks stood in packs at the roadside and watched. They waved and sang 'This Little Light of Mine' in time with the marchers and clapped. Some had to wipe at their eyes. A woman in a white rain scarf raised her arms above her head and wept at a sight she could scarcely believe possible.

The clouds bunched up and a drizzle let down. As they turned onto Oak Street and narrowed their column, people stood in front of their clapboard homes and waved endlessly. Stoops were broken down. Every other porch board was missing. Homes sagged on their block foundations and tiny faces peeked from broken windowpanes stuffed with rags. Staples was reminded of the homes around Marrowbone. The children possessed the same knowing eye.

In the business district, no one was there to watch them. They could hear 'The Star-Spangled Banner's though they were still blocks from the capitol.

Here and there, white women in fitted skirts

began to appear on city sidewalks. They watched and talked while their husbands stood in suits and smoked cigars and tried to keep their customary smirks in the face of all that change.

On Dexter Street, Mary trained her camera on the far-off stage, where Rosa Parks had just stepped out to a roaring ovation. When she spoke of hiding from the Klan as a girl, Mary ran out of film. She lowered her camera. Only then did she feel the weight of where she was.

Harold looked all around, past the Guardsmen and the plywood barriers lining the wide street. He looked in the windows of the office-supply company and the big bank building. Now all the faces were white. On the balcony of the Jefferson Davis Hotel the white men gathered. Some slumped on the rail and some stood tall. None wore his customary smirk. And Harold beheld in them the open-mouthed realization that a new day had truly come. 'This is it,' he said to himself, a whisper amongst the masses.

Like everyone else, the three of them locked arms. And like everyone else, they roared when Martin Luther King took the stage and declared that segregation was on its deathbed in Alabama.

Staples nearly broke down listening to the man. It was as if King were a prophet sent straight from God. As television cameras rolled, he stood and gave a history lesson to the country.

He told of how those in power had engineered Jim Crow to keep poor whites separate from poor blacks.

343

He reached back and drew a line from slavery to the very place they stood. 'We are on the move now,' he said.

Time fell away for Staples. He could have listened for a thousand years.

The people raised their voices in 'Glory Hallelujah' again and again, and the three who had driven from West Virginia vowed to carry back with them what they now possessed.

As they filed away from the white columns of the capitol, a voice came over the loudspeaker. The voice said, 'Stragglers must not remain.' Hurried travel was now in order, for it was true that to be caught in Alabama after dark was death.

APRIL 1965

Staples had come home from Alabama inspired. He coughed less. Said things like, 'We witnessed, in the course of a few hours, a permanent change in the South. Things will never be the same.' He wanted to take that energy and organization he'd seen and funnel it into the War on Poverty in Wayne County. Huntington, too. 'In Alabama,' he said, 'they've got a drive to register voters. Here, we're going to de-register.' Everyone knew that the rolls in Wayne were stacked deep with dead folks and out-of-district names. It was one of the ways men like Charlie Ball stayed in office.

When you got the votes of dead men, you damn sure got elected.

But it was difficult to sustain Staples' energy. Harold went back to Morgantown, and Mary was quiet as ever.

On a cold Saturday, Staples worked the gift shop cash register. The *No Sale* flag was stuck again. He slid a one under the bill weight, smiled, and handed a dime to the customer.

They'd opened the shop inside the community

center for tourists, who'd started showing up. Like most Saturdays, rich folks from Huntington had come out to the Cut in droves. Word had spread that the 'commune' was selling its wares, and everybody wanted to gawk. Ledford said that was just fine with him, as long as they bought a bag of marbles or made a donation to the food and clothing pantry. Most didn't. Most only took pictures.

Ledford eyeballed a fat woman at the display counter. She was admiring a blue paperweight he'd blown. Her pocketbook straps left red imprints on her forearm. He wondered what she hefted inside.

At the register, Staples rang up a twenty-five-count marble bag and a Ringer cross rack. 'Thank you kindly,' he said to the man across from him. The man wore expensive sunglasses and his hands were shaky. Staples told him, 'Come on back out tomorrow for church services if the feeling grabs you. I'll be preaching on the righteousness of fair play.'

The man nodded and walked away.

Ledford walked over to Staples. 'You ought to have told him we'd be picking up serpents,' he said.

Staples nodded. 'That's just the kind of thing we need in the papers.' He coughed hard, then got it under control.

'I take it you haven't seen today's paper?'

Staples said he hadn't. There was a crash at the open door. The wind had blown it shut, the brick door stop too light to hold. Mary tended to it. She was stationed there, handing out pamphlets on community action.

Ledford pulled a rolled-up newspaper from his back pocket and slapped it on the counter. 'Why don't you go on break, do a little reading.'

Staples picked it up. 'Don't you need to be up at the furnace?'

'Stretch is tending.'

'All right,' Staples said. 'I'll get another brick for that door on my way back.'

Ledford watched him go. He walked past the fat woman who had moved on to a miniature marble tree. It was a display item, and she dropped a marble on top and listened to the musical plunks. When it got to the bottom, she picked the marble up and cupped it in her hand. Then she dropped it into her open pocketbook and walked toward the door. Mary offered her a pamphlet as she left, but the woman declined.

Ledford left the register and walked to the tall display shelf. The blue paperweight was missing. He walked over to Mary and pointed at the fat woman where she strolled across the Cut. 'See her?' he said. 'She just stole a paperweight and a marble from us.'

'Why?' Mary smiled at an approaching couple.

Ledford sidestepped to let them in. 'Welcome,' he said. Then stepped back to the open doorway and put his arm around Mary. 'Why?' he said. 'Hell if I know. But I'll bet you a dollar she's walkin to a Cadillac over there at the lot. Full tank a gas. Stocked fridge at the house. Lord knows she's well fed.'

'Be nice Daddy,' Mary said. She jabbed him in the rib cage.

'Just tellin it like I see it,' Ledford said. 'If you can figure why somebody'd do what she just did, you can figure how to fix it.'

Staples retired to his bed for an afternoon nap. He spread the paper before him and read the headline. *US* Jets Challenged by Migs in Viet Raid, it read. Below, another article charged Russia with harassing U.S. warships. Reds were in the air and on the water. They were east and west and in between, and they were looking for a fight. Staples quit after a sentence and looked for something else. Down the page, a smaller headline read *Burnt Cross Found in Yard of Martyr*. It hadn't been enough to murder Viola Liuzzo in Alabama on the night stragglers should not have remained. Now they'd tracked her to Detroit and lit a pyre of hatred while her husband and children slept inside.

If there was any residual hope left from Staples' moment in Montgomery, it was fast being drained.

Rachel came to his door with some canned tomatoes and pickled beets she'd put up back in August. The beets were his favorite. She was worried about the old man.

He told her thank you, handed her the paper to take away, and lay back down on the bed. 'They make it awful hard, don't they?' he said.

Rachel looked down at the newspaper. 'I guess they do,' she said.

MAY 1966

Someone had set fire to the glass tree. Its stump was black and jagged. Its limbs littered the ground. Here and there, warped hunks of glass cooled, wrapping themselves around twigs and swallowing groundcover, translucent. Mack shot water at the steaming mess from a wide hose. He thought back to the cross burnt on his West End yard. 'More slack!' he hollered to Jerry, who unwound hose from the big coil.

Dimple and Wimpy bent at the knees and touched the ground and sniffed their fingertips. Nothing. Somebody had known how to cover his tracks.

Staples stood on the top step of his chapel and looked down at them. He wore an old bathrobe with holes in the pockets. Above him, the moon was a sliver. He looked at it, then back at the burnt stump. Flashlight beams waved at the ground around it. It was four a.m. 'Well,' Staples aid. 'I reckon the evil spirits can no longer be warded away.'

Ledford sniffed at a hunk of singed bark. There was something familiar to it. He looked up at the ridge in the distance. He had an idea who had set the fire, and he knew why. Interim election primaries were a week off, and this had been a message to stay home. To cease giving poor folks a voice at meetings, and a reason to walk to the polls.

The headlights of a truck shone through the front gate. It pulled into the lot and went black.

'It's Paul Maynard,' Staples said from his perch. 'I called him.'

Dimple and Wimpy went back to tracking, but both of them knew there was nothing left behind.

When Paul had said his hellos and surveyed the damage, Ledford took him aside. They stood next to the chapel stilts and spoke in hushed tones. 'I don't want this kind of thing gettin started again,' Ledford said. 'It'll turn Dimple and Wimpy a way we don't want to see.'

'I know it,' Paul said.

Ledford tried to read the other man's loyalties. All he could see in the face before him was sadness. Maybe fear.

'Shine a light over here,' Mack called out. 'I think I see a footprint.'

Paul walked over to the rest of them.

Ledford turned and headed for the ridge.

The sun was coming up by the time he crawled through Shorty Maynard's front window. His boots were muddy so he'd taken them off, left them on the wide porch. He surveyed the laundry room and got what he came for. He admired the living room, sat back in the wing chair, and put his feet up on the coffee table.

When Shorty came downstairs, he didn't notice

Ledford. He walked to the kitchen and yawned and stretched. Started a pot of coffee.

Ledford watched him walk to the side door and look out the thick pane. He wore a T-shirt and briefs. 'Nice new house you got here Shorty,' Ledford said.

Shorty's nerves electrified. He whirled on Ledford, a look of true panic in his eyes.

'What?' Ledford said. 'You didn't think somebody'd show up right off?'

Shorty wished to God he'd put his pants on before he came down. 'Where are your shoes?' he asked.

'On the porch. I didn't want to soil your prime floors.' Ledford repositioned his back. 'I could sit in a wingback like this here all day,' he said.

'What the fuck are you doing in my house?' Shorty eyeballed the rifle over the fireplace mantel.

'Collecting evidence,' Ledford said. He pointed to a pile of clothes beside the chair legs. He'd gotten them from the laundry room, folded and stacked them on the floor. 'Gasoline, scorched thumb on the work glove. There's even a length of wick in the shirt pocket,' Ledford said. 'Why you didn't think to burn your getup, I'll never know. You just set it right there by your fancy laundry machine.' He pointed past the kitchen. 'I guess you figure anything'll wash out in such a contraption.' He smiled at Shorty. 'But my bet is you don't even know how to work it. You was waitin on your wife or daughter to rise and shine.'

Shorty breathed fast through his nose. He could hear a squirrel scurrying in the chimney. He

351

thought about the rifle again. Wondered if Ledford had a pistol on him.

The grandfather clock chimed seven o'clock. Its gong echoed in the corner. The two men were still as they listened.

'Look here Shorty,' Ledford said. 'I don't intend to do a damn thing about this. Far as I'm concerned, you set fire to a tree, and that isn't enough to put me over the edge.'

Shorty picked up a road map from the dining room table and covered himself with it.

Ledford continued. 'I've made a promise to Don Staples, to myself and my family, that I will not be baited. I will not raise my hand in anger any longer.' He held his hands up as if to show evidence. Shorty looked at them, blank. Ledford stood and walked to the back door. 'I still can't figure how you covered your tracks like you did,' he said. He nearly slipped in his socks on the polished hardwood. 'But it doesn't matter. This is over. I was never here.' He looked at the pile of stinking clothes on the floor one last time, then opened the door. He stepped onto the porch, sat down, and pulled his boots back on. The laces were half rotten. He was careful not to pull too hard.

He knew Shorty Maynard watched him cross the yard to the woods, and he wondered if his head was centered in the sights of the big mantel rifle. It didn't matter. He'd said what he came to say, and he'd gotten out with nobody dead. He'd be home by nine.

Mary would be studying her sociology book.

Willy would be out on a run. Orb would be at the Ringer circle.

Ledford walked through the woods and pledged to himself that he'd keep his temper down. He'd make them all safe. The oldest, he'd chaperone at rallies. The middle, he'd keep in the gym. The youngest, he'd forever watch over, sure to avoid anything that would cause him to bleed.

Halfway up the ridge, the rain picked up. It soon beat down in torrents, tearing through leaf canopy like the downpours at Guadalcanal. It had the same sound, the same smell on the air.

The floods were coming again.

People pulled the plastic curtain hard as they stepped inside the rectangle. It was not unlike a shower stall, the voting booth. Inside, they made their selections quickly. Most voted the slate, and most had no idea who they voted for. School boards, county clerk, names typed on paper, names they'd seen their whole lives and been told to vote on. Primaries, mid-term or not, brought out more corruption than the general elections. No Republican stood a chance. A Democrat who won in May could rest easy that he'd win again in November. Voters fell in line like always. They had to. Every polling official at Poke Branch School had been picked by Noah and Charlie Ball, and every one of them whispered a word or two to voters as they took their paper ticket.

Staples and Ledford had sent a handwritten letter

to the president and the Department of Justice, pleading for the federal government to send in poll observers, listing instance after instance of past vote fraud and intimidation. It hadn't worked.

Now they stood against the gym wall at Poke Branch. They observed and wrote in spiral notebooks. Beside them, Mary rolled film.

At other polling stations, Marrowbone residents worked alongside young people from VISTA and the Appalachian Volunteers, writing down any suspicious behavior.

By noon, there was already word that a boy from New York had gotten his nose broken for smart-mouthing one of Noah Ball's men. It was the first violence to visit in a year.

Since Ledford had spoken to Shorty Maynard, there had been relative calm on the land. Floods had come and washed the footbridges away, but their waters had stopped an inch shy of the threshold of the Land of Canaan Congregational.

At three p.m. a janitor pushed ammonia water across the gym floor. Staples had a coughing fit and had to be helped outside. Ledford stood with him by an oak tree on the school lawn, the old man hacking blood and struggling to breathe.

When it was apparent he wouldn't catch his breath, Ledford stuck his head in the gym doorway. 'Mary,' he called. 'I've got to get him to a hospital. Mack'll be by shortly.'

And then they were gone.

Inside a minute, a man with a crew cut and a

lisp approached Mary. 'Turn that thing off,' he said, pointing to her camera. He was barrel-chested. Sweaty. He grabbed her by the elbow and pulled her to a voting booth. Noah Ball stood inside. The big man closed the curtain behind them and put his hand over her mouth. He'd tucked her camera in his armpit and he held Mary so that she faced him, her chest pressed to his, her backside pressed to Noah Ball.

Noah smelled of Aqua Velva and gin. The big man smelled of day-old sweat and mildew. Mary tried to bite the hand across her mouth, but it was pressed too hard. She tried to swing her arms and legs, but the men only squeezed her tighter. She was in a vise.

'I'll rip that film out of your movie machine,' Noah said into her ear. 'And I'll rip your blue jeans and panties off too.' He pressed his groin further into her backside, his arms locked around hers.

Tears welled in Mary's eyes. Her breathing went shaky against the big man's hand.

'Big Jim here'll have you first,' Noah whispered. He stuck his tongue in her earhole. 'Hussy like you can take on two in a row I'd imagine.'

Mary went still. She listened for the footfalls of Mack Wells on the gym floor, but there was nothing.

Big Jim pressed his face to hers. 'I'm goin to take my hand away,' he said. A chunk of his nose had been bitten off in a bar fight. He had no eyebrows to speak of. 'You make a sound, I'll do to you what he said I would.' His eyes said he meant it. 'You stay quiet, we'll leave you be.'

He took his hand away. Mary shook and whimpered a little. The two men stepped back enough to let her fall to the floor, and then Noah took the camera and tore the film out. He put it in his coat pocket and dropped the camera beside her. He said, 'There is no way a bunch of Communist longhairs is going to sway an election in Wayne County.' The gin was starting to wear off and his voice lacked the meanness he'd intended. 'You keep what happened here to yourself, or it'll get uglier for everybody at Marrowbone.' Even as he said it, Noah Ball heard the weakness behind his words. He already regretted agreeing to Charlie's plan of intimidation, and he already feared what would come if the girl didn't abide.

Mary gathered her camera as they stepped from the booth and re-pulled the curtain. She smelled them on her skin. She couldn't catch her breath. What would her daddy do, she wondered, when she told him about this?

The Clydesdale collars were ill-fitted for Boo and Silver, but the horses pulled steady nonetheless. Behind them, Dimple bent his knees and rode the drag harrow's T-bar, which he'd fashioned from a downed hickory limb. It was near big as a telephone pole. Trailing him, the heavy chain drug the earth below, loosening the hillside where corn would soon grow. He gripped the leather traces and kept the slack even. In his thumbs, he could feel Silver and Boo strain with each step – the movements of their muscles conducted through the leather like electricity. His palms tingled.

Dimple had bought the half-rotted collars from old W. D. Ray up the road. W. D. appeared to be liquidating his every possession. He'd wanted five dollars for both collars, and he threw in the brass hames and traces at no charge. When Dimple had offered more, the old man told him, 'Rapture's a comin. Your paper money won't mean a thing.'

At the end of the last row, Dimple told the horses, 'Whoa,' and stepped off the harrow. He fed them both browned apple slices from his jacket pocket and scratched at their muzzles. Boo had tiny white warts growing all over hers. Papilloma, Staples had called the warts one day. Dimple often wondered how the man knew all that he did.

He unhitched the horses, relieved them of their harnesses, and turned them loose in the pasture.

He watched them eat grass, his boot perched on the bottom rung of the split-rail fence. The section swayed a bit, and Dimple shook the post. Another one too wobbly for his liking. He'd have to come back with his sledgehammer.

Ledford approached from behind. He had a Thermos of coffee and two tin cups. 'Thought you could use a little,' he said.

Dimple nodded his appreciation and took what was offered. It was fresh, and it opened his airways when he sniffed it. Burned his throat when he swallowed.

'Listen,' Ledford said. 'I wondered if I might talk to you about Noah Ball.'

'The mortician?' Dimple had a toothache. He wasn't in the mood to talk around things.

'That's right.' For two days, ever since Mary told him what happened to her, Ledford had been praying for the strength to stay calm. He'd been trying to figure how to keep blood off his hands.

Dimple smelled trouble.

Everybody knew Noah Ball to be a greedy man, and everybody knew he lined the pockets of his friends at the county court. He made their dead kin look pretty in their coffins, and they made him head of the poverty commission. What nobody knew, including Dimple and Wimpy, was what Noah Ball had done to Mary in the voting booth. Ledford had decided to change that.

Across the pasture, Boo neighed and butted her head against Silver's haunches. He ignored her.

'Noah disrespected Mary over at Poke Branch in the primary,' Ledford said.

'Disrespected her how?' Dimple asked.

Ledford breathed deep. 'He put his hands on her,' he said. 'Told her he'd do worse if she squealed.'

Dimple frowned and regarded the horses. He'd always thought Mary a beautiful child. There was a burning sensation behind his eyes, and he wondered why Ledford hadn't paid Noah Ball a visit. 'Something got to be done on that,' he said.

Ledford agreed. 'It's taken everything I have not to do it myself, but I made a promise . . .' He didn't finish the thought. It sounded absurd on the air. Neither man spoke for a moment.

'What's Paul Maynard say on it?' Dimple asked.

'He doesn't know about it. Nobody does.'

Dimple looked out over the hillside pasture. They'd cleared a good bit of land for it and the cornfield too. The wind picked up. 'Cold front comin,' Dimple said. He shot back the last of his coffee. 'Me and Wimpy'll pay Noah Ball a visit day after tomorrow.'

Ledford looked at the ground below his feet. 'I appreciate it,' he said. He thought for a moment. 'I believe we could keep this kind of thing between me, you, and Wimpy, and that'd be it,' he said.

Dimple watched the horses. The tips of their ears swiveled. He shook the loose fencepost again. 'Should have dug these deeper,' he said.

The Ball Mortuary was housed in an old, two-story Victorian on Salvation Street in Elmwood. The gables were trimmed in intricate circles, like a line of bull's-eyes. There were cornices across the top tower and the porch wrapped around the left side of the house. Its boards creaked under Dimple as he fingered the gingerbread trim along a windowsill. 'I hate this kind of house,' he told Wimpy, who followed.

'I think it's pretty,' Wimpy said.

When they got to the side door, Dimple gave the knob a try. It was unlocked. When he opened it, the stained glass seemed to move in its lead cames, as if the whole panel might fall.

There was music inside the house. The further in they stepped, the louder it got. It was coming from below.

The Bonecutters took out their bandanas.

Down in the basement, Gene Autry was on the phonograph. Noah Ball loved Gene Autry songs, and if there was a duet, he always sang in time with the woman. 'I've got spurs that jingle jangle jingle,' he crooned, slightly louder than the record player in the corner. He moved his feet on the checkbox linoleum floor, never picking up Gene Autry's intended rhythm. Noah was a vain man, as evidenced by his manicured mustache and nose-holes plucked clean of strays. He wore yellow rubber gloves and flicked his middle finger against an orange tube he'd inserted into the carotid artery of the dead woman before him on the table. She was old. Her skin was gray. He'd yet to trim her toenails, which had gone black and curled over the ends of her toes like snail shells.

He went on singing. 'And that song ain't so very far from—'

The cold nose of the Smith & Wesson was at his neck.

'Walk over and shut it off,' Dimple said.

Noah did as he was told, the revolver's barrel stuck to him all the way. He was careful not to scratch his record when he lifted the needle.

In an instant, the room was silent. Out of the corner of his eye, Noah made out a second man at the foot of the stairs, and in the silver reflection of the embalming tank to his left, he could see a dark figure behind him.

'Cover her up,' Dimple said. He hated to see a dead woman like that, her parts out in the open.

Noah threw a sheet over the body. He'd yet to utter a word. He thought momentarily of the secret room he kept behind the bookcase.

Dimple took the gun from his neck and stepped back. He cocked his right leg as far as he could and swung it forward hard, his shinbone connecting dead center between the man's legs. Noah emitted a sound like that of a vacuum turning on and dropped to the floor.

The brothers wore the black toboggans Rachel had knit them three Christmases back. It was the first time they'd ever put them on. They wore their bandanas clear up to the eyes. Paisley red, and old. Each had on a common barn coat and blue jeans. Their oldest, most nondescript boots.

Noah stared up at them from the floor, where he clutched at the rising bruise in his stomach and tried not to retch. He thought his eyes might be playing tricks on him. These two were out of a movie.

'See here, Noah Ball,' Dimple said. 'And I mean listen. Or next time, I'll take those crushed nuts of your with me like a souvenir, and I'll rip your dick out, too, you hear me?'

Noah just breathed heavy.

'Hear me?' Dimple roared.

Wimpy pulled a seven-inch dagger blade from

his belt. He raised it up and swung it down, iron-wood handle heavy as its name. The knife tip stuck in the linoleum with a dull thud.

'Yes, yes, I hear you,' Noah managed. He pissed himself a little, wondered if there was blood in it.

Dimple crouched to him. His revolvered hand went lazy. 'You ever lay a finger on another Marrowbone woman,' he said, pointing with his gun, 'that knife'll be up to the hilt in your danglers.'

Noah shuddered. He made a quiet, whimpering sound, then managed to stay relatively still.

Dimple stood up. They'd started to walk up the stairs when he turned back. 'You tell your cousin Charlie or Shorty Maynard about this, you'll be might sorry,' he said. 'Do you think I mean what I say?' he asked. It had gotten sweaty under the bandana. He could smell his own foul breath.

'Yessir,' Noah said. He was prone, his chin tucked. From the stairs, they could only see the ugly crown of his balding head. 'Me and him both got no problem stabbin' a man like you,' Dimple said. 'Gets easier ever time we do it.' He glared over the bandana's rim, stepped down from the stair, and walked to the record player. He lifted the arm and set the needle down. The whistles waddled happy. 'Try not to sing the ladies' part this time,' Dimple said. 'You ain't got the pipes for it.' He ascended the stairs behind his brother.

Gene Autry sang, 'Yippy yay, there'll be no wedding bells today.'

JUNE 1966

C harles Town Race Track was a half-miler in the state's eastern pan-handle. Erm had first bet its windows in 1948 – a side trip from some business in Baltimore. 'Bush league,' Chicago bookies said of the West Virginia track. The purse on a day's races wasn't half that of a track like Hawthorne. But by 1966, Erm owned and stabled three horses at Charles Town, and he had everyone on the take.

He had two Airstream trailers out back of the stables. One was for Fury. The other was for Erm and his girl of the month.

At five a.m., Fury shoved a doughnut in Willy's mouth and flicked him in the forehead. The trailer smelled of beer. 'Let's go,' Fury said. 'We're going to miss the morning workout.'

The sun rose over the steel plant smokestacks, casting shadows across the track's turned dirt. Exercise boys in dusty T-shirts mounted horses on the afternoon card, and a man with a cigarette behind each ear called out the day's scratches. 'Ain't no rain comin,' he said. 'Stay on your mount or that dirt'll snap your neck.'

He pulled the cigarette from his right ear and lit it with the one in his lips.

Erm leaned on the rail by the finish pole. He studied his short form and talked to a fat man in a bowler hat. 'Him,' Erm said, pointing to a young jockey working out Tuna Melt, one of his three horses.

'Smart,' the fat man said. 'Save two bills makin him git up this early.'

'Damn right,' Erm said. The exercise boys commanded a two-dollar rate for morning work, but a prospective jockey got nothing.

Erm watched the kid around the quarter turn. His stirrups were too low.

Willy squinted at the sun. He'd never been to the eastern panhandle, and its relative flatness didn't agree with him.

'Here,' Fury said. He handed Willy a paper cup of steaming coffee.

'Thanks.'

'You see the kid on the brown filly? That's the new jock.' Fury pointed to the same rider his father was watching.

'Did you ever want to be a jockey?' Willy scorched his tongue on the coffee.

'What the fuck are you talking about? I'm five foot ten.' Fury snorted morning snot and spat it on the ground.

'Oh. Yeah,' Willy said. He gripped the track's rail in his hand, knocked his cast against it. Across his forearm, in black paint on plaster, were the words

364

ORB WAS HERE. Willy had punched a wall at the gym and broken two bones in his hand and wrist. The doctor had shaken his head at the X rays. 'You've fractured both a carpal and metacarpal,' he'd said, pointing with his pencil to something Willy couldn't see.

His temper had gotten the better of him again. He'd been on edge, in the first place – Josephine was keeping him a secret from her family. Something had happened to Mary that no one would speak to. Then, Hambone Maynard had sold Orb a cup of lemonade for a nickel. After watching him drink it down, Hambone told Orb that he'd pissed in it. Orb ran off to sit with his dogs. Chester found him there, reported the event to Willy at the gym. 'The hefty boy called Orb a bad name,' Chester had said. 'He called Orb a dough-baked half-wit.' That's when Willy punched the wall. He'd lain in bed for three days after the cast. He'd taken up smoking again.

He'd be a freshman at Marshall in August. Fury wasn't going to college. He'd enlisted in the Marine Corps. Vietnam awaited, and this was Fury's last hurrah.

By the day's third race, the sun cut through the grandstand opening. Fury and Willy sat on benches and ate hot dogs with onion and mustard. 'Watch this,' Fury said. He pulled a gold-handled magnifying glass from the big paper sack at his feet. It was difficult to find the right angle, but eventually Fury found it. The sun's rays came through the glass in a pin-point of blue-white light.

Willy watched the target just below them, a man wearing overalls in the infield.

'Watch his neck,' Fury said. A circle the size of a ladybug danced on the tanned neck of the over-alled man. Fury got it still. The man twitched and twisted free. His arm shot back and slapped his burnt skin.

This delighted Willy. He laughed RC Cola right out his nose-holes.

Fury shushed him and hid the magnifying glass. The man had turned around and was searching wildly for the yellowjacket that stung him. Fury said, 'Stupid railbird hillbilly. Half wit'll spend his last dollar on a longshot cause he likes its name.' He knocked back the end of a beer.

Willy quit laughing.

Inside the riders' room, four tiny men sat at a card table playing five-card draw. All smoked. All wore undershirts and jockstraps. Four Styrofoam cups bled rings on the cheap laminate top, screwdrivers all around. They anted and called and the youngest laid out his cards. 'Four eights, King high,' he said.

There was a groan, then the sliding of quarters into a pile.

Three other jockeys were in the room, pulling on socks in front of their lockers. Two were overweight and one was bald. They'd not been invited to play.

Erm came through the door. 'Take a walk,' he said to the men at the lockers.

'But we got to get in our silks,' the bald one answered.

Erm stuck his face in the bald man's direction. 'I said take a fuckin walk.'

They did so.

Erm pulled a chair to the card table and produced four envelopes from his inside pocket. 'Just do what we talked about,' he said.

Back by the grandstand, a ticket stooper looked up women's skirts. 'Look at this bum,' Fury said, pointing to the man. 'Anything for a beaver shot I guess.'

When the announcer called 'Twenty minutes to post,' Fury reached into his brown bag and produced a fat roll of bills.

'Why don't you just keep that in your pocket?' Willy asked.

Fury didn't answer. He was peeling off fifties. He licked his thumb just as he'd seen his father do a thousand times. He handed six fifty-dollar bills to Willy and put six of his own in his shirt pocket. 'Remember,' he said, 'all you have to say is one sentence – 'Twenty-five on Tuna Melt to win, fifteen on First Edition to place, ten on Heav'nly King to show.' Say it back to me.'

Willy repeated it word for word. He'd have to say it six more times in the next twenty minutes.

When they got to the betting bay, lines were longer than Fury had anticipated. 'Fucking payday,' he said under his breath. They'd have to work fast. 'Look,' he said to Willy. 'Stagger your lines. Got it? Go to that one first, then skip down two lines to that one, skip two more, and so on.' He pointed as he explained. 'Keep your ballcap on at the first, take if off at the second, and keep rotating that way.'

'Got it,' Willy said.

'Most of these ticket sifters are in the know,' Fury said. 'But you can't be too careful.'

Fury slid into the bathroom. Inside a stall, he pulled an overcoat, fedora, and sunglasses from his brown bag. He put them on and headed for the betting windows.

In all, they placed the same bet to twelve different countermen. Fury changed in the bathroom again, and they walked back to their seats with eighteen tickets apiece.

When the gate opened, two of the paid-off jockeys yanked hard on their reins. They kept their elbows tucked so as not to be obvious. Their horses would never recover from such a start. The kid on Tuna Melt got a great break from the three position. After the morning workout, he'd adjusted his stirrups, and now he was riding hard all the way.

On the three-quarter turn, the last of the bribed jockeys wheeled wide and dropped from second to fourth. He bumped the bald jockey on his way, pushing him from contention. That left three. Tuna Melt was the superior equine. The only question was who would place and who would show.

'C'mon, you fucking midgets,' Fury said. He held binoculars to his eyes.

The two jockeys Fury watched were middle-aged farmhands. Their horses were broken-down fillies at glue factory's gate. Odds were 20 and 30 to 1.

But none of that mattered if First Edition didn't pass Heav'nly King in the next two seconds.

Tuna Melt led gate to wire and won by six lengths. At 9 to 1, she'd pay out nicely. Place and show were too close to call. They were going to a photo finish.

Willy watched Fury slam his binoculars into the bag. It sounded as if the glass cracked. 'Please please please,' Fury was saying, his head bowed, his fingers laced in prayer.

When the results went official, Fury leapt from his seat, punched the air and hollered 'Thank you Jesus!' First Edition had placed by the tip of her flaring nostril. Fury sat down and gathered himself. Went silent for a moment. 'This is a big one,' he told Willy.

They went back to the windows and collected using the same stagger and disguise method they'd employed to bet.

In all, with the boys' winnings and what he cleared through his local bookie, Erm left Charles Town that Friday with almost ten grand.

'Not bad for a day's work,' he told the boys as they pulled onto Middleway Pike. At the last stoplight in town, Erm peeled off two hundred for each of them and passed the bills to the backseat. They were already loose on beer he'd bought them at the ABC store. 'Here,' he said when he handed Willy the cash. 'Maybe you'll get your prick wet.'

By midnight, both boys were passed out drunk. Erm took his time driving through Charleston.

Kanawha Boulevard was quiet. He could smell the river.

He parked the Cadillac in an empty Shoney's parking lot. The headlights of a passing car reflected off the restaurant window. The blacktop was rain-slicked.

Erm looked at the two boys in the rearview. Willy snored.

He checked his watch. Charlie Ball was late.

The white Impala rolled up at a quarter to one. Charlie stopped with a jerk in the space next to Erm and waved a hand. There was a woman in the backseat.

Erm got out of his own car and into the Impala. A fifth of whiskey sat upright on the seat, and the upholstery stank of sweat. Charlie Ball was dead drunk. The woman in the backseat was not his wife. This one was blond, young. She was asleep, her bra straps loose around her biceps, her mouth open.

'You play it pretty loose for public servant, don't you, Charlie?' Erm said.

Charlie smiled and unscrewed the top of his whiskey. He knocked back a big one. 'Erm, I want you to meet Ginger,' he said. He whistled. Ginger didn't stir, so he whistled again, louder. She opened her eyes.

Erm looked at the young woman, spoke his customary line. 'How do you do?'

She said, 'How do we do? We do it dog style so we can both see the television.'

The two men laughed hard. Charlie could

scarcely stop. 'Hot damn, she's got a mouth, doesn't she?' he said.

She licked her dry lips, looked at Erm, and said, 'That's how we do.' She picked up her pocketbook and rooted for cigarettes.

Erm watched her fall back asleep before she could get her cigarette lit. It rested between her fingers, twitched a little. He turned and looked out the front windshield. A giant statue of a boy was atop the restaurant. He hoisted a hamburger. *Fat Boy* was written across his shirt. Erm wanted to point out his likeness to Charlie. 'I've got your money,' he said.

Charlie nodded. 'You're a smart Italian man.'

Erm pulled the old leather envelope from his inside pocket and unzipped it. Handed over twenty grand in hundreds, rubber-banded.

Charlie thumbed the edges. He winked at Erm, put the money in his own inside pocket. 'This is good land,' he said. 'Good for horse racing.'

Erm didn't care that Charlie knew nothing of tracks and dirt pack and leveling terrain. He was a politician, and like the rest of them, he would push gambling on the hayseeds because he knew there was money in it. Come payday, they'd line up at the betting windows.

Erm stuck his hand out for the shake. Charlie took it. The grip made him cringe, and when he looked Erm in the eyes, he knew he'd made a mistake.

'Okay, so,' Charlie said. He looked away and cleared his throat. 'Shorty Maynard's got the original deed. That acreage is more than we thought, and I don't believe Shorty'll have any trouble getting his name on all of it. The developers are in line to—'

'You told me that none of this land cuts into Ledford's property.' Erm took his hand off the door latch.

Charlie tried to sharpen up. 'Oh no, of course not,' he said. He smiled, looked back at Ginger.

Erm opened the door and stepped out. 'Sit tight a minute,' he said.

Charlie took deep breaths and watched Erm open the big Cadillac door. He leaned across the seat for something on the floor. Charlie saw two figures asleep in the back, but he couldn't tell who they were. He began to panic.

Erm returned and stood at the Impala's open passenger window with his hand in his jacket. He stuck his face in and gave Charlie the eye. He pulled a box of cigars out fast. Charlie flinched. 'Be a good boy, Charlie,' Erm said.

Before he drove away, he called, 'Get a neck strap and hand those out at the legislature.'

FEBRUARY 1967

Everything was about to change.

Four men stood inside the rusted fence of the Bonecutter burying ground. Ledford, Staples, Dimple, and Wimpy. Staples had called the graveside meeting, and none of them knew why. They feared he was losing his mind.

Their eyes squinted to read the dark etchings. Hand-carved names like *Gertrude, Della, Woodrow,* dark-mossed rock lined by water. Their years marked another time: 1801 . . . 1864.

Ledford thought of the headstones of his mother and father and brother, imagined them grown over with weeds. After they went in the ground, he'd visited the gravesite only once in his life, at fourteen. A terrible feeling had come over him, and he never went back.

'I've left detailed instructions with my brother Bob,' Staples said. He wore a toboggan knitted by Rachel. It was pulled low over his ears and eyebrows. He hadn't been out of bed in a while. 'I wish to be buried right there,' he said, pointing to a corner.

The Bonecutter brothers registered no reaction

at first. Then, both men nodded. That was fine with them.

Staples turned to Ledford. 'I already told you about my desk drawer, haven't I?'

'Yes, you have.'

Staples turned to the brothers. 'Something in there for him,' he told them. 'I want him to take heed of me, dead or not.' He smiled and pointed his pipe at Ledford. It was always in his hand in those days, always empty. He stuck it in his teeth and kept it there a while, unlit but comfortable.

Ledford nodded. Looked away. Staples seemed so old to him. His skin was drained – no sap left. 'Let's get you inside,' Ledford said.

It had gotten cold.

A black sedan came down the road. It was new, shiny. The four of them watched it pull to a stop at the gate, plates reading *C of E* before the number, blue on white. Two men stepped out in overcoats. They waved.

The goats had gotten loose again, and they ran straight for the tall man. He jumped onto the hood of his car like he'd never seen a goat before.

Dimple laughed. He and Wimpy walked over, and the other two followed.

The men had documents with them. *U.S. Army Corps of Engineers*, they read. *Acquisition, Relocation.* The tall one with the mole on his cheek said, 'We wanted to give you some time to ponder all this before we put notice in the newspapers.'

Congress had approved it. The Corps of Engineers was stepping in the way of all the floods. They were going to build a dam at Lavalette and back up the forks of Twelvepole Creek. They were going to make a 2,000-acre lake.

'Marrowbone Creek don't flood but once ever two years,' Dimple said. 'And when it does, we manage just fine.'

The short one nodded. His fedora was loose on his head. 'I hear you,' he said. 'But this is mandatory acquisition we're talking about. You won't have to clear out for a couple years, but come '69, well . . .' He didn't elaborate.

Wimpy wore an odd expression. 'Are you tellin' us that Marrowbone will be underwater?' he asked.

'Yessir, that's what I'm telling you.'

Staples said, 'I worked for the Conservation Corps.' He grunted. Stifled a cough and tried to stand straight.

Ledford had him by the arm.

Two thoughts were in Ledford's mind. The first was that it was twenty degrees and he ought to get Staples back indoors. The other was that he liked the thought of Marrowbone underwater.

'What about our kin?' Dimple looked back to the burying ground. For him, everything depended on how the two men answered this question.

The short one took off his hat and held it in both hands at his waist. 'Well, yessir,' he said. 'We would be happy to cover cost of excavation and reburial, make that an easy process for you.'

Dimple said, 'I'd just as soon leave em where they are.'

Staples nodded his head. 'Under a lake,' he said. He patted Dimple on the shoulder and laughed. 'I always wanted to be buried at sea, but I reckon a lake's close enough.'

The short one cleared his throat and looked at the tall one, who shrugged and put in a stick of gum. The short one said, 'I'm sure we could work something out Mr Bonecutter.'

Staples started coughing and Ledford led him away.

Wimpy watched them go. He'd seen neither surprise nor anger on their faces at news of the damming of Twelvepole Creek. Wimpy wondered if Ledford felt what he did about Marrowbone. He wondered if the younger man regarded the chimney stack every morning like he did, knowing it didn't belong, and knowing, deeper down, that maybe none of them belonged.

The goats had walked clear up the main road. A direct, steady amble, as if they'd planned it. When they were almost out of eyeshot, they turned and stared at Wimpy.

He knew they'd wanted to run for years, and now was as good a time as any to let them go. He waved a hand.

JUNE 1967

The Marrowbone Action Group was meeting at seven inside the community center. There was to be discussion of the coming dam and lake, and a vote had been ordered to oust Noah Ball from the poverty commission. Nobody had seen Noah in months. Word was he would make a run for state senator in a year's time. The Ball cousins wanted two districts to rule.

It would be a tough row to hoe. In the year since the interim elections, things had changed. The *New York Times* had gotten wind of Wayne County. They ran an article about local corruption and called it 'The War on the War on Poverty.' Don Staples was quoted: 'The politicians and the businessmen can holler communist plot all they want to. We got a different name for it. Poor Power is what we call it.' Walter Cronkite mentioned Marrowbone on his show, ran a full minute of footage showing the factory and the community center and the gym. Stretch Hayes' silhouette was right there on national television – through the open gym window, you could see him shadow-boxing. There was mention of Douglass High

School in town, which was slated to become a community center of its own. Cronkite had said, 'Theirs is not a movement for rural whites alone.' The *Charleston Gazette* ran Harold's law school graduation speech. He'd finished first in his class. He spoke of the CIP and Smalley's Cafeteria. He spoke of the power of lawful resistance.

The state road commission and the board of education took note of the attention. Marrowbone was real. Up at Poke Branch, the state rebuilt two swinging bridges. Knob Drop Road was patched and paved, and a guardrail was put in at dead man's curve. School buses started running deep into hollers.

For a short while, it seemed that the energy they'd found in Alabama would come back again. There had even been talk of a visit by Martin Luther King, whose Southern Christian Leadership Conference had noted Marrowbone's work.

But nothing much had truly changed. Staples had finally gone to the doctor, where he heard the word he'd been waiting for. *Cancer*. The war in Vietnam went on, and the poor stayed poor. Noah Ball may have been peeking at the world through his mortuary curtains, but Charlie was out working overtime, lining pockets and buying votes.

He'd been talking to Shorty Maynard about how to shut Marrowbone down for good. He wanted to own that land before the government bought it up. Charlie had gambled away the land development money, Erm's included.

Marble sales were down. The cost of natural gas

378

was up. The factory's chimney stack needed a good cleaning.

Ledford watched the smoke cloud through the community center window. His shinbone was acting up. It was as if the pain came from inside the bone, an angry shrapnel souvenir that the Navy doc at Espiritu Santo had missed all those years ago. He propped it on a folding chair and checked his watch. Inside an hour, there wouldn't be any empty seat in the place.

He told Orb to rub his leg a while.

The television was on. They'd raised it, a ten-brick stack underneath. The newsman spoke on Vietnam like he did every night. Cue cards. Numbers instead of names.

Harold opened chairs and set them in a line. Herchel pushed a broom double-time, a cigarette stuck in his lips. Jerry taped a cord to the floor and switched on the microphone. He tapped it to the tune of 'Oil It Up and Go.'

Ledford told Orb to shut off the television.

'What about *Gunsmoke* at seven-thirty?' Orb asked. Puberty had changed his voice.

Ledford shook his head no and stood up. He winced. 'We're having a meeting in here Son. Go on over to the chapel to watch,' he said. He pointed his finger at Orb. 'Spend a little time with Staples, like you used to. Dying man needs company boy, you hear?'

Orb heard.

'And don't turn the old man's set on till *Andy*

Griffith,' Ledford said, and headed for the door. There was a good bit on his mind. In an hour, he'd be telling the people that he had no answers for them. That when the government told you they were flooding you out, maybe there weren't answers anymore.

Outside, it was humid. The creek was low.

The gym door opened and Willy stepped out. His handwraps hung loose at the wrist. He was shirt-less. Behind him, Josephine Maynard stuck her head out the door and hollered that Huntington girls were no-good whores. She spat on the ground and stepped back in the gym. Willy walked for the creek. He didn't return his father's wave.

Stretch Hayes stood in the gym doorway and made a gesture to console Josephine. 'He's just young,' he told her. 'You give him some time, he'll come back to you.'

Over at Herchel and Jerry's, Bendy was packing up the last of her things. She pushed open the screen door with her backside, spotted Willy coming. 'I never step foot on this land again!' she screamed at him. She had an Army duffel slung over her shoulder and a knife block in her hands. The little metal handles glinted in the sun.

Out back in Herchel's garden, Willy knelt and smelled the marijuana plants. They were a good foot shorter than the stickweeds around them and from far off they looked like rattlesnake ferns. Willy had been picking at the camouflaged buds for four years. He knew that Herchel knew he did it, but neither had ever said a word.

At the big garden, Mary walked the rows, her mother trailing behind. Each woman had her hands clasped in back, head bowed to the ground. They were inspecting, eyeballing leaf holes. Categorizing by size and shape, discerning what manner of critter had been into the seedlings this time.

'Slugs are feasting,' Rachel said.

Mary nodded. She took note of yellow-edged mustard greens and ugly broccoli stalks. 'We need Mrs Wells and her death traps,' she said. Mary thought of Harold then. She looked to the chicken coop. It was quiet, a think swirl of dust along the gate. The clouds above covered the sun and Mary shut her eyes and imagined Harold was there, walking the grounds in his undershirt, wise beyond his years.

'Is this cat poop?' Rachel asked.

'No.' Mary walked on down the row, her eyes unfocused, her bare feet marking a trail.

They passed each other at the middle. Rachel regarded her daughter. 'Are you all right Mary?' she asked. Rachel's head was cocked, her eyes squinted.

'I'm fine.'

Twice in the last week, Rachel had peered through the keyhole of Mary's bedroom door. Each time, she could make out the top of her head, so still where she sat on the floor. Next to her, the projector ran, its rolling clicks a dull lullaby. Its beam cast a picture on the far wall. Rachel could only make out bits and pieces. Orb mouthing 'Amazing Grace' onstage. Staples on his soapbox. Harold, smiling.

Mary bent next to a cabbage seedling and took a handful of salt from her gardening belt. There were holes along its front, the potato sack material unraveling. There was no need for pepper any longer. The cats had abandoned Marrowbone. Mary held the salt over a fat brown slug. She opened her fist and the salt poured in a thin line across its back. The slug twisted into a U shape, its feelers reaching for its tail. Mary poured the rest and watched the slug's sheen disappear, replaced by a thick film of white.

Her mother stood above her, watching. 'Are you sure you're all right?'

'I'm fine,' Mary said.

Above the Cut, high on the ridge, Dimple and Wimpy bellied dirt and passed the binoculars back and forth. They were watching Shorty Maynard, who was two hundred yards off. He stood on top of Big Shoe Rock and looked through his own bincoulars at something down below. It was the third time in two weeks they'd seen him spy.

'What's he trained on?' Dimple said.

'Can't tell.' Wimpy was hungry. He sighed, rubbed his sore neck.

At the clearing, Shorty decided to have one more look before calling it a day. He rolled the wheel with his pointer finger and watched Ledford step back into the community center. Chickens darted across the lawn, chased by a dog. He rolled it again and watched his daughter step from the boxing gym. She was moving funny. Shooting her arms like something had upset her. Josephine had a flair for the dramatic.

It was two weeks prior that Shorty had gotten the anonymous letter. *Your daughter is dating a Marrowbone boy behind your back,* it read. Nothing more. Shorty suspected the strange Russian woman had penned it, and he suspected the boy she referred to was Willy Ledford. He wanted to see for himself.

Shorty had steered clear of Marrowbone ever since Ledford's shoeless visit to his house. But Charlie and Noah Ball had lately been getting in his ear. They said he ought to seize full ownership of the Maynard Coal and Coke tract, to strong-arm old man Paul if he had to. Charlie was in the business of land development, dam or no dam, and he was promising money to Shorty. He told Shorty to bust the Marrowbone people on something, to seize their land, to use the old bogus property deed he kept in a safe deposit box in town. 'Where there's land, there's money,' Charlie had said.

Shorty had friends in the state police. He knew a county magistrate who issued warrants on next to nothing. He could smell the office of sheriff. He could smell all that money.

There was a rustle in the trees down the hill. He looked, then put his eyes back in the binoculars. It took him a minute to relocate Josephine. What he saw made his throat seize. He rolled the focus wheel again to be sure. A black boy had stepped from the gym. He wore nothing but a pair of cutoff blue jean shorts, and Josephine walked straight to him where he stood on the lawn. She put her head to his chest. He wrapped his arm around her.

That was all it took. In Shorty's mind, from that moment forward, it wasn't Willy Ledford that Josephine was dating behind his back. It was Stretch Hayes.

He let the binoculars fall to his chest. He wondered if he ought to stick his finger down his throat to rid himself of this sickness. Then he wondered if he ought to come right down the mountain and shoot Stretch Hayes in the face.

It was the second idea that took.

Wimpy watched him unsling his rifle and start down the hill. 'He's got his gun out,' he told Dimple. 'He's on the move.'

They followed, their boot soles quiet against the ground.

Fifty yards down, Shorty found the source of the rustling sound. High up the trunk of a giant black locust tree, a family of black bears played. Shorty counted four young cubs. They circled each other, playing peek-a-boo around the thick tree's middle. Behind some leaves, on a sturdy limb, their mother sprawled, tired in the shade. Her balance was magnificent. Shorty reckoned she must have weighed four hundred pounds.

A sow that size would make a prize kill.

He raised his rifle.

Up the ridge, Dimple and Wimpy had stopped moving when Shorty did. 'What's he looking at now?' Dimple asked.

It took ten seconds for Wimpy to locate the bears in his own eyepiece. By that time, Shorty had raised his weapon. 'Oh hell,' Wimpy said. He dropped the binoculars to the ground and unslung his Winchester. As best he could through the tree cover, he centered the ivory bead on Shorty Maynard's head.

'Hold on a minute,' Dimple whispered.

In Wimpy's mind was a singular question. Could he rightfully kill a man over that man's aim to kill a bear? It took only a second to know. If that bear was a mother of four, the answer was yes. Wimpy put his finger on the trigger.

'Hold on,' Dimple said. He'd picked up the binoculars and surmised the situation. 'He lowered his gun.'

It was true. At the moment Shorty Maynard was about to squeeze his trigger, just before the moment Wimpy would have squeezed his, something had happened. The big sow had moaned and scratched at her eye with a paw. The way she sounded, the way she moved, somehow matronly and not unlike his own mother – it unsettled Shorty, and then it settled him back again. For a moment, his anger went missing. The smallest cub made its way to the sow. Shorty couldn't fire. He didn't have it in him.

He slung the rifle back over his shoulder and hiked up the ridge, where he'd crest and go down the other side, the picture in his mind playing over and over again – Stretch Hayes wrapped around his only daughter. He took out a half-pint of Old Grand-Dad and drank, fast.

Coming down the other side, Dimple and Wimpy didn't speak. They'd decided to leave the bears be, though both had wanted a closer look.

Wimpy was on edge. Every chipmunk scurry pricked his neck hairs. Every birdsong rang sinister. They were halfway down when he said, 'I believe I ought to have kilt Shorty Maynard just then.'

Dimple regarded the hillside creek. Its bed was the color of rust. 'That ain't the smartest thing you've said.'

'Well,' Wimpy answered. 'Might've saved the world some trouble, if I had kilt him.'

'Might've,' Dimple said.

Orb was the first to spot one. He was following the dogs as they sniffed the edges of the newly planted field. Tug wandered to the base of a nearby maple tree and started snouting something he'd found there. The dog sneezed and shook his head. When Orb walked over to see what it was, he noticed that the tree trunk was covered in what looked like wood roaches. But these were a lighter brown, and they weren't moving, except for one. He leaned in close. They were empty shells, split husks of some creature he'd never encountered. High up, one pulled itself from its shell and emerged a sickly pale color. It was red-eyed and cripple-winged.

Orb craned his neck. Up the trunk there were more, but these weren't pale in color. They were black with golden wings. Their eyes were red as blood. Up higher, they were everywhere.

Orb had read Exodus. He'd listened to Staples preach on Moses stretching his hand over Egypt. To him, these bugs meant hell was about to break loose.

He ran and whistled for the dogs to follow.

Dimple was down the hill, working the foot pedal on a grindstone. He took swallows from a tin cup and spat water in a line to the sandstone. He touched the blade of his axe there and ground a new bevel. When Orb came running his direction, dogs trailing, Dimple laid off the pedal.

He thumbed the axe bevel and chunked it into the top of a fencepost he was mending. He regarded the boy, his strange hollering. When he got within ten yards, Dimple could make out what he said.

'Locust plague! Locust plague!'

Dimple put in a wad of tobacco. 'Slow er down,' he said. The boy's voice was cracking wild, his long legs clumsy as a foal.

The dogs were in a strange state. They preferred a calm Orb to an excited one. They whipped their heads and nipped at one another. Tug hadn't stopped sneezing.

Wimpy was further down the hill, helping Mack split telephone wires. He heard Orb and ran up to him, shirtless. His chest hair had gone white. 'You say you seen a locust swarm?' he asked.

'They invaded a tree.' Orb was out of breath.

'Show me,' Wimpy answered.

Dimple shook his head.

When they got there, Wimpy took his time examining the shells. He crouched and worked his way from the bottom up. He crushed an empty husk in his fingers and blew it to the wind. On his tiptoes, he reached for a live one and cupped it. It banged around inside his hand and called a fast chirp, low and steady.

'It'll bite you,' Orb said.

'These ain't locusts. These is cicadas.' Wimpy smiled as he opened his palm and the cicada walked slow to his fingertip. 'Can't hurt a thing,' he said.

'Where did they come from?' Orb had his hand to his brow. He searched the sky above.

'Wrong way,' Wimpy said. He pointed to the ground. 'They come up through them holes. Happens ever seventeen years.'

Orb dropped to his knees and began sticking his finger in the holes he found. They were quarter-sized, some a little bigger. Mounds of dirt encircled their dark openings.

Above, more cicadas began to call. 'This is only the beginning,' Wimpy said. 'Couple weeks, you won't be able to spit without hittin one.'

Orb wore an expression of marvel. He had found something besides marbles to pass the time.

He took off his shirt and had Wimpy hoist him to his shoulders. There, he scraped as many cicadas as he could reach into the shirt, cinched it, and headed for home. 'I've got to make a box,' he said.

He passed Dimple on the way. He was sitting on a big flat rock, an open canteen in his hand. 'Too old to play with bugs, Orb,' Dimple said.

JULY 1967

Chester was out at the Ringer circle again. He'd had enough of Orb's library book on cicadas. It had to be the most boring book ever printed, *The Periodical Cicada*. Orb hardly got his marbles out of the bag since he'd borrowed it. He spent most days inside the four-man tent he'd pitched on the lawn. Zippered up inside, reading his book, a hundred or more cicadas humming and circling him. They hung from the tent ceiling and absorbed the sun's heat. They mated. They spoke to Orb, and he read aloud to them, words like *singing apparatus* and *enlarged genital hooks*.

He'd named his favorite, the biggest among them. Crawly Slowpoke Junior he called the cicada with a bent wing.

Chester toed the line and shot his taw. His game was solid. A boy from Beech Creek shook his head and knew he'd lose.

The VFW Marble Tournament was coming up in a week, and this was Chester's last year of eligibility. Orb's too. Neither had ever entered the tournament. Chester didn't want to be the one to integrate it, and Orb had always said he just didn't want to.

Everybody had known for years that he could win easy and go to Nationals. Maybe win there too. But now his game was rusty on account of the cicadas, and he'd turned fourteen. By next year's tournament, he'd be too old to compete.

Chester's opponent watched his stranded shooter gleaming in the sun. He wasn't allowed inside the circle as long as Chester kept up his streak. He'd been sticking kids for a week, running the table.

He shot the last of the marbles out of the circle, lined up the other boy's taw, and knocked it clear to the grass.

'You're damn near as good as Orb,' the boy said. He was barefoot and shirtless. Folks said he had bedbugs. He gathered his marbles, bagged them, and offered the bag to Chester.

Chester shook his head. 'We ain't playing keepsies,' he said.

The boy smiled. 'You ever play against Ham Maynard?'

Nobody called him Hambone anymore. Just Ham. He was nose tackle on the Junior High football team. He'd won the VFW Marble Tournament three years straight. 'No,' Chester said.

'He's the best I've seen.' The boy picked his nose and flicked boogers at the Ringer circle. 'He won fourteen dollars at Shuffie's pool hall last week.'

Chester looked at the smoke from the factory stack. It was tinted red by the rays of the fading sun, thick but see-through.

'You hear about Ham's sister Josephine?'

Chester didn't answer. He bent to tie his sneaker lace.

The boy went on. 'She got both her eyes blacked. Swole shut. Everybody says it was her daddy that done it.'

'The police man?' Chester said. The cicada chorus heightened. The boys had to shout to be heard.

'Mean son of a bitch,' the boy said. He tossed his marble bag in the air and caught it behind his back.

Chester said, 'See you later,' and walked for Orb's tent.

Over at the chapel, Harold and Ledford dusted the pews and swept the floor. Paul Maynard tended to Staples. He was in bed with a fever, and they didn't want him getting up. They'd unplugged his television the night before. Riots raged in the streets of Newark, and Staples stared at the screen for hours, turning the knob and sweating through his nightshirt, muttering about the end of days.

He slept, and Paul Maynard sat in a ladderback chair reading the paper.

At four, on break from the furnace, Stretch Hayes brought by a Thermos of onion soup. He handed it to Paul. 'I didn't feel like soup today,' he said. Stretch's mother had always claimed onions would sweat out a fever. She'd fed it to him as a boy, and now he made it for her each

391

night, hoping to bring her back from where she'd gone. Deathbed, just like Staples.

Paul nodded a thank you.

'Is he going to pull through?' Stretch asked. Behind him, the dogs ran free, snapping at the air, their teeth clacking a trail behind the wings of brave cicadas.

'Oh yes,' Paul said. He watched relief on the young man's face. 'Don't you worry Son,' he told him.

Harold finished sweeping and walked the length of the aisle. The lectern was chip-edged and wobbly. It was the same one he'd stood behind as a boy. Now he was back, thoroughly schooled, but more confused than he'd ever been on the ways of God and man. He stood at the podium and watched Ledford run a rag across faded pew seats. He was on his knees, wincing at the pain in his bad leg.

Harold wobbled the lectern and marveled at how small the chapel looked from up front. It had seemed so big as a boy. His parameters had changed. Inside a month, he'd been inside both the County Circuit Court and the State Supreme Court. He'd listened to the oaths bounce off the wide walls and vaulted ceilings. He'd been admitted to the practice of law.

In September, he'd be a general practitioner in the cramped Huntington office of Bob Staples.

Harold knew he'd be giving the sermon on Sunday, and he straightened his posture like he would when the seats were filled. Staples' cough echoed through the wall behind him. It was a weak sound from an old man, the only one left at Marrowbone who truly believed in the words of peace that parted his lips. Harold no longer believed in what folks called passive resistance, though he still championed its virtues in public.

He watched Ledford stand and wince and limp to the door. He imagined the Ledford he'd seen at Smalley's four years back, the muscles in his forearms popping as he pressed the cattle prod to the throat of a sinister man.

Behind him, Staples coughed some more. It mingled with the sound of the dogs barking outside, and the cicada calls crested again, and Harold couldn't imagine a single thing of use to tell those who would soon come to worship with him.

SEPTEMBER 1967

Stretch Hayes tipped a one-hundred-pound bucket of cullet into the hole. It roared and kicked a cloud of dust. He'd forgotten to put on his safety glasses.

Ledford watched from the corner, where he cleaned a handmade taw. He checked his watch. Forty minutes since the last load. Stretch was running slow.

Ledford walked over and said, 'Why don't you knock off early this evenin.'

'Thanks,' Stretch said. His eyes were bloodshot from crying, and his hands were shaky. It was only the day before that he'd buried his mother. It had been four days since she'd suffered an aneurysm and died before Stretch could get to the hospital.

Ledford watched him go. Then he turned and eyeballed the furnace. It didn't take long to know it was too hot. There was no need to add striking colors. Every marble in this batch would have its color burnt out.

Ledford re-angled the fans and adjusted the line knob. He inspected the marbles coming off the rollers. They were dull. Some had cold rolls.

He'd let the factory get away from him.

He couldn't even recall why he'd built it in the first place. It seemed secondary now, a day job. An office.

When he'd gotten the temperature right, Ledford sat in a folding chair and stared inside the belly of the furnace. His feet propped on a worktable, he reclined and let the heat from the hole radiate through the soles of his shoes. He unfocused his eyes like he had as a youngster, then closed them and watched the pictures dance. He imagined Shadrach, Meshach, and Abednego stepping into Nebuchadnezzar's furnace and then stepping back out unscorched. Staples had once told their story so convincingly, but Ledford never truly believed such stories. They were made up to see folks through hard times.

The room around him hummed, fans and fire. On the workbench was a table lamp carved from driftwood. Wimpy had made it with his paring knife. It formed the face and long beard of a mountain man. When he'd accepted it as a gift, Ledford had asked, 'Is it John Brown?'

'Hell no,' Wimpy had answered. 'That's big Ben Chicopee.'

On the pegboard behind the lamp were framed pictures of Rachel and Mary and Willy and Orb. Harold too. Baby pictures and younger years. Everybody was smiling. The frames that held them were lined with dust, and the braided wire they hung on was frayed. Ledford had looked at these photographs every day for thirteen years, and each time he did, he remembered the empty walls of his Mann Glass office. Somehow, both places smelled the same.

He stood and stepped to the furnace hole. He held his hand so close that the hairs on his fingers curled, then ceased to be.

A cicada walked along the brick face of the furnace. Ledford wondered why it didn't ignite and turn to ash. He wondered how it could still be alive, all the others having perished two months back, their life spans predetermined, predictable.

The cicada lighted on the chairback and went still. Ledford watched it watching him. There were black pinpoints in the middle of its red eyes. The gold legs matched the wings, tucked into a pyramid against the cicada's back. One wing was bent, and it was the biggest cicada Ledford had ever seen. He had an idea.

It crawled onto his finger and he carried it to the workbench. There, it settled onto the hardwood surface. Ledford grabbed a jar full of brad nails and picked one out. It wasn't much wider than a needle. He stuck it through the back of the cicada and tapped the top with a cross-peen hammer. It stayed put, working its tiny legs to gain ground that was no longer there. The bug was nailed down solid.

Ledford went to get his clay and boxwood tools. He would carve its likeness.

If it was to fit inside a playing marble, his cicada figure could be no larger than one half inch. He knew that most thought sulphides were useless as shooters, that the air bubbles around the figures inside caused cracking. But Ledford had mastered the art of making marbles by hand, and if he could pull this one off, Orb would have a taw that truly suited him, one that would bring him back to Ringer.

Mack Wells walked in as Ledford sculpted the wings. He regarded Ledford, bent over the workbench, an old jeweler's loupe stuck in his eyesocket. He held it there by scrunching his face. Mack leaned over his shoulder. 'You a strange man,' he said.

'I'll be with you in just a second.' Ledford had a cutter tool in one hand and a wood rib in the other. He finished the wing and put them down. Switched off the desk lamp and dropped the loupe lens in his shirtpocket.

Mack pointed to the nailed-down cicada. 'Don't think he's going to win the race,' he said. The little legs still worked to find their footing.

'I'm making a new sulphide for Orb.'

Mack had assumed Orb was done with marbles, that he'd outgrown them. 'Cicada sulphide,' he said. 'First one in history?'

'I doubt it,' Ledford answered.

The fans quit running. It was suddenly quiet inside the factory. 'Damned power went out again,' Mack said.

Ledford shook his head and turned to his clay cicada. He wondered if he could finish it without the lamplight.

'The Packard's ready to go,' Mack said. 'I cleaned

397

up your pistons, replaced the one with the cracked skirt. Got you some new compression rings.'

'I appreciate it.'

'Stretch Hayes helped me out. That boy has come to know a car.' Mack made shapes in the floor dust with the toe of his shoe. There were mouse droppings mixed in. 'You think he's all right?'

'I think he will be,' Ledford said.

'I'm afraid he's a tickin bomb.' Mack thought of Harold, home now, but still far away in the way he talked and looked at things. Mack cracked his knuckles. 'When you going to get yourself a new automobile?' he asked.

'When they make one as fine as the Packard.'

'They do,' Mack said. 'It's called the Studebaker.'

'Does it have suicide doors?'

'Now what the hell does that matter?'

The power came back, and the fans' rotation built, and inside the roar, the two men stood and stared at the insect crucified on the workbench. Its legs slowed, and its wings twitched, and finally, it was still.

OCTOBER 1967

O n the stoop of a secondhand plumbing store, the proprietor and his sons stood and watched people file into Douglass High School. Above the gymnasium door was a sign that read *Grand Opening: Carter G. Woodson Community Center.* One of the man's sons asked him, 'Why there so many white folks?'

The man shrugged. He had a can of black paint in his hand. 'Steady the ladder,' he told his sons. When he got to the top, he dipped his brush and touched up one of the twenty hand-painted signs covering the old house. *We Cut and Thread Pipes While Your Waiting* it read. Below him, the boys paid little attention to the creaking ladder. There was too much happening across the street. A blue school bus had just pulled up.

It was bitter cold for that time of year.

Inside, J. Carl Mitchum stood on the stage and thanked the Neighborhood Youth Corps for their help in getting the center ready. 'These young men and women have found that the value of work goes beyond monetary compensation,' he said. He thanked the country's poverty commission for their help, though many in attendance knew such help was reluctant and slow. There was not a single politician present. 'And,' J. Carl said, 'I'd like to thank the Marrowbone Marble Company for their significant contributions, of both the financial and sweat varieties.'

He pointed out the Ringer circle and the Ping-Pong table in the corner, and when he finished speaking, people milled around the gym, eating ham biscuits and cupcakes and signing their names to paper lists meant to mobilize. The center would offer typing classes and legal advice.

There was an old, duct-taped heavy bag hung in the corner. Little boys beat on it with their fists, then blew on scraped knuckles. A man held his baby girl up to the speed bag and pushed her fat hands against it. She laughed at the way it swung to and fro. Orb and Chester inspected the Ringer circle and eyeballed the crowd for any marble players.

After the cicadas had all died off, Orb found himself rusty inside the circle. He hadn't yet discovered his old delivery, and he was afraid to use his new cicada taw. He didn't want it to shatter.

Chester pointed to the bleachers stacked against the wall and said, 'I bet you I could backflip off that. Bet you them little boys would pay to see it.'

Willy and Stretch stepped outside for a smoke. They watched the man across the street repaint his signs. Willy pointed to one. *We Buy Sell or Swap Anything.* 'You really think he means anything?' he asked. 'Think you can swap knives and guns?'

'He ain't got no guns,' Stretch said. He pointed to the corner. 'You seen my house since Mom died?'

Willy shook his head no. They walked down Tenth Avenue to the corner of Sixteenth Street. They had their coat collars up to keep out the cold.

Stretch pointed east to a brown brick two-story. 'Bank owns it now,' he said. He'd moved out to Marrowbone full time.

'Looks empty,' Willy said. The windows were shuttered with plywood.

Stretch crossed the street and Willy followed. Cars howled by and paid them no mind.

They circled the house. Stretch knocked on the plywood as if someone might still be inside. A length of downspout hung loose at the back corner and he kicked it free.

In the alley, four boys pitched nickels on the apron of a rotten garage. Stretch knew one of them. 'What's goin on, Larry?' he said.

They all looked sideways at Willy and went back to the game.

A middle-aged man in a torn toboggan walked over from the housing projects. His limp reminded Willy of his daddy's. The man walked in front of a slow-moving car as if he hadn't seen it. 'Loose squares,' he was calling as he came. 'Who need loose squares?'

The nickel pitchers ignored him.

'I'll take one,' Willy said.

Stretch gave him a look.

'A quarter,' the man said.

'A quarter?' Willy knew better. 'I'll give you a dime.'

'Fifteen cent.'

Willy handed over the change. The man pulled a small brown Ball jar from his coat pocket and fished out a cigarette.

He hollered at passing cars as he left, 'Loose squares, who need em?'

One of the nickel pitchers stood and told Willy, 'You better off throwing that fifteen cent on the ground right here so I can take it.' His fingertips were gray from playing. 'Don't you know that man soaks his cigarettes in cat pee?' he said.

Willy sniffed the cigarette and all the boys laughed.

Stretch was the first to stop. He said, 'You all know about the community center across the street?'

'What about it?'

'It's open,' Stretch said. 'Basketball, boxing, help with your schoolwork. Marbles.' The word sounded juvenile on the air. He wished he hadn't said it. 'You shoot marbles like you pitch them nickels, you'll be doin all right.'

'Marbles?' one of the boys said. He hooked his thumbs in the pockets of his blue jeans. 'We don't play no marbles.'

'You can lay bets on Ringer just like you can lay bets on anything,' Willy said.

The tallest boy frowned. 'What you know about layin bets pecker-wood?' he said.

'Plenty,' Willy answered.

Stretch told them to have a good one and he and

Willy walked back across Sixteenth Street. 'Better watch your mouth around here,' Stretch said. 'How the hell you even know what loose squares was?'

'I know a lot of things,' Willy said. He'd learned some of them from Fury, who'd sent him six letters from Vietnam, each one more erratic than before.

Up ahead, the plumbing-store proprietor was showing Ledford a set of four tires. 'Lightly used,' he was saying. 'Uniroyals, good rubber.' He stuck a penny in the tread and half of Lincoln's head disappeared. 'See?' he said.

Ledford turned to Mack. 'Got room for em in the bus?'

Mack said he did.

'I'll take em,' Ledford said. They shook hands and Ledford looked around the yard at the other wares for sale. Bathtubs and sinks were everywhere. There were toilets and smokestacks lining the house's foundation. Pipes blackened by weather leaned against the siding and reached almost to the roof. Ledford spotted a hand-crank wringer-washer like the one from his boyhood home. He walked over and turned it, watched the teeth line up and roll. For a moment, he considered sticking his hand inside to see what would happen.

Orb had gotten inside an old clawfoot tub on the side lawn. He looked as though he might fall asleep there. Chester was climbing a four-holed industrial sink leaning vertical against the house. When he got to the top, he back-flipped to the ground below as the two boys who'd steadied their father's ladder looked on, wide-eyed.

A police cruiser rolled past. The officers inside surveyed people as they filed from Woodson Community Center. They drove at a crawl and watched Mack and Ledford roll tires toward their blue Short Bus. They watched Orb sling his leg over the side of the tub. The officer in the passenger seat told his partner, 'See there, circus does come to nigger town.'

They laughed. In the backseat, Shorty Maynard was in street clothes. He liked to go for ride-alongs with Huntington officers. He called it 'jungle safari.'

They rolled past Stretch Hayes as he lit another cigarette. Shorty made a gun out of his hand and pointed it at Stretch. 'Circus is about to be shut down,' he said.

At sundown, the Short Bus was running hard. Mack put it to the floor coming up Knob Drop Road. 'Listen to that,' he said.

It sounded to Ledford like the engine might explode. He leaned over and eyeballed the needle. The drop-off was coming and Mack was still at fifty miles an hour. 'Drop-off's comin,' Ledford said.

'Damn right it is.' Mack didn't appreciate a back-seat driver, but he knew that when a man's family dies in an automobile crash, he's liable to be careful at the wheel. 'I'll slow er down,' Mack said. He let off the gas.

The seats of the bus were filled. Rachel pulled her coat under her legs. The Naugahyde was hard and cold. Lizzie shuffled cards. She and Rachel were playing high-low.

In the back, Willy watched the trees whip by. Orb and Chester watched Willy and tried to act like he did. 'Don't slow down so much,' Willy said.

'You think this is a airplane?' Mack shot them a look in the wide rearview. He had his eyebrows raised.

Chester said, 'What are you talking about?'

'The drop-off,' Willy told him. 'Dead man's curve.' He whispered to Chester and Orb, 'I can take it at thirty miles an hour.'

The tires banked a rut. Everyone shook in their seats. Ledford wondered what Willy whispered. He knew the boy drove the Packard too fast.

Mack slowed to fifteen by the time they got inside the hard right. The boys all craned at the window to see the drop-off. The new guardrail had already started to rust. There was a long black streak where some drunk fool had tested its strength.

Coming through the straight stretch, Mack counted two cars in the front yard of the Ray place, and the Rays didn't own but one. It sat where it always did, dead as ever. Trunk-popped and hawking goods. But the other one was a white Impala. 'You see that Impala?' Mack said.

Ledford had his eyes on. 'I see it.'

Mack pulled into the drive and shut off the bus.

W. D. Ray was standing by his wares, talking to Noah and Charlie Ball. All three squinted to see who had pulled in.

'Stay on the bus everybody,' Ledford said. He stepped from the open door. Mack did the same.

The drive was laid with fresh gravel. Ledford leaned into Mack as they walked. 'Who you think put in this rock?' he asked. Then he straightened up and waved a hand. 'Afternoon, Charlie, Noah. Mr Ray.' He nodded to each. They got in hand-shaking distance and Ledford stuck his in his pockets. 'I would say it was fancy seein you out here Charlie,' he said, eyes wide and leveled, 'but I reckon you can buy votes in any district.'

Charlie shot Noah a look. Word was out. Noah was making a run at the legislature. Charlie cleared his throat and said, 'Somebody's got to make things right out here.'

Ledford laughed. He produced his tobacco and stuck a plug in.

Mr Ray walked slow back to his porch.

Charlie breathed deep. 'Your laugh meant to suggest something, Ledford?' He was talking like he did to people who worked for him. He was puffing up. 'You think you're the man to make things right?'

'I think I'm thrice the man you are, for that or anything else,' Ledford said. 'I ought to run against Noah, whup him in the primary.'

The words had come quicker than Charlie expected. He searched for something to say.

Ledford tongued his plug. 'He won't step inside my polling booth, that's for certain.' Noah wouldn't meet Ledford's stare, so he turned it back to Charlie. 'You want me to spit on your shoes again Charlie?' he asked. 'If Shorty Maynard was here, he could draw his hanky and wipe it off, I'd imagine. Shine em while he's at it.'

There was silence, and the feeling that somebody might pull a gun.

Mack felt his blood surge. He'd not been this close to a fight in some time.

Charlie stepped forward like he was going to do something.

Ledford squared him up. 'You going to draw your sidearm like Shorty does?'

'He never did draw it,' Charlie said, spittle at the corners of his mouth.

'Had his hand on it though, didn't he?' Ledford winked at him.

Charlie's teeth were grit.

On the bus, Rachel shut her eyes. She prayed for silence. She prayed there'd be no gun clap. Beside her, Lizzie did the same.

Ledford turned to the open trunk of the rusted Chevy. Inside, black-stamped cardboard boxes had been split open at the seams. 'Chewing gum and coffee,' he said. 'Straight out of the box. Which one you buyin, Charlie?'

Charlie looked at Mack for the first time. He started to ask him what he was staring at, but thought better of it. 'I don't drink coffee and I don't chew bubble gum,' Charlie said.

'Then why you standin here for?' Mack said. 'I don't see no box in that trunk labeled *Ballots*.'

Charlie's lip quivered. He sniffed hard.

Mack told him, 'Say it. Say what you want to say to me.'

But Charlie Ball didn't say a word. He looked at Noah, then over at Mr Ray, and then he walked to his car.

Ledford smiled at Mack. 'Well, I guess we'd better move so these gentlemen can clear on out.' He waved at Mr Ray. 'Mr Ray, I believe we'll be talkin soon.'

Charlie was furious. It was time to talk to Shorty Maynard again, time to give the go-ahead.

Back on the bus, Mack swung the wheel as he reversed them onto the road. 'Good people of Marrowbone,' he said to them all, 'what kind of man doesn't drink coffee or chew gum?'

'A stupid one,' Chester hollered.

They all laughed. 'That's right,' Mack said. He'd backed up on Knob Drop to let the other two out. He wanted to see them drive away.

'A stupid son-of-a-bitching one,' Orb said.

They all laughed again, Willy the hardest.

Orb was straight-faced. Deadly serious, watching the Impala disappear down the hill.

'That's right Orb,' Ledford said. 'A stupid son-of-a-bitching one.' He'd never heard the boy speak such words. Orb was the one with an even temper. He turned to Mack at the wheel. 'Pull back in,' he told him.

Ledford walked alone to the Rays' front door. He carried a pressure cooker full of Lizzie's half-runners.

They'd forgotten to set them out at Douglass. When W.D. opened the heavy door, Ledford said, 'Forgot to give you these beans.'

Inside, it smelled of rotten wood and cornbread. Ledford sat down in a schoolroom chair. The desktop had been removed, but the metal arm stuck up sharp. He situated himself across from W.D. and said, 'Who laid your gravel?'

'I did.' W.D. snorted and looked behind him at the kitchen. 'Fix Loyal some coffee,' he said, but no one was there.

'Where'd you get the rock?'

W.D. didn't answer. His false teeth were in, and he worked his gums doubletime. He looked at his hands, stuck them in the pocket of his overalls. He looked at the broken clock on the wall, then turned to the kitchen again. 'Where is that damned woman with the coffee,' he said.

'W.D.,' Ledford said. 'You don't have to be afraid of the Ball boys, or Shorty Maynard either. I—'

'I ain't afriad of none a them,' W.D. shot back. 'Maybe at one time I was, but rapture's a comin, and those three have fire at their feet already.'

Ledford nodded. 'I believe you're right,' he said. Floorboards creaked above. A greasy yellow cat padded down the staircase. Ledford thought hard about what to say. 'Mr Ray, we've known each other a while now. You know what we've tried to do around here for folks that need it, folks that the Ball boys and Shorty Maynard have—'

'Look here Ledford,' W.D. said. Then he stood

up and walked to the front windows. He looked out between two flat squares of cardboard. Did the same at the side windows. He sat back down. Scratched at his white stubble. 'For years I been givin information to them three on who could be pushed around and who couldn't. I been tellin em things they wanted to hear, you know what I mean?' W.D. shook his head. 'And they give me money here and there, gravel, what have you. You know they give me a telephone?'

'No, I didn't.'

'A damned telephone. Paid for the man to come out and wire it up. Shorty Maynard said for me to ring him or Noah anytime I heard of something fishy over at your place. Wrote down their numbers for me, one of the numbers for emergency. Told me they'd pay me pretty good for that.' He shook his head again. 'I ain't never told em nothin on you, Ledford.' He was telling the truth. 'That's God's people you got over there.'

Ledford thanked him.

'I'm through with it,' W.D. said. 'All of it. What you done out here has changed things, far as I'm concerned.'

Ledford didn't know what to make of all the man had said.

'Listen,' W.D. said. He pointed to the phone where it hung on the wall. 'I ain't used that telephone but once, just to see. My fingers is too big for the holes.' He held up his knotty hands. 'Anyway, damned if that Shorty Maynard wasn't here in his police car in five minutes' time.' He laughed. 'Huey Church had stole from me, so I told him Huey was runnin moonshine, and I reckon he used that to go and scare the Churches, keep em in line and votin how they should.' He smiled. 'Keep em away from the likes a you,' he said. 'But I've had it by God. I'm too old for it.' He stomped his foot to the floor and smacked his knee.

Before Ledford left, he thanked Mr Ray for his time. 'You hold on to that pressure cooker,' he said. 'Rachel's got another one.' He told the old man not to rip his telephone out. To keep the Ball boys and Shorty Maynard close, let them think he was a pushover. 'You give em false information if you want to,' Ledford said, 'but keep em around.'

W. D. Ray stood tall as he waved to the bus from his porch. Rapture could wait a while. He was part of something.

The Keith-Albee Theatre seated two thousand, and when Willy walked the aisle on the Saturday before Halloween, every one of them was full. It was the midnight show. *Point Blank*. Folks had heard about Lee Marvin's role, how he wielded his gun like it grew from his hand. How he threw men off rooftops.

Stretch Hayes waved to Willy from the front row, where he'd saved him a seat. Next to Stretch was his brother, Clyde. He craned his neck at the screen. It was his first full day of parole. Inside the penitentiary they didn't show moving pictures, and to Clyde the color looked neon.

He didn't speak when introduced.

There was a coming attraction for *To Sir, With Love*. When Sidney Poitier's face filled the screen, someone in the middle rows hollered, 'Baboon!'

Clyde tore the ring-pull off his second can of beer and tossed it on the floor. He worked his jaw between swallows.

The crowd was young and rowdy. Halfway through the movie, someone threw a stink bomb vial at the wall.

By the time Lee Marvin punched a downed man in the balls, Clyde had drunk eight beers. 'That ain't how it is,' he said to Willy and Stretch. 'Don't no real punch sound like that.' He'd found flaw in gunshots and bloodspills all night.

On the movie screen, a black nightclub singer screamed his riffs. A few rows back, someone imitated a chimpanzee. Someone else let fly an egg. It smacked the screen and trickled down, slow and thick and yellow.

Clyde stood up and turned around. Two thousand empty faces. Another egg let fly. It broke against his Adam's apple and filled his shirt collar with yolk. 'Motherfucker,' Clyde said.

Two white boys stood up and ran.

'I know where your mommas live,' Clyde called after them.

'Sit down, nigger!' somebody yelled.

Clyde threw his beer on the floor and raised a hand to block the projector booth beam. Dust swirled, glinting here and there, the stirring of an invisible storm. 'Say it again!' Clyde called, searching the empty faces.

And it *was* said again, and another egg let fly – this time from the balcony – and soon enough, chairbacks were stepping stones and fists weren't picky.

Willy followed Stretch through the fire exit door. Stretch had followed Clyde, who'd opened the door with the face of a big, buzz-cut white boy who'd decided to take a swing. He'd missed. Now that boy was face down on the alley bricks, his letterman jacket soaking up a puddle, his nose cartilage refashioned.

He was the starting middle linebacker at Huntington East. His father was chief of police.

The alley spilled to the street, and Fourth Avenue became a stomping ground. Someone kicked the sideview off a Thunderbird, picked it up, and swung it against the back of Stretch's head. He dropped to his knees.

Willy got him by the armpits and they crossed Tenth Street, running.

Clyde was nowhere to be found.

Sirens sounded quick. The officers on duty had radioed when the first chair was jumped. Inside five minutes, there were seven squad cars in front of the theater.

By the time someone lobbed a brick through the

front window of Kiser's Drugstore, the police had donned riot helmets. Some gripped clubs and others shotguns. They moved east on Fourth Avenue, by car and by foot, and when they got to Sixteenth Street, one car headed south.

Shorty Maynard was on a ride-along, and he was happy to navigate.

He spotted Willy and Stretch in J. Carl Mitchum's front yard. The old man was pressing a handkerchief to Stretch's bleeding scalp. When the headlights lit them up, J. Carl stared down the beam. He was big, his white undershirt amplified. 'You boys go inside,' he said.

But they didn't go inside. Stretch turned and faced the car.

Next to Shorty in the backseat, the buzz-cut linebacker had stopped his own bleeding with a grease rag. 'That's him,' he intoned. He pointed a blood-streaked finger. 'That's the one that did it.' His daddy gunned the cruiser.

Stretch took off in the direction of Douglass Community Center. His logic was clouded by the hot buzzing inside his skull.

The tires on the squad car were bald in back. It fishtailed on the sidewalk and straightened, then bore down hard, tore two stripes on Douglass's front lawn before stopping a foot short of the door. It was there that Stretch Hayes pulled at the brass handles with no luck. He just kept pulling, as if the locks might decide to give, as if refuge was more than a word used by preachers.

Shorty Maynard was on him before Willy and J. Carl could cross the street.

Stretch turned from the door and faced him. 'You going to black my eyes shut like you did your daughter's?' he said.

Shorty swung his club and missed, Stretch slipping it like he would a boxing glove, his fists at the ready. The second swing caught him, put him on his knees. He threw a straight left that missed. Shorty's third swing put him to sleep.

The police chief and his buzz-cut boy held J. Carl and Willy off, kept them where they couldn't see. J. Carl tested the chief's resolve and walked toward the squad car. 'Don't take another step,' the chief said, his eyes fixed down the squat barrel of his revolver. J. Carl froze where he stood.

'Stretch?' Willy called, craning to see. 'Stretch?' He could only see the back of Shorty's head and shoulders, so tall above the roof of the car. It was the first time he'd seen him since he'd beaten up Josephine. Willy stared at that long neck and head, imagined those big hands striking Josephine. He wished for a moment that he carried a gun.

The blue and red lights spun on the squad car's roof, a beacon of fear to those peering through windows. Willy watched the mirrors and bulbs. They threw shadows on the bricks of the community center. The howl was relentless.

At nine p.m. on Halloween night, the raid came.

State policemen lined Marrowbone's main gate

and spoke through bullhorns. 'Step out of the house with your hands over your head,' they said. Dimple and Wimpy crouched on the floor in their longjohns. They peeked through the high window and surmised the number of men outside. They laid their rifles on the floor and did as they were told.

Up the Cut, Orb was running the dogs. They caught wind of the state police and came running, hard.

The dogs sensed a siege. From a hundred yards off, they saw Dimple and Wimpy on their knees, men in dark uniforms standing behind them.

When they leaped the creek by the lower foot-bridge, full bore and snarling, three officers opened fire. Jim-Jim, Doo-Dad, and Pug were struck in the head and neck.

They died where they fell before Orb could get there. Tug was hit in the back leg and retreated to the creek bed. Orb climbed down to him, held the dog while he whimpered, blood leaking slow into cold water.

Across front yards, the state police put people on their knees. They made neat lines of the residents of Marrowbone, careful to go easy on women and children. Ledford crept in the chicken coop's shadow, his .45 drawn. When he saw their number, he tucked the gun in along his spine, emerged, and demanded a warrant. One was produced, and Ledford went prone like the rest.

They caught Herchel in a circle beam of flashlight as he hacked at his marijuana plants with a hand axe. They hauled him off in cuffs.

They had proof that Marrowbone housed criminals.

Herchel looked at the ground as he stumbled along, barefoot and shirtless, gripped at the elbows. A trooper shined his light on Herchel's chest scar and stared. The skin there reflected light.

Orb was the only one Herchel glanced at. The boy's crying was too much to ignore. None had ever heard such a thing from Orb.

As he stepped into a squad car, Herchel nearly cried himself. They shut the door on him, and through the glass, he watched Orb go from one dog to the next where they lay on the ground. The boy bent and put his ear to each one, but there was nothing.

Tug followed alone, limping, Orb's shirt wrapping his back leg. He nudged each dog with his snout. They lay where they'd fallen, in a line across the cold crabgrass. Tug licked at their bloodied ears and lips.

When Orb stood up and buried his face in Rachel's sweater to quiet his cries, Tug stayed put, his eyes on his brother and sisters. He whined. He limped back and started down the line again, pushing his snout against each dead dog, certain they'd wake up soon enough.

FEBRUARY 1968

The carpet in Bob Staples' office was white, coffee stains marking a trail from door to desk. Reverend Thompson sat across from him in a highback leather chair, and beside him was Paul Maynard. Both would be character witnesses should Herchel or Stretch's arrests go to trial. The Reverend would speak on behalf of Marrowbone. Paul would do the same for Stretch Hayes.

Bob Staples and Harold did nothing but study case law and review the actions of the police. The rest at Marrowbone organized against a shutdown.

'These meetings and community marches ain't doing a goddamn thing for anybody,' Paul said. He looked at Reverend Thompson. 'No offense.'

'None taken.' The Reverend shifted in his seat. 'I wish your brother was well enough to soapbox, Bob. He'd whip up results.'

'I know it,' Bob said. 'I wish he was too.'

The West Virginia Human Rights Commission had backed J. Carl Mitchum. He'd accused the Huntington Police Department of brutality the night of the theater riot. The papers weren't listening. The accusation had not stuck.

418

Stretch was out on bond. His brother Clyde had decided to run. It wasn't the first time he'd broken parole.

In the office corner, Harold sat on the floor behind a semicircle of stacked paper. 'I got a woman here who saw Stretch Hayes on his knees when Shorty swung the club, but she won't testify to it.' He hadn't slept in two days.

Paul shook his head. 'None of that'll stick on Shorty,' he said. 'We got to go after him with bigger than that.' Lately, he'd been wishing he'd lined pockets like the rest of them. He didn't have friends in the state police. He couldn't get a warrant based on nothing but shared hatred.

'I think we've got to fight it out in the paper, on the nightly news,' Reverend Thompson said. 'Stand up for Marrowbone and what it's done for people.'

The results of the raid were disheartening. The local news had been calling Marrowbone a Communist training ground full of dope-smoking beatniks. Some residents and already moved away. Mrs Wells and Herb were among them. They wanted nothing to do with such trouble.

Talks with the SCLC and Martin Luther King had been stalled by word of a drug bust. Marrowbone was no longer a stop for the Poor People's Campaign.

Paul Maynard looked at the floor. He twiddled his thumbs. He knew that scared black witnesses and newspaper editorials were useless. He knew his nephew had to be dealt with in blood.

MARCH 1968

Wimpy's stomach wasn't right. It was making sounds of the squeaking variety and he feared he'd shit himself if he let one rip. The fire trots, as he called them, were back again. They often accompanied trouble, frayed nerves.

He sat inside the outhouse, reading a beat-up copy of *Letters from the Earth*. Morning sun shone through the cut half-moon on the door and illuminated the open book. Something moved there, cast a shadow on his page across the word *microbe*. Wimpy looked up.

A cicada traversed the moon's edge.

'Hello there,' Wimpy said. 'Where did you come from?'

A cloud covered up the sun. Next to the cicada, a splinter of wood twitched in the wind. The little bug turned to face him, its red eyes like drops of blood. Wimpy had an uneasy feeling. 'Party's over,' he said. 'You're a year late.'

He finished up and followed the cicada to where it flew. He lost sight of it out front of the house.

Dimple was there, working a posthole digger at

the parking lot's edge. The floods had eroded another chunk of land. He wiped sweat from his nose with a hanky. 'Gettin too damned old,' he said to his brother, but Wimpy looked past him to the gate. 'What is it?' Dimple said. 'What the hell you lookin at like that?'

Wimpy didn't answer. His face had lost its color, and he walked past his brother, on out to the gate. He stood and stared at what he saw there.

Dimple followed. A cicada flew around the gatepost, then off to the trees behind the burying ground. Dimple leaned in close next to his brother. Together, they examined the tiny clawed feet perched on the crossrail. 'What in the devil?' Dimple said.

Wimpy reached out as if to touch the things, their points stuck in the wood, their lengths sticking up where a body should have been. He stopped short.

Dimple pointed. 'Is that foot missin a toe?'

It was the left. 'This was the redbird I told you about,' Wimpy said. He couldn't understand what he saw. 'Do you think somebody shot him?'

'No,' Dimple said. He leaned in closer. Sniffed. 'There ain't no smell of birdshot. Looks to me like something ate him, left the feet behind.'

Wimpy was certain the cicada had led him there. And now, in the trees beyond the burying ground, he could hear more of them, grinding their call – crying, it seemed to Wimpy. Orb's book had confirmed that cicadas only came once in seventeen years, but here they were again. The book said they did not eat trees or plants like some supposed, but only struck egg slits in saplings and small bushes. In fact, the book said cicadas did not consume a thing, but here was the redbird, eaten alive.

It was beyond peculiar, the little feet on the gatepost. Both brothers studied them for some time. Wimpy regarded them as a sign, but he didn't know what of.

Neither spoke a word.

A car kicked mud and came fast down the road. Dimple walked back to his repair site. He'd left his shotgun and binoculars there.

He put the binoculars to his eyes and had a look. 'Erm's Cadillac,' he said.

When it got within fifty yards, the Cadillac finally slowed. It stopped at the gate. The front bumper hung loose on one side. There was an imprint on the hood in the shape of a man.

The car whined in neutral, and the door swung open. Fury stepped out, dirty and bearded. His hair grew to his shoulders. He'd lost twenty pounds.

'Morning, fellas,' Fury said. In his waistband was a little Colt .25. 'Anybody up for playin cards around here?' He laughed. Then he went straight-faced, his hollow eyes flinching. He turned and looked at the trees as if they might uproot and come after him. 'Is Ledford around?' he asked.

Inside the factory, Fury sat down on the workbench, his skinny ankles dangling pale from his pantlegs. He blinked incessantly while he spoke, and everybody could smell his foul breath. Mack and Ledford exchanged a look. They recognized a man in love with morphine.

'So I ran as fast as I could from Uncle Sam after that,' Fury said. He'd been chronicling his tour in Vietnam. His injury after walking into a trip wire, his decision that the war was wrong. 'And wouldn't you know it,' he said, itching at his filthy beard, 'I came back to Chicago and found nothing but more war.' Uncle Fiore had been shot and killed in his toolshed. Erm was running scared. 'The only thing that's kept Dad alive in the last ten years is Uncle Fiore,' Fury said. 'Now that he's gone, it's open season on Dad.'

Ledford threw a hunk of wet newspaper in the wastebasket. He wiped his hands on his overalls. 'And you took his car?'

'Probably not the best idea,' Fury said. He smiled. His teeth were yellow.

'Where is your daddy now?' Mack asked. He didn't trust the Bacigalupos. He didn't want them around.

'I don't know,' Fury said.

Stretch came in the back door and took his place at the welder's table. He pulled the mask over his head and torched up.

Fury twitched at the sound of combustion. He bit at his lip. 'Listen,' he said. 'I have seen things with my eyes closed, things that changed me.' He chuckled. 'I talked to God,' he said. He looked from Ledford to Mack and back to Ledford. 'Listen.' He shook his head and took a deep breath. 'Dad's all torn up about this land deal with Charlie Ball. He wants to come clean, but he doesn't know how.'

'What are you talkin about?' Ledford said.

'The land development deal. It's all fallen through. Dad had wanted to build a racetrack out here, be your neighbor, but it turns out Charlie Ball gambled away the money.'

Ledford glared at the young man. He wondered if he was being set up.

Fury rocked back and forth, knocked over a jar of brads. 'Sorry,' he said. 'I run off at the mouth a lot.' He gathered up the nails. His fingers shook.

Mack and Ledford looked at one another again.

Ledford said, 'Are you tellin me Erm was in cahoots with Charlie Ball behind my back?'

Fury grimaced and clutched at his stomach. 'Where's the restroom?' he managed.

Mack pointed to the back. Fury hopped down from the table and ran.

When Ledford kicked open the door two minutes later, Fury was sitting on the floor with his belt around his biceps, a needle stuck in the crook of his arm. He smiled with his eyes closed.

Staples was bedridden, didn't have much breath left to draw. But he liked to be kept abreast of developments. Rachel, Mary, and Lizzie tended to him most, alternating blocks of hours, watching him sleep and wheeze and waste away.

On a Monday afternoon, it was Lizzie's shift. She pressed a cold washcloth to his forehead and said,

'So, Ledford explained to the young man that dope isn't allowed out here. He and Mack searched the car, the duffel inside it, the clothes. They flushed what they found and stomped on his needle plungers.'

Staples nodded. 'Good,' he managed. 'Good.'

Lizzie looked out the window. A cold front was coming in. The tree limbs swayed. 'I mean, can you imagine? That young man showin up with drugs, after they hauled Herchel outta here?' She shook her head. 'They've got him locked up in Willy and Orb's room. Keepin a watch on him, lettin him sweat out the demons.'

Staples' chest rose and fell slow. 'What's happening with the case?' he asked.

'Nothing,' Lizzie said. 'Your brother has done a fine job. Harold is learning from him every day.' Wind whistled through the doorjamb. She turned to him. 'Bob thinks that warrant was bogus. He thinks the raid, Herchel's arrest, all of it will be thrown out just like they threw out Stretch's.' Harold had subpoenaed police department shift logs and proved that Shorty Maynard was not approved for ride-alongs, much less baton swinging. Stretch was cleared of all charges.

'Good,' Staples said. 'Law.' He believed in it. He closed his eyes.

Lizzie felt the washcloth. It was no longer cold. She stood and ran water in the sink. Looked out the window again.

Up the Cut, inside Willy and Orb's room, Fury

had awakened. He was naked, a film of dried sweat on his skin. He was alone in the room.

The door was locked. He tried the window. It gave. He'd waited long enough.

Dimple and Wimpy were the first to spot him. Fury leaped from the window to the porch roof, then rolled off and hit the ground hard. He got to his feet and ran past the dog kennel at a speed none knew he possessed. He wore no clothes, his parts exposed and jostling for all to see. Dimple gathered his reins and turned Silver to the west. 'That boy's naked as a jaybird,' he said.

He made a clucking sound and took off across the footbridge, Wimpy in tow on Boo.

They got to him at woods' edge. Dimple rode close and kicked Fury to the ground. He got up and they circled him. Wherever he turned, they blocked his route. 'Give it up,' Wimpy told him.

After a while, he did.

That night, the worst came. When they'd secured Fury on the bed again, a fever gripped him. The Ledfords watched him through the night, twitch-fits grabbing hold and cold sweats coming every half hour. Rachel melted six ice cubes on his head and neck alone. Mary cinched more in a dishrag and pressed it to his belly. Willy and Orb watched from the open doorway to their bedroom. Fury was red-streaked, diagonal. Like war paint, Orb thought. Zebra stripes the color of scabs.

Down the hall, Ledford slept hard. He'd been up two straight nights with Fury. Had felt it was his duty. 'He's my godson after all,' he'd told Rachel.

Now, while the rest of the family tended, Ledford got locked inside a nightmare. Fury's talk of gook ears and land mines had brought it on. Never had Guadalcanal visited him like this. He could smell it, and he could feel it on his skin. Effluvium, rotten fish, mildew. 'Atabrine! Atabrine!' someone shouted incessantly. Then there was McDonough, who was dressed in civilian attire. White shirt, collar buttoned tight, the veins in his neck swollen and pulsing. 'I can't breathe,' McDonough said. 'Put a hole in me.' Then he laughed and his face turned dark and he said, 'Have you kneeled at the feet of the Lord? Have you called on him since they nailed him up there?' He pointed and Ledford turned to look. There was nothing but a hillside of mud, a hundred or more people crouched on its face. 'Asses and elbows,' McDonough said. It was all you could see – bent backs, bottoms of feet. The people wobbled and twitched. They were digging holes in the ground.

Ledford asked what they were digging for and got no answer. He turned back to McDonough, who said, 'Dig for ticks.' Then, just as it had on the banks of the Matanikau River, McDonough's face exploded.

Ledford screamed and sat up in bed.

Down the hall, Fury sat up in the same instant. His eyes were shut and he mumbled something about rain. Rachel pressed him back to the bed. His skin was hot to the touch, his voice hoarse and dry. 'Shhhhhh, shhhhh,' Rachel said.

Tears welled in Mary's eyes. She walked to the hall and sat against the wall. The ceiling fixture hummed above her. There were air bubbles behind the wallpaper.

Willy and Orb went to the kitchen and came back with a pillowcase full of marbles. An hour prior, they'd drenched it in tap water, filled it with old marbles and stuck it in the icebox. Orb had come up with the idea. Now it crackled and unstuck as they rolled it onto Fury's chest, frozen glass spreading like chain mail. Fury wheezed.

Ledford stepped into the room. There was hatred in his eyes. He stepped to the bedside and leaned in close on Fury. He studied the young man's face. Sniffed him. He took a wad of Fury's beard in his fingers and began to sift through. It took only a minute before he found it on the chin, swollen to the size of a grape, its head burrowed deep. 'Get me my tweezers from the hall closet,' Ledford said.

When he yanked the tick, blood burst and dotted Ledford's fingers. It dripped from the ends of Fury's beard and gathered at his collarbone.

Ledford set the tick down in an oversized yellow-glass ashtray on the nightstand. Fury grit his teeth and his fever surged again.

Ledford said, 'Willy, go to the Bonecutters. Tell them how it's gotten.'

Willy ran hard. His sneakers pounded cold ground and the thump of his heart reminded him of training days. A board on the footbridge cracked under his weight.

428

Something caught his eye at the edge of Herchel's garden. There was a glint in the moonlight, and Willy stopped dead to eyeball it. Ground-cover rustled, and someone ran for the woods. For a moment, Willy thought about running after them, but Fury was burning alive, and he'd have to let it go.

Dimple said he'd ride the ground's perimeter. Wimpy mounted Boo bareback and Willy swung on behind him.

When they got there, Wimpy dismounted and walked quick to the backyard. At the dogwood tree, he took out a Buck knife and a tin cup. Scraped at the bark until he had enough.

In the kitchen, he boiled water and infused the dogwood scrapings. He followed Willy to the bedroom, the tea balanced gingerly in a soup bowl.

They all watched as Fury choked and gasped on the steaming concoction, Wimpy forcing it on him. It seemed that more spilled down his jaw than got inside, but Wimpy assured them it would do. Mary turned away. She wouldn't watch a man drown in a scald of bitter water.

When he'd finished with the tea, Wimpy stood. He took both of Fury's hands in his own. 'My grandmother was a fever doctor,' he said. 'I seen her do this more than once.' He looked at each of them. 'If you don't like it, leave.' Wimpy closed his eyes and squeezed Fury's hands until the knucklebones knocked together. He seemed to shudder just as his patient did.

Willy stood in the open doorway, Rachel and

429

Mary just inside. Orb moved closer to watch. He held his daddy's hand.

Wimpy tucked his chin to his chest. He made a grunting sound. Then, looking up at the ceiling, he said, 'There came a angel from the east bringing fire and frost. *Go in*, frost. *Go out*, fire.' His voice grew louder. 'In frost, out fire.' It seemed to reverberate off the windows and walls. 'Go *in*, frost. Go *out*, fire.'

They watched as the crimson stripes disappeared. The color of Fury's face went from red to almost pale. His wheezing seemed to settle and the tendons in his neck relaxed.

'Good Lord,' Rachel said.

Mary had her hands to her face. For a moment, she thought Wimpy had killed the young man.

'How did you do that?' Orb asked. He was squeezing Ledford's hand so hard his fingertips went numb.

Wimpy did not answer. 'Leave him be now,' he said. 'He's got to sleep for a day or more.' He did not tell them that the fever was the hottest he'd encountered, nor did he tell them of his fear that when Fury awoke, he'd not be the same man. Wimpy looked at the dead tick in the yellow ashtray. 'You burn that,' he said. 'I don't care how dead it is. You burn it.'

The insects of Marrowbone were coming after them now. Wimpy was certain of it. Out of the ground and the trees they came, marking the land and its people with their signs.

APRIL 1968

The walrus-tusk knitting needles had been snapped in two. Like dry branch kindling, they'd broken and splintered so as never to be repaired. Rachel bent to the ground and thumbed the sharp edges. She found them this way, out of the bag where she'd left them when the kitchen phone rang. In pieces on the back lawn next to her rocking chair. She'd taken to sitting out back instead of out front. She'd just as soon watch the trees and birds as the people, whose numbers had shrunk considerably. Now her tools had been sabotaged, her grandmother's walrus needles rendered useless by an unknown entity. She looked into the woods. Listened. There was nothing but the usual, katydids and crickets, an ebb and flow, a melodious din.

It was April Fool's Day. The air smelled of a skunk.

Rachel wondered if the ruined knitting needles were someone's idea of a joke.

'Rachel?' Wimpy had come up behind her.

'Good Lord,' she said. Her hairs stood on end, her heart electrified.

He laugherd at how she'd jumped. 'Almost came out of your shoes, didn't you?' he said.

Rachel smiled at Wimpy. Noticed something wrong in his eyes.

'I brung you somethin,' he said. He handed her a mess of newspaper tied with twine. It was the funny pages, and Wimpy had put something inside. Paper flared at the top like a hard candy wrapper.

'Well thank you Wimpy,' she said. 'Should I open it now?'

'If you want to.'

She tore the paper with her fingernails. Inside was a tiny, drawstrung pouch fashioned from hide and sinew. She emptied its contents into her open palm.

It was the redbird's feet.

Wimpy had lacquered them and attached hooks made from thin wire. 'They're earrings,' he said. 'I don't know if that gauge is too big, but . . .'

Rachel was horrified. She stared at the missing toe, fought the urge to drop the feet on the ground. 'I'm not sure what to say. Did you kill him Wimpy?'

'No. That's what I come to talk to you about. You remember that redbird?'

'Yes. I could never forget it.'

'Well, he never come to visit me this year. And then, last week, I found those.'

'Earrings?'

'No, his feet. Just perched on a gatepost, pretty as you please, no body in sight. No feathers, nothin.'

Wimpy still could not rectify that picture in his mind. He'd tried to shake it loose, but it had begun to visit his dreams.

'What happened to his body?'

'Don't know. Best we can figure, something ate it.'

Rachel didn't know what to think, but she was newly glad about the earrings. Found it thoughtful of Wimpy to give them to her

'I've spoken to you on my talks with the bird,' Wimpy said. He motioned to the dogwood tree. 'I'd like to lean,' he said.

'Do you want a chair?' For the first time, she noticed he was an old man.

'No, I'd like to lean.' They walked to the tree and Wimpy put his back against its trunk. 'I believe,' he said, 'that the bird come to warn us, but something got him fore he could.' His eyelids were heavy. 'I believe it's them cicadas that got him.'

Rachel wondered if his mind was fading. 'What was he coming to warn us about?' she asked.

'That's what I can't figure. But you'll see it if you look hard enough. It's in all of them.' He swept his hand in the air as if to mark something.

'All of them?'

'Birds, bugs, snakes. It's in the way they're coming out of their nests and holes and runnin scared. Zigzag, like something has shook them.'

For a moment, it seemed to Rachel that Wimpy might cry. He'd sunken so far into the tree that he almost seemed a part of it. His chin was to his chest.

He watched a black oil beetle crawl across his boot top. It stopped and looked up at him. It roared.

An hour after the news report that Martin Luther King had died, Don Staples drew the last of his shallow breaths.

Ledford was with him when he went, holding the old man's hand in his own. He did not cry. Instead, he remembered the words Staples had spoken to him again and again in his last months. 'When I go,' he'd said, 'I want you to open my desk drawer. In it you'll find my papers. You do what's written.'

Ledford let go the cold hand and stepped to the little oak desk next to the broken television. He opened the middle drawer. A thick stack of lined yellow paper had been folded and tied in twine. *For Ledford* was scrawled across the front.

He sat down on the edge of the bed and split the twine with his daddy's dogleg jackknife. He would read it with Staples next to him. It would only take a moment to know that the man's words were sage and true. He'd written them in black ink, slow and neat.

Most men are fools. They unknowingly ruin their sons, who get a good start in life from the nurturing of their mothers, women, who are not fools. Why do men ruin their sons? Because their fathers ruined them. Why did their fathers ruin them? Because once upon a time a foolish man tried to claim a square of dirt as his own, and another man took issue. We accepted this as how things worked. The wool was pulled over our eyes, and we've yet to tear it away. Instead, we went on claiming those squares of dirt, stealing oxen and sheep, coveting our neighbors' houses. And the squares of dirt got bigger and bigger, heartily planted with crops or laid with factories by the hands of the black slave and, the white poor. We went on killing over those claims and crops and factories, and the poor were tricked into killing one another, and whenever one of us called for cessation, he was labeled less of a man. But this is a lie. The great lie, as I once explained it to you, Ledford. I put my hand to you and told you what a real man is, what a real man does. His heart must be cleansed of the lie of violence, and his hand must not wield war. A man like you has the chance to use heart and hand for peace, for helping those that need it most. You are on this path. Do not step away from it, even as the world falls apart around you, as it surely will in the days to come. There will be fire. There will be riot in the streets. You must not let it ruin you or what you have begun to build. You must keep peace in your heart and hand.

Twenty-five were present at the Bonecutter burying ground to watch Don Staples lowered into a hole. Jerry had built his coffin from scrap wood. The women cried.

The wind blew through the Cut and the people

435

huddled together. Harold stood before them in a black suit and tie. There was a lump in his throat. He held a sheet of yellow paper in his hand. It trembled. Staples had wanted Harold to give his eulogy, and so it was done.

He looked down at the words and read. 'Don Staples left behind a son.' Harold looked at the people and continued. 'A man who lives and works in California. Beyond these facts, he knew nothing of the grown child he once abandoned. He asks that all of you look to your children today. Hold them and teach them the laws of Moses and the model of Jesus, who fed the hungry and clothed the naked. Remember the words of the Book of Malachi – "and the Lord will turn the hearts of fathers to their children and the hearts of children to their fathers, lest I come and smite the land with a curse."'

Harold folded the paper and stuck it in his pocket.

Jerry, Stretch, Willy, and Chester pulled the ropes taut and scooted the coffin above the hole. They let lengths of rope out, inches at a time, sliding across their work gloves with a whirring sound, and the box sank in increments to its designation.

Mary shivered, her arms crossed in front. She'd worn a green dress, refusing black. Staples had liked her in green.

Harold looked at her, then back at the hole in the ground. He closed his eyes and listened to the thump of dirt on wood. Shovelfuls. Loud at first, then muted.

Mary was the first to walk away. Her mother

followed, calling her name. Their heels sunk with each step into a ground made soft by spring rain. Mary wiped at her eyes and ignored her mother's call.

It was quiet inside the community center. Mrs Wells had come out to pay her respects. She poured Dixie cups of her Rum-Tum-Goody Punch. Rachel had made ham salad on saltines, Staples' favorite. Fury handed out plates and cups, nodding graciously. He wore one of Ledford's old suits. He'd gained fifteen, pounds. Trimmed his beard and put his hair in a ponytail. As Wimpy had predicted, Fury was a changed man after the fever broke, but the change was for the better.

The television was on. The newsman said 300,000 were in attendance at the funeral of Martin Luther King. Orb and Chester sat on the floor and watched as Machalia Jackson sang a few lines of 'Take My Hand, Precious Lord.' Then the newsman said riots were raging in the nation's capital. They were ranging too in Baltimore, and in Louisville. In Kansas City and Chicago. Orb's eyes scarcely blinked. He watched buildings smolder, their windows blacked and jagged. Soldiers stood on street corners, their rifles slung over their shoulders.

Fifteen remained at Marrowbone full time. The rest had left.

The Corps of Engineers had posted a date on which everyone had to be out. That date was January 2nd, 1969.

JULY 1968

The parking lot of Veterans Memorial Field House was nearly full. The sun hung orange over the dye factory next door, where men finished their shifts and stepped into the street. They walked past the Ford dealership, smoking and gripping lunch pails. Their hands were stained blue.

Inside the field house, area boys knuckled down and narrowed the competition. Ham Maynard was too old to compete, and everyone wanted to see who'd take his place as champion.

There'd been a power outage, so floodlights hung on basketball rims, extension cords snaking to a generator. Two men were on their knees inside the Ringer circle. They ran concrete floats across the surface to certify it was level. A big man in a suit vest walked around them. He called out the semi-final matchup on a whistling microphone. On his head was a piss-cutter hat with *USMC Korea 1st Marines* monogrammed in red. He'd sweated through his shirt. 'Let's give these boys a hand,' he said. The crowd responded half-heartedly. The big man looked at them, bent-backed on wooden

438

bleachers. He'd expected more and couldn't figure why the crowd had shrunk as the day went on.

The answer was in the parking lot. Sixty or more people had heard whispers that Orb Ledford was going up against Ham Maynard once and for all. They gathered in a bunch at the parking lot's north-west edge. Some sat on the hoods of cars, others on the roof of an abandoned body shop. A dozen boys pressed against the chain-link fence in the alley. There was a patch of dirt in the body shop's side yard, perfect for Ringer. Fury and Stretch had worked on it all afternoon. The lines were painted. The cross rack was loaded with thirteen marbles.

Orb stepped to the pitch line with Chester behind him. 'You got nothin to worry about,' Chester said.

Orb was sweating, wiping at his forehead with the backs of his hands.

Ham Maynard toed the line next to him. He wore a sleeveless T-shirt, and his arms were the circumference of Orb's thighs. Ham hadn't said a word since he pulled up in the bed of a truck full of football players.

Over at the fence, Willy had Tug on a short leash. 'Sit,' he told the dog. Orb had insisted on bringing him. He never went anywhere without Tug in those days. Willy regarded the two boys. Ham had lost all his baby fat and sprouted to six feet. Orb was tall and skinny as ever, frail some might call him. It had surprised Willy that Orb wanted to face Ham at Ringer after all this time. He'd been hard to figure ever since the raid.

Fury leaned a chalkboard against the brick wall. It was the size of a record album. He stepped to it and marked changing odds. He kicked at a rusted sign lying face up in the yard. *Drink Royal Crown Cola*, it read.

Fury held up a fistful of dollar bills. 'Anybody else?' he called. 'Last chance before we start.' Nobody answered. 'Scared money never wins,' Fury said. He had energy to spare. He'd been off dope for three months, but he'd doubled back on small-time gambling. 'Okay fellas,' he said. 'I'll ask one more time after the lag.'

It was quiet. From across the parking lot, the generator could be heard through an open field-house door.

'Lag!' Fury hollered.

Ham tossed first, and his black taw rolled within an inch of the lag line.

Orb followed suit, his cicada taw rolling a hair closer.

There was a low cheer, some mumbling. One boy fell from his perch on the chain-link. In the bed of the truck, two others cracked open beers and whooped and hollered.

Orb and Ham retrieved their taws for the match.

A car swung into the alley. It was Shorty Maynard's police cruiser.

'Shit,' one boy said. 'Put up the beer.'

Ham squinted at the oncoming car. 'It's my dad,' he said.

Charlie Ball was in the passenger seat, Noah in

the back. The three of them knew that Ledford and Mack were at the Friday meeting of the West Virginia Human Rights Commission. It was an important one, a fund-raiser in memory of Bobby Kennedy.

They wouldn't run into Marrowbone brass, Charlie had told Noah.

They were tired of hiding, and they were drunk. Had been since an Independence Day party the night prior.

The car rolled to a stop in the alley. The sun was getting low.

Tug stood and tested the leash. A low rumble started in his chest. Willy gripped the leash tight.

Charlie Ball stepped from the open door in a three-piece white suit, fat as ever. 'Evenin boys,' he said. He smoothed his thinning hair and pulled up his pants. 'I hope nobody's into anything illegal around here.'

Shorty stepped from the driver's side and propped his arm on the roof. He wasn't in uniform. Noah stayed in the car.

Stretch felt his blood rush. He hadn't seen Shorty Maynard since the night he beat him into the ground. Nobody had. In the fallout from the theater riot, Shorty had been shamed out of running for sheriff. He'd kept his job as deputy, but most days, like this one, he just drove around. Drunk. Trouble in his eyes. His family had left him.

Charlie had been nearly as scarce. He made

public appearances when he had to, won the primary, along with Noah, but otherwise he'd taken to hiding behind his curtains, just as his frail cousin had before him.

He walked through the fence gate and regarded the Ringer circle.

'Regular dirt engineers around here,' he said. 'I heard the two best marble men in the state was having a side match. I guess I found it.'

'You want to lay a little down?' Fury asked.

Charlie laughed. He up-and-downed the young man, his long hair, his sandals. 'Hippies know how to count paper money?' he said.

Fury laughed too. 'When they grow up the son of a Chicago bookie they do.'

Charlie swallowed. He hadn't recognized the boy. 'Oh,' he said. 'Well, your daddy and me go back a ways.'

'Maybe you want to consider wagering on this match,' Fury said. 'From what I hear, you could use the scratch.'

Shorty whistled a signal.

'Excuse me,' Charlie said. He walked back to the alley.

Some in the crowd got nervous and left. Others whispered about boxing and bench presses and who would whip who in a fair fight.

Tug's snout twitched, his eyes on the police car, his hackles halfway up. 'Sit,' Willy told him.

The two men at the cruiser called Fury over.

'Don't do it,' Stretch said.

Willy just stared at Shorty Maynard. He didn't advise either way.

'It's cool Stretch,' Fury said. He strode to the alley alone.

When he got to the car, Shorty asked him, 'Ever hear of a barber?' His breath smelled of whiskey on an empty stomach.

'Ever hear of Lavoris?' Fury answered.

'How much can we put on Ham to win?' Charlie asked.

'As much as you got.' Fury looked from one of them to the other. 'As much as you believe he can beat the likes of Orb Ledford.'

Shorty laughed. 'The retarded one?'

Fury didn't like the word. He'd come to marvel at Orb's concentration inside a Ringer circle. He knew he couldn't be beat. 'What do you want to wager?' he asked.

'I don't know if you can cover it.' Charlie took out his billfold.

'I can cover it,' Fury said. He was lying. He was flat broke.

He walked back to the circle with two thousand dollars in his back pocket.

Orb knuckled down. He shut one eye and cocked his elbow. Pressure built inside his thumb, and he shot.

The cicada taw zipped across the ground like a bullet. It struck a center marble, sent it to the grass. But something was wrong in the sound of the strike. It was too loud. It turned Orb's stomach.

The cicada shooter lay in the center of the circle in pieces. There had been an unseen air bubble somewhere. Glass lay in shards next to the tiny clay wings.

Orb crawled to it on his knees. He nearly cried, seeing the clay insect like that. Exposed, artificial. One bent wing, same as his favorite cicad. He stuck it in his pocket. He'd had enough.

'I forfeit,' Orb said.

'What?' Fury couldn't believe his ears.

Orb stood up. 'I forfeit.' He walked for the parking lot.

Chester followed. 'Orb,' he called. 'Orb, you can use my taw.'

Orb would not use anybody's taw but his own, that was known.

'You owe us four grand,' Shorty Maynard hollered from beside the car.

'Hold on a minute.' Fury tracked down Orb. Chester did the same. The three of them stood between two pickup trucks and talked in whispers.

Fury came back with an offer. He stood at the police cruiser again, between the state senator and the deputy, who took slugs from a brown pint bottle between cigarettes. 'In the event of a forfeit,' Fury said, 'it's customary to allow an alternate player.'

'Spit it out,' Shorty said.

'Chester will go against Ham.' He pointed to Chester.

Shorty smiled.

'The colored boy?' Charlie said.

Fury nodded.

444

'Deal.'

They strode to the circle.

Ham won the lag, and on his first shot, he knocked a marble clear of the ring line. Then another, and another. He was meticulous. But on his fifth shot, his angle was off, and the marble stopped short of the line.

Chester got down in his stance. One leg was straight behind him, toe pointed. The other was tucked under his chest. His sneakers gripped the dirt, his armpits dripped sweat. He blew on his hand and knuckled down.

Chester never missed a shot. He knocked the remaining nine marbles out of the circle with ease, and then he knocked out Ham's shooter.

'He was hunching!' Charlie hollered. 'His thumb came over the line.'

A chorus of low mumbles moved over the crowd. 'No he wasn't,' some said.

'This is a goddamn fix,' Shorty Maynard said. He spat out his words. 'It's a setup. That fuckin hippie's a yankee hustler, and this boy's his nigger sidekick!' His chest heaved.

Tug shot forward on the leash. A current came through Willy's elbow and shoulder, tendons wrenched, but he managed to hold on and dig in. The dog erupted, bellowing from deep, his front paws off the ground.

Shorty Maynard's hand went to his gun. Everyone watched as he kept it there, frozen under his shirt in back.

Noah stepped out of the car's backseat and watched from the alley.

'All right,' Charlie said. 'Let's get going now.'

'We ain't goin nowhere,' Shorty said.

Stretch had his hands fisted.

Chester hadn't moved. He stayed on one knee by the ring line.

Orb walked to Tug and tried to calm him.

Boys in the crowd were wide-eyed. One ran down the alley.

'C'mon!' Noah hollered. 'We got to go.'

Ham Maynard stepped to his father. 'Daddy,' he said quietly, 'he beat me fair and square.'

'The hell he did!' Shorty felt their eyes on him. He wanted to smack his boy for talking to him like that. 'Get in the car Ham,' he said.

'But I came in the truck with—'

'Get in the fuckin car fore I kick your ass over there to it!'

Ham did as he was told. His chest sunk and he hung his head. Orb thought he saw tears welling.

'Boys, you all go on home now,' Charlie said. He was trying to smile, trying to go on pretending his life was in control. He gave Fury a look and followed Ham to the cruiser.

Shorty worked his jaw. He stared at Stretch Hayes, then Fury, then Willy. 'You'll all get what's comin to you,' he said.

Tug growled low.

'You keep that dog away from me,' Shorty said.

The sun had set behind the dye factory's

446

outbuilding. Boys walked away in near darkness, retelling what they'd just seen.

While Shorty strode backwards to his car, Orb searched the ring's perimeter for Ham's shooter. He knew it was Ham's favorite, the big black onyx.

He found it in a patch of greased-over grass. He started toward the alley to return it. 'Hold on,' he called, holding up the marble. He jumped a rotten railroad tie in the lot.

'What's he doing?' Fury asked.

Chester stood up and brushed off the knees of his blue jeans. 'Orb don't play for keepsies,' he said. 'Never has.'

Inside the cruiser, Shorty Maynard stuck the shifter in first and turned to the backseat. He eyeballed his boy. 'You make me sick,' he said. He left off the clutch and mashed the gas before he'd turned back around.

Ham and Noah yelled, 'Wait,' but it was too late. There was a crunching sound at the front bumper.

For a moment, it was still inside the car. Then the screams came from over at the circle.

Shorty's face went white. 'It was that dog,' he said. 'I told em to keep that dog lashed.' He knew it wasn't the dog. He shifted into reverse and howled backwards down the alley. He jerked the wheel hard when he got to Twenty-sixth Street, straightened, and gunned it up Fifth Avenue.

The car's grille had hit Orb in the legs and buckled him forward, then back. His head had struck the alley bricks, dull and hard. When they

447

got to him, he was out cold. A pump knot was already rising on the back of his head, big as a tennis ball. Willy put his hand under it. He screamed for someone to call an ambulance. Chester ran for the Field House.

The nurses and doctors called it 'the bird,' but Rachel hadn't asked them why. She stared at it, a small green box on the rack next to Orb's bed. It had knobs like those on her old radio. A tube ran from its side, across her lap, and into Orb's mouth, where the tape had caused a rash. Rachel listened to the little green respirator blowing and sucking. She watched her boy, his eyes unmoving under the lids, his chest rising and falling unnatural. His hand was warm in hers, and she rubbed her thumb there, squeezed once in a while, hoping he'd squeeze back.

She sang to him. Mostly 'Shortenin Bread' and 'Twinkle, Twinkle,' like she had when he was a baby.

They'd cut a piece of his skull bone away, and they hadn't put it back. A tube ran from his brain to another little machine. It measured pressure, let them know if the swelling came back.

When they'd looked at his pupils, one was a pinprick. The other, a planet.

Rachel looked at the stack of books on the side table. Mary had brought them from the house. Comic books mostly. *Doctor Dan the Bandage Man* was in the middle of the stack. They hadn't read it in years. Rachel picked it up and opened the front cover. Mary had taped two fresh Band-Aids inside.

'Dan is a busy fellow,' she read. In one hand she held the book at the spine, in the other, Orb's hand. 'He is always on the go, but one day in a big backyard cowboy fight, he fell.'

Ledford stood in the open doorway, arms across his chest. Behind him, in the hall, an old man pushed a walker and shuffled along, an inch at a time. Ledford didn't speak to him.

Orb had been in the hospital for four days, but to Ledford, it seemed they'd lived there a year. The sound of the respirator orchestrated his dreams.

When he wasn't in Orb's room, he was outside, lighting the next cigarette off the one in his mouth. The Bonecutter brothers had been looking for Shorty, Charlie, and Noah for three straight days. Mack brought their reports to Ledford at the hospital. No sign of any of them. Not at their homes or hangouts. All three men were on the local news nightly. It was widely known that drink was a problem in both the Ball and Maynard clans, and now there had been a hit-and-run.

In the lobby, Mary poured coffee from the pot to the Thermos. Her eyes were red as blood.

Fury stood behind her and asked again if there was anything he could do to help.

'No,' Mary said. She walked toward the elevator.

Fury watched her go. He wondered where Willy was.

In his billfold was a slip of paper. On the paper was a telephone number. Erm had given it to him years before, told him, 'You call this number if the shit ever really hits the fan.' Fury had tried it twice a day for the last four days. No one had ever picked up.

He paid for a pack of Teaberry in the gift shop and regarded his billfold. He slid the little paper out and walked to the bank of pay phones. He had a feeling this time. His fingers found the holes, 3, 1, 2. He'd memorized it by now.

On the fifth ring, someone picked up. 'What is it?' he said.

'Dad?' But Fury knew it wasn't him.

'Who the fuck is this?'

'Loaf?' Fury asked.

'Who wants to know?' He blew his nose.

Loaf the associate, still around. They'd gotten to Uncle Fiore, but not his henchman. Fury had never been so happy to hear that voice. 'It's me, Fury,' he said. 'You've got to get Dad.'

Harold sat in the chapel's first pew, reading the paper. The radio was on beside him. Hank Aaron had hit his five-hundredth home run in Atlanta.

Harold checked his watch. It was almost eight p.m.

Herchel walked through the chapel door. It was his first time back at Marrowbone. Everyone had advised him to stay away until his arrest was sorted out. It had been. The original search warrant was deemed bogus by a circuit judge. There'd been no probable cause, he'd said. The warrant was based, he'd told the court, 'on nothing more than hogwash and palaver, and a bunch of old boys gettin too big for their gun britches.'

'Evenin Harold,' Herchel said.

'Evenin.' Harold turned off the radio.

'Where is everybody?' Herchel sat down in the second pew and thumbed at a hymnal left on the seat.

Ledford came through the sanctuary door and nodded to them. He'd been in Staples' old quarters, reading and writing.

Ledford had called this meeting. From Orb's hospital room, he'd told Mack to spread the word – 'Sunday, eight p.m. I want every man there,' he'd said. 'But listen, let's try to keep the young ones out of it.'

Orb had been in the hospital for nine days. He showed no signs of waking. Twice, he'd had to be resuscitated.

By 8:15, the front two pews were filled. Mack, Harold, Herchel, Jerry, and Fury. Dimple and Wimpy had declined. They wanted to guard the gate. 'There's women and children still about,' Dimple had said.

The men sat and talked to one another quietly about Hank Aaron, about Vietnam, Tet. Ledford stood and faced them. 'Harold,' he said. 'I believe you ought not involved yourself in this. You're a man of the law.'

Harold looked Ledford in the eye. He nodded. 'God's law first,' he said.

Ledford nodded back. He took a deep breath. 'I made a promise—'

The door swung open. Willy stepped into the aisle, followed by Stretch. They proceeded forward, Willy on drunk legs, and sat down in the second pew.

'Son,' Ledford said, 'this isn't for you.'

Willy just sat there. His hair was messy, unwashed. He reeked of sweat and beer.

'Son,' Ledford said.

Nobody moved.

Ledford took another deep breath. 'I don't have all night, so I'm just going to say what I have to say.' He wanted to get back to the hospital. 'My mother used to tell me things happened, bad and good, in threes Well, lately, it's been all bad, and it's been a mite more than three.'

The men sat still in the pews. None fanned himself, despite the heat.

Ledford said, 'Don Staples guides me from the grave.' He cleared his throat. 'I wrote something back to him, and I want you to hear me read it right here in this church.' A knot was building in Ledford's throat. He spoke through it. 'You all know I lost my own family when I was still a boy, and Staples was the closest I ever had to a daddy after that. And you all know I listened to him more than most did, even when it was hard to. But things being what they are, well . . .' He took out his daddy's old batch book. He'd been writing in it all week at the hospital. He decided to get on with it.

'What I have to say will take away everything Staples stood for, everything he taught me. But it would be a greater disservice to him if I didn't speak what's on my mind.'

Herchel felt like he'd walked into a dream at Marrowbone. None of it seemed real, from the sight of Orb and his dead dogs right up to this moment. There was a pinching sensation behind his scar.

Harold and his daddy sat hip to hip and listened. Both could remember their first time in the chapel. It had seemed so strange then, so foreign.

Jerry's notepad and pencil were in his pocket. He'd not written in it since Staples passed, and he wouldn't start tonight. He knew what he was about to hear were not words of God.

Fury tried not to fidget. Stretch did the same. Willy cracked his knuckles against his thigh.

'What's on my mind is evil,' Ledford said. His voice was steady and loud. It carried to the windows and the trusses. He spread the batch book on the lectern and looked to it. 'Evil men abound in these parts. There's no sense any longer in denying them or turning away from what they've done. They have set fire to a tree on this very lawn, and before that, they set fire to a home full of people. They are the same kind of men that set fire to a cross at my boyhood home.' He looked up at Mack and Harold Wells, then back at the book. He continued. 'They have put their hands on my daughter.' He grit his teeth. The words were stuck in his throat. 'They have struck down my son. They will pay for all of it.'

Ledford looked at all of them then. He gauged in each a willingness to abide, and then he kept going. 'In response to the acts of these evil men, some would point to the words of Jesus. They'd tell me to turn the other cheek, as so many have done in recent years, whether they were set upon by dogs or hoses or batons. And I would tell those who call for peace that they are good and righteous people. Staples was one of them. But my praise of peace and righteousness would be followed by different talk.' His head bowed deeper as he went. 'Staples told me there was peace in my heart. He was wrong. There is no peace. There is only war. Right or wrong, this is the burden man must carry. And I will carry it up and down the Cut and along the ridge. I will take it to them where they hide if I have to.'

He looked out the window. There was darkness in the ridge folds. 'Women and children have got to leave here, and those who aren't a part of what's to come. But for those who stay, I'll tell you what.' He looked at them. 'We can stir the creek and wake up the trees. We can be a people freed.'

It was quiet, and then, there came the sound of hooves on the chapel lawn. They stopped. There was a blow and snort, the sound of Boo the mare.

Footsteps pounded up the chapel stairs. The door opened, and Wimpy stepped inside. His shirt was stuck to his skin and he gripped his rifle by the stock. 'Ledford,' he said, out of breath. 'You got to come see this for yourself.'

Ledford descended the front stairs. He swung onto Boo and held fast. The rest of the men stayed behind.

The horse came up on the gate. It had gotten dark, but Ledford could make out Dimple, standing with his shotgun at his side. He was talking to another man, and behind him, there was a long white car. Ledford squinted. It was Charlie's Impala.

The man Dimple spoke to was Erm.

They dismounted. Ledford regarded his old friend, who smiled. His teeth bridge was missing – nothing but emptiness. His eyes were hollow. His suit stitching was pulled out in spots, hanging loose on his frame.

'Hey Ledford,' he said. 'I know you're mad at me for the land deal, but I didn't know that your property was—'

'Isn't my property,' Ledford said. 'Belongs to the Bonecutter brothers.'

'Right,' Erm said. He looked at the brothers, nodded.

He'd never cowered like this. He'd never shown such respect.

'Is that Charlie Ball's car?' Ledford craned to see the inside.

455

'Yes it is.' Erm turned and walked through the half-open gate. They followed him.

He swung open the driver's door and folded the bench seat forward. On the floor was a green wool blanket. He pulled it back. Charlie Ball was in a prone position, stuffed between the backseat and the front. His mouth, hands and feet were duct-taped. He kept his eyes on the upholstery in front of his face. Breathed hard through a clogged nose.

'Found him at his foul-mouthed girl's place in Charleston,' Erm said. 'I followed him there once, couple years ago.' He shook his head. 'Son of a bitch is gone two weeks at a time, his wife doesn't blink an eye.'

Ledford looked at the Bonecutters. It was clear they'd already seen what was in the car. He looked at Charlie again. 'Cover him up,' he said.

Erm did so and slammed the door shut. 'It's a wonder a man so fat can fit back there,' he said. 'Listen, Ledford—'

'Can we fit the Impala in the crib barn?' Ledford called.

Dimple said they could.

'Let's get the car in here, then get him up to the chapel.' Ledford looked up the main road. It was dark and quiet. 'Nobody tailed you?' he asked.

'Nobody.'

'You know he's on the news – they're searching for him.'

'I found him first,' Erm said.

They got the car in the barn, rolled Charlie up

in the blanket, and carried him up the Cut, a man on each end. He swung like a hammock between them.

In the chapel, they dumped him in the aisle with a thud. Everybody stood from the pew and looked.

Fury nodded to his father, who smiled at him, toothless and grateful for the phone call.

Ledford unrolled the blanket and Charlie grunted and seized on the floor. The church lights confused him and he shut his eyes tight.

'I'll be damned,' Mack said.

'Is that Charlie Ball?' Herchel was the first to approach him. He knelt and looked at the man on the floor, as if some species he'd not encountered before. Herchel poked him in the cheek where the tape stretched, peeled at the edge by sweat. 'Pee-yoo,' Herchel said. 'I believe he's pissed himself.'

Dimple stood in the open chapel doorway. 'Runs in the family,' he said. He turned his head and spat tobacco juice down the stairs. 'I'm going back to the gate just in case.' He was gone.

They sat Charlie in the back pew. He'd yet to open his eyes.

They gawked and mumbled on his predicament. Then, Willy bolted for him. He stopped a foot away, planted his feet and swiveled his hips. He brought every thing he had in a roundhouse right, and it landed at Charlie's cheekbone. Things broke, in face and hand both. It was an awful sound, amplified by all that empty wood. Charlie fell to the floor and Willy hopped in a circle, clutching his rebroken hand and cursing.

'Let's get a handle here,' Erm was saying, and everybody stayed frozen where they were. He looked at Charlie, who'd crawled under a pew. 'You boys need to calm down.' He pulled a flask from his jacket pocket and held it aloft. 'Takers?' he asked.

Ledford stepped forward and took it from him. He unscrewed the cap and stuck it to his lips. Turned it over and looked to the trusses. They watched his Adam's apple bob.

After a while, Erm gathered the men in the front pews and asked questions about all that had happened – the Ringer match, the hit-and-run, the disappearance of Shorty and the Ball cousins. Fury hadn't elaborated on the phone.

Erm looked at Ledford. 'I'm sorry this had happened,' he said. He stood and walked down the aisle. He locked the chapel door and checked Charlie on the floor. 'Still sawin logs,' he said.

He called Willy, Stretch, and Harold to the back, and they came and stood with him. He pointed to Charlie Ball. 'One,' he said. Then he pointed to the three of them. 'Two, three, four.' He pointed to himself. 'Five.'

They looked back at Erm, blank.

He put a hand on the pewback and leaned. 'Two of five are dead men,' he said. 'One, inside a week, the other a year.' He let it sink in. 'But you three are boys.' He pointed at the men up front.

'Harold,' he said. 'Your old man was a boy once, but he went to Germany and came back a man. Willy, yours wasn't even a boy when he went overseas, and he sure as hell wasn't one when he came back.' He looked at Stretch. 'I don't know about you.'

Stretch said, 'My daddy's in prison and my brother broke parole. I just beat a assault rap against Shorty Maynard.'

'Enough said.' Erm liked the young man. He looked at Harold. 'This isn't law school.' He looked at Willy. 'And it isn't the racetrack. This is something you don't come back from.'

They said they understood. He led them to the front pews.

Erm sat down on the risers in front of the men. He was tired. This would be his last hurrah. 'Gentlemen,' he said, 'I was just telling the young ones that they were looking at a dead man.' He took off his shoes and rubbed his feet. 'But there are some things in this shit life I'm good at, times when I know what to do.' He looked Ledford in the eye. 'This is one of those times.'

'I've got to get back to the hospital,' Ledford said. The whiskey had both settled and frightened him. He couldn't look in Willy's direction, and he could feel Don Staples through the church wall.

Erm nodded. 'I'll put this thing together quick if you fellas will give me a hand.'

Mack was uneasy. He wished Harold had never come back to Marrowbone.

'Listen,' Erm said. He sensed he was losing them. 'Some men you can put in the ground and nobody notices. I've known those men, and I'm one of em.' He was free to tell the truth about killing. His own coming end had made it that way. 'Another kind of men,' he went on, 'you can't just make them disappear and expect your life to go on.' He motioned toward Charlie down the aisle. 'You have to plan,' he said. 'You have to know what you're doing.'

Ledford knew that Erm was right.

They listened to him talk. Then Erm asked them questions. None could understand his reasons.

'Who knows about cars?' he asked.

Mack and Stretch raised their hands.

'Who knows someone in Charlie's pocket, maybe Shorty Maynard's too?'

Ledford raised his hand.

'Good,' Erm said. 'Let's get down to brass tacks.'

The green bird respirator clapped and hissed. It had sung Rachel to sleep in her chair again. Her hand was wrapped tight around Orb's, her arm accustomed to the discomfort of extension. She'd not miss the squeeze she knew was coming.

It was dark in the hospital room. One tube light above Orb's head. Moonlight through windowblinds was scarce. Mary sat in the corner chair. She'd bought her mother a new pair of size-six knitting needles and was waiting for her to wake up. The needles were wood, not bone, but Wimpy had made a case for them that Rachel would surely like.

It was a carved rosewood fish, its head the screw-off cap. Mary thumbed the sanded gills, ran her fingers over the tiny scales. She listened to the respirator. She would not look up from her lap. She would not look at Orb anymore.

Ledford came through the door. He walked to the bed and put his hand on Orb's forehead. There was heat and there was swelling, and though a machine did the boy's breathing, Ledford bent to him anyway, and he put his head to Orb's nose and listened. 'That's a boy,' he whispered. He kissed him where the wrap revealed tiny black hairs, sprouting new. They'd shorn his whole head for the surgery. 'I love you Orb,' Ledford whispered.

He straightened and looked at Rachel, who slept sitting up, her mouth open. He whispered that he loved her too, and then he walked over to Mary in the corner and kissed her on the forehead. 'I used to sit in the driveway of the house where you were born,' he said. 'I used to watch your mother hold you and kiss that little head.' He almost smiled, and then he left.

Mary couldn't be sure, but she thought she'd smelled liquor on his breath. She thought she'd seen tears in his eyes. Both were firsts, and she didn't know what to make of her daddy then. She rubbed the wooden fish and hummed 'Amazing Grace' and tried not to think at all.

At a quarter to midnight, on July 20th, in the kitchen of W. D. Ray, Charlie Ball sat in a schoolroom chair

461

with no desktop, a .45 pressed to his temple. Ledford held the gun steady. He watched W.D. read numbers off a scrap of paper. The old man forced his fat fingers into the holes and dialed.

He held the receiver to his head, and after a while, he hung it up. 'No answer at the second one neither,' he said.

'Well, then dial the third number,' Ledford said.

'The emergency one?'

'I'd say this qualifies,' Ledford said. 'Wouldn't you Charlie?'

Erm leaned against the icebox and smoked.

Charlie kept his mouth shut. He couldn't figure what they were up to. They'd had him for a week. At first, he was tied in the crib barn next to his car, taped, fed water and bread twice a day from the hands of the Bonecutter brothers. But after four days, they'd loosed the knots and peeled off the tape. Erm had walked him at gunpoint to an empty Marrowbone house. In the bathroom, he'd told Charlie to strip and shower. 'Scrub good,' Erm had said. 'Get all that tape residue off.' Someone had laundered Charlie's clothes, and he re-dressed and slept in the empty house under watch of revolving guards. It occurred to him that maybe they wouldn't kill him after all.

On the third ring, there was an answer. 'Shorty?' W.D. said. He was wide-eyed, looking from Ledford to Erm.

'Just say what we practiced,' Erm whispered.

462

It was Noah on the other end. He asked W.D. what he wanted.

'I've got something,' W.D. said. He was talking loud, like a child might to a tin can phone. 'Something big that's goin to get you all off the hook on this hit-and-run thing. But I've got to see Shorty in person. Can't talk about this on the telephone.'

Charlie opened his mouth as if to shout warning.

Ledford stuck his .45 inside.

Charlie pissed himself again.

Erm nodded at W.D., let him know he was doing just fine.

'Charlie's here now . . . yes,' W.D. spoke into the receiver. 'No, they've all gone to Charleston for the weekend. Ledford, Mack, all of em. Some other benefit up there at the Capitol for that other killed Kennedy boy.' He nodded. Gave Erm a thumbs-up. 'All right. I'll see you soon.' W.D. hung up the telephone.

Ten miles away, in Elmwood, Noah Ball and Shorty Maynard gathered themselves. They shuffled in the dark to find their shoes. Empty Mason jars were everywhere. Canned peaches and green beans and tomatoes polished off. Shorty kicked one over reaching for his gunbelt. Glass shattered. 'This better be good,' he said.

The room smelled like a cave. It was a secret room, a bomb shelter Noah had dug out in 1951. Its doorway was hidden behind a bookcase in

463

his basement. The smell of embalming fluid was embedded in its walls. He'd stocked it sufficient with food and water and liquor.

They'd been living inside for two weeks, emerging only to empty piss and shit buckets in the mortuary sink. Their second day inside, they'd listened as the Bonecutter brothers searched the basement, mumbling and scooting equipment across the floor.

Shorty got his gunbelt buckled. 'We'll take my car,' he said.

'I don't know if that's a good idea.' Noah scratched at his neck stubble. It had grown in every which way. 'We could take my—'

'We'll take my car.' Shorty unlatched the shelter door and pulled it open. He pushed hard on the back of the bookcase.

They'd hidden the squad car under a tarp in a locked garage down the street.

In the shadows of the old trees lining Elm Avenue, they ran there.

Erm patted W.D. on the back. 'You were perfect,' he told him. 'Now go on upstairs and lock the door behind you. You remember how to turn on the television?' Erm had bought the old man his first set the day before.

'I remember,' W.D. said. He walked up the stairs, greasy yellow cat at his heels.

Erm looked at Ledford and Charlie. 'Keep that gun on him,' he said. 'I'll be back.' He walked through the living room and out the front door.

From the porch, Erm pointed his flashlight to a wide patch of gravel alongside Knob Drop Road. He pushed the button three times, on and off.

Inside the Packard, Stretch said, 'That's it. Let's go.' He sat in the passenger seat. There was a toolbox at his feet, and next to it, an old kerosene blowtorch.

Willy fired the ignition. Before he drove away, he stuck his own flashlight out the driver's window. He aimed it west, up the road toward Marrowbone. He switched it on and off three times.

Harold was at the wheel of the blue Short Bus, tucked by a hedge in an abandoned lot. He signaled back with the headlights.

Erm watched the Packard drive east. He stepped down off the porch and walked to the back of the house, flashlight in hand. He lit up Mack, who was sitting in a broken wrought-iron chair, his toolbox at his feet. 'Ten, maybe twenty minutes,' Erm said.

Mack nodded.

'Did you get that?' Erm asked loud.

'Got it,' Dimple answered. He and Wimpy crouched behind a rhododendron bush.

'Good. You other three come with me.' Erm came back in the house with Herchel, Jerry, and Fury behind him. Each carried a short-barreled shotgun. 'Get in position,' Erm told them.

Jerry climbed the staircase and turned a corner. He put his back against the hallway wall and tried to breathe normal. The air stunk of wallpaper glue.

He could hear the television from behind a closed door.

Herchel and Fury sat down behind the old couch in the living room. Dust bunnies gave way. The two of them tucked tight and stared at the old cookstove against the wall.

When Erm walked into the kitchen, Ledford stepped away from Charlie Ball. He kept the .45 aimed at his head.

'Charlie,' Erm said. 'Look at me.'

Charlie looked at him.

'If you do what I tell you to do, you'll walk out of here alive.'

Shorty had insisted on driving with the headlights off. 'No tellin' who's out lookin,' he'd said. He'd gone three times to the pint of bourbon under his seat.

Noah braced his arm against the dash around turns. His feet were planted hard on the floor.

They rounded dead man's curve at twenty miles an hour. Something caught Shorty's eye. When they'd passed, he asked, 'You see that?'

'What?'

'I thought I seen something over there. A little orange light.'

'I didn't see anything.' Noah's nerves were shot. He was ready for all this to end.

Shorty came up the straight stretch in blackness. He coasted quiet onto the Rays' gravel drive, one hand on the wheel, the other on his sidearm.

He saw Charlie's Impala in the yard. 'He's here all right,' Shorty said.

They parked next to the Impala and got out slow. Crickets sang in unison, a deafening call. The porchlight was on.

'W.D.,' Shorty said, his pistol drawn.

The old man stuck his head from an upstairs window, and Shorty aimed at him. W.D. swallowed hard and said, 'I'll be down presently. Got a case of fire trots I'm afraid. Charlie's in the kitchen.'

Noah looked at Shorty, who kept his gun drawn and walked slow onto the porch. He looked through the window slats before going in. 'Charlie?' he called from the doorway.

'In the kitchen,' Charlie hollered.

They walked through the dark living room. Floorboards whined below their feet. At the kitchen doorway, Shorty raised his gun. He saw Charlie's wingtips and stepped over the threshold. 'Why are you sitting like that?' Shorty asked. He holstered his gun.

'Like what?' Charlie stared at the icebox. There was a pencil drawing taped there, and in it, a bearded man in the sky extended his arms wide. Lightning bolts erupted from his hands, and below him, stick-figure people ran about.

'Like a statue,' Shorty said.

Noah gripped the doorjamb and frowned. Something wasn't right with his cousin.

Ledford and Erm stepped from the walk-in

pantry with their guns leveled at Shorty Maynard's head. 'Keep that pistol holstered,' Erm said.

Noah thought about running but didn't.

'Hands up high,' Erm said.

They did as they were told.

'Now,' Erm said. He held his .38 in a manner bespeaking seriousness. 'Everything is going to be fine. Ledford's going to take your revolver, pat you down, that's it.'

Ledford pulled Shorty's gun from its holster and stepped back. He put his own weapon in his waistband and emptied Shorty's of its rounds, which he dropped in his pants pocket. He returned the gun to its holster and patted both men down. 'Just that one,' he said.

'Okay fellas,' Erm called.

In the living room, Fury and Herchel stood from behind the couch. They rested their shotgun barrels on its back. Jerry stepped from the landing and stuck his through the stair rail.

'Step in there and have a seat,' Erm said.

Outside, Mack cut through the sideyard in a quiet crouch. He set his toolbox down by the squad car's front tire. He put his creeper board at the bumper and lay down. There was a small dent in the grille, and Mack thought of Orb. He rolled under, switched on the flashlight tucked in his armpit, and located things. Axle. Fuel line. Brake line.

Ledford and Erm were by the front door. They glanced to the yard once in a while, where the

Bonecutter brothers stood guard. None spoke a word until Mack rolled out and nodded.

Charlie, Noah, and Shorty sat in a row on the couch, shotguns at the base of their necks, another one staring from the stairs.

'Here's what we're going to do,' Erm said.

Noah Ball couldn't take it. The silence had gotten him. 'Please,' he said. He wore a pathetic look. 'I was just in the car. I wanted to go back and check on the boy, but it happened so fast—'

'Shut your mouth,' Ledford said.

Charlie Ball was numb to it all. He sat as he had in the kitchen. Statue straight.

Shorty shook his head in disgust at Noah, who clasped his hands and bowed his head and prayed in a whisper. It was hard to make out, all 'dear Gods' and 'thank you Lords.'

Erm didn't like all the movement. He didn't like the look on Shorty Maynard's face. 'You might want to pray like your friend here,' he said.

Shorty looked from Erm to Ledford. His eyes were dead. He clasped his hands and looked at the ceiling. 'Thank you God,' he said. 'For everything. But thank you most of all for James Earl Ray.' He put his hands back in his lap, snorted, and spat on the crooked coffee table.

Ledford only blinked at him.

'Here's what we're going to do,' Erm said again. 'You three are going to get in that police car out front, and you're going to drive out of here alive. You're going to go to Huntington and turn

469

yourselves in at the station on Fifth Avenue. Ledford and I are going to follow you in Charlie's Impala to make sure you get there safe. Understand?'

They didn't understand. But when they were told to get up and move, they did so.

At gunpoint, they walked outside in a line, where there were further guns pointed, these in the hands of the Bonecutter brothers, whose stares were something to behold. As the three men stepped into the cruiser, Dimple whistled the tune to Gene Autry's 'Jingle Jangle Jingle.'

Shorty turned the key.

'Why are they letting us go?' Noah asked from the backseat. He got no answer.

Out on Knob Drop, headlights lit up the road. The Packard pulled from the gravel patch and drove the same direction it had before. Willy and Stretch would drive a quarter mile and block the road from the east.

The Short Bus pulled out at an angle and stopped. It blocked the west.

Shorty put the car in gear and watched. 'Keep us from runnin, I guess,' he said. 'Box us in.' He could hardly keep from smiling. No one knew Knob Drop like he did. There were four dirt turnoffs between the Rays' place and Route 52, and neither Charlie's Impala nor the Packard had tires for any of them.

Shorty was glad they'd driven his car.

He pulled onto the main road and checked his rearview. The Impala was riding him close. 'Let's see what they got,' Shorty said. He laid the pedal to the floor.

They hit fifty quick on the straight stretch, and Shorty didn't touch the brake pedal until dead man's curve was thirty yards ahead. When he did, nothing happened. He looked down at his feet and mashed it again and again. He tried to cut the wheel, but it was no use. Charlie pressed his fingers to the roof and Noah grabbed the head-rest, and when they hit the guardrail, it may as well have been made of tinfoil.

Stretch's blowtorch had done its job.

Erm slowed the Impala and for a moment, they watched the car soar. It rode solid ground, then it rode nothing, and then it was gone. No squeal, no crunch, no siren. Gone.

Ledford said, 'Pull up close to the edge.'

He shined the flashlight there. It looked natural enough, a section of guardrail missing, jagged-edged. Long lag bolts glimmered in the beam, pulled from the wood embankment where Willy had wrenched them loose. Ledford tossed the flash-light to the floor. 'Let's go get the boys up the road,' he said.

Back at the Ray place, Erm wiped the Impala down with a rag, inside and out. He left the keys in the ignition, the car on the lawn. 'Remember,' he told W.D., 'when they ask, you tell em all three men left here in the squad car at midnight, drunk as rummies.'

W.D. nodded. 'And I can phone Sheriff Maynard,' he said, 'tell him it's done?'

'You got it,' Erm answered. 'He's expecting the call.'

He and Ledford got in the Packard. The rest had already walked to the Short Bus where it waited on the road. Mack turned it around in the gravel patch, and they all drove home to Marrowbone. No one spoke a word on the way.

They parked in the lot and walked up the Cut in a pack. Dimple and Wimpy watched them go. They were tired, and there was no one left to guard against.

Erm wanted one last meeting at the chapel. He said you could never be too thorough, too prepared for questions.

Ledford stopped at the bottom of the chapel stairs and watched the rest of them climb. 'Go on and start without me,' he said.

Willy looked back at him. 'Where you going?'

Ledford beheld the face of his oldest boy, lit by the yellow bulb above the door. *Land of Canaan Congregational* it read. It stopped his breathing, seeing Willy like that. He was hard beyond his years. He'd become what Ledford had feared he would become. 'I've got to check something up at the factory,' he told him.

Ledford had known for some time that he'd already run his last batch of marbles. The place was a blight on the earth, the ugly side of Marrowbone. He watched the smoke billow as he walked. It sabotaged the sky, put a film over the stars.

Inside the factory, he kicked over buckets of cullet, blue and green and red and yellow glass scattering on the floor like minnows. There were wheelbarrows full of glass. He dumped those too.

In the corner, he pulled the tarp from the mountain of newspapers. He stared at all those words on paper, piled chest high. He lit a cigarette and tossed the match on the pile. It fizzled. He lit another and tossed again. This one took, and the paper blossomed, and the words began to disappear.

Ledford stepped away as the roar came in earnest. He walked to his workbench where the pictures hung. In one of them, Orb crouched at the Ringer circle, his knees muddied, a look of determination on his face. In the picture glass, Ledford watched the growing fire's reflection. It danced up the wall and across the ceiling. It stuck to everything.

He stepped to the furnace and stared at the glow inside the square. He thought of Shadrach, Meshach, and Abednego, and he wondered if he could put his hand inside and pull it out unscorched. If the lives he'd ended were meant to be ended. He stared into the furnace fire until his peripherals went white. He stepped again toward the opening, and its heat singed his arm hair. He closed his eyes and watched the little swirls dance across the black stage of his eyelids. There was a bird in flight. Something sickening in its movements. It was after a thing he could not see, its beak open and pointed and foul. And then, on the backs of his eyelids, there formed two pinpoints. They were the color of the sun, and they grew outward. For a moment, Ledford thought that if he opened his eyes, he'd be back on the swingshift at Mann Glass. There was a rumble beneath his boots. His knees gave, and he pitched forward, bending at the waist. He put a hand out to steady himself. He opened his eyes to see his fingertips catch fire inside the furnace square. The nails turned to ash, the flesh dripped as wax, and white bone went black as the fire crept high to his knuckles. Ledford felt nothing. His sight ceased to be, and he dropped to the floor.

The factory door opened.

Fury and Harold ran past the growing flames in the corner. They got to Ledford and hooked him by the arms and dragged him outside to the grass. The fingers on his right hand were gone. A black stump smoldered, red cracks wisping white smoke.

The rest had come running by them. Willy stared at his daddy's hand, mostly gone. Bones jutted, sharp. The color of ash. 'God oh God,' Willy said.

At the water station, Jerry unrolled the hose. Mack knelt to the ground and opened a heavy door by its latch. Inside was the gas line's shutoff valve. As the factory windows exploded and the flames licked the roof, Mack reached inside the hole. He grabbed the black knob and turned it.

DECEMBER 1968

A twenty-foot red spruce tree stood in the middle of the community center. Dimple and Wimpy had cut it down the day before. Its base they'd fashioned from cinderblocks, and it stood straight with help from fishing line lashed to basketball rims. From a stepladder, Lizzie had thrown lead foil icicles over its wild branches. Mary had strung popcorn and encircled the circumference in loops. There were ten long lengths of bubble lights, blue and red and yellow and green, pointy-topped bulbs filling empty spaces.

It was their last Christmas Eve at Marrowbone.

The top doors on the RCA Victor were wide open, and on the phonograph, Nat Cole spun. Harold turned the volume knob high for 'Hark! the Herald Angels Sing.' As a boy, he'd thought the song was about him.

Outside, it had gotten dark and cold. The sky was cloudless. Ledford looked up at the moon. Its edges were crisp. He blew his cigarette smoke at it, took a last drag. He held the cigarette in his hooks, stubbed it out against the bottom of his boot. His physical therapist liked the phrase 'shift in

475

handedness,' but he'd be damned if he smoked with his left. The hooks pinched a square just fine.

He leaned against the siding and scratched his back. The harness straps were itching him again. They formed a figure eight across his spine and held the prosthesis tight to his stump. The doctor had taken the hand off at the wrist, replaced it with steel and rubber.

Ledford made sure the cherry on his cigarette was out. Then he stuck the hooks in his pocket and opened them, dropped the butt inside.

He watched Orb run a circle on the lawn, Tug at his heels. Since he'd come home from the hospital, the dog had not left his side. Orb liked to run, and his physical therapist said it was good for him. He and Ledford had overlapped in their respective recuperations. Physical, occupational. Both had exceeded expectations. But Orb wore a perpetual look of nothingness. He had not spoken a word, and the doctors said he likely never would.

The boy had surprised everyone when he squeezed his mother's hand one hot August night. Rachel was watching the hospital television. On the screen, Chicago policemen tear gassed a crowd of protesters, and Orb squeezed her fingers. She'd looked at him, and he'd looked back.

Ledford whistled, and Tug came running. Orb followed. 'Let's get inside where it's warm,' Ledford said. He held the door for them, then followed.

The ceiling lights were shut off, and for a moment everyone stood in darkness. Then Mack plugged

476

in the tree lights, and faces were lit in hues of yellow, uniformly looking up at the blown-glass star. It threw blue lines across the ceiling beams, and Ledford pulled Rachel close, her back against his chest, his chin on her head. 'Merry Christmas,' he said.

The steel hooks were cold through her sweater. She smiled, cried a little. Thought of the new home they were building at Beech Fork. It was big, and when the dam was built and the lake came, their yard would back up to the water. Ledford said he'd build a boat dock.

Nat Cole's 'Silent Night' ended, and the record crackled before going quiet.

Orb ran a circle around the base of the big tree. Chester approached and stood in his path. Orb stopped and stared. 'Here you go Orb,' Chester said. He handed his friend a gift. The wrapping paper was silver-and-gold striped. Orb just looked at it. 'I'll open it for you,' Chester said, and he did. The paper dropped to the floor in strips. Chester held up a wood-framed photograph of the two of them. Mary had taken it on the day the Woodson Center opened. It was black and white. It froze in time a moment at the junk-strewn yard of the secondhand plumbing store. In the photograph, Orb peeked over the edge of a clawfoot tub, and behind him, eight feet up, Chester rotated backwards through the air, a blur of hands and knees and feet. 'I carved the frame myself,' Chester said. Wimpy had taught him how.

Orb stared at the photograph. Then he looked

right through his friend and kept on running around the tree.

Ledford walked over to Chester. 'That's the best kind of gift there is,' he said. He patted the boy on the back. He was glad Chester was staying. Not many were, but there would be enough. Up at the new grounds, they'd plant and harvest next to a two-thousand-acre lake that never flooded. No factory, no televisions, no post office box with the name of a newspaper on the side.

Ledford looked closer at the picture. Chester's blur reminded him of a photograph he'd once seen of his own father. Six years old, swinging on a rope. 'Mary take this picture?' he asked.

'She's good, isn't she?' Chester said.

'Yes she is. That reminds me.' He stepped to the tree and pulled a box from underneath. It was wrapped sloppy in old paper – he'd done it himself, hooks and all. He called Mary over and she opened it. Inside was a new Bolex 16mm movie camera.

She didn't know what to say.

'I thought maybe you could get film of the whole place before it winds up underwater,' Ledford said. 'Moving pictures of Marrowbone.'

Mary nodded.

In the corner, Herb Wells ran a bow across his fiddle. Jerry turned the big Stella twelve-string, and Herchel plucked the clothesline on his gas-tank bass.

'Good people of Marrowbone!' Mack hollered. 'The house band would like me to apologize in advance. They don't know but one song, and it ain't a Christmas tune.'

Mrs Wells sat in a folding chair and ate an iced cookie. She watched her boys and smiled. Willy walked over and asked if she needed a refill on punch. She looked him in the face and said, 'You got the same eyes now you did as a three-year-old child.'

'I do?'

'Yes indeed.' She nodded her head and wiped her mouth with a napkin. 'Matter of fact, I bet you still pee on a fire to put it out, don't you?'

'Yes ma'am,' Willy said. He laughed. It felt good. He hadn't done it in days, not since the phone call from Fury in Chicago. Erm had been found in his old bookie office, on the floor next to Loaf the associate. Their necks were cut, earlobe to earlobe. Willy told Fury to come back to West Virginia, that they were building a new place. Fury said he couldn't. It was in his every syllable – he was shooting heroin again.

The three-piece started in on 'Oil It Up and Go,' and folks tapped their feet in time with the bass. Even Dimple and Wimpy shuffled their shoes a little. They stood by the door with their arms crossed. Stretch stood next to them and did the same.

The old Ringer circle was gathering dust. Inside it, Harold danced with his mother. He dipped her, and then, halfway through the song, he hugged her and walked away toward the tree.

Mary watched him come, and when he asked if she cared to dance, she answered, 'I'd be delighted.'

479

They stepped to the circle and she lay her head against his chest and together they swayed, slow, though the song was fast.

When it was quiet again, the door opened, and Bob Staples came in carrying a store-bought fruit-cake. 'What are you people doing?' he called. 'Turn on the damned television.'

Jerry pulled the knob and sat on the floor. Orb sat down next to him. The two of them often sat together. The mutes of Marrowbone. Jerry wished the boy could remember the signs he'd once taught him, but it wasn't to be.

On the screen was a gray-white curve of light. A voice spoke the words, 'And the spirit of God moved upon the face of the water.'

Dimple and Wimpy walked over from the door. They'd never looked at a television before. 'What is that?' Wimpy asked.

Bob Staples said, 'It's the surface of the moon.'

Wimpy shook his head to be sure he wasn't dreaming. 'Good Lord in heaven,' he whispered.

The remaining people of Marrowbone gathered in front of the television and stared at the horizon of the moon. Ledford knew for certain that he would leave the RCA behind. He would never turn on a television again. The broadcast of the Apollo 8 astronauts would be the last thing he ever watched.

They read from Genesis as they orbited. 'Merry Christmas,' one of them said. 'God bless all of you. All of you on the good earth.'

JANUARY 1969

It was New Year's Day. In twenty-four hours' time, the Corps of Engineers would own the land. Mary walked the grounds of Marrowbone, her new camera in hand. She stood in front of the burnt-down factory, a place they'd all avoided since July. She filmed the circle of glass on the dirt. Snow fell.

Beside her, Ledford knelt and tapped his hooks on the thick glass. 'Go get your ice skates on and have at it,' he said.

Mary smiled. She filmed her daddy. He looked up at her, said, 'Shut it off.'

Across the Cut, the Bonecutter brothers rode Silver and Boo at woods' edge. Saddlebags hung full over the horses' haunches.

'Put your camera on those two,' Ledford said. 'That's the last you'll ever see of em.'

The brothers had said their goodbyes the night before. They would not elaborate on their plans, only said they were leaving Marrowbone for good. Riding to the hills. Living off the land and moving on when the time came. 'It's how we were meant to live,' Wimpy had told Ledford. 'It's what the bugs

ACKNOWLEDGMENTS

In this book, I wrote of many things that I can never truly know or understand. In making the attempt, I consulted the books of several authors who did in fact know and understand, and I cannot thank them enough. The same goes for the expertise of a couple of kind souls who put up with my phone calls full of questions.

I am not a glass man, and so I appreciated the wealth of knowledge in *Calling to Memory . . . The History of the Owens-Illinois Huntington, WV Plant #2* by the KYOWVA Genealogy and Historical Society. I also consulted the online source *Batch, Blow, and Boys: The Glass Industry in the United States, 1820s-1900,* particularly *Batch recipe book of D.J. Crowley, ca. 1890s.* In addition, for all of his help, I'd like to offer my sincere thanks to Jim King, a real marble man in Sistersville, West Virginia.

I have never been to war, and so I owe a debt of gratitude to *The Story of World War II* by Donald L. Miller, *Guadalcanal* by Richard B. Frank, *Goodbye, Darkness* by William P. Manchester, and *Blood for Dignity* by David P. Colley.

I was not yet born at the time of the Civil Rights

movement, and so I would like to acknowledge *At Canaan's Edge* by Taylor Branch, *Selma 1965* by Charles E. Fager, The Library of America's *Reporting Civil Rights: Part Two*, particularly 'Letter from Selma' by Renata Adler, and Steven Kasher's *The Civil Rights Movement: A Photographic History*. Also, Bruce A. Thompson's master's thesis, *An Appeal for Racial Justice: The Civic Interest Progressives' Confrontation with Huntington, West Virginia and Marshall University, 1963–1965* was of great help. I consulted the archives of the *Charleston Daily Mail*, the *Charleston Gazette*, and the *Herald-Dispatch* as well (thanks to my friend Bob Brumfield for pointing me in the right direction on the Keith-Albee incident). And, for both his profound knowledge and lived experience of the time, I humbly thank C. Michael Gray, fellow Huntingtonian.

I offer my gratitude to Huey Perry, for his book *They'll Cut Off Your Project*. It was the basis for so much herein, and it was immeasurably helpful and inspirational in writing about those folks who most choose to forget.

There are several other books that have, in various and odd ways, influenced me over the last couple of years, and without them, I could not have possessed the necessary wisdom for an endeavor such as this. They are, *The Telltale Lilac Bush* by Ruth Ann Musick (for 'Hickory Nuts'), *Folk Medicine in Southern Appalachia* by Anthony Cavender, *Concise Guide to Self-Sufficiency* by John Seymour, and *Horseplayers* by Ted McClelland.

I would be remiss if I did not acknowledge my consultation of *The Periodical Cicada* by Charles V. Riley and *Handbook of Severe Disability* by Walter C. Stolov and Michael R. Clowers.

To my marvelous agent, Terra Chalberg, I thank you. For so many things. To everyone at Ecco who worked on this book, I appreciate it. In particular, I'd like to acknowledge Ginny and Dan, who simply do things right. Dan, you're the man, and I thank you.

To Dot Jackson, I say thank you, for everything, for being who you are.

I'd like to thank my family–all of them, by blood or by marriage, from kinfolks who are gone to those still here, from my sisters to my sons–and a special thanks to my parents, Maury and Carol. My wife, Margaret, is beyond thanks. She is, simply, the best.

The Blackwell Guide to the

Philosophy of Religion

—— Blackwell Philosophy Guides ——

Series Editor: Steven M. Cahn, City University of New York Graduate School

Written by an international assembly of distinguished philosophers, the *Blackwell Philosophy Guides* create a groundbreaking student resource – a complete critical survey of the central themes and issues of philosophy today. Focusing and advancing key arguments throughout, each essay incorporates essential background material serving to clarify the history and logic of the relevant topic. Accordingly, these volumes will be a valuable resource for a broad range of students and readers, including professional philosophers.